BURI

Also by David Hodges at Pharaoh Press

Flashpoint

DAVID HODGES

BURNOUT

PHARAOH PRESS

BURNOUT

ISBN 1 901442 14 4

First published in 2005 by Pharaoh Press

The right of David Hodges to be identified as the author of
this work has been asserted in accordance with the
Copyright, Designs and Patents Act 1988

This novel is entirely a work of fiction.
All the characters in this book are fictitious,
and any resemblance to actual persons, living or dead,
is purely coincidental

Conditions of Sale

Typeset in Plantin Light 9.75 on 12pt.
Produced by John Saunders Design & Production, Abingdon OX13 5HU

Cover concept/photography © Adam Clutterbuck

Printed in Great Britain by Biddles Ltd., King's Lynn

THE AUTHOR

A former senior police officer with Thames Valley Police, David Hodges gained wide operational and management experience in his thirty years with the force, serving in all ranks from constable to superintendent and retiring as head of Corporate Communication.

A prolific writer, who has achieved several successes in the prestigious Queen's Police Gold Medal Essay Competition, including the first prize and the award of the gold medal, *Burnout* is his second published novel.

David lives with his wife, Elizabeth, in Somerset, where he can fully indulge his passion for thriller writing.

To my beloved wife, Elizabeth,
for all her love and support over
so many years.

Before...

Hate, paranoia, cruelty – the eyes held it all and in their fixed unblinking stare Ron Ferguson also saw death.

'Please,' he blurted hoarsely, his voice cracking open with a gasp of pain as the cage of chicken wire binding him to the frame of the wrought iron bed cut into the flesh of his sweating near naked body. The figure did not move, but in the glare of the moonlight flooding into the bedroom through the open window the thin lips curled into a contemptuous sneer.

'Please,' he begged again. 'I'll do anything you want, but don't –'

A black gloved hand rose to eye level, as if in a placatory gesture, but this was only illusory and a fraction of a second later his tormentor was thrusting a large square can towards him as the other hand proceeded to unscrew the cap in a very slow deliberate motion. In the stillness of the room the metallic scrape of metal on metal was plainly audible and, heedless of the wire cutting deeper into his flesh, he thrashed madly from side to side in a futile attempt to snap the vicious strands.

The stench of petrol enveloped him even as the fiery spirit launched itself from the spout in a glittering cascade, seeping into the patchwork of lacerations that covered his trunk and lower limbs, soaking into the mattress and dribbling over the edge of the bed into the thick pile of the carpet. His choking screams held a mixture of agony and terror as they erupted from gnawed blooded lips through a torrent of drink laden vomit and fled into the humid night, losing themselves among the pines of the thickly wooded hillside, and carrying with them the remnants of his own sanity.

He was too far gone to hear the click of the lighter, to see the tiny flame born in the doorway where the dark figure had retreated, briefly illuminating the cold pale face and the triumphant gleam in those fixed staring eyes. But he was aware of the sheet of flame that leaped from the floor at the foot of the bed and swept over him with the frenzied roar of a tidal wave, stoking up its energy on the greasy fats seeping on to the rubber mattress from his writhing blackening flesh and exiting from the incinerated inner shell of his body through every conceivable orifice in fiery twisting tongues that raced up the walls and across the ceiling of the old house in a gleeful orgy of destruction.

For Ron Ferguson death was relatively swift, but justice was to take a lot longer...

Chapter 1

The telephone rang at precisely 3.00 am. 'Chief Inspector Dexter?' The voice sounded nervous, unsure of the likely reaction.

The hand that snatched the receiver from its cradle re-emerged from under the bedclothes and shook off the sheets in which it had become entangled. 'Who wants to know?' came the truculent reply.

'Jamie Briggs, sir. Headquarters Control Room Inspector,' the caller continued in a rush. 'We've got a nasty incident. Detective Chief Inspector Lawson asked for you to be called. Apparently the press are already on the scene.'

Dexter levered himself up on to one elbow, conscious of his wife stirring beside him. 'What sort of incident?' he queried, the interest suddenly evident in his tone.

A barely perceptible sigh that sounded very much like relief. 'Suspicious fire at Alden House, Bellingham, sir. They've got a stiff to go with it, I'm afraid.'

Dexter frowned heavily in the darkness. 'I should know that address, shouldn't I? Isn't it one of our vulnerables?'

'Yes, sir. Judge Lionel Berwick's place, and it looks like he's the stiff.'

Dexter was wide awake now and hauling himself up into a sitting position against the headboard. 'Berwick?' he exclaimed louder than he had intended.

'So I'm told, sir, though they've yet to do a formal ID, of course.'

Dexter cast a guilty sidelong glance in the direction of his sleeping wife, then turned away from her, cupping the telephone mouthpiece in his other hand. 'No chance he was smoking in bed, I suppose?' he said dryly.

A hard laugh. 'Shouldn't think so, sir, not unless he was using petrol in his lighter.'

'Gordon Bennett! So who's the the Senior Investigating Officer?'

'Detective Superintendent Moffat is SIO, sir.'

Dexter groaned. 'That's all we need,' he grated. 'Bloody' *Super Plod.*'

'Yes, sir,' Briggs replied politely, but without further comment.

The bedside light snapped on and a hand grabbed Dexter's arm. 'Big mouth!' his wife, Tania, hissed in warning. 'Tape!'

He blanched slightly, remembering, too late, that all calls to the Control Room were recorded as a matter of policy, something even Tania had immediately appreciated.

'Are you still there, sir?' Briggs queried innocently.

Dexter cleared his throat. 'Yes… er… I'm on my way, Jamie. About an hour I should think.'

There was laughter in the other's voice now. 'Thank you, sir,' he acknowledged. 'I'll tell Chief Inspector Lawson just that, shall I?'

Tania's blue eyes studied him frankly as he put the telephone receiver back. 'Nice one, Mike,' she said tartly. 'For the Press, Public Relations Officer, you certainly know all about tact and diplomacy, don't you?'

He swung his feet over the edge of the bed. 'Yeah, yeah,' he growled. 'But at least I don't make a profession out of being a prat like Moffat. He couldn't detect a fart in a storm.'

'You'll be the prat if someone has cause to listen to tonight's tape later on,' she retorted, then added after a moment's pause: 'So what was that about Judge Berwick?'

He felt acid churn in his stomach. Damn, he had been hoping she hadn't heard him mention the name. 'Nothing for you to worry about, love.'

'Michael,' she snapped as he stood up. 'I'm not a kid.'

He made a face before turning. 'I know that, dear, but I don't want you upsetting yourself after all this time.'

'What's *happened*?' she persisted tersely.

He sighed and sat down again. 'There's been a fire at Berwick's place and they think he died in the blaze. It's just an accident, probably an electrical fault or something. Dick Lawson wants me over there to handle the press.'

She swallowed hard and he could see a flicker of something in her eyes he hadn't seen for a long time. 'A fire?' she echoed, a tremble in her voice. 'But if it was accidental, why are CID –?'

'A precaution, nothing more,' he cut in hastily, anxious to put an end to the line her thoughts were taking. 'Usual procedure with incidents like this. Now can we drop it? I have to get ready.'

She hesitated, then gave a weak smile. 'Yes, you go ahead.' She leaned across and kissed him on the cheek. 'I'm just being silly. Judge Berwick's name gave me a jolt, that's all. Touch of déjà vu.'

He nodded, studying her narrowly for a moment. 'I'll get back as soon as I can, okay?'

Another smile and she ran her hands through her tousled auburn hair. 'Yes, of course. Give my best to Dick Lawson, won't you? Tell him it's a long time since he and Janet were over for a meal.'

Standing at the bathroom mirror a few minutes later, Dexter gripped the edge of the wash-hand basin and stared at his face in the rapidly clouding glass as the basin filled with hot water. Time was beginning to tell on him. He could see that in the thinning grey-black hair and the pouches under the haunted brown eyes. Even his neat military style moustache was turning grey and there was an overall tightness in his face that seemed to accentuate the sharpness of his cheekbones giving his cheeks a sunken failed appearance. Just forty-six years of age, that was all, and yet he was beginning to look like sixty. The strains and stresses of the job were killing him, he knew that, but the thought of letting go now and having to admit to himself – and even worse, to Tania – that he couldn't hack it anymore just didn't bear thinking about.

The biggest joke of all was that everyone thought he had it made. Always up there being interviewed in front of the TV cameras, quoted almost daily in the national press and rubbing shoulders with the high and the mighty at virtually every major event in the force calendar. Yet they didn't know the half of it. As the Chief Constable's confidant, he was envied and resented by every senior officer in the force; seen as a renegade by the rank and file because of his links with the press and mistrusted by the press themselves because he was the police spokesman. He walked a tightrope between the two camps and he was acutely conscious of the fact that, if he made one wrong move, there would be a queue of people waiting to plunge a knife in his back. No wonder he was worn out and now, to add to it all, it looked like the past was coming back to haunt him. What was that quote one of his shift sergeants always used to come out with when the chips were down? 'Life's a bitch and then you die.' Yeah, well sometimes you could be dead and not even know it.

Thick fog was waiting for him when he left the house twenty minutes later and there was a sharp chill in the air that went right through him. He shivered as he made his way down the drive to the double garage by the gate.

Tania had been right about the déjà vu bit. Even he felt it and it was certainly ironic that Berwick of all people should have died the way he had. How long was it since the Challow case? It had to be over twenty years he reckoned. He had been just a rookie detective then. 'Keen and green,' his crusty old detective inspector had called him. Probably true at the time too. But he had still nailed that crazy fire-freak, hadn't he? *And* got a crown court commendation after Berwick had put the bastard away.

The engine of his blue Volvo started first time and a few seconds later he was through the gate and bumping along the unmade lane towards the main road. He glanced at the bare trees reaching over the hedgerows on either side to form a skeletal tunnel and shivered again.

Why the hell did poor old Berwick have to go and get himself cremated? The last thing Tania needed was to be reminded of the Tulse End nightmare all over again. For so many years she had struggled to come to terms with what had happened, taxing every ounce of patience and resilience he possessed and demanding the best psychiatric support that could be provided. Now, when the pair of them had at last managed to establish a normal life for themselves, there was every chance that everything could go to rat's shit, just because of this.

'Damn you, Eddie Challow,' he said aloud. 'Damn your rotten stinking hide.'

Alden House was a big Georgian place set well back off the road in wooded grounds and he could smell the fire even before he saw the imposing pillars of the entrance gates. A group of shadowy figures scuttled towards him as he pulled up, peering in through the open window.

'What gives then, Mike?' a bearded reporter in a gabardine raincoat queried when he saw who was behind the wheel.

Dexter grunted. 'I don't know myself yet, Tom,' he replied, recognising the news agency man. 'Catch you later, eh?'

He ignored the host of shouted questions from the others and edged towards the iron gates. A uniformed constable pushed his way through the reporters and shone a flashlight in his face. Turning away from the glare, Dexter showed him his warrant card.

'Chief Inspector Dexter,' he snapped sourly, seeing rings in front of his eyes. 'Headquarters Press Office.'

The policeman stepped back smartly and leaned on one of the gates 'Sorry, sir. Just follow the drive round to the right. You are expected.'

His instructions proved to be unnecessary, for the flashing blue lights of the emergency vehicles became clearly visible through the trees a hundred yards into the grounds and seconds later Dexter was pulling up in loose gravel behind one of half a dozen fire appliances. Alden House was no longer alight, but a smoky haze still drifted lazily across the beams of the powerful spotlights trained on the building and yellow helmeted figures moved among the ruins, raking out debris. The familiar stench created by a combination of wet smoke, charred wood and scorched stonework was only too apparent and Dexter knew that, even with dry-cleaning, his clothes would carry the smell for days afterwards. He made a mental note to extract some cleaning tokens from the Senior Admin Officer's tight fist as soon as he got back to the office.

He found Detective Chief Inspector Lawson standing talking to a couple of senior fire officers in their distinctive white helmets a short distance from what had once been the front door of the building, and the tall gangling CID man turned quickly at his approach. 'Mike, my man,' he exclaimed. 'Didn't wake you up, did we?'

Dexter grimaced, nodding at the two fire officers. 'No, you arsehole, I always stay up until 3.00 am!'

Lawson sighed. 'Oh dear, the trials and tribulations of being a press, public relations officer. And there's me thinking it was all TV interviews and Masonic dinners.'

He placed an arm around Dexter's shoulders and walked him over to a police area car parked a few yards away, its headlights and blue flashing beacon already dimming as the battery started to run down. 'Stupid sods,' the detective commented and reached through the open window to turn everything off. 'Should have left the lot on and let them walk back to the nick.'

'You're all heart,' Dexter observed dryly leaning back against the door and shaking his head at the packet of cigarettes thrust under his nose.

Lawson studied him for a moment as he lit up. 'So, how's Tania these days?' he queried quietly. 'Does she know about all this yet?'

'Oh she knows all right. I just hope it doesn't put her back to square one. You know, association of ideas and all that.'

Lawson nodded. 'I'm just sorry I had to be the one to stir things up again, Mike, I really am, but you were down as on call tonight, so I had no choice.'

Dexter sighed. 'Forget it. I'm always on call for incidents like this and Tania would have heard about it sooner or later anyway.' He stared past him at the remains of the house. 'Bit of a mess, isn't it?'

Lawson turned briefly to follow his gaze. 'It's a lot more than that, old son. Going to take some sorting out too.'

'No ideas then?'

Lawson shrugged. 'Too early yet. We know the fire was started about four hours ago but we're still at the theorising stage. When the Home Office Pathologist deigns to arrive we should know a little bit more.'

Dexter stiffened. 'Are you saying this thing had been going on for three hours before I was even called?'

Lawson nodded. 'Bit isolated out here and the old boy lives – lived alone. His wife died two years ago and there were no house staff, just a domestic who came in three days a week. Unfortunately, the place was well alight before a bloke spotted it from the road as he was driving by.'

'But *three hours*, Dick? Surely someone could have let me know a damned sight earlier than they did? This will be a major press story.'

'Yeah, well, I must admit things weren't handled particularly brilliantly. Our first unit on the scene after the fire service was a bloody dog man and he seems to have farted about for a while before calling CID. Probably tried to get the dog to piss on the fire! I only got here an hour ago myself – minutes before I had Headquarters Control Room telephone you, in fact – and the governor *still* hasn't arrived.'

'Well, every cloud has its silver lining.'

Lawson chuckled. 'You and Moffat really don't like each other, do you?'

Dexter snorted disparagingly. 'The man is a catastrophe waiting for a place to happen, you know that as well as I do. I haven't been to one major enquiry yet that he hasn't cocked up.'

'Now you're being unkind.'

'Am I? Then why did you lot christen him *Super Plod*?'

Lawson chuckled again, but ignored the question. 'You've got Mr Moffat all wrong, Mike. He's quite a nice bloke when you get to know him. He just doesn't like the press, that's all.'

'Well, I don't happen to *be* the press. I'm a copper like you and if

I'm to do my job properly, I need to know what is happening – which reminds me, what's all this I hear about petrol being used to start the fire?'

Lawson tossed his cigarette away into the darkness. 'You're certainly on the ball tonight.'

Dexter raised his eyebrows mildly. 'Well, *was* it petrol?'

The CID man hesitated, then shrugged. 'All I can tell you is that there was apparently a strong smell of the stuff when the first fire appliance arrived and they found some empty cans lying inside the house.'

'Then it *was* arson?'

Lawson laughed harshly. 'You don't get a detective superintendent and his side-kick out of bed for a routine house fire.' He frowned. 'This is a pretty strange business though.'

'In what way?'

'Well, it seems that whoever did this job wanted to advertise the fact that the fire was started deliberately.'

'Why the hell would anyone want to do that?'

'Beats me, but there it is.'

Dexter scowled in the darkness. 'Something you're not telling me, Dick?' he said suspiciously.

'Should there be?'

'Not if we're on the same side, no.'

'Then you've answered your own question.'

'So what can I tell the press?'

Lawson gave an exaggerated shrug. 'You'd better ask the governor about that when he gets here.'

'Oh great. And what's *Super Plod* going to say, eh? No comment, as per usual?'

'That's his prerogative.'

'No it bloody well isn't, not when you drag me out of my pit at three o'clock in the morning.'

Lawson chuckled. 'Well, you'll have your answer soon. His BM has just drawn up.'

The CID man was conspicuous by his absence when the rotund little man in the heavy parka got out of the BMW car and walked quickly towards Dexter. 'Chief Inspector,' he acknowledged curtly and with heavy formality. 'Was that Mr Lawson I just saw walk away?'

Dexter nodded. 'He was just filling me in on the circumstances. Bad business this, sir.'

Moffat's gold-tinted glasses glittered in the light of a spot-lamp blazing from a nearby fire appliance. 'What are *you* doing here?' he queried icily, ignoring the other's attempt at conversation.

Dexter shrugged. 'I was called out to deal with the media. You seem to have a fair few camped by the main gate at the moment and it will get worse as the day progresses.'

'So, get rid of them then.'

'I beg your pardon?'

'Well, that's what you're paid for, isn't it?'

Dexter bit his tongue. 'No, sir, it isn't. I'm here to keep them off your back and to do that I need something to give them. Can we cobble together some sort of brief statement after you've had a look around?'

Moffat stared at him. 'Statement?' he echoed. 'I have no intention of giving those hyenas anything, Mr. Dexter.'

'It would be easier if we did, sir. At least then they'd be happy.'

There was a hard edge to the CID man's voice when he replied. 'I'm not here to make them happy, Chief Inspector. I'm here to investigate a serious crime. They are a total irrelevance.'

Dexter controlled himself with an effort. 'The Chief Constable has an open policy towards the media –' he began, but Moffat cut him off in mid-sentence.

'Don't you quote force policy to me, Mr Dexter,' he snapped. '*I* am in charge of this investigation and *I* will decide who is told what and when. Is that understood?'

Dexter gritted his teeth, but stuck to his guns. 'I still need something to tell them,' he retorted.

Moffat moved closer to him and studied him fixedly. 'Then tell them we are investigating a house fire,' he sneered. 'And when I need to tell them any more than that, you'll be the first to know.'

Before Dexter could argue the point, the little man turned on his heel, heading towards the house and the two fire service officers Lawson had already rejoined. 'Pompous little sod,' Dexter breathed and pulling his mobile from his pocket, he quickly dialled a number.

The telephone at the other end rang for ages without any response and he swore to himself. 'Come on, Kitty,' he muttered impatiently. 'Don't tell me you're at another flaming party.'

Abruptly there was a click, a loud sniff and a female voice answered in a halting slurred voice. 'What now, Michael?'

He grinned in spite of the frustration that still ate away at him after his encounter with Moffat. 'How did you know it was me?'

'With respect, you're the only rotten pig that would ring me at... Hell, it's five-thirty in the morning!'

'Sorry, Kitty, but I need you straightaway.'

A loud sigh. 'Just because you suffer from an over-active libido, is no reason to wake me up at five-thirty in the morning, Michael.'

He emitted a soft chuckle. 'Alden House, Bellingham, Kitty,' he continued. 'Know where it is?'

'I should do. I only live a mile from Bellingham. Pass the place every day on my way to work.'

'Good. Then I'll meet you at the main gate shortly.'

A loud yawn. 'Got something tasty there, have we?'

'Just a cremated crown court judge.'

'Oh... nice one. ETA twenty minutes. Okay?' But the telephone went dead before he could answer.

The fog had thinned appreciably by the time Dexter drove out to the main gate and he found that what had originally been a small knot of journalists was now a sizeable crowd, armed with cameras and microphones.

The bearded agency man in the gabardine raincoat was first off the starting line and he got to Dexter even as he climbed out of his car. 'What can you tell us, Mike? Was it arson?'

But the question was immediately drowned by a chorus of other voices, all seeking different answers. 'Can you confirm Judge Berwick is dead, Chief Inspector?'... 'Could this have been a revenge attack?'...'Any idea as to who may have been responsible?'... 'Who is leading the investigation?'... 'Will there be a press conference?'... 'Can we have an interview?'

Dexter made no effort to say anything. Instead, turning his head away from the firing-squad of flashing camera bulbs, he raised both hands in front of him to try and put a stop to the excited clamour. It took a few moments, but finally he succeeded and there was a strained silence.

'All I can tell you at this stage,' he said, now facing the cameras, 'is that there has been a serious fire at Alden House, which the fire service have managed to extinguish. A body has been found on the premises, but it needs to be formally identified before we can release any details. A police enquiry has been set up under the command of Detective Superintendent Brian Moffat and –'

'Moffat?' someone shouted incredulously to spontaneous laughter. 'Not *Super Plod* himself?'

Dexter winced. Though he knew the senior detective was not the most popular CID man in the force because of his reputation as a bungler and his arrogance towards his staff, he hadn't realised someone had been indiscreet enough to pass his nickname on to the press, which was totally out of order. It was all right having a joke internally at another colleague's expense, but it did the force no good at all to have its dirty linen washed in public. He made no comment in relation to the jibe, however, instead batting it off with an abrupt: 'That's it for now, ladies and gentlemen, I'm afraid. Talk to you later.'

But they weren't going to let him off that easily and the questions resumed immediately, as he knew they would. 'Who reported the fire, Chief Inspector?'... 'Who found the body?'... 'Where did the fire start?'... 'How was it started?'... 'You haven't said whether it was arson or not?'... 'Is this now a murder case?'

He took a deep breath and tried to wave them to silence, but without much success. 'I can tell you nothing more at this stage,' he said in a louder voice. 'As soon as I have more, I will let you know.'

'Off the record, Mike,' the agency man said close to his ear. 'Is the dead man Judge Berwick or not?'

Dexter shook his head wearily. 'I can't tell you anything, Tom,' he replied. 'Not until he has been formally identified.'

'So it is a *he* then?'

'No comment at this stage.'

'Any chance of a quick interview?' another voice chimed in and he saw that the speaker was a petite brunette in jeans and a leather jacket.

'Not at present, love,' he replied. 'Nothing I can say.'

She tapped a heavy tape recorder hanging over one shoulder by a leather strap and held up a microphone. 'Local radio,' she explained. 'I just need a few words for the AM news.'

He shook his head again. 'Sorry. Later maybe.'

She glanced down briefly to fiddle with the dials of her recorder, apparently deaf to his refusal. 'Two minutes, that's all I need, Chief Inspector,' she said, now thrusting the microphone towards him.

His mouth tightened. 'I've just said no,' he snapped, turning back to his car and ignoring another microphone thrusting towards him through the small crowd, 'so leave it alone, will you, love.'

'I'm not your love,' she snapped, realising she was getting nowhere. 'Especially not now.'

Back in the relative security of his car, Dexter watched the crowd of reporters break up into smaller groups and drift away. They wouldn't go far though, he knew that, and if Moffat didn't come up with something positive in a few hours, like a press conference or a more illuminating statement, they would start to get nasty. Blast the man for his stupid arrogance, he thought. It put his small press team in an impossible situation and damaged his own credibility in the eyes of the media.

Starting the engine of his car, he flicked on the lights and swung in a complete circle to head back towards the main gate of the house. 'Watch that lot,' he said through the open window as the young bobby once more swung one of the gates back to admit him. 'They'll be over the wall given half the chance.'

He glimpsed the shadowy figure in his headlights as he rounded a sharp right-hand bend in the driveway. At first he thought it was a police traffic motorcyclist, but the helmet appeared to be black and the leather jacket was certainly not uniform issue. Then the figure was racing off along a narrow track that curled away among the trees to his left.

'Now who the hell are you?' he breathed and spun the wheel hard over as he gunned the car in immediate pursuit.

The track had not been intended for anything more sophisticated than a tractor and the Volvo was soon lurching and pitching on the lumpy pitted surface like a live thing, all but wrenching the steering wheel out of his hands and sending mud and stones clattering up under the wings with a noise like machine-gun fire. The figure was still racing ahead of him, glancing behind every few seconds, but making no attempt to veer off the track into the woods.

'You know where you're going, don't you, me lad?' Dexter commented through gritted teeth, swerving round a projecting low level branch and nearly losing control on the sharp bend that cut away to his right.

Now he could see the shape of a shed or barn of some sort through the mud-spattered windscreen and seconds later he was forced to come to a jolting halt when the track ended abruptly before a pair of large double doors. The trees seemed to press in on him as he scrambled out of the car and the muffled shouts and bangs from the direction of the house, where the fire service were evidently still working to make the building safe, had a strange disembodied quality, as if part of another world.

His quarry seemed to have completely disappeared and he studied the building in front of him dubiously. On his own, with no prospect of backup, it would simply be asking for trouble to poke his nose in there, but the adrenalin was already flooding through his veins, much like the old days when he had been a young bobby on the beat, and he knew he couldn't just walk away and leave the job undone.

Grabbing a torch from the glove compartment of the car, he went round the back and opened the tailgate, rummaging around until his hand closed on the wheel-brace lying among the litter of tools and other rubbish left permanently in the vehicle. Then, moistening dry lips, he approached the double doors of the building, and, masking the beam of his torch in one hand, looked for some sort of handle or latch. That turned out to be unnecessary, for one of the doors was already open slightly just enough to allow him to slip through.

He was met by a heavy blackness and the strong smell of diesel fuel. He listened intently, his torch now switched off completely, but there was nothing save the thudding of his own heart. The cold steel of the wheel-brace seemed to burn in his tightly clenched hand as he stepped forward a few paces, his eyes trying to accustom themselves to the darkness. He walked into something and made a grimace as the wheel-brace clinked against metal. Still nothing moved, but his sixth sense told him someone else was there with him, listening, waiting. His mouth tightened. Well, he wasn't prepared to fool about anymore. Taking a deep breath, he switched the torch full on and swung it in a half-circle.

An ancient rusted tractor, crouching like some enormous insect directly in front of him; stacks of chopped wood along one wall; saws, billhooks and other tools hanging from a crossbeam; and, in one corner, a workbench laden with boxes, cans and bits of dismembered machinery – but more importantly, a crash-helmeted figure lunging towards him from one side of the tractor, swinging a long piece of wood in both hands.

Fire in his head and the stench of spilled diesel in his nostrils as he hit the ground. Then, incredibly, a hard laugh and a voice saying, 'Not this time, my friend,' followed by the snarl of a motorcycle engine starting up. He surfaced through a red mist that became a powerful tail-light and managed to get himself up on to one elbow in time to see the motorcycle nosing its way out through the double doors. Grabbing the front wheel of the tractor, he hauled himself to his knees, but already he was too late and the next second his assailant was gone, revving repeatedly as he faded into the darkness.

★

'You really are a prize idiot, you know that, don't you?' Dick Lawson snapped.

Dexter made no effort to deny it as he sat under a spotlight on the step of the fire appliance while the young fireman cleaned the gash on his temple and put a large plaster in place. 'Story of my life,' he replied with a weak smile.

'But what the hell did you think you were doing out there?'

Dexter pushed the fireman's hand away and watched him walk off with an indifferent shrug. 'How about trying to collar an arsonist who thought he'd sneak back to gloat?'

'And what makes you so sure he was our man?'

'Why else would he be lurking in the woods with a damned motorcycle stashed away in a shed nearby?'

'He could have been press.'

'Pressmen don't go around clobbering coppers with bits of wood.'

'A would-be looter then.'

Dexter snorted. 'What, on a trials bike? He'd have been able to carry a lot away on that, wouldn't he?'

'You're sure it was a trials bike?'

'Positive. Even in the dark it was unmistakable.'

Lawson produced his packet of cigarettes again and lit up. 'That would certainly explain how he managed to escape through the woods. Probably got in and out of the grounds via Stud Lane, which runs along the back of the property, and he was long gone by the time I managed to get the troops down there to have a look. I'll have another search carried out when it's light.'

'Bit pointless really.'

'Yeah, well, we have to go through the motions and they might find something of interest. In the meantime, all we've got is your pretty vague description, which I've had circulated, and the thousand to one chance our man will be picked up by a traffic mobile for speeding.'

The CID man studied his old friend for a moment. 'I should warn you, Mike, that the governor's not too happy with you over this business. You're lucky he's tied up with the Home Office Pathologist at the moment or he'd tear your ears off.'

'What the hell have I done now?'

'Well, while you were chasing your phantom motorcyclist, a

23

couple of reporters got into the grounds. They were intercepted only yards from the house.'

'So, what does *Super Plod* expect me to do? Handcuff them all to the main gates?'

Lawson made a sharp exclamation. 'Get real, will you, Mike. It should never have happened and you know it.'

Dexter glared at him, unrepentant. 'Yeah? Well, let me tell you something. It's going to go on happening as long as your boss behaves the way he does. Cooperation is a two-way street, Dick, and he's broken the first rule already.'

Lawson drew deeply on his cigarette and directed a succession of smoke rings at the spotlight. 'Look, Mike,' he said patiently, 'I know he tends to act a bit cavalier at times, but that's just his style.'

'Cavalier?' Dexter retorted, climbing gingerly to his feet. 'More like *Don Quixote*, if you ask me.'

Lawson helped him up and chuckled softly. 'Why don't you go back to bed and get out on the right side next time, eh.'

'Don't tempt me. I might just decide to stay there.'

The CID man followed him to his car. 'After that bang on the head, no one would blame you if you did, you know that, don't you? It's a nasty gash and by rights you should have gone to hospital.'

Dexter grunted. 'Maybe, but I've got an appraisal with Assistant Chief Constable Operations at ten o'clock and I don't think he'd appreciate it if I didn't appear.' He half-turned. 'By the way, speaking of things medical, shouldn't you be with Moffat and the Pathologist at the moment?'

The other shook his head. 'Gordon Graves has finished the job he came to do and I've seen and heard all I need to at this stage.'

'Which is?'

Lawson shrugged. 'The man was burned to death. Simple as that. Post-mortem might establish more, of course, but that won't be until later today.'

'So what else has Moffat got to talk to Graves about?'

Lawson grunted. 'Since I was politely told to bugger off, I suspect it's funny handshake business. Both of them are evidently members of the same Masonic lodge, so maybe they have some top secret problem to discuss – like who's the next worshipful master.'

Dexter feigned surprise. 'And there's me thinking all these years that you were a fully paid-up member of the club yourself.'

Lawson gave a short laugh. 'Is that right? Well, I'm sorry to disappoint you, old friend, but unfortunately I've never been asked.' He slammed the car door shut as Dexter slid carefully behind the wheel. 'Now go and get some breakfast and make sure Tania's okay, eh? Catch you later.'

It looked as though Alden House had been laid to siege when the young constable let Dexter out through the main entrance and the army of reporters surrounded his car in seconds, bombarding him with questions he couldn't answer. Despite the crush, he glimpsed Kitty Morrison's distinctive yellow sports car almost immediately and edged his way forward to park beside her. The slender black girl, with the dread locks the Chief Constable loved to hate, joined him in the front passenger seat even before he came to a stop, a broad grin on her face and her brown eyes sparkling behind the big square-framed glasses. Her grin widened even more when she saw the bulging plaster on his forehead.

'Hey, what happened to you, Michael?' she chortled with a total absence of sympathy. 'Don't tell me you and old *Super Plod* had a punch-up?'

'Just leave it, will you,' he retorted sourly. 'I'm not in the mood. Now, do you want to hear what's been happening or not?'

His briefing about the situation was short and to the point and, despite her initial humour, she listened carefully, making a written note of what he had told the press in the light of a small pocket torch she had brought with her.

'Just keep the *Rat-pack* happy until we know where this thing is going,' he finished up grimly, 'and try to humour Moffat. He'll need us soon enough when he starts thinking about public appeals and I want to be right there when the press give him two fingers.'

A flash of white teeth as she climbed out of the car. 'You know, if there's one thing I've always admired about you, Michael,' she chuckled, 'it's your deep sense of Christian charity.'

Chapter 2

Tania was sitting at the kitchen table with her back to the hall door when Dexter finally arrived home. She was still wearing her nightdress and staring out of the window into the grey wintry morning as if in a dream. She appeared not to hear him come in and visibly jumped when he spoke more sharply than he had intended. 'Should you not be getting ready for work?'

She returned the half-empty cup of tea she was holding to the saucer, almost tipping it over with uncharacteristic clumsiness in the process. 'I – I don't feel like going in today,' she replied hesitantly.

'Oh?' He frowned and placed both hands on her thin hunched shoulders, planting a kiss in the midst of the tousled auburn hair, which hadn't yet seen a comb. 'And why is that then?'

Her hand reached up to clasp his own and he squeezed it briefly, sensing what was going on in her mind, but in no hurry to bring the subject out into the open. 'I haven't slept since you left,' she explained. 'I'm just all in.'

He grunted, fully aware of the fact that she hadn't taken a day's sickness from her job at the local hospital laboratory in Heaton for at least two years. 'Well, if you're ill…'

'It's not that.'

'What then?'

She swivelled round in the chair. 'Why didn't you tell me, Michael?'

He turned towards the teapot on the worktop, anxious to avoid the gaze of those penetrating blue eyes. 'Tell you what?' he prevaricated, selecting a mug from the cupboard above his head with exaggerated care.

'You said that the fire was due to an electrical fault.'

'I said probably.'

'Well, whatever. The fact remains that you knew it was arson from the start.'

He poured the tea slowly, grimacing to himself. 'I didn't know for sure. It was only suggested as a possibility when Control Room rang me. Anyway, what difference does it make?'

He risked turning towards her, trying to conceal his embarrassment behind the mug.

Her freckled face was pale and drawn and there was a haunted expression in her eyes, which now widened appreciably. 'What on earth have you done to your head?'

He gave her a weak schoolboy grin and felt the plaster tenderly. 'Oh *that*. Walked into a ruddy tree at the fire, nothing serious.'

She nodded. 'It looks more like the tree walked into you, Michael. What have you been up to?'

He gulped some tea, then winced as it burned his mouth. 'I've told you what happened,' he snapped, suddenly irritated, 'and that's it. Now why don't you go back to bed and rest?'

She continued to study him fixedly. 'They said on the radio that Judge Berwick was burned to death and police are treating the case as murder.'

His eyes narrowed. 'Who the hell said that?'

'It was on the local station.'

'That damned bitch,' he grated, remembering the female reporter with the over aggressive microphone. 'That isn't what I told them at all. They've just put two and two together to make five.'

'Are you sure, Michael?' she persisted. 'Or is it that they made four and you don't like it?'

He scowled. 'Okay, so it's likely that Berwick was murdered, but that's nothing for you to worry about.'

She shook her head wearily. 'Michael, why are you always trying to protect me? I'm a big girl now, you know.'

He sighed and, returning the mug to the worktop, met her gaze with a wry smile. 'Big enough for me anyway, love,' he teased, eyeing the sharp little nipples straining against the thin fabric of her nightdress.

She flushed. 'I'm being serious, damn you!' she blazed. 'I'm fed up with being patronised. You don't honestly think I've ever forgotten what happened all those years ago, do you? Time is not the great healer it's meant to be, Michael. You just run out of tears, that's all.'

He nodded, leaning back against the worktop and looking very uncomfortable. 'I realise that,' he said carefully, 'but what's the sense in raking it all up again? Berwick died in a fire, simple as that.'

'Started by someone deliberately.'

He shrugged. 'Okay, so it was deliberate. But there must be loads of people who have an axe to grind against a crown court judge.'

'But it was a fire, Michael, a *fire*. Doesn't that strike you as odd?'

'Ironic maybe, but not odd. It's the ideal way of trying to conceal a murder – burn the corpse.'

She started to say something, but he waved her to silence. 'Listen to me, Tania,' he said firmly. 'Eddie Challow was put away for what he did and he's still inside. He can't hurt you anymore, if that's what you're worried about, so why all this nonsense, eh?'

She bit her lip. 'But what if he's not still inside? We already know he was moved from the top security special hospital at Broughton Lake to that psychiatric unit at Bramley Heath. What if he's managed to escape?'

Dexter stepped forward quickly and, taking her in his arms, gripped her tightly. 'Now you're being ridiculous. Don't you think we'd have heard by now if that had happened? For flip's sake, it would have been headline news everywhere.'

She stared up at him, her eyes wide and fixed. 'So, what if the authorities have simply released him? After all, he has been locked away for twenty years and he *was* sent to Bramley Heath for further assessment.'

He sighed heavily and stroked her hair. 'What if, what if, what if. You're full of *what ifs* today and you're simply torturing yourself for no reason. If he had been released, we would have been the first to be told about it. The hospital has an obligation to keep the victim informed of things like that. This business is just coincidence, nothing more; a cruel quirk of fate. You must start seeing things for what they are and not what you imagine.'

She released her breath in a long trembling sigh and gently pushed him away. 'Yes – yes, I know. I'm just being silly again, that's all.' She forced a smile. 'Look, let's forget it, shall we? I'll get you some breakfast. Brown toast okay?'

He hesitated, still not happy. 'You sure you're going to be all right?'

Another little smile and she nodded her head firmly. 'I'll be fine. I might take Gwenda out later. Get a bit of fresh air.'

That didn't seem to ease his mind either and he frowned again. 'You sure you can manage that damned horse? She can be pretty spirited sometimes and –'

She laid a hand on his arm. 'Stop fussing, Michael, and sit down. I'll make a fresh pot of tea.'

He grunted and, pulling out a chair, reached for the paper. 'Any post?'

She shook her head. 'Only junk mail really – oh, but we did get a wedding anniversary card.'

He started, his face reddening as it always did when he had a secret planned. 'Anniversary card?' he murmured a little too casually, keeping his eyes firmly on the newspaper. 'Who from?'

'You do know it's our anniversary on Sunday?'

He gritted his teeth, sensing her watching him, hoping he would give something away. 'Of course I do… er… who's the card from? Bit early, isn't it?'

She leaned over him and dropped it on to his paper, kissing him briefly on the cheek. She seemed to have put all thoughts of Judge Berwick and Eddie Challow from her mind and, casting her a swift sidelong glance, he saw mischief in her eyes. '*I* think it was probably sent by a certain husband not noted for his razor-sharp memory,' she whispered, rubbing herself against him provocatively. 'That's why he made sure it caught the post in plenty of time.' She chuckled. 'Trouble is, in his panic he forgot to sign it.'

He pulled away from her, outwardly concentrating on the card. 'Don't be so daft,' he snapped, irritated by the question and scared to death he might let something slip if he said anymore. 'I had nothing to do with it. Now, will you let me read the flaming thing?'

She made a face and, twisting the lobe of his ear, flounced across to the toaster. 'As I said, it's not signed anyway,' she retorted, 'so there's nothing there *to* read.'

He glowered at the card with its entwined hearts and the words "Happy Anniversary" on the front, less interested in who might have sent the thing than in the fact that it had put him severely on the spot. The printed message inside read: "Fond memories on our special day", but there was no handwritten message and the card was unsigned.

'*Our* special day?' he queried.

She half-turned, the bread-knife in her hand and the mischief back in her eyes. 'Precisely the point I was making, dearest,' she said with silky sarcasm. 'I don't remember us sharing our nuptials with anyone on our wedding night, do you?'

He gave her an old-fashioned look and grunted. 'More likely they got the wrong address.'

She laughed outright, a pleasing sound after her earlier mood. 'Oh come on, Michael, I hardly think a husband or wife would forget where their other half lived.'

He gave a brief self-conscious smirk, feeling suddenly foolish. 'Doesn't say "wedding anniversary" here anyway,' he said defensively. 'Words "our special day" could mean any sort of anniversary.'

She adjusted the toaster to take the two slices of bread she had just cut. 'I can't think of any anniversary that calls for a threesome,' she retorted, still laughing. 'Unless you've arranged something really different for ours?'

He ignored the comment and a moment later a fresh mug of tea arrived in front of him and a hand ruffled the hair at the back of his neck. 'Exactly what have you got planned, my sweet?' she teased. 'I do hope it's something nice.'

He turned his head to glare at her. 'You ought to see someone about that nose of yours,' he snapped. 'It's getting very long and pointed – oh, by the way, the toast is on fire.'

She was still raking out the cremated remains in the toaster when the telephone rang, putting paid to any further conversation about their anniversary. 'Saved by the bell,' he breathed as he picked up the receiver.

'Mike, is that you?' The voice was familiar and sounded agitated.

'It's me, Sarah,' he confirmed, recognising his deputy's brittle tones.

A sigh of relief. 'I'm at work, Mike, and it's going absolutely mad here. There's been an overnight raid on an explosive store at Littleton Camp, a fatal traffic accident involving a child and a police car at Heaton, and now this Berwick thing. We've actually got BBC Television camped outside and the phones are going non-stop.'

He made a wry face, visualising the pandemonium in the general office now that the absence of Kitty and himself had reduced the staff to two. 'Doesn't surprise me. Is John in yet?'

A loud snort greeted the question. 'What do *you* think – oh, sorry, he's just walked in.'

He grinned. John Durrell, the rotund balding ex-police sergeant, who had joined the office as a civilian two days after retiring from the job, was not noted for his punctuality. Unlike Sarah, however, he was an indispensable unflappable member of the team – when he deigned to turn up on time.

'I'm on my way, Sarah,' he said. 'Twenty minutes. Okay? Just keep taking the tablets.'

Tania's second attempt at toast succeeded and ignoring her disapproving tut-tutting and head shaking, he wolfed down two buttered slices and half a mug of tea before heading for the door.

'Michael,' she called after him and he stopped dead in the hallway, turning briefly. 'Don't worry about me, okay?'

He nodded, throwing the door wide. 'Just be careful on that damned horse.'

'And Michael?'

He swore, turning again. 'What now?'

The devilment was back in her eyes and her freckled face wore a broad grin. 'Where *are* we going on our anniversary?'

'There and bloody back,' he snapped, slamming the door shut with unnecessary force, but he was also grinning as he strode quickly down the driveway.

*

The car park at the front of Police Headquarters had all the appearance of a film set when Dexter drove into his allotted space. The press were everywhere and he counted at least three camera crews, plus a big green film unit van.

He managed to get into the building without being spotted and found Sarah at fifty thousand feet and still climbing. Her shoulder-length black hair had the dishevelled appearance of someone who had repeatedly run their hands through it and the thin hatchet face was flushed and twitchy. She was on the telephone when he walked into the open-plan office, talking animatedly to someone at the other end. One hand immediately shot in the air when she saw him, the thin fingers with their long red fingernails clicking together to attract his attention.

He nodded, but ignored the imperious summons, receiving a wink from John Durrell as he passed the retired sergeant seated on the edge of his desk, with one telephone receiver at his ear and another on the adjoining desk off the hook. The individual telephone consoles were all ablaze with flashing yellow lights and the office buzzed with waiting calls.

The desk in Dexter's own office seemed to be buried in paper and he glanced at it sourly as he hung his coat on the back of the door. Press releases, incident reports, letters and newspaper cuttings

seemed to have been dumped on the polished teak surface in piles –
as if a chute had opened in the ceiling to disgorge the lot – while the
telephone was almost covered in sticky yellow memos, asking him to
ring half the world at once.

'Michael, we really must get some help in here.' Sarah marched
into his office, her voice already several decibels higher than usual.

He slumped into his chair and looked at her, saying nothing, the
intense activity of the last few hours after hardly any sleep at last
beginning to tell on him.

'I mean, listen to it,' she persisted in her best *Sloane Ranger* voice.
'It's like World War III starting.'

He smiled grimly. Poor old Sarah was certainly hyped up this
morning. Maybe her reporter boyfriend wasn't giving her one as
often as she would have liked. But there again, she had never been
able to handle stress in the six months he had known her anyway. An
ex-journalist for a national newspaper, Sarah Hamilton-Lancing, the
younger daughter of the Hamilton-Lancings of Frome, had only got
the job because of her pedigree and the fact that in the top echelons of
the police service bullshit often baffled brains. She was superbly
miscast in the role of Deputy Press Officer, despite her undoubted
journalistic talents. But as Assistant Chief Constable Operations had
declared after chairing the selection board, 'She certainly comes well
recommended,' frowning when Dexter had retorted: 'So did *Lucrezia
Borgia*, sir!'

'Are you listening to me, Michael?' Sarah snapped, stamping her
foot.

He nodded. 'Sarah, I wouldn't dare do anything else,' he
murmured dryly. 'But you're out of luck. With Carol not due back
from leave until the day after tomorrow, there *isn't* anyone else, as
you well know. We're just going to have to manage as usual. One of
the privileges of being part of a chief constable's secretariat.'

'I just can't see why you called out young Kitty,' she went on. (Ah!
So *that* was it.) 'After all, she *is* only employed as a press liaison
assistant.'

'Yeah, yeah, yeah, whereas you are my deputy,' he cut in wearily,
then held up his hand before she could say anymore. 'Look, Sarah,
the reason I called out Kitty was because most of what she will be
doing is manning the press lines at the incident room, which is bound
to be set up shortly, for a good twelve hours a day. You're too
valuable to commit to something as mundane as that. I shall be

dashing about all over the place in the next few days and I need someone in this office I can trust.'

'You do?'

'I do,' he lied. 'Now tell the switchboard you're putting all the phones on hold for a few minutes and I'll give you and John a quick briefing.'

She nodded, staring at him. 'By the way, what happened to your head?'

He sighed. 'I picked a spot,' he replied. 'Now can we get on?'

Dexter's quick briefing actually lasted just under five minutes, for his direct telephone line rang seconds after he had provided the basic information. 'Mr. Dexter?' the soft voice purred and he quickly glanced at his watch, his stomach trying for a pole-vault gold. 'Sorry, Laura,' he blurted, recognising the cultured tones of Laura Tensing, secretary to Assistant Chief Constable Operations, and realising he was already five minutes late for his appraisal, 'I'm on my way.'

'Oh good,' came the slightly amused reply. 'Mr. Parkes *will* be pleased.'

★

Dennis Stanford Parkes BA was not a man who liked to be kept waiting and the irritation showed on the smooth baby face when Dexter stepped into his office after a brief knock and an announcement by the ever correct Miss Tensing. The pale blue eyes studied him coldly through the silver-framed spectacles and the thin violinist's fingers toyed unceasingly with the gold coloured Parker pen that, unbeknown to Dexter, had just been used for nothing more momentous than the completion of the other's essential mileage claim form.

'You really must learn to manage your time more effectively, Michael,' Parkes said tightly, leaning back from his desk in a leather chair that seemed ready to smother him. 'I'm a busy man, you know, and you're now seven minutes late.'

'Sorry, sir,' Dexter replied, accepting his waved invitation to sit down in the nearest of two less imposing armchairs facing each other across a mahogany coffee table. 'We're a bit busy downstairs at the moment.'

Parkes deserted his desk and settled himself in the armchair opposite Dexter, a thick blue file on his lap. 'I can imagine,' he drawled, without being able to imagine anything of the sort. 'Judge Berwick, wasn't it?'

33

Dexter shrugged. 'As far as we know. We're waiting for the post-mortem and formal ID.'

'Of course, of course. Bad business.' Parkes hesitated, as if trying to find the right words. 'Publicity not doing us much good at the moment though, is it?'

Dexter's eyes narrowed. 'I'm not sure I follow you, sir?'

Parkes sighed impatiently. 'Haven't you seen the papers yet, Michael?'

'I haven't really had much time, sir. I was called out at three o'clock and –'

'Yes, yes, yes, I appreciate that. Part of a PRO's job though, isn't it?'

'What being called out at three o'clock in the morning or reading the papers, sir?'

The pale blue eyes studied him contemptuously. 'Don't be obtuse, Chief Inspector. You know very well what I mean. It's your job to make sure we present the right image. Judge Berwick was very well connected and in any event you must be aware how committed the Chief Constable is to maintaining a good relationship with the media.'

Dexter's mouth tightened. 'Only too well, sir, but Detective Superintendent Moffat is the SIO and –'

Parkes cut him off again. 'I'm sure you would not want to bother me with trifles, Michael. Suffice it to say that you are the representative of the Chief Constable and you will always be fully supported if you are doing your level best to ensure his policy is maintained. Do I make myself clear?'

'Yes, sir.'

'Good, then let's move on, shall we? Busy, busy, you know. Other people to see. And our appointment *was* to talk about you, after all.'

'Yes, sir,' Dexter agreed, furious that the blame for the bad press was being laid at his door while his problem with Moffat was simply being side-stepped, as per usual.

Parkes opened up the blue file and flicked through one or two papers, apparently engrossed. Dexter knew differently, however. The ACC would have thoroughly read the file well in advance of the interview. All this was carefully staged for his benefit. Designed to keep him in suspense, feeding the chief officer's own personal power complex.

'So,' Parkes said finally, leaning back in his chair and deftly twirling his pen between two fingers. 'How's the Press Office?'

Dexter shrugged. 'Busy as usual, sir. We could do with another member of staff actually, especially during incidents of this kind.'

'Challenge of management, Michael,' Parkes smirked and, clenching his other fist, raised it to emphasise the point. 'Got to get to grips, man. Test of the old organisational skills.'

Dexter frowned. 'Yes, sir, but –'

'No buts, Michael. Every faith in you. Now, what about the future, eh? How do you see yourself in, say… a year's time?'

His attempt to make a case for an additional press liaison assistant expertly kicked to touch, Dexter was caught off guard by the sudden change of direction. 'Well, sir, I am keen to progress.'

Parkes returned to the blue file and flicked it open again, obviously looking at nothing in particular. 'I've read your self-appraisal, Michael,' he went on. 'Nice to see a man with ambition.'

'Thank you, sir. I feel I still have a lot to offer the service and I would like to make the crown before I retire.'

Parkes looked at him in dismay. 'The crown? Superintendent, you mean?' He shook his head slowly and sat back, twirling the pen again. 'Yes, I realise from your own career assessment that you are keen for promotion, but,' and he made a face, 'trouble is, you see, the service is changing; looking for… ah… different qualities.'

'What sort of qualities, sir?'

For the first time Parkes himself seemed caught off guard, but he recovered just as quickly. 'Michael, Michael,' he patronised without answering the question, 'you're doing an excellent job where you are. Round peg and all that. Promotion is not the only thing, you know. Job satisfaction is much more important.'

'Are you saying you won't be recommending me for the next board, sir?' Dexter was conscious of a peculiar twisting feeling in his gut.

Parkes sighed heavily and looked out of the window, still twirling his pen. 'You have to understand,' he went on, apparently more interested in the antics of a pigeon on the window sill than in his press officer, 'that there is a lot more competition for the superintending ranks these days.'

He forced himself to meet Dexter's gaze, but then immediately returned to the blue file, apparently referring to a list of postings. 'You've done very well in your career so far. Three years on CID and then Detective Sergeant on both the Regional and National Crime Squad. Back to CID as the Detective Inspector on Winslake police area, Chief Inspector Operations at Headquarters, then back to Winslake as second-in-command before coming here as the force Press, Public Relations Officer. Four chief constable's commendations and three from different crown courts. Quite a bit of achievement there, I would say, and it will certainly be borne in mind in the future.'

He treated Dexter to his most reassuring smile. 'As you will know, the Chief Constable intends civilianising your post within the next few months, in line with the trend nationally, and I am quite sure we can find another challenging role to suit your talents when that happens.'

Dexter's expression remained bleak. 'Thank you, sir. So you're not recommending me, I take it?'

A muscle twitched irritably in the baby face and the gold pen stopped twirling. 'I think you know what I'm saying, Michael,' Parkes replied. 'Be satisfied with what you've got. All right?'

'Then can I have a reason, sir?'

The good-natured façade was discarded completely now and the pale blue eyes were once more cold and hard. 'This appraisal is not about giving reasons, Chief Inspector,' Parkes snapped. 'It's about assessing your overall performance. So let's get on with it, shall we?'

The rest of the interview was very much like all the other annual appraisal interviews Dexter had attended under the new enlightened performance system – a sprint through around a dozen different sections, each numerically graded and dealing with such topics as leadership, innovative ability and time-management. Each section was covered by a middle of the road assessment and given a careful grade that put him above average, so he couldn't complain, but not high enough to warrant consideration for the next rank. Clever bastards, he thought bitterly as he signed the bottom of the form and walked out with his copy tightly clenched in his hand. Clever, smooth, cheating, unscrupulous *bastards*.

He called by the gents toilet on the way back to his office to splash some cold water over his face and take the angry redness out of it. No sense advertising the fact that things hadn't gone well. It was humiliating enough to know that he wouldn't be going up on the next board with people like Dick Lawson, without telling the whole world in advance. The blast of the tannoy (you couldn't even escape it in the bog, he thought savagely) forced him out of his hideaway within minutes, however. 'Chief Inspector Dexter, report to Press Office urgently please. Chief Inspector Dexter...'

Lurching away from the wash-hand basin, he flicked some water on his hair and hurriedly dried his face on a paper towel. Then, taking a couple of deep breaths, he headed out into the corridor, almost bowling over the force's civilian Statistics Officer on the way in. 'Sorry, Fred,' he jerked over his shoulder, forcing a grin. 'Urgent tannoy.'

Fred Larsen turned briefly to stare after him. 'What, Sarah ladder her tights again, Mike?' he chortled.

The origin of the call was certainly his number two (surprise, surprise) and she was waiting for him in his office, hands on hips and a tighter than usual expression on her face.

'Michael,' she snapped. 'Why didn't you tell us about the cuffs?'

He stared at her blankly.

'I mean,' she exclaimed, 'if we're not to be trusted with confidential information, *okay*, but it's made us look totally stupid with the press.'

He raised his hand to stop her. 'Cuffs, Sarah?' he queried. 'Do you mind telling me what you're talking about?'

Before she could answer John Durrell slipped between them and dropped a newspaper cutting on to Dexter's desk. The headline and first short paragraph told him all that he needed to know.

BODY HANDCUFFED IN FIRE

The body of an elderly man, believed to be a retired crown court judge, was found in the shell of a burning house in the early hours of this morning, handcuffed to the frame of his bed. Police are treating the case as one of murder.

'The lying two-timing snake,' he breathed, sitting down heavily in his chair.

'You mean it's untrue?' Sarah exclaimed. 'Then how –?'

'Oh I bet it's true all right,' he grated. 'It's just that Lawson hadn't got the guts to tell me and that prat, Moffat, was obviously naïve enough to think no one would find out. Have they set up an incident room yet?'

'The old Bellingham nick, just down the road,' Durrell replied. 'They're in the process of doing it now.' He left the office quickly, returning with a scrap of paper. 'Kitty called from there a short time ago. Apparently the place was closed two years ago as a main station and it's only used now by the local beat officers. Ideal place for an incident room really.'

Dexter all but snatched the piece of paper from him and stabbed the buttons of the telephone as if he wanted to push them through and out the other side. 'Kitty? Get me DCI Lawson, will you? And tell him I don't want any rubbish about him not being available.'

He put the phone on hold and turned towards his deputy as Durrell dashed back into the other office to deal with another call. 'What's the damage so far?'

Sarah snorted. 'Half of Fleet Street are up in arms. I don't know where they got their information from, but they're hopping mad we won't confirm it.'

He grunted. 'You know as well as I do that you can't keep things like this quiet.' He raised one hand fractionally and punched his extension button on the telephone. 'Yes, Kitty? Damn! Yeah, well tell him to call me soonest.'

He slammed the receiver down hard. 'Lawson's back at the scene apparently. I'll just have to go down there and try and get hold of him.'

'So what do we tell the press?'

'What *can* we tell them? I can see why Moffat wanted this kept quiet. If he nicks anyone, he'll want something up his sleeve for the interview. But he should have told me about it anyway. How can I guard his back now?'

Durrell poked his head into the office again. 'Call for you, Mike,' he said almost apologetically. 'Says he's an old friend.'

'Tell whoever it is that I retired last week.'

'News guy, named Quentin Fuller.'

'Fuller?' Dexter echoed, suddenly interested. 'Okay, put him through.'

'Mike?' The voice at the other end was halting and disembodied, obviously on a mobile. 'Lost... police handcuffs... lately?'

Dexter grinned in spite of the way he felt. 'What are you after, Quentin?' he queried.

'Meet you... lunch today...'

Dexter automatically shook his head, forgetting it was a phone call. 'Can't, Quentin. Busy.'

'In your interests... Vital we speak... Say midday...Trout Inn... Maybury...'

Dexter glanced quickly at his watch, then tapped the top of the desk with the fingers of his other hand, deep in thought. Quentin Fuller was one of his best media contacts and their trust and friendship went back years. The shrewd little journalist had even been a guest at his wedding. When Fuller said he had something to impart, it was usually good and he never used words like vital lightly.

'Mike?' floated back again.

'Yeah, okay,' Dexter agreed. 'See you there.'

'Out to lunch then?' Sarah snapped waspishly as he replaced the receiver.

He raised his eyebrows. 'Jealous?'

She snorted and, turning on her heel, went to rejoin Durrell in the main office. 'I hope you choke on it, Michael,' she threw back over her shoulder.

Chapter 3

The Trout at Maybury was an old coaching inn, allegedly dating back to the seventeenth century. It was renowned for the international cuisine provided by its *French* chef, whose detailed knowledge of that country was quite surprising, since he had been born in West London and had only visited France twice on boozy day trips with his live-in girlfriend. Nevertheless, he could certainly cook and no one who had twenty-five pounds a head to spend on a meal really cared where he came from as long as he continued to serve up the gastronomic delights for which The Trout was justly famed.

Dexter, who preferred food he could easily recognise and hated voyages of discovery through uncharted seas of anaemic sauces, ignored the tantalizing aromas drifting out of the open door of the restaurant and made straight for the smoke-filled public bar, where he found Fuller already tucking into an enormous ploughman's lunch in one corner. Ordering a ploughman's for himself and taking a pint of shandy back to the table, he propped himself on the stool opposite his old friend and raised his glass in mock salute.

'Michael, my boy,' the thin grizzly-haired journalist chuckled loudly through a mouthful of his portion of French stick, fragments of bread already clinging to his gingery beard. 'Glad you could make it.'

Dexter took a long pull on the shandy, then made a face, eyeing the other's pint of frothy beer enviously. 'So what's all this about, Quentin?' he queried, leaning forward across the table to make himself heard above the general hubbub.

Fuller tapped a huge piece of cheese with his knife. 'Nice bit of strong cheddar with this lot, Mike,' he said. 'You'll enjoy it.'

'I'd enjoy it a lot more if you said what was on your mind,' Dexter retorted. 'When I told you on the phone that I was busy, I wasn't exaggerating.'

Fuller nodded, suddenly serious. 'I can imagine,' he said. 'Horrific job at Alden House. Makes you wonder what kind of a person would do something like that.'

'If you think –' Dexter began, then stopped and leaned to one side as his ploughman's arrived. 'If you think,' he continued after the young waitress had disappeared, 'that I've come here simply to be pumped by you, you've got another think coming.'

Fuller shook his head and waggled his fork in his direction. 'I reckon we can help each other, old son,' he corrected. 'How's Tania?'

Dexter unwrapped his sealed pat of butter and began spreading it on his roll. 'As well as can be expected after what has happened.'

Fuller finished eating and pushed his still half-full plate to one side, going for his pint instead. 'I sympathise,' he replied. 'It must have brought the whole rotten business flooding back.'

'Something like that. But we're not here to talk about Tania, are we?'

Fuller ignored the censure in his tone and blithely carried on in the same vein. 'What is it, Mike, nineteen years since they put Eddie Challow away?'

'Twenty.'

The journalist lit a cigarette and offered the packet across the table, pocketing it without comment when the other refused. 'I was a buck reporter on the local paper when it all happened,' he reminisced, his blue eyes half-closed in thought. 'I met you for the first time at the scene, if you remember.' He chuckled again. 'You threatened to nick me if I didn't bugger off.'

Dexter loaded his fork and started eating. 'Should have done too,' he growled. 'You became a regular pain in the arse.'

'Yeah, but I did do a nice supportive piece on you when you were pilloried by everyone for getting personally involved with the key witness, didn't I?'

Dexter nodded slowly, a distant look in his eyes as he remembered the frail ghost-like figure lying in the hospital bed, eyes wide open, yet seeing nothing. He must have fallen in love with Tania at that moment, he reckoned. Perhaps it was her vulnerability that had touched him first, but he had got to know her well over the next few weeks and a marvellous bond had developed between the two of them. The powers that be had tried to shift him off the case, of course, putting a woman detective there in his place, which they said was more appropriate in the circumstances, but Tania would only respond to him, so he had stayed with it in spite of them all.

Then just a few months after the long drawn-out court case, they had finally married and moved to their present home at Elvington. There, with the support of the local psychiatric hospital in which she had spent some time as a voluntary patient, he had set about repairing the mental damage that had been done. It had been a terrible period, sapping every ounce of energy he possessed as he tried to deal with the recurring nightmares, the bouts of depression and the near suicidal moods; where only patience, the willingness to listen and the constant reassurance of his solid dependable presence had had any real effect.

'Biggest story I'd ever seen at the time, you know,' Fuller's voice droned on as he puffed on his cigarette, 'and when my editor came in and said his senior reporter had broken his leg, which meant I'd have to handle it, I just couldn't believe my luck.'

Dexter surfaced with a jolt, his face suddenly cold and hard. 'Luck?' he said savagely, food spilling off his loaded fork. '*Luck*? It wasn't lucky for Tania when she was attacked and raped by that perverted bastard while she was out jogging and it certainly wasn't lucky for her poor devil of a father when his house was burned to the ground with him inside it!'

He had unwittingly raised his voice and a number of customers were looking towards the pair of them with evident curiosity. Fuller snatched his cigarette from his mouth and laid a hand on his friend's arm. 'Yeah, I know, Mike,' he said hastily. 'Sorry, okay? Sometimes I've got the tact of an elephant. Forget what I said.'

Dexter relaxed and made an apologetic grimace. 'No problem. I've had a bad day, that's all.'

Fuller drained his pint and pointed at Dexter's half-empty glass. 'Same again?'

Momentary hesitation, then a resigned: 'Yeah, okay, just a half, thanks.'

As Fuller headed for the crowded bar, Dexter found his mind wandering off, taking him back to the horrific crime that had rocked the county all that time ago and which, in a strange terrible way, had been instrumental in bringing Tania and himself together.

In his mind's eye he could still see the hideous blackened corpse of her father, twisted into an impossible position in his final agonies, lying on the iron frame of the big double bed to which he had been tied with chicken wire. He could still remember the stench of charred wood and furnishings in that small gutted room and the nauseating odour of something else, unconnected with the burned furniture, curtains, carpets and roof beams, that had brought the bile racing up into his throat in a fiery torrent. He had made a fool of himself at that incident, he knew that only too well, but just for once the carefully cultivated, macho policeman's mask had slipped and, unbeknown to Tania, he had been living his own private nightmare ever since.

'I should get out of there if I were you.' Fuller's voice at his elbow made him jump and he stared at the journalist, his expression blank and uncomprehending as the other set another glass in front of him.

'Wherever it was you were off to,' Fuller explained, the dwindling cigarette butt in the corner of his mouth forcing him to affect a lopsided grin. 'Going by the look on your face, you certainly weren't enjoying it.'

Comprehension dawned and Dexter sighed heavily. 'Oh, I see. No, just thinking about what we were discussing, that's all.'

'Nightmare still as vivid then?'

'I can't see it ever fading. I reckon I'll take it with me to my grave.' The policeman hesitated, then went on in almost a rush. 'I know this sounds awful, but do you know, every time I look at Tania I see that swine, Challow, grinning at me over her shoulder.'

Fuller took a mouthful of beer, smoke trailing from the cigarette now held between two fingers of the same hand, then returned the glass to the table with a bang. 'Hardly surprising after what he did to her,' he replied, 'though I have to say, I've never stopped wondering what made him flip. I mean, he wasn't exactly the sort of person you would see as a budding psychopath, was he?'

'They never are. That's the problem.'

'Even so, you have to admit that this guy was about as unremarkable as you can get. A twenty-six year old bachelor, living in a crummy end terrace with his elderly mum, and working as a driver for the local haulage firm, I ask you. So, he was a bit of an indecency merchant and he had a couple of minor convictions for setting fire to hay barns, but –'

'Hardly *minor*. They were revenge attacks on a farmer who gave him a good belting for touching up his teenage daughter – and that MO is pretty significant when you think about what he did to Tania and her dad later on. He was also strongly suspected of a number of other arsons and sexual assaults in the area and his name certainly came up in connection with the murder of that girl in the quarry at Tulse End.'

43

Fuller made a dismissive wave. 'Okay, okay, but it was all suspicion; nothing was ever proven. Anyway, he was hardly Public Enemy Number One, was he? Yet suddenly, out of the blue, *pow*! Proper *Jekyll and Hyde* stuff.'

Dexter finished his first shandy and watched the residue slide back to the bottom of the glass. 'Yeah, it was that all right,' he agreed, 'but a whole lot more besides. I got sight of the psychiatric report before they put him away and it made pretty disturbing reading, I can tell you. According to the shrink who prepared it, Challow must have been suffering from some sort of psychotic disorder for years. Something to do with sexual repression and an unhealthy mother fixation, whatever that means. It was only just hidden beneath the surface apparently and he could have gone over the edge at any time. All it needed was for someone to press the right buttons.'

'Then along came Tania.'

'Dexter grunted. 'Yeah, naïve little Tania, the original collector of waifs and strays, who was always looking out for the underdog and would have found an inadequate loner like Eddie Challow an irresistible challenge. By rights, of course, she shouldn't have been anywhere near Tulse End, but at university, studying for her finals. Then the sudden death of her mother forced her to return home for the funeral.'

'And she stayed on afterwards.'

Dexter nodded. 'She couldn't bring herself to abandon her father. The death of her mother had hit him pretty hard and she felt it was her duty to stay and look after him.'

'Some girl!'

'You can say that again. To give up her finals and everything she had worked for to remain in Tulse End took real guts. But she didn't hesitate, even taking over her mother's former admin job at her dad's haulage firm so she could keep an eye on old man Ferguson and make sure the business was ticking over properly.'

'Then she ran into Eddie Challow.'

Dexter made a grimace. 'Couldn't really miss him. He was always hanging around the village between driving jobs when she went to the shop for anything. Being Tania, it didn't take her long to feel sorry for him – especially when he told her he lived at home, supporting his elderly mother after his father had been killed at the quarry just before it closed down –.'

'Oh yes,' Fuller interjected quickly, 'I remember that incident. I was at school in Grazely when it happened, but it was in all the local papers. The old boy was a blaster, wasn't he? Blew himself up after one too many whiskies from his hip flask. Tragic business.'

Dexter was unsympathetic. 'Bit messy, I should think,' he agreed, 'but hardly tragic. He was a drunk, and violent with it too. Used to knock his wife and son about on a regular basis by all accounts, and he managed to booze away not only his own wages, but most of the money she made as a cleaner at Heaton General Hospital as well.'

'Small wonder that young Eddie turned out the way he did then, eh? Pretty awful life for a kid.'

Dexter treated him to a withering stare. 'Which is exactly what the shrinks said in their assessment of him,' he said coldly. 'Poor little misunderstood Eddie. It wasn't his fault that he'd turned out the way he had. It was all down to the years of abuse he'd suffered as a child.' He shook his head slowly. 'And the tragedy of it all was that at the beginning, Tania thought the same. So much so, that when he told her he had got the sack from his job as a tanker driver with the big petroleum company, TQ International, she went straight to her dad to persuade him to take *poor* Eddie on as a relief driver with Ferguson Freight.'

Fuller crushed the remains of his cigarette on the side of his plate. 'One hell of a mistake,' he commented.

Dexter nodded. 'The biggest, for Challow was nothing like all the other pathetic misfits she had helped in the past. He was a nasty little pervert whose twisted mind interpreted her natural kindness towards him as a come-on.'

The policeman started on his second glass of shandy, sipping it slowly as he continued to reminisce. 'The scumbag became so obsessed with her that he made her life a misery, leaving love letters and presents on her desk at work like some adolescent schoolboy and pestering her to go out with him at every opportunity. Being Tania, of course, she tried to humour him for a while, anxious not to hurt his feelings –'

'Until he lost it one night and actually got physical.'

Dexter nodded. 'He came back from a long-distance run and found her working late, checking the tachographs on the lorries in the garage parking bays. Seeing no one else about, he thought he was on to a winner and tried to force himself on her.'

'But old man Ferguson was working late too.'

'Yeah, in his office above and, hearing her screams, he ran down the stairs and caught the little turd at it.' Dexter shook his head slowly. 'What Ron Ferguson should have done, of course, was to call in the police. Challow could then have been charged and locked up. But true to nature, Tania pleaded with him not to, so instead he simply sacked Challow on the spot.'

'Another big mistake.'

'A fatal one, because it humiliated Challow in the eyes of his elderly mum and with a mother-worshipping psycho like Eddie Challow, that was the very last button that needed pressing. A few nights later he raped Tania as she was jogging back from the village, then with cold ruthless premeditation, went on to her home and torched her father in his own bedroom after lashing him to the bed with chicken wire.'

Fuller grimaced as he remembered the crime scene all those years before. 'He was certainly one vicious article,' he agreed, lighting another cigarette, 'but there must have been some spark of humanity in that crazy brain of his or he wouldn't have left Tania alive after the rape. After all, he must have known she would testify against him.'

Dexter's eyes narrowed. 'You're beginning to sound like his defence counsel.'

Fuller shrugged. 'Nothing of the sort. I just wonder – in fact, I've always wondered – whether he actually *was* the clever scheming psychopath he was made out to be or simply a social inadequate with a loose cog, who finally lost what little control he had of himself.'

Dexter snorted. 'Now you're beginning to sound like a bloody psychologist.'

Fuller frowned. 'I'm not making excuses for him, Mike,' he retorted. 'I'm merely saying that the facts speak for themselves. Don't forget, he always maintained that he was invited to Ron Ferguson's house on the night it all happened – something to do with being paid off – but that he left when no one answered the door.'

'How very convenient.'

'Maybe, but with Ron's death, his story couldn't be tested either way. He always admitted sexually assaulting Tania, I know, but maybe he just got carried away when he saw her out running and took her on impulse. Perhaps the murder of Ron Ferguson was a spur of the moment thing too. He was already wound up after the rape and it's more than likely that the hatred he felt towards the man who had sacked him simply spilled over into the uncontrollable violence that resulted.'

Dexter glared at him. 'So that makes it all right, does it?' he grated. 'If Challow didn't actually plan what he did, he didn't deserve to be put away for doing it? Maybe he should have been given probation or community service then, eh? Even better, a conditional discharge or a small fine?'

Fuller reddened appreciably. 'That's not what I'm saying at all.'

'Good, because I want to tell you something about this social inadequate of yours, who only acted on the spur of the moment and probably didn't really mean to hurt anyone in the first place. After everything he'd done – deliberately burning an innocent man to death, raping a helpless girl who had only ever shown him kindness – do you know what he said to me when I nicked him at his home? Well, I'll tell you: sweet FA, that's what! Oh, his brief said plenty in his defence at his trial, but when I took him in, he never even batted an eyelid at the enormity of his crimes. No denial, no admission, no expression of remorse, not even the feeblest attempt to justify anything. He just smirked at his mother, got his coat and climbed into the CID car as if he were getting a lift to work.'

Fuller gave a slight shiver and drew heavily on his cigarette. 'Scary.'

'Dexter nodded. 'Yeah, it was scary all right and for Tania it still is. Her only consolation is that the little bastard's nuts will have shrivelled up before he ever sees the outside world again.'

Fuller took a deep breath. 'I wouldn't count on that, Mike,' he warned. 'Ever is a long time.'

The icy blade that sliced into Dexter's stomach twisted several times before it was withdrawn. 'What the hell are you saying?' he said in a voice that suddenly did not sound like his own. 'Don't tell me they're thinking of letting him out?'

The pressman looked almost apologetic. 'I'm afraid he's out already,' he said quietly. 'Six weeks ago, in fact.'

Dexter jerked forward in his chair, the colour draining from his face as he gripped the edges of the small table with both hands. 'Six weeks ago?' he gasped. 'That's just not possible.'

Fuller shrugged. 'Sorry, old friend, but my source is impeccable. There's absolutely no question about it.' He frowned. 'I thought you and Tania would have been the first to be told.'

Dexter slumped back into his chair, shaking his head in disbelief. 'The last we heard, he had been transferred from maximum security at Broughton Lake Special Hospital to a secure unit at some psychiatric place called Bramley Heath.'

'Then surely you must have suspected his release might be on the cards with such a move?'

Dexter reached for his glass of shandy again and drained half the contents before replying. 'Of course we suspected it might be on the cards one day. But that transfer was not even two years ago and with all the bad publicity that's been going down lately about discharged psychos re-offending, we understood Challow would be lucky if he made it before the next total bloody eclipse.'

Fuller shrugged. 'Maybe he made remarkable progress?' he commented dryly.

Dexter glared at him. 'Remarkable progress, my arse!' he snarled. 'He's a bloody psycho and always will be, whatever weird and wonderful tricks he does to impress the shrinks.' He stabbed an accusing finger at the pressman. 'And what I want to know is how those morons can actually justify turning a sadistic animal like that out on to the streets without even warning his victim of the fact?'

A brittle smile. 'Probably because they feared just the sort of reaction from the mild-mannered British public that you're giving me now.'

Dexter's anger intensified. 'Damn right I am – and can you blame me? *You* know what that filthy scumbag did. He's not human. He should have been kept inside until he rots.'

Fuller winced. 'Keep your voice down, Mike,' he murmured without looking up. 'Unless you want to involve the whole pub in our conversation.'

Dexter downed the remainder of his shandy and stood up, shaking his head several times. 'I've got to get some air,' he choked. 'I can't get my head round this.'

Fuller finished his own pint and followed him out into the pub car park. 'So how are you going to play it with Tania?' he queried, studying him out of the corner of one eye as he lit up another cigarette.

The policeman leaned back against the side of his car. 'Don't ask,' he said tightly. 'She was in a bad enough state when she heard about Berwick's death, Heaven knows what she'll say when –' He broke off and stared at the journalist fixedly, his eyes widening. 'Holy shit!' he breathed. 'Berwick! That's why you're really here, isn't it? You think Challow torched the Judge?'

Fuller shrugged again. 'Well, I have to admit it did occur to me, especially after the threats he made when he was finally put away. Don't forget, he always denied the arson. Claimed someone else in the village was responsible.'

'Cobblers! Like who, for instance? He never actually named anybody, did he?'

'There were enough residents up in arms over Ferguson's artics trundling through the place at all hours of the day and night.'

'Yeah, so I suppose the local WI and Mothers' Union got together to form a hit squad, led by the Vicar wielding a fiery cross? Get real, Quentin. You conveniently forget that Challow's prints were found all over one of the petrol cans dumped at the scene.'

'Which, Challow said the police had planted to get a conviction.'

'Oh come on, that's the sort of thing every villain says these days and you know it as well as I do. I suppose the police also planted the gear stolen from Ferguson's house in the back of Eddie's van? *And* the flaming great roll of chicken wire that was later matched to the stuff used to tie the old man to the bed?'

'But our man wasn't exactly liked by the local bobby, was he?'

'It wasn't a question of like or dislike. Tom Meredith was simply doing his job by keeping tabs on him. No one wants a pervert living in the community when there are kids about and there were enough complaints about his exploits in the village.'

Fuller frowned. 'But wasn't there some sort of personal dimension to Meredith's interest? I seem to remember –'

Dexter snorted his irritation. 'That was a smear job by Challow's defence counsel. Meredith's fifteen year old daughter was indecently assaulted one night on her way home by a masked man. Challow was strongly suspected of being the culprit, as he was with several other similar assaults in the area, but there wasn't enough evidence to do anything about it.'

Fuller wasn't really listening and suddenly he snapped his fingers. 'Yes, I remember now. Challow alleged that Meredith had started hounding him afterwards and had actually threatened to fix him at the first opportunity.'

'That allegation was a load of crap, like everything else he said. If you think back, he also claimed that Tania herself had egged him on, had actually enjoyed what he did to her. But he only said that so she'd have to re-live the whole vile business in graphic detail in the witness box. You can't get much sicker than that.'

'And assuming he still is that sick, handcuffing and torching Berwick would be just the sort of revenge that would appeal to him, wouldn't it? That's why I contacted my man at Bramley Heath Hospital – to check whether he was still inside.'

Dexter's eyes glittered. 'And when you found he wasn't, you thought: "Bingo, another nice little scoop in the offing". That's about right, isn't it?'

Fuller winced. 'It's my trade, Michael,' he retorted coldly. 'It's what I do.'

Dexter grunted. 'Yeah, but do you have to be so bloody transparent about it? I suppose you thought you would just give good old Mike Dexter a ring, buy him a pint, then con him into coughing up all the juicy bits about the Alden House fire, eh? I bet you've already started your write-up; some explosive new feature about a psycho's revenge maybe? Just waiting for the day we nick Eddie Challow?'

The journalist flushed. 'That's not it at all,' he retorted indignantly. 'I came here to tell you about Eddie Challow in good faith, primarily for Tania's sake.'

'*And* to cut a deal.'

Fuller sighed. 'Okay, so I think it would be advantageous to both of us if we could share our information in the future, but that's not exactly a crime, is it? We could be barking up the wrong tree anyway. The fact that Berwick died a few weeks after Challow's release might be nothing more than coincidence.'

'Coincidence?' Dexter exclaimed. 'Coincidence be damned! You don't believe that anymore than I do.' He straightened up and released his breath in a sharp hiss as something else suddenly occurred to him. 'Just a minute, I must have actually been within a hair's breadth of nabbing the little swine just a few hours ago.'

Fuller started. 'What, Eddie Challow? But how could you? You didn't even know he was out.'

Dexter stared at him wildly, his thoughts racing. 'He was the right sort of height and build too,' he breathed, thinking of the incident in the woods, '*and* he was riding a motorcycle. Challow used to be into motorcycles, didn't he? Had a scrambler, if I remember. It must have been him.'

Fuller shook his head, frowning heavily. 'You're talking in riddles, Michael.'

Dexter gripped his arm tightly. 'We've got to find out where he's gone to ground, Quentin – and fast.'

The journalist studied him narrowly, reading the panic in his eyes and at once seizing his opportunity. 'Okay, okay,' he reassured. 'I'm working on that already and I'll ring you when I have something.

Now what's all this about a man on a motorcycle? And what happened to your head?'

Dexter didn't answer him, but released his arm and turned quickly to yank open the driver's door of his car with savage force. 'I've got to get back,' he exclaimed, scrambling behind the wheel. 'Tania's on her own. Hell, she could be out on that damned horse even now.'

Fuller grabbed the edge of the door before he could close it. 'Take it easy, man,' he shouted as the powerful engine thundered into life. 'You'll be no good to anyone if you kill yourself on the way.'

Dexter nearly trapped his fingers in the door as he slammed it shut. 'No,' he threw back at him. 'And I'll be no good to Tania either if Eddie Challow gets to her first.'

*

Dexter repeatedly tried his home number on the car phone as he raced back through the network of country lanes, but there was no reply and his stomach was churning by the time he swung through the gateway of the detached slate-roofed cottage he and Tania had called home for so many years.

'Tania?' he yelled as he slammed to a halt in a swirl of gravel and jumped out of the car. But the autumn afternoon was very still and all he could hear was the ticking of the hot engine and the distant call of a wood pigeon.

'Tania!' he yelled again, still with no response.

An empty house greeted him as he raced from room to room, futilely shouting her name, and he stopped short in the kitchen, breathing heavily. It was spotless, everything cleared away and not even the remains of a snack in evidence. Gwenda, it had to be. That bloody horse!

The gate at the side of the house had been left open and he raced through like a madman, slipping and sliding on the muddy track that plunged between high grassy banks to the left of the half acre of garden before disappearing into a copse of mature conifers.

Tendrils of cold grey mist greeted him like a ghostly army as he entered the trees and the cry of the wood pigeon seemed to be directly overhead, insistent and strangely mournful. Then the broken-down drystone wall which bordered the copse on the far side loomed up in front of him and a few seconds later he was through and into the lush green field beyond.

51

Now he could see the barn where Tania kept the grey mare she had rescued from the gypsies three years before, a long low building nestling in a shallow depression flanked by skeletal hawthorn hedges. The place looked deserted and he could see no sign of any movement in the adjoining fields, just a dismal misty landscape stretching away in every direction like a vast smudged etching.

Stumbling through the ankle-deep wet grass, tripping on hummocks and concealed hollows, he headed diagonally across the field, ignoring the well worn track that skirted the edge and heedless of the water soaking through his shoes as the ground was compressed beneath his feet like a sponge.

He heard the terrified screams when he was just over halfway to his objective and he reached the barn as a figure, clad in riding kit and a green waxed jacket, burst through the side door in a panic, falling on to one knee, then staggering upright and cannoning into him with a force that almost bowled him over.

'In there,' Tania choked, pointing back at the barn and shuddering as she held on to him tightly. 'In the stall. I was rubbing Gwenda down and –'

Firmly pushing her away from him and ignoring her whispered, 'Be careful,' he strode to the door and ducked his head inside. He was greeted immediately by the smell of old straw and damp wood, mixed with the sour odour of horse sweat and as his eyes accustomed themselves to the gloom, he saw Gwenda's big head peering at him over the single stall, which had been constructed in the corner. The horse gave several short snorts and stamped her feet uneasily, but nothing else stirred. He stepped into the barn and went over to the animal, patting her nose to reassure her. She whinnied softly and nuzzled his chest.

'Has it gone?' Tania called tremulously from the doorway.

He turned quickly. '*It*?'

She gulped. 'The biggest rat I've ever seen. It was – it was sitting on that bale over there.'

He relaxed with a soft curse and shook his head slowly, staring at the floor. 'Do you mean to tell me that's why you screamed?'

She shuddered again. 'Well, you know how terrified I am of rats.'

'Yeah,' he snapped irritably, 'but I thought –'

He broke off abruptly, but he was already too late. 'Thought what, Michael?' she breathed, then added: 'And what are you doing here anyway? Surely you should be at work?'

A timber cracked not too far away and he threw a startled glance into the shadows at the far end of the barn.

She followed the direction of his gaze, frowning, 'Michael, what is it?'

He hesitated, staring at her fixedly and trying to find the right words to say. Gwenda whinnied and stamped her feet again. Outside rain began to patter on the roof of the barn and as Tania's gaze locked on to his own, he knew she had already read the answer in his eyes.

Chapter 4

Quentin Fuller almost missed the turning. The crooked signpost was on top of him before he realised it and the nearside wheel of the big Mercedes tore a sizeable chunk out of the grass verge as he swerved hard right on to the recently surfaced road with tyres scrabbling for a grip.

Roof height hawthorn hedges raced past him on both sides and, slowing for a sharp right-hand bend, he found himself passing through a plantation of closely packed pines, braking heavily when a small muntjac deer erupted from a gap in the hedge to his left and darted straight across the road in front of him.

'Twenty years,' he murmured to himself, thinking of the last time he had driven down the same road and scarcely able to believe how long ago it actually had been. 'Twenty bloody years.'

A lot of turbulent water had passed under the bridge since then and no mistake. Two failed marriages, a brain tumour and a couple of heavy libel cases for creative journalism had aged him well beyond his forty-two years, but somehow he had struggled through to make a success of everything. A thriving news agency in the *Smoke* after fifteen years' graft on the nationals, money in the bank and a pseudo-Tudor house in Surrey. He had a lot to be thankful for. Yeah, and in a perverse sort of way, it was all down to Eddie Challow, for if the Tulse End job had not landed in his lap, he might still have been a dispirited hack on the Heaton Gazette, reporting on council meetings, civic functions and minor crime cases at the local magistrates court.

A cock pheasant scurried along the verge beside him, trying to pick the right moment for committing suicide under his wheels, then abruptly changing its mind and flying off over the hedge with a panic-stricken flurry of heavily beating wings.

Exactly what had drawn him back to Tulse End, he hardly knew himself. Nostalgia maybe? He frowned. Heaven forbid. That would have made him as depraved as Eddie Challow. Morbid curiosity then? Possibly, but even that was a bit too unpalatable to accept. No, he preferred to think it had more to do with the chance of picking up some information on Eddie Challow's likely whereabouts so he could save himself the expense of bribing some highly placed official for the right address. He could live with that. At least being a tight-arse was a tad more respectable than the other two alternatives.

The only problem he faced was where to get his information from. Challow's mother, he knew, was long gone. She had died of a heart attack shortly after her son's trial – some had said at the time as a result of the harassment she had received from hostile neighbours. As for the rest of the village, twenty years was a hell of a time and most of the original residents would also be dead or have moved on by now. Still, it was worth a try, if only for the excuse of downing his third pint of the day at the local hostelry and anyway, there just might be some old stager around who could tell him something he didn't already know.

That prospect began to look increasingly unlikely as he entered the village, however. Where once there had been run-down country cottages, with potatoes and cabbages growing in the front gardens, he found a development of modern red brick houses opposite a very smart looking golf club. The village centre, with its large well-kept green, Norman church and primary school, was much as he remembered it, but the old shop had been replaced by a mini-mart, with a small twin-pump petrol station next door, and there were double yellow lines everywhere, prohibiting parking at any time.

As for The Goose Inn, outwardly its thatched old-world image had been preserved, but the interior had undergone total refurbishment, with an upmarket restaurant, yuppie-style bars and inflated prices to go with it all. The licensee (George Brookes, according to the sign above the door) turned out to be the fifth incumbent in twenty years and that was about the only information volunteered by the surly uncommunicative Londoner, who was obviously more interested in keeping his bar takings up than gossiping with customers. Fuller left after only twenty minutes, totally disillusioned and convinced that even the beer had been watered down by someone.

His next stop was Halls Close – when he finally managed to find it – and for several minutes he sat staring at the row of four terraced cottages sandwiched between the old village hall, which bore signs of substantial renovation, and a new block of flats, which, by the look of them, needed renovating already. It was the end cottage that interested him though and he frowned as he tried to visualise the wire chicken runs that had once occupied the adjoining land on which the flats now stood. The cottage looked dark and sinister in the autumn light and the single lamp that burned in an upstairs room only served to enhance its forbidding appearance. He shivered slightly, wondering who might have bought the place and whether they knew that Eddie Challow had once lived there.

'Problems, sir?' The young bobby appeared suddenly at the open window of his car and he jumped, his eyes flicking briefly to the rear-view mirror and noting the big police Land Rover that was now parked a few yards behind him. He had been so absorbed in his scrutiny of the cottage that the sound of the approaching vehicle had hardly registered with him.

He shook his head, automatically reaching for the key in the ignition, then relaxing and wondering why he always felt the need to drive away when approached by the law. 'No problem, officer,' he returned with a smile. 'Just having a rest for a moment, that's all.'

The other nodded, his suspicious gaze probing the car's interior. 'Why here, sir? It's a cul-de-sac.'

Suddenly Fuller remembered the couple of beers he had sunk and inwardly cursed his stupidity, jumping in quickly before *PC Plod* could smell the evidence on his breath and ask the fateful question that would put paid to his driving licence for twelve months. 'Actually I'm press,' he blurted with a forced smile and, reaching into his inside pocket, flashed his press card. 'Quentin Fuller. I covered the Eddie Challow case here twenty years ago. I was in the area and just thought I'd look by.'

'Eddie Challow, eh?' The bobby tilted his flat cap back a little and shook his head, leaning on the roof with both arms outstretched as he continued to peer in. 'I was told about that business when I transferred down here from the Met. Bit of a nutter, wasn't he?'

Fuller grunted. 'Yeah, you could say that. He used to live in that end cottage with his mum . Worked as a driver for Ferguson Freight before he did old man Ferguson in and raped his daughter.'

The policeman nodded. 'So I understand, sir. Up on Quarry Wood Hill, wasn't it? Torched the place after being sacked and got put away in a mental hospital? Long time ago though and the whole place has been taken over as a wildlife reserve now.' He gave a short laugh. 'I reckon I must have been about five when all that happened.'

Fuller studied the schoolboy face and nodded. You look as though you're still in the sixth form now, he thought uncharitably, but he had the good sense not to voice his opinion. Instead, he lit a cigarette and waved an arm towards the cottage. 'Funny to see someone else living here now though,' he said. 'Maybe they don't know about Eddie Challow.'

'Oh, I reckon they know well enough, sir,' the other replied, 'but a house is a house and property round here is at a premium. Last owners didn't care, so why should the present ones, eh?'

He straightened and turned away from the car. 'Anyway, I must be getting along now. My dinner will be ruined. Drive safely, sir.'

Though relieved to see the bobby going, Fuller had to satisfy his curiosity. 'Do you know who lives in the house now, officer?' he called after him.

The bobby half-turned. 'Yes, sir,' he replied with a grin. '*I* do.' Then sauntering diagonally across the road, he nudged open the gate of the end cottage with his foot and disappeared round the side of the house with a wave of one hand.

*

'So I'm to be a prisoner then, is that it?' Tania took another sip from her glass of brandy and studied her husband across the kitchen table. He met her gaze with a heavy frown. Her reaction to the news about Eddie Challow's release had been more controlled than he had expected, too controlled, in fact. There had been none of the anticipated hysteria and to all intents and purposes she seemed to be holding up remarkably well. But he knew differently. Her eyes were unnaturally bright, her face almost bloodless and the hands that gripped the brandy glass were subject to fits of trembling. She was very near the edge, he could see that, and it wouldn't take much to tip her over completely.

Reaching across the table, he gripped her thin wrists with both hands and squeezed them reassuringly before letting go. 'It isn't like that at all,' he said quietly. 'I am merely saying we should take a few elementary precautions until we have a bit more information – like making sure all doors and windows are kept locked and that you don't go wandering about on your own, for instance. It's just common sense really, nothing more.'

'And what about my job? Am I to chuck that in as well? Lock myself away in this house like a recluse?'

He shook his head firmly. 'Absolutely not. I can arrange to take you in and collect you each day and when you're actually there, you'll be with other people anyway.'

She gulped some more brandy. 'What you really mean is that Eddie Challow has done his time and I have to start doing mine now?'

He sighed. 'Don't you think you're overreacting just a bit? Challow probably had nothing at all to do with Judge Berwick's death. It may even turn out that Quentin Fuller's info is duff and our man is actually still inside. I will need to get an official check done before we can be sure of anything.'

She made a grimace. 'Don't patronise me, Michael,' she replied. 'If you really believed that, you wouldn't be suggesting we take your so-called elementary precautions and you certainly wouldn't have come flying back here the way you did.'

He started to say something, but she interrupted him. 'And there's something else as well.'

She pushed her chair back slightly and, opening the single drawer in the table, produced the wedding anniversary card they had received that morning. 'I just noticed it after you'd left,' she said, handing it to him.

He re-read the card quickly, turned it over, then shook his head in puzzlement. 'Noticed what?' he said.

'Look at the footnote on the back of it.'

He did so and immediately tensed, his mouth compressing into a thin hard line. The two-line boxed inscription sent shivers creeping up and down his spine.

> Designed by patients at Bramley Heath Psychiatric
> Hospital. Your purchase will help us to help them.

'Bramley Heath,' she said. 'The place Eddie Challow was transferred to.'

He avoided her gaze and, tossing the card back on to the table, reached for his half-empty coffee cup. 'Okay, so it looks like it could have come from him,' he acknowledged grudgingly. 'But that doesn't mean anything. He is simply trying to put the frighteners on you. He wouldn't risk going back inside by doing something stupid after all these years.'

She shook her head in disbelief. 'Is that what you really think?' she exclaimed and leaned forward to emphasize her point. 'Michael, he specifically sent this card to warn us he was out, you must see that.

The card actually says "Fond memories on our"- not *your* – "special day". That wasn't a mistake after all. He was not referring to the anniversary of our own wedding, but to the anniversary of the – the things he did all that time ago. Michael, he wants us to know in advance that he is coming after me.'

'Cobblers!' he snapped, his patience suddenly failing. 'If that was his intention, then why didn't he sign the flippin' thing in the first place?'

Her expression registered a mixture of frustration and despair. 'Surely that's obvious?' she said, her eyes suddenly brimming with tears. 'Without a signature, he couldn't be directly connected with it. But he knew that one of us would spot the inscription on the back sooner or later and come to the obvious conclusion.'

He made one last lame attempt to allay her fears. 'Look, it's a charity card. There are hundreds of different types about. Anyone could have sent it.'

'Oh be your age, Michael,' she choked. 'Who else but Eddie Challow would have sent us a card like this from Bramley Heath? He's playing a game, do you still not understand?'

He nodded quickly and laid a hand on her arm, alarmed by her deteriorating emotional state and anxious to prevent her working herself up anymore. 'All right, all right,' he said soothingly, 'then we'll play a game of our own, shall we? What did you do with the envelope the card came in?'

She pulled her arm away and used the backs of both hands to dry her eyes. 'In the bin, I think, but I don't see –'

Climbing to his feet, he went to the pedal bin in the corner and lifted it on to the worktop beside the sink. 'If we can find out where he posted the card, it may give us an idea where he is living,' he explained, dipping into the plastic liner. 'It's not conclusive, of course, but – ugh!' He removed his hand and washed something off his fingers under the tap. Then a second or two later he emitted a grunt of satisfaction and held up a crumpled yellow envelope. 'This it?'

She hoisted herself wearily out of her chair and joined him by the sink. 'It looks like it, yes. It's the right colour anyway.'

He used the dishcloth to carefully remove some jam from the top right-hand corner, then peered at the stamp.

'Birmingham?' she exclaimed over his shoulder before he could hide what he had seen. 'When was it posted?'

He hesitated, reluctant to add to her fears.

'Michael!' she snapped.

He sighed. 'Yesterday afternoon.'

'I knew it,' she breathed. 'And Birmingham is less than two hours away from here.'

He turned to lay a reassuring hand on her arm once more. 'Look, Tania, don't you think you're taking this fantasy a little bit too far?'

She shook her head firmly and stared past him out of the window. 'It's no fantasy, Michael,' she said. 'He's out there somewhere, watching us, I just know it.'

He snorted angrily. 'Now you *are* being ridiculous,' he snapped, though he couldn't help casting a swift sidelong glance in the same direction. 'If you don't get a grip on your imagination, you'll end up...'

He broke off, seeing the hurt in her eyes.

'End up where, Michael?' she said, a hard edge to her voice. 'The *funny farm*? Is that what you're saying?'

He looked away from her. 'No, of course not. Look, I didn't mean –'

'Then exactly what *did* you mean?'

Before he could think of a suitable reply, the telephone came to his aid for the second time that day. 'Yeah?' he responded almost eagerly.

'Mike?' Sarah's voice queried excitedly. 'Where the hell have you been? I've been trying to get you for over two hours.'

He winced, suddenly remembering that he had left his mobile phone in the car. 'Why, what's up?'

'What's *up*?' There was an explosive snort. 'Detective Superintendent Moffat is what's up. He's been asking for you for most of the afternoon. He needs a press conference set up to appeal for witnesses.'

'Fat chance of any of those in this case. But I thought he had no intention of talking to the press?'

'That was before ACC Ops started leaning on him. Judge Berwick wasn't exactly your ordinary run-of-the-mill murder victim, you know.'

'So it's the old school tie again, is it?'

An impatient hiss. 'Never mind about that, just listen. I've fixed up a venue in the old parade room at Bellingham nick for four o'clock. Kitty will be on hand, of course, but you had better get over there yourself if you value your skin.'

He scowled, glancing quickly at Tania, then at his watch. 'Yeah, okay, I can probably just make it.' He hesitated. 'Thanks for covering for me.'

'I didn't do it for you,' came the tart reply. 'I did it for the department.

And you're still in deep poo, Michael, I hope you realise that.'

'What's new?' he retorted bitterly, but the telephone had gone dead.

★

Quentin Fuller left Halls Close feeling a lot more satisfied than he had expected to be. Though his visit to Tulse End had so far failed to produce any leads to Eddie Challow's whereabouts, he had at least established one thing: there was no way the little psycho was going to return to his old haunts with one of the county's finest ensconced in his former cottage.

Fuller couldn't help chuckling at the irony of the situation, thinking that the surprising fortunes of Number 4 Halls Close would make a nice little piece for one of the less prestigious tabloids, in addition to the main story he was already pursuing. "Cops Collar Crime Cottage", he murmured. Yeah, that was the sort of headline the cheapos loved (provided some local hack hadn't done the business already, of course) and it would put a few quid in his pocket, if nothing else. But before he got into that sort of trivia, his present investigation still had to be completed and there was one final port of call he needed to make.

Turning left out of Hall's Close, he headed away from The Goose Inn and the road which had brought him into Tulse End, making for the blind end of the village instead. He found what he was looking for almost immediately. Just past the Norman church, on the far side of the village green, a concrete road struck off at a forty-five degree angle between the ivy-clad walls of the small cemetery and the adjacent vicarage. The original wooden signpost had long since gone, of course, and no one, it seemed, had thought fit to replace it, but even after so many years, he didn't need a sign to tell him that this was the entrance to Quarry Wood Road – it was etched indelibly on his memory – and he made the turn almost as a reflex action.

Accelerating to meet the steep incline which, he knew, would take him right up to the old Ferguson haulage yard, past the long-abandoned quarry workings, he couldn't help thinking about Ron

Ferguson and the ingenuity of the man. The shrewd ex-stockbroker had actually acquired Tulse End Quarry for a song – essentially because very few developers had seen much potential in an isolated twenty-five acre property disfigured by a massive hole almost as big as the crater of Vesuvius. Within just two years, however, he had managed to renovate the ruins of what had once been the home of the former and very much deceased quarry owner, Thomas Selby, develop the site to accommodate his fleet of articulated lorries and, against considerable local opposition, establish a viable transport business that had remained profitable until his untimely death.

The cruel irony was that Ron had become a victim of his own success. If he hadn't taken the gamble to purchase the old quarry in the first place; if he hadn't managed to persuade the local authority to allow him to develop the site and run his articulated lorries in and out of Quarry Wood Road; and if the business hadn't taken off quite as well as it had, his only daughter would not have been doing her customary jogging along this lonely stretch of road the night she was raped by Eddie Challow and Ron Ferguson himself would not have ended up being incinerated in his own home. The big *if*, but then, that was life, wasn't it?

Fuller darted frequent glances at the broken-down chain-link fence bordering the verge to his left as he negotiated the lethal obstacle course of poorly filled potholes and assorted debris now scarring the wide concrete road pushing up through the woods. It was impossible to see very far into the densely packed pine trees, but he wasn't deceived. He knew only too well that they shielded an ugly moon landscape of abandoned workings, which ultimately fell away into an enormous pit, blasted out of the hillside by the quarrymen so many years ago. The savage grey scar had become something of a local landmark and it was clearly visible from his old home town of Grazely, five miles away on the other side of the valley.

When the quarry had finally closed, the local kids had taken to haunting the place on boring Sunday afternoons, disobeying parental orders to keep away from the workings, which were known to be unsafe, and using the old lorry tracks for dare-devil exploits on their mountain bikes or skinny-dipping in the deep black pool at the bottom. Accidents had been common, but no one had actually died – at least not until he was in his late teens and reporting for the Heaton Gazette. Then the missing girl was found strangled and sexually assaulted in undergrowth at the bottom of what the locals chose to call *Hobbs Kitchen* The police manhunt had lasted eighteen months, but despite their enquiries and the massive publicity that had resulted, no one was ever brought to book. There were plenty of suspicious mutterings, of course, and Eddie Challow's name had come up more than once, as it always did with every local incident involving anything of a sexual nature, but in the absence of any real evidence, the police had been forced to admit defeat. Even now though, Fuller could not help wondering whether Challow *had* actually been responsible for the crime. Maybe Ron Ferguson's little girl had been a lot luckier than anyone had realised. At least she had lived to tell the tale.

About half a mile above the village, the concrete road ended in a T junction, the right arm of the T rising even more steeply towards the summit of the hill and the left disappearing under a pair of half-open wire gates. Spinning the steering wheel to the right and pulling out over the faded white line marking the junction, he braked sharply and turned in his seat to study the gates. He wasn't surprised to see that they still carried the familiar warning sign: "Danger. Keep Out. Quarry Workings", but there was another, and apparently fairly new, blue and white notice on a post to the left of the gates, which declared that the site had now been designated a wild bird sanctuary. He smiled wryly as he pulled away again, thinking of *Hobbs Kitchen* and wondering whether parachutes were standard equipment for twitchers.

A further half mile, and the steep road he was following levelled out and ended altogether in a wide turning area. Directly in front of him un-gated stone pillars valiantly tried to hold back a tangled mass of brambles and ivy which all but smothered the seven foot high perimeter wall of the long abandoned property he had come to see.

Pulling over on to a patch of grass, he switched off and sat there for a moment, studying the entrance dubiously. In the fading autumn light it looked particularly uninviting and he almost re-started the engine and bolted. But curiosity got the better of him and, grabbing his anorak and a torch from the back seat of the car, he locked up and went closer.

The heavy iron gates were no longer there, but their imprint was just visible in the ankle deep grass that looked as though it had been trampled down in places. His heart missed a beat as it dawned on him that someone had been this way before, and evidently not too long ago either.

Stepping gingerly over the fallen gates and into the belt of woodland beyond, he paused to listen. A bird of some sort lifted off a branch way above his head with the thudding of large wings, but otherwise there was only the distant hum of traffic on the dual carriageway far below to intrude upon the sepulchral stillness. He shivered and, zipping up his anorak, moved on, following another broken concrete road that made off among the trees, his torch gripped tightly in one hand like a cosh and his eyes searching the shadows for the slightest movement.

Moments later he glimpsed buildings through gaps in the trees ahead and as the woodland finally came to an end, the driveway blossomed out into a broad concrete hardstanding now sprouting a generous amount of grass and ankle-height scrub and overshadowed at one end by the huge hangar-like shed that had once garaged Ron Ferguson's small fleet of articulated lorries.

Apart from the inevitable graffiti from spray cans, the ugly windowless building seemed to have stood up pretty well for itself over the years and, even though the misplaced energies of mindless vandals had ensured that the adjoining two-storey office block where Tania had worked so hard to keep the family business on track had suffered the usual fate reserved for vulnerable unoccupied buildings, the shed's half-open steel entrance doors had proved too much for them. Rusted and battle-scarred, they remained more or less intact, defying all attempts to tear them down, and inside the building the thick black lines marking the lorry bays were still visible, despite the debris that strewed the floor from the partially collapsed corrugated iron roof.

At the rear of the shed, thorny scrub tumbled down a steep slope towards the old nineteen-seventies MOD firing range, which occupied six to eight wooded acres of mixed woodland between the quarry workings and the busy dual-carriageway, and he could just make out the ragged track that led off the dual-carriageway to snake its way among the trees in the direction of the quarry. The range had been closed on safety grounds when the ten mile link to the motorway had been driven through the countryside and although the MOD had still hung on to the land, he remembered it being let out at one time to the local police force for riot training. Maybe it still was and he smiled faintly as he tried to visualise the reaction of the twitchers in their hides when scores of bobbies, dressed in full para-military gear and carrying protective shields, descended on the MOD site next door to storm specially constructed barricades under a hail of missiles and petrol bombs. Somehow he didn't think it would be seen as the ideal complement to an afternoon's bird-watching.

Conscious of the lengthening shadows, he ignored the roofless shells of the two single-storey warehouses to the right of the lorry shed and headed towards a high bank bordering the hardstanding on his left. Skirting the remains of the derelict fuel pumps, which stood out in the gloom like *Isaac Asimov* creations from another world, he turned up a steep driveway between the ruined staff canteen and a much smaller building with slatted steel doors that looked as though it had once housed some sort of generator. Ten to fifteen yards further on the driveway levelled out and then suddenly the horror house, with its big empty windows and pretentious wrought iron balcony running the length of the upper floor, was there, staring at him bleakly across a ruined garden still littered with the now partially overgrown debris that the fire service had raked from its sodden but smouldering shell all those years before. Part of the slate roof had long since collapsed in on itself and the broken chimneys rose like ragged tombstones into the darkening sky as a grim testimony to the ferocity of the blaze that had engulfed the building. He fancied he could still smell the odour of wet smoke; still hear the roar of the flames and the crash of exploding windows as the teams of yellow-helmeted fire-fighters struggled with their leaping hoses, while the heat of the blaze roasted their faces and clawed at their throats with smoky steel talons.

Heading for the rectangular gash that had once been the front door, he ducked under a liquorice assortment of hanging cables into the long hall, his torch switched on and probing the shadows nervously. He passed a couple of door openings, one on either side, and paused briefly at the foot of the angled shaft, which was practically all that remained of the staircase, directing the beam of his torch up through a criss-cross of ravaged beams and half devoured floorboards into the upper rooms. The iron bed to which Tania's father had been lashed with chicken wire was probably still up there, but he couldn't see it and he shivered, lowering the torch and skirting the shaft to make his way along the corridor towards the back door.

As he did so, he noticed that the unpleasant lingering smell of wet smoke was now even more apparent than before and he shook his head in disbelief, hardly able to credit that it was still present after all this time. It seemed to be growing stronger as he moved towards the back of the house too and it wasn't long before he found out why. Freezing in the kitchen doorway and extinguishing his torch, he stared across the litter of broken glass and rubble which covered the floor, his gaze riveted on the small pile of logs in one corner which hissed and crackled as the flames feasted hungrily on the sodden wood, sending myriads of sparks in all directions and a plume of smoke curling up through the naked beams where the upper floor had been. What looked to be an old mattress lay in front of the fire and beside it a pile of blankets, but there was no sign of anyone in the room and he guessed that they had made good their escape on hearing his approach. Or had they? What if Eddie Challow had come back here? What if the fire and the mattress were his? He turned quickly to look along the hallway behind him, fumbling with his torch in a sudden panic. For some reason it refused to work, but he was too late anyway, because a dark figure was already lurching towards him from an adjacent doorway.

*

The press conference was a total farce. It was plain that Detective Superintendent Moffat only intended going through the motions, making the customary public appeal for witnesses to avoid criticism later and with no real intention of telling the media anything. He completely shut out Dexter and Detective Chief Inspector Lawson sitting on either side of him, insisting on responding personally to every question fired from the close-packed ranks of journalists crammed into the police station parade room and treating each one with the same characteristic contempt. In fact, he made so much use of the hated term "no comment" that one frustrated journalist asked him if it was the only phrase he knew and there was uproar when he refused point-blank to confirm or deny the earlier press report that the body of Judge Berwick had been found handcuffed to the bed.

Throughout the whole embarrassing event Dexter fidgeted uncomfortably in the hard creaking chair, grateful for the long parade room table standing between him and the flashing cameras. This at least provided something of a psychological comfort zone, but he was acutely conscious of the fact that, regardless of his non-participation, he would nevertheless be identified with Moffat over the fiasco for evermore. There were at least two video cameras trained on them and though he tried to edge slightly away from the bumbling senior detective, he knew he would still be in shot for the evening news. His only hope was that the television producers would refuse to show any footage of the conference on the grounds that it was a complete non-event, which would tarnish their own reputations as prime-time broadcasters.

He could hardly conceal his relief when the ordeal came to an end and he was actually the first to get up from the table and head for the side door leading to the old administration offices at the back of the building, leaving Kitty Morrison with the job of ushering the infuriated reporters and camera crews out the front. He didn't get far, however, for Moffat caught up with him even as he tried to close the door behind him.

'Not so fast, Mr Dexter,' the obnoxious little man said sharply, stepping in front of him to bar his progress. 'I want a word with you.'

Dexter half-turned to close the door completely, then faced his superior with a bleak expression on his face. 'A word, sir?' he prevaricated, guessing what was coming and knowing he hadn't got a leg to stand on this time.

Moffat's eyes glittered with pure venom behind the gold-tinted glasses. 'Let's cut the crap, shall we?' he snapped. 'Where the hell have you been all the afternoon?'

Before Dexter could answer, the parade room door opened again and Detective Chief Inspector Lawson squeezed past them, directing a sympathetic wink at his colleague as he did so.

'Well?' Moffat persisted. 'Lost for an answer, are we?'

Dexter studied him silently for a moment, waiting until Lawson had disappeared through the door at the far end of the corridor before replying. 'Not at all, sir,' he said finally. 'The fact is, I had to nip home for a few minutes. My wife hasn't been at all well and I wanted to check that she was okay.'

Moffat gaped at him. 'Your wife?' he echoed incredulously. 'Your *wife*?'

Dexter made a grimace, appreciating only too well how lame his answer must have sounded. 'Yes, sir. Unfortunately I forgot to take my bat-phone indoors with me, so I had no idea I was being called. I can only apologise for that.'

Moffat shook his head in disbelief. 'Let's get this straight, Chief Inspector,' he breathed. 'I am in the middle of a major crime enquiry, with the incinerated body of a retired crown court judge lodged in the fridge, a five hundred thousand pound listed property burned to the ground and the national press actually camped on my doorstep, and you take it into your head to *go home?*'

'It wasn't like that at all, sir. As I've explained to you, my wife wasn't well. I had no choice.'

Moffat snorted. 'No choice?' he echoed. 'So what was wrong with calling a bloody doctor? Dealing with sick people is what they're paid for, isn't it?'

Dexter's mouth tightened. 'It wasn't that sort of illness,' he said coldly. 'My wife has a psychological problem – '

Moffat cut him off with a dismissive wave of one hand. 'I know all about your damned wife, Chief Inspector,' he retorted. 'There is hardly anyone in the force who doesn't. And it's about time you stopped using a rape trauma, which happened over twenty years ago, as an excuse for your own shortcomings.'

Dexter controlled his rising anger with an effort. 'I am not using it as an excuse for anything, sir,' he grated. 'I had a legitimate reason for going home and it so happens that Tania's regression is directly related to this murder investigation. Perhaps if you'll just listen a moment –'

'*Me* listen?' the little man cut in again, his face contorted into an unpleasant snarl and a line of spittle forming on his lower lip. 'You've got a nerve! No, *you* listen, Chief Inspector. I'm not interested in your pathetic attempt to change the subject. You're in deep shit over this and you know it. Furthermore, it's the second time since this investigation began that you've shown you can't be trusted. Only a few hours ago, when you should have been keeping the media in line, it seems you were actually blundering around the woods in pursuit of some imaginary arsonist, leaving your press cronies to swarm all over the crime scene, hampering the search teams and destroying vital evidence.'

'There was nothing imaginary about the character I saw,' Dexter retorted vehemently and tapped the plaster still attached to his forehead. 'Do you really think I did that all by myself?'

Moffat thrust his face towards him with characteristic belligerence. 'I don't care whether you were mugged by a deranged tree fairy,' he rasped. 'You're not paid to play hide and seek in the woods, but to be the force PRO and so far you've made a pretty lousy job of it.'

Dexter bit and bit hard. 'Well, maybe I'd do a lot better job if I thought the effort was worthwhile,' he threw back at him, his anger and frustration now surfacing in a rush. 'But there's little point in even having a PRO when senior investigating officers like you have no intention of telling the media anything in the first place.'

Moffat gave a self-satisfied smirk. 'And if I had my way there wouldn't be one,' he sneered. 'But since the Chief Constable, in his infinite wisdom, has decreed otherwise, we have no option but to play along with the whole stupid charade.'

Dexter emitted a short humourless laugh. 'And you certainly got into the swing of things with that conference just now, didn't you, sir?' he retorted. 'It must have been the biggest charade the press have ever seen.'

Moffat's smirk froze into a savage putty-like mask. 'You think you're so damned clever, don't you?' he almost whispered. 'Well, let's see if you're still laughing tomorrow morning after I have had the chance to speak to ACC Operations about your behaviour. Mr Parkes is not noted for his sense of humour.'

Then he had turned on his heel and was heading off along the corridor in the direction taken by DCI Lawson a short time before, his short quick strides and swinging arms registering his inner fury with each step he took.

'Nice one, Mike,' Kitty Morrison murmured sarcastically at Dexter's elbow as he watched Moffat fling open the door at the end of the corridor and slam it with unnecessary force behind him. 'You handled that really well, didn't you?'

Dexter glanced behind him at the now half-open parade room door and made a wry face. 'Yeah,' he agreed. 'Sometimes I reckon I'm a bit too much of a diplomat.'

Chapter 5

Quentin Fuller sat down carefully on the upturned wooden crate and studied the bearded weather-beaten face of the old tramp in the glare of the fire.

The man had given him quite a start when he had first appeared out of the shadows of the ruined hallway, but it had quickly become apparent that Shammy, as he chose to call himself, was quite harmless. In fact, he seemed to be a lot more frightened of his unexpected visitor than the other way about and sitting uneasily on a broken stool on the other side of the fire, his gaunt frame hunched over tightly crossed legs and both arms clasped together round one knee, he presented a pathetic vulnerable figure who was likely to be more of a threat to himself than anyone else.

'Strange name, Shammy,' Fuller commented, trying to get some sort of dialogue going.

The other grunted. 'What's strange about it?' he said sullenly. 'If your name's Leather and you're in the Navy, that's what you get called, like it or lump it. Chamois leather – Shammy, see?'

'Yeah, I rather think I'd gathered that,' Fuller replied dryly, 'So, you were in the Navy then?'

'That's what I said, didn't I?'

The pressman abruptly changed tack. 'Live here, do you?' he queried, reaching over the pile of blazing wood to hand him a cigarette and a box of matches.

The tramp nodded, hesitating a moment before accepting the offer, then keeping one eye firmly fixed on him as he lit up. 'For now,' he muttered, brazenly pocketing the matches. 'Move about a lot.'

'So how long have you been dossing in this place?'

The question had been meant to sound casual, conversational, but Shammy scowled. 'You ask a lot of bleedin' questions,' he said suspiciously.

'Just curious, that's all.'

'Why, you the *Old Bill* then?'

Fuller laughed. 'Hardly. Actually I'm a reporter.' He reached into his pocket and handed over his press card in its worn leather holder. The tramp studied the card closely in the firelight, then flipped the wallet back to him, narrowly missing the curling flames.

'I'm up here from London – on a story,' Fuller went on. 'You know, that business with Judge Berwick.'

Shammy frowned. 'Judge Berwick? What business is that?'

'You mean you haven't heard?'

A harsh cynical laugh. 'No, me morning paper weren't delivered today.'

Fuller winced. He had asked for that. Damn fool thing to say to a tramp in the first place. 'Someone torched his house last night,' he said, using his lighter to light his own cigarette. 'He died in the blaze.'

Shammy visibly stiffened. 'Berwick's been murdered?' he said incredulously. 'But why would anyone want to do a thing like that?'

Fuller raised his eyebrows. 'I would have thought that was pretty obvious,' he retorted. 'There must be quite a few ex-cons who have him to thank for a stretch inside.'

'Yeah, but torching him, that ain't decent.'

There was a strained silence for a moment, broken only by the crackle of the fire as Shammy stared into the dancing flames, drawing slowly on his cigarette. 'He wasn't a bad bloke, you know,' he said at length, 'for a judge anyway. Always fair.'

Fuller's heart began to beat faster. 'You knew him then?'

Another harsh laugh. 'Well, he knew me anyway. Put me away a couple of times, he did. Only come out three months ago.'

'You did time yourself then?'

The tramp threw him a contemptuous glance. 'No, I went to bloody university. What d'ye think?'

Fuller smiled faintly. 'What were you in for?'

'That's my business.'

Fuller acknowledged this fact with a slight nod and didn't pursue the point. 'So, why come here?' he went on.

'Why not? It's as good as anywhere else.'

'I wouldn't agree there. This house has a pretty rotten history.'

Shammy grunted. 'The fire, you mean? Yeah, I know all about that.' He grinned suddenly. 'Folk avoid the place, think it's haunted. That suits me fine. Bit of haunting is the best thing for some peace and quiet.'

71

'So you've never seen anyone else wandering about up here?'

The tramp's grin faded and his expression was very wary again. 'Like who?'

Fuller tossed his cigarette on to the flames and shrugged as casually as he could manage. 'Like anyone at all.'

A piece of wood fell off the fire and the tramp stared at it for a moment. 'How much is it worth?'

Fuller's heartbeat quickened and he fumbled in his pocket for his wallet. 'How about a tenner to start with?'

Shammy reached over quickly to take the proffered note, but Fuller folded his hand over it in a single snap movement. 'Well, *has* there been?'

The tramp hesitated, then nodded briefly. 'Some geezer in an old army Land Rover, that's all. Been up here a couple of times. Brought some planks and stuff with him.'

'Planks?'

'Yeah, doin' some work upstairs by the sound of it. Lots of banging anyway.'

'Why would he be doing work on a derelict like this?'

Shammy shrugged. 'Dunno. Maybe he's thinking of movin' in. I minds me own business, keeps out the way.'

'What does he look like?'

Another shrug. 'Smallish. Wears a black leather jacket and some sort of blue cap. Couldn't see much else of him as he weren't that close.'

Fuller opened his hand and let him take the note.

'If he comes again, let me know, okay?' He extracted a business card from his wallet and jotted something on the back of it before handing it over. 'Ring me at my hotel or on my mobile any time, day or night. Got it? I've written the hotel number on the card.'

'An' how am I supposed to do that up here?'

'Fuller sighed heavily. 'Ever heard of a telephone kiosk?' he said patiently and fumbling in his trouser pocket, he pulled out some loose change, which he reached across to place in the other's open palm. 'There's one in the village. If the call's to my hotel room, you can always ask the operator to transfer the charge and I'll accept it. Do you know how to do that?'

'I ain't stupid. So how much is it worth?'

'Depends on how good your information is. But let's say a straight twenty if he's still here when I arrive.'

The tramp nodded slowly and, pocketing the change with the ten pound note and business card, he threw him a quizzical glance, one eye half-closed in thought. 'Why you so interested in who comes up here? I thought you said you was doing a story on Judge Berwick?'

'To borrow the phrase you used earlier, that's my business.'

'No it ain't, not when you're tryin' to drag me into it.'

Fuller studied the set stubborn face and took a chance. 'He could be the same guy who torched this place originally.'

'But I heard he was inside, got sent to some nuthouse up north.'

'He was released a few weeks ago.'

Shammy stared about him in the gloom and shivered. 'An' you think he might have done the Judge?'

'It's possible, yes. Berwick was the one who put him away.'

'But why would he come back here?'

'Nostalgia maybe.'

'That's sick, that is.'

Fuller nodded grimly as he stood up to leave. 'Yeah,' he agreed, 'and they don't come much sicker than Eddie Challow.'

Crouched on the charred beams of the room above their heads like a great black spider, the leather clad figure, who had been listening so intently to their conversation, carefully eased himself into a more comfortable position, his dark eyes narrowed and thoughtful.

*

'Enjoy your heart to heart with the governor?' Dick Lawson dropped into the chair beside Dexter's desk and met his colleague's glare with a broad grin.

Dexter eased his own chair out of the kneehole on its squeaking casters and swivelled to face him. 'I suppose you want a drink?' he said dryly and reached into the bottom right-hand drawer of his desk for the whisky bottle he always kept there.

'I wouldn't say no.'

'You never flippin' do.'

Armed with two generously charged glasses, the two old friends studied each other in silence for a few seconds, sipping their drinks slowly.

The vast Headquarters building was deathly still. It was already gone seven o'clock in the evening and most of the staff that crammed its honeycomb of small claustrophobic offices during the day had long since left for home.

'I just hope the Chief doesn't walk in,' Dexter commented suddenly, eyeing the glass in his hand with a frown.

Lawson shook his head definitely. 'Saw him leaving just as I arrived,' he replied.

'That still leaves ACC Operations.'

Lawson chuckled. 'Then maybe you had better get hold of a *Babycham* in case he wants to join us, eh?' he suggested maliciously.

Dexter set his glass down on the polished teak surface of his desk. 'Why didn't you tell me Berwick was handcuffed to the bed?' he queried softly.

Lawson finished his drink in one gulp and made a grimace as the harsh spirit attacked the lining of his throat. 'Not my decision, Mike,' he said, placing the glass carefully on the edge of the desk.

'Bullshit!'

Lawson shook his head. 'Nothing of the sort. Moffat wanted it that way. Didn't want any leaks.'

'Leaks?' The colour rose to Dexter's cheeks immediately. 'You cheeky sod.'

'Only telling you what the man said.'

Dexter shook his head slowly. 'Yeah, but you could have slipped me the wink,' he said bitterly, also emptying his glass. 'So much for friendship.'

'That's not fair,' the detective snapped. 'Moffat is the SIO on this one and, as such, he calls the shots. You should know that better than anyone.'

Dexter leaned forward. 'Maybe, but this time there's a lot more at stake than an incinerated stiff.'

'Like what?'

Dexter slumped back in his chair and swivelled to face the window. The enclosed car park was empty except for a crash-helmeted traffic man checking the tyre pressures of his BMW motorcycle before going out on patrol. 'Tania is on the edge,' he said abruptly. 'She is convinced Eddie Challow is coming after her.'

'Eddie Challow? But he's inside.'

'*Was* inside.' Dexter faced him again. 'He was released six weeks ago.'

'How the hell do you know that?'

'I just do and I'm convinced the information is legit.'

'But even if it is, to come back here after all these years? It doesn't make sense.'

'Doesn't it?' Dexter leaned towards him. 'Berwick was handcuffed to the bed, Dick. *Handcuffed.* Have you forgotten how Tania's old man died?'

Lawson poured himself another drink and shuddered. 'How could I ever forget something like that?' he retorted. 'Anymore than I could forget Berwick's grisly end. I was the local DS when Ron Ferguson was torched, if you remember. The damned corpse was still smouldering on the remains of the bed when the fire service took me inside.'

'I saw it too, Dick,' Dexter said grimly, 'and I still dream about it.'

'So what do you want me to do, recommend a suitable shrink?'

'No, I want you to listen, that's all. Remember the man on the motorcycle in the woods?'

Lawson looked puzzled. 'You're not suggesting that your assailant was Eddie Challow? You said you never saw his face.'

'I didn't, but Challow was into bikes, wasn't he? Did a lot of scrambling. And there was something that the character said too: "Not this time, my friend". Strange sort of phrase to come out with, don't you think?'

'Not particularly.'

'Then there's this.' Dexter handed him the anniversary card that had been delivered earlier.

Lawson examined it and shrugged. 'Okay, it's an anniversary card. Congratulations.'

'Look on the back.'

Dexter studied his colleague's face as he read the inscription and had the satisfaction of seeing his eyes narrow. 'Well?'

Lawson flicked the card on to the table with a heavy sigh. 'So it's from a psychiatric hospital called Bramley Heath.'

'Where Eddie Challow was transferred just two years ago.'

Lawson shrugged. 'If you say so, but the card's not signed and could have come from anyone.'

Dexter scowled, remembering that he had said much the same thing to Tania earlier. 'Get real, Dick,' he snapped irritably. 'Who else but Eddie Challow would have sent us this crap? It's a threat, you must see that?'

Lawson held up his hands in a conciliatory gesture. 'Okay, okay, perhaps Challow did send it, but it still doesn't prove he torched Berwick or is coming after Tania.'

Dexter gritted his teeth to control his exasperation, then began counting off points on his fingers. 'Look at the facts, for heavens sake. One, Challow was put away by Judge Berwick and within six weeks of the little psycho's release Berwick is torched in his own home. Two, Berwick was secured to his bed just like Challow's original victim –'

'Ron Ferguson was tied up with chicken wire.'

Dexter snorted his exasperation. 'Handcuffs, chicken wire, what's the difference? The principle is the same. Three, Challow had a passion for motorcycle scrambling and I end up getting clobbered at the scene of the crime by a guy riding a trials type motorcycle. And four, Tania and I receive an anniversary card this morning from the very place where Challow was last detained. Surely that's enough for you?'

Lawson shook his head. 'Frankly, Mike, no it isn't – and it certainly won't be enough for Mr Moffat, especially as you're so personally involved in this thing.'

'Sod Moffat!'

Lawson sighed heavily. 'Be reasonable, Mike. I'll grant that the anniversary card is a worrying aspect and I can see why you're so concerned about it. But otherwise, you've got absolutely nothing; there's not a single solid fact to latch on to.'

'So you're going to do sweet FA about it?'

Lawson drained his glass a second time and returned it to the desk. 'I never said that,' he replied standing up. 'I'm investigating a murder and I would be negligent if I ignored any information that was passed to me. But before I can do anything about Eddie Challow – and that includes speaking to the governor – I have to confirm that he has actually been released. I can't just take your word for it. So let me get that out of the way first, eh?'

'And then?'

'That will depend on what I find out.'

'Or whether he gets to Tania *before* you can find it out.'

Lawson stared at him keenly. 'Just leave it with me, will you, Mike,' he said. 'Don't go charging off like a loose cannon. I promise I'll get back to you as soon as I can. And for heaven's sake, keep out of Moffat's way. You're not his favourite person at the moment.'

'I can't think why,' Dexter retorted bitterly. 'Something I said?'

*

It was completely dark by the time Quentin Fuller left Tulse End and he sighed wearily as he settled back in the soft leather seat of his

Mercedes, thinking of the shower and three-course dinner that awaited him at The Lamb Hotel in Claydock where he had booked a room for a couple of nights. The urgent shrill of his mobile telephone was the last thing he wanted to hear and, swearing as he reached across to the instrument in its hands-free cradle, he stabbed at the answer button as if he were trying to summon a lift.

The call was short and sweet, but its effect on him was dramatic. Abandoning any prospect of a shower and a three-course dinner, he turned left at the next intersection, heading away from Claydock and The Lamb Hotel towards the dual-carriageway. Fifteen minutes later he had left the dual-carriageway behind and his tail-lights had merged with a hundred others speeding north along the motorway, another cigarette in his mouth and an excited gleam in his eye.

He only stopped once during the next hour, slipping briefly into a rain-swept service area for a hamburger and coffee, followed by a sizeable withdrawal from his business account through the services' own hole-in-the-wall. Then ten minutes on, he exchanged the motorway for a winding unlit B class road and within two to three miles his headlights picked out a large oblong sign through the squalling rain, telling him that "Bramley Heath Welcomes Careful Drivers".

He successfully negotiated his way round a torturous one-way system, which seemed determined to take him on a complete guided-tour of the town, and then, about half a mile along the straight road out, he spotted the blue and white "Hospital" sign. Seconds later the straggle of shops and garages on his left gave way to an imposing brick wall, which hugged the edge of the road and seemed to stretch away into infinity. On impulse, he slowed right down and swung into the wide entranceway, pulling up with his engine running to peer through the streaming front passenger window.

He was confronted by a pair of iron gates, which seemed to be as high as the wall itself and looked as though they might be electronically controlled. Through the bars he glimpsed a small lodge and beyond it, a long floodlit drive, which cut across open parkland to an enormous turreted mansion, pin-pointed by even more powerful spotlights. In the darkness and the rain, the place had a forbidding aspect and he shivered slightly as he read the large sign on the right-hand wall: "Bramley Heath Psychiatric Hospital. Keep Clear. Restricted Area".

He was still staring at it, as if mesmerised, when a flashlight blazing in his face from the other side of the gate alerted him to the fact that he was attracting unwelcome attention. Promptly pulling back on to the road, he accelerated swiftly away, wondering why on earth he had decided to stop there in the first place. 'It isn't the nutters in the can you have to worry about, Quentin, my boy,' he said aloud. 'It's the ones on the outside.'

For the next few miles his eyes constantly strayed to his rear-view mirror, watching for the headlights and flashing blue beacons he expected to see closing on him at any moment, and he became so preoccupied with his anxiety about police pursuit, that he almost overshot the entrance to the roadside café he was looking for.

At the last minute he spun the steering wheel hard left and bumped across the potholed car park, passing between several vans and articulated lorries before lurching to a stop in front of a long prefabricated shed-like building that, according to the garish flashing sign above the door, served as "Jack's Diner".

The air inside was heavy with the smell of fried food, and cigarette smoke drifted in bluish clouds among the closely packed bodies – mainly lorry drivers by the look of them – crouching round the dozen or so small tables. He spotted Fred Baines almost immediately. He was sitting apart from the rest at a table in the far corner, close to the door marked "Toilets". His raincoat was thrown carelessly over the opposite chair to indicate it was taken and he was staring moodily into a large mug in front of him, his bald head gleaming in the light from an adjacent wall lamp and his heavy slab like features and bulbous nose giving him all the appearance of a defector from the old post-war KGB.

Fuller bought a mug of coffee he didn't want and went over to him. 'Couldn't you have picked somewhere more salubrious than this?' he complained as he scooped the raincoat up into a ball and tossed it on to the chair next to him.

'Only place I could think of that the rest of the staff would never come to,' the other retorted in the soft lilting tones of the Welsh valleys. 'Can't afford to be seen with you now, can I?'

The pressman lit himself a cigarette, then slid the packet and his lighter across the table. 'So, exactly what have you got for me?' he demanded. 'It had better be good to drag me all the way up here.'

Baines selected a cigarette and lit up, drawing the smoke down in a slow thoughtful motion. 'Oh, I don't think you'll be disappointed,' he replied.

'That's reassuring anyway,' Fuller said dryly. 'I gather from what you told me on the phone that you've finally managed to find out where Eddie Challow has gone to ground?'

'That and more besides.'

'I'm listening.'

Baines blew smoke rings and threw him a sideways glance. 'Money first,' he said bluntly.

Fuller's eyes narrowed. 'You always get paid when you come up with something of interest and you know it,' he retorted.

The Welshman met his gaze defiantly. 'Maybe, *bach*,' he said with emphasis. 'But this one's costing you a lot more than usual because of the risks I had to take raiding confidential patient files. So I don't want any misunderstandings on what I'm owed, see.'

Fuller nodded slowly and produced an envelope which he carefully placed on the table in front of him. 'You're certainly getting to be a greedy bugger, aren't you?' he commented, keeping his hand firmly on top of the envelope.

Baines' eyes flicked to the envelope, then back to the pressman's face. 'I've never let you down before, have I? Don't forget it was me that tipped you off about Eddie Challow's release in the first place.'

'Yeah, six weeks after it had actually happened.'

Baines stiffened, an angry scowl on his heavy features. 'You know damned well I couldn't help that. I'd been away on secondment for three months. Didn't realise he had actually gone until I got back.'

'You should have kept your finger on the pulse then, shouldn't you?'

Baines gave a short derisory laugh. 'Is that so?' he retorted. 'Well, it may interest you to know that, for some strange reason, hospital management didn't see fit to send me a personal e-mail and, as I'm not flaming clairvoyant, keeping my finger on the pulse from two hundred miles away would have been a bit difficult.'

Fuller stubbed out his unfinished cigarette and took a sip from his mug, grimacing at the strong bitter taste and thinking the stuff was more like creosote than coffee. 'Let's just get on with what we came here to do, shall we?' he said, anxious not to get bogged down with pointless recriminations. 'I've got a long drive back.'

'Money first,' Baines repeated stubbornly, his anger still evident.

Fuller shook his head. 'I don't work like that.'

'I could always go somewhere else.'

The pressman released his breath in a sharp exasperated hiss and, returning the envelope to his pocket, started to climb to his feet. 'Then you do just that,' he snapped, calling his bluff. 'I'm not pissing about with you all night over it.'

The Welshman's sudden grip on his arm was surprisingly strong and there was now a hint of alarm in his restless dark eyes. 'Okay, okay, no need to get touchy,' he said hastily. 'We'll do it your way.'

Fuller deliberately hesitated, then sat down with exaggerated reluctance. 'Ten minutes,' he warned, 'then I'm away.'

Baines nodded and, glancing quickly round the room, leaned towards him across the table. 'Eddie Challow should never have been let out of Bramley Heath in the first place,' he said darkly.

Fuller frowned. 'Then why the hell was he? I thought all restricted patients like him had to undergo some sort of rigorous psychiatric assessment before being recommended to the Home Secretary for release?'

Baines grunted. 'Oh they're assessed all right,' he confirmed, 'and not just as a one-off either. It's a continuous ongoing process from the very start of their detention, right the way through, and every single aspect of their mental and physical behaviour comes under the microscope.' He smiled faintly. 'Bit like rats in a laboratory tank really. Only difference is that the rats have no right of appeal and are never likely to see the light of day again. We, on the other hand, tend to decide the fate of our patients through mental health tribunals and actually let a few of them go from time to time.'

Fuller grimaced at the unsavoury analogy. 'So, if you're right about Eddie Challow, how come he managed to slip through the net?' he said coldly.

Baines shrugged. 'No assessment process is infallible,' he replied. 'Furthermore, psychopaths can be very cunning – that's what makes them so dangerous – and Eddie Challow is a lot more cunning than most. During his time inside, he learned a great deal about psycho-analysis and the techniques that are used in the assessment process. So he simply played the so-called experts at their own game. Put every effort into convincing them that all the psycho-therapy sessions and other psychiatric and pharmacological treatment programmes had worked. Presented himself as a completely changed and psycho-logically re-adjusted person – a star patient they could be proud of, in fact.'

'Maybe the treatment he received actually did work?'

Baines slumped back in his chair and shook his head. 'Once a psychopath, always a psychopath,' he said. 'These people can't be cured, only trained to recognise and deal with their own particular psychosis. And in Eddie Challow's case, he's as crazy now as he was when they first put him away.'

Fuller raised his eyebrows. 'Nice caring sentiments for a member of the nursing profession,' he said mildly.

'Maybe that's because I'm not as naïve as some of my colleagues.'

'Or maybe it's because you simply don't like Eddie Challow.'

Baines shrugged again. 'Think what you like,' he retorted, 'But I *know* him and what he's capable of. Don't forget, he was put on my wing when he first came to the Heath and I've been in this job long enough to be able to spot a bad 'un when I see one.'

'Pity no one else could do the same thing.'

'As I've already said, no assessment process is infallible and some serious blunders were made, and not just at Bramley Heath either.'

'I don't follow you.'

Straightening up, Baines removed a tobacco fibre from his tongue and flicked it on to the floor. 'Bramley Heath is a secure psychiatric unit for restricted mental patients who are being considered for eventual release,' he explained. 'It has a lower category status than the top security special hospitals like Broughton Lake, where Challow was initially banged up, but it is nevertheless an important next step in the discharge process. A patient is never released into the community straight from a special hospital, see, and the fact that Eddie Challow was transferred to us from Broughton Lake, means that the Broughton RMO – the Responsible Medical Officer – must have been satisfied with his progress to feel that he was suitable for a more open regime.'

'Bramley Heath didn't look particularly open to me just now,' Fuller commented dryly.

Baines' eyes narrowed. 'So you had a little peek, did you?' he replied softly. 'Bit of a risky thing to do under the circumstances, I would have thought.'

'Call it journalist's curiosity.'

'Journalist's stupidity more like. What if you'd been checked out and they'd linked you to me?'

'Well, I wasn't and they didn't, okay? Anyway, if it's such an open regime, why would they want to check anyone out in the first place?'

'I wasn't suggesting it is entirely open. I said it was more open than Broughton Lake. But it's still a secure unit and there has to be some sort of basic security for obvious reasons. Where it differs from a special hospital is that it can provide a more flexible care programme, tailored to individual patient needs and driven by the patients themselves rather than by an arbitrary systemised process.'

'What does that mean in English?'

Baines pursed his lips thoughtfully for a few moments before replying. 'In essence, it's all about stimulating development through step-by-step incentives. The greater the progress a patient makes, the more licence he or she is likely to be given. Exactly what that entails will depend to a large extent on the patient themselves, but to start with, it could mean them being allowed out into the grounds for, say, a few hours a day and later for short periods outside the hospital itself; first with and then without supervision. Ultimately, they could earn enough brownie points to be given the opportunity of actually working in the local community for a couple of days a week as a way of acclimatising themselves to life beyond the institution and preparing them for their day of discharge.'

'And Eddie Challow, what did *he* do to distinguish himself?'

Baines gave a bitter smile. 'Anything and everything he could do to impress the hospital management. Apart from cooperating with the shrinks at every stage of his treatment programme, he got himself elected on to the Patients' Council, helped in the hospital library and chapel, and actually managed to finish off an HND in electronics he had started at Broughton Lake. He even managed to squeeze in a bit of caring for others as well, by befriending a nasty little pervert called Gilbert Trench who was being ostracised by the rest of the patients because of a major BO problem. That earned him some major brownie points, I can tell you.'

'And not one single person smelled a rat?' Fuller exclaimed. 'That's a pretty damning indictment on the professional competence of the mental health service.'

Baines nodded. 'You can read into it what you like,' he said, 'but the fact remains that a dangerous psychopath is on the loose and I reckon he means to get even with all those who had a part in putting him away.'

Fuller thought of Judge Berwick and felt excited, then guilty at feeling excited all at the same time. 'And what makes you think that?' he said, trying hard not to appear too interested, but failing miserably.

Baines' eyes gleamed. 'Not much escapes me,' he boasted.

'Challow kept an old scrapbook of press cuttings about his trial in the drawer of his desk. Got a quiet look at it when he was clearing out his stuff before being moved to another wing. Interesting thing was, the names of all the main players in his case – the woman he raped, the trial judge, the senior police investigating officer – were all highlighted with a yellow marker pen, then listed in ink on the inside cover of the scrapbook. He'd obviously kept them in mind all the years he was inside. Didn't think that much of it at the time. Then I heard on the radio this morning about the body of an elderly man being found after a fatal fire at the home of Judge Lionel Berwick and I *knew* Challow had started. That's when I rang you.'

Fuller felt slightly light-headed as he experienced a sudden surge of adrenalin and he gulped down some more of his coffee to conceal his excitement. 'But how could Challow have known where to find Berwick in the first place?' he went on. 'It wouldn't have been exactly public knowledge then.'

Baines grunted. 'It's not difficult to find out the addresses of public figures like Lionel Berwick,' he retorted. 'You only have to make a few discreet enquires locally, or check the electoral role or telephone directory. Information's pretty easy to get hold of today, as you should know.'

Fuller ignored the barb. 'Even so, surely someone must have been keeping an eye on Challow since his release? What about electronic tagging, for instance?'

Baines shook his head. 'Tagging's not considered appropriate for patients like Eddie Challow. Instead, he's been made the subject of what they call supervised after-care. That includes living where he's told to live, regularly taking any prescribed medication, reporting for counselling sessions, and obeying set restrictions, like keeping away from his former victim. All a load of crap really, but at least it keeps the Home Office happy.'

'So he would have had ample opportunity to top Berwick after getting out?' Fuller reflected grimly.

Baines nodded. 'Between attending counselling sessions, of course,' he added with heavy sarcasm.

But Fuller hardly heard him; his mind was already racing on to other things. 'So where is he living now?' he said.

Baines took his time stubbing out his cigarette. 'Near a place called Maple Bucksters.'

'Never heard of it.'

Baines smirked again, obviously enjoying his few moments of privileged knowledge. 'I gather it's a small hamlet about twenty miles north-west of Heaton, close to the Mid-Shires Canal at Curling Lock.'

Fuller raised his eyebrows. 'But that's within spitting distance of his old stomping ground. I'm surprised the authorities allowed that.'

'It wasn't in their interests to object. Apparently Challow has a cousin, Tommy Lee, who owns a small boatyard just up from the lock. He operates and maintains canal boats for the tourist industry when he's not servicing tractors and other machinery for local farmers. Bit of a born again Christian by all accounts and as part of his Christian duty, he agreed to store Challow's personal stuff for him at the boatyard when Eddie was put away. He was also our man's only visitor after his dear old mum snuffed it and when Challow was due up for release, Lee offered to provide him with a job until he got himself sorted out. He even made one of his older canal boats available for him to live on. Jobs and accommodation are not that easy to come by for ex-mental patients, so the care team nearly bit his hand off.'

'I bet they did.'

Baines reached into his jacket pocket again and this time handed over a small black and white photograph. 'Challow has got himself a new ID too. Calls himself Alan Salter now. I pinched a spare mug shot from his personal file to make sure you'd be able to recognise him again. The hospital won't miss it.'

Fuller glanced quickly at the picture. A familiar cadaverous face, with tight curly black hair, now streaked with grey, and deep-set brooding eyes, stared back at him. Challow may have aged a lot over the years, but the unnerving intensity of those strange dark eyes was still the same and he shivered involuntarily.

'The boat's called *Water Gypsy*, I gather,' Baines went on, 'and it's permanently moored upstream a few hundred yards east of the boatyard. Apparently, you can get to it via a woodland track leading off the boatyard access road called Bottom Lane.'

Fuller nodded appreciatively. 'You've certainly done your homework, I'll give you that,' he acknowledged. 'But one thing I cannot understand is why the authorities haven't ordered Challow's recall to hospital long before now or at the very least alerted the police?'

'And why would they do that?'

'Well, they must have ample grounds after you told –' Fuller broke off and stared at the hard slab-like face, his eyes widening. 'You haven't actually *told* anyone about this, have you?' he breathed. 'You've kept the whole damned thing to yourself?'

Baines met his stare without flinching. 'Oh, I tried,' he said grimly. 'Believe me, I tried. Right at the very start, when Challow was first lodged on my wing, I made a point of warning the hospital management that he was a dangerous con artist. But I had no evidence, see, so they wouldn't listen. Then, when I pushed it, they bloody well moved him to another wing. Said I had a down on him and that my judgement couldn't be trusted. Too damned clever for their own good, that's their trouble. Think they're the only ones who know anything about anything and can't accept that anyone could be as smart as they are – especially a lowly nursing assistant like me.'

'But that was before you'd seen the scrapbook with the list of names.'

Baines emitted an angry snarl. 'They had their chance months ago and they blew it, so as far as I'm concerned, they can stew in their own juice.'

'But it's your duty to –'

'Duty?' Baines' expression was suddenly venomous and he leaned across the table again. 'Let me tell you something about duty, *bach*,' he snarled. 'Fifteen years I've worked in this filthy job. Cleaning up nutters' crap every day, sticking needles in them when they flip and watching my back every single second, just in case one of them tries to get lucky. And what have I got to show for it? Bugger all, that's what. Still the same salary scale, still the same rank, still the same crap. Good enough to do the dirty work, but not good enough to be listened to or recommended for anything better.'

Fuller stared at him in disbelief. 'All this isn't just about money, is it?' he breathed incredulously. 'You want to get your own back, don't you? Punish the system for not giving you a better deal. That's why you didn't make too much of an effort to contact me when Challow was first released. It had nothing to do with your being on secondment. You knew in advance that Challow was going to be let out, but you wanted him to get clear first; so he could do whatever it was he had planned. Then you could gloat when the hospital got egg all over its face in the full glare of the publicity provided by me.'

Baines jerked back in his chair and studied Fuller with a sneer. 'Should have treated me better then, shouldn't they,' he retorted.

'But a man has died, don't you see that?'

Baines nodded slowly. '*I'm* dying too, bach,' he said soberly. 'Got word from the clinic last month. Hepatitis B. Must have got it from a needle at the hospital. Only a few months left apparently and I mean to enjoy them.' He laughed without humour. 'So don't try that moral bollocks with me. It doesn't wash anymore.'

Fuller dumped his envelope back on the table. 'Then you'd better start spending your blood money now, hadn't you?' he said without a trace of sympathy. 'I wouldn't want you to leave any unspent.'

The smirk was back on Baines' face as he pocketed the envelope and stood up. 'Don't you worry about that,' he retorted. 'I'll make good use of it, you can bet on it.'

Fuller snorted his contempt. 'Aren't you going to count it then?' he grated.

Baines bent close to him as he reached across the table to pick up his raincoat. 'Oh, I think I can trust you, Mr Fuller,' he said softly. 'But can you trust yourself, that's the point? I mean, do you go straight to the police with what I've just told you – save further lives and all that – or do you keep it all to yourself until you have enough for the story of a lifetime?' He straightened up. 'Sod of a decision, isn't it?'

Then he was heading for the door without a backward glance, leaving Fuller staring into his cold cup of coffee and wondering why Baines had to be such a perceptive arsehole.

Chapter 6

Silence. Heavy, almost threatening. Broken only by the soft lapping of water and the occasional creak of a tree.

Quentin Fuller eased his right leg into a more comfortable position and peered once more through the lattice-work of branches behind which he had been concealed for the best part of two hours. Twenty feet away the canal boat tugged gently on the ropes holding it fast to the grassy bank, mist rising around it off the dark water like steam in the cold frosty dawn.

He still felt guilty about his decision to follow up on the information he had been given instead of going straight to the police and he despised himself for being such a blatant hypocrite and doing exactly what Baines had guessed he would do. Yet, looking at things logically, he took comfort from the fact that there was very little he could pass on to them anyway. Everything Baines had told him was based on supposition and the police were unlikely to be able to do anything with it even when they had it, except maybe to ask some difficult questions as to where he had obtained his information in the first place. No, guilt or no guilt, he had little choice but to press on with his investigation until he had some concrete facts to lay before Detective Superintendent Moffat and his team. Exactly how he was going to get hold of those facts, he was not entirely sure, but the prospect of securing a major exclusive story was an excellent motivator.

A couple of rabbits emerged from the undergrowth further along the towpath and stood looking in his direction for a few moments before disappearing back under cover. Seconds later a moorhen trailed a noisy passage across the water. But nothing stirred aboard the canal boat and he actually began to wonder whether he was in the wrong place after all. Then he shook his head definitely. The name, *Water Gypsy*, was now clearly visible on the prow of the boat and the tarpaulin in the stern could in no way disguise the angular shape of the big motorcycle. No, this had to be the right one. He just needed to be a little more patient.

In fact, that patience was rewarded just twenty minutes later when a glimmer of light showed through the heavy curtains drawn across the boat's rectangular windows. Fuller tensed, carefully preparing the camera slung round his neck for a quick shot with the telephoto lens.

Still no one appeared from inside and he relaxed slightly. A pair of mallards flopped down the far bank into the canal, quacking noisily, and he froze as a man, muffled in a duffle-coat and cloth cap, stomped heavily past his hiding-place, heading towards the boatyard round the next bend. The world was waking up, it seemed.

More ducks joined the other two and he reached into his anorak pocket for his hip flask, shivering not for the first time, as the damp rose like a miasma from the marshy ground and seeped into his bones.

Then suddenly there was movement on the boat and someone in a black leather jacket pushed open the double doors and stepped up on to the tiny for'ard deck. In the camera's viewfinder the figure seemed to lunge across the towpath as Fuller adjusted the telephoto lens for maximum magnification and he jumped involuntarily as familiar deep-set dark eyes stared directly into his own from under the peak of a blue forage cap.

'Bingo!' he muttered under his breath. It may have been twenty years since he had last clapped eyes on Eddie Challow, but even without the photograph given to him by the avaricious Baines, he would have known him anywhere.

Challow chose that moment to pause to light a cigarette and Fuller managed to capture half a dozen shots of those pale almost skeletal features before his subject had clambered from the boat and headed off along the towpath in the same direction as that taken by the other man.

Silence once more, but still Fuller waited, just in case Challow decided to return. Ten minutes and fragile sunlight began to creep among the trees. A heron swooped low over the canal, but chose not to land and something small scurried through the sodden undergrowth close to Fuller's foot.

He stood up slowly, stretching his aching muscles. Time to move. Parting the thin branches in front of him, he stepped out on to the towpath, glancing warily left and right before cutting across to the canal side.

The boat seemed to sigh gently as he scrambled aboard and he dropped to a defensive crouch, swivelling round to re-appraise the towpath. Nothing. So far so good. From beyond the bend he could hear the sound of hammering and the chug of some sort of light engine. Evidently the boatyard had started work for the day and that suited him just fine.

A quick check revealed that the double doors were locked, but he wasn't deterred. Shaking the handle, he felt them give a little. He smiled grimly and felt for the clasp knife in his pocket. Eddie Challow should have asked the police for some crime prevention advice, he mused, as he inserted the blade into the gap and sprang the lock.

He was greeted by the characteristic old boat smell of damp musty furnishings and recently treated wood, laced with the whiff of Calor gas and the distinctive odour of a poorly maintained chemical toilet. Not a very welcoming atmosphere, he mused with a grimace, but then that was the least of his worries. He was more concerned about the wall lights that had been left burning inside the heavily curtained living area, for it suggested that Challow didn't anticipate being away too long. He would have to work fast, but it would have helped to have known what he was looking for.

Using the flashlamp he had brought with him to supplement the dim glow provided by the lights, he began a swift but methodical search, going through every cupboard and drawer he could find and even checking the chemical toilet. It didn't take him long to find something either. Eddie Challow had obviously not expected his new home to be turned over by anyone, so he had made very little real effort to hide the evidence away.

The green canvas holdall had been stuffed into the linen box under one of the bench seats and Fuller unzipped it almost half-heartedly, guessing from the weight of it that it probably contained nothing more than tools for boat repairs. But he could not have been more mistaken and as he cleared it out, item by item, very carefully placing the contents on the nearby pull-out dining table, he felt his skin crawl. The holdall did in fact contain a couple of very small screwdrivers and a pair of pliers. These had nothing whatsoever to do with boat repairs, however, of that he was certain, any more than the rest of the stuff – which included a small cardboard box containing a sausage-shaped substance resembling Plasticine and smelling strongly of marzipan, a reel of fine electrical wire, packets of batteries, a collection of strapless watches in a plastic bag and a boxed miniature radio transmitter and receiver – had anything to do with electrical maintenance. As for the large Ordnance Survey map, which he opened out curiously and weighted down at each corner with ashtrays and an empty vase, that had as much to do with rambling as the sawn-off shotgun had to do with game-keeping.

For a few moments he simply stood there staring at the sinister collection of equipment, an icy hand clawing at his insides as the strong marzipan smell took him back to his time as a feature reporter with the army in Ulster when that sickly odour had introduced him to plastic explosives for the very first time. It had been the practice then for the security services to grade the individual quantities recovered by them as to their potential destructive energy and from his experience of those exciting terrifying days, it wasn't difficult for him to see that there was enough of the stuff here to blow up a whole fleet of canal boats, let alone just this one.

Now he *knew* what Eddie Challow was up to and with that knowledge came the realisation that only he could avert the hideous catastrophe the little psychopath was planning. The enormity of the responsibility pressed down on him heavily and his first instinct was to pack the stuff back into the holdall and dump the lot into the canal before taking to his heels. But that was no real solution, for it would have meant destroying the evidence and letting Challow get off scot-free to commit his awful crime another day. No, what was needed above all was evidence and that meant photographs.

Adjusting his camera to the correct setting, he forced himself to keep as calm as possible and began snapping pictures of the table and its contents with hands that were suddenly ice-cold and trembling. Just half a dozen pictures, however, and the camera refused to function as the film expired. Cursing under his breath, he flicked open the back and dropped the expired roll into his anorak pocket, then reloaded with a new one. But his luck was about to run out and he had only managed a further five shots before a creaking floorboard made him whirl round to face the cabin doors.

The deep-set dark eyes beneath the peak of the blue forage cap were cold and hard and the large bowie knife in Eddie Challow's hand gleamed in the lamplight. 'I do hope you've used the right exposure?' he said softly.

*

Assistant Chief Constable Dennis Stanford Parkes BA was not amused, that much was obvious, and it seemed that the coffee table and easy chairs were to be denied Mike Dexter this time. Instead, the head of force Operations remained firmly behind his big mahogany desk and he directed his PRO, with an imperious flick of the wrist, towards the leather chair set directly in front of it.

Dexter slumped into the chair with a weary resignation. It was obvious what was coming and he really didn't care anymore. He was already in the doghouse with Tania for arriving home late the previous night, still smelling of the whisky he had shared with Dick Lawson, and he hadn't helped matters at breakfast the next morning by stubbornly refusing to apologise, then dismissing her fears about being left alone after dark as neurotic nonsense. The blazing row that had followed had ended with Tania grabbing her coat and storming from the house, her car keys in her hand and her mind set on going back to work 'where she was needed'.

Feeling a total heel for the way he had behaved, he had worried about her all the way to Headquarters, trying several times to get her to answer her mobile telephone, but each time receiving the same metallic voice telling him he could not be connected. Then, finally arriving at the office half an hour late with a speeding ticket from a vigilant traffic motorcyclist in the glove compartment, he found a memo in the middle of his desk, ordering him to report to Assistant Chief Constable Operations immediately.

'Do you have a death wish, Chief Inspector?' Parkes snapped abruptly, cutting in on his reverie.

Dexter studied him levelly. 'Death wish, sir?' he said with little real interest.

'Parkes stabbed a finger at a report lying on the desk in front of him. 'Detective Superintendent Moffat came to see me earlier this morning,' he went on. 'And he's far from happy with you at the moment or with the service he's been getting from the Press Office.'

'That *is* a surprise, sir.' Dexter replied dryly.

Parkes glared at him. 'Don't try to get clever with me, man,' he warned, a sudden harshness in his tone. 'I am in no mood for it this morning.' He snatched up the report and waved it in the air. 'First, he tells me, you failed to control the press properly at Alden House, with the result that they were all over the murder scene like a rash. Then you went missing for hours, ignoring the repeated attempts that were made to contact you. Finally, when you eventually *did* decide to put in an appearance at a press conference he'd more or less had to set up himself, you failed to manage the press effectively and were insolent towards him when he tried to speak to you afterwards.'

Parkes tossed the report back on to his desk. 'What the hell's going on with you, man?' he exclaimed. 'You seem to be going to pieces.'

Dexter sighed. 'With respect, sir,' he began, 'the facts you've been given have been distorted.'

'So you're saying Mr. Moffat is a liar?'

'Not exactly. I did lose contact with Headquarters for a time, because I left my mobile telephone in the car, but –'

'You went home, I believe.'

'My wife was ill, sir, as I have already explained to Mr Moffat, and in any event, I had been on duty since half-past three in the morning, so I feel I was entitled to a meal break like everyone else.'

'That's as maybe, but Headquarters Control Room should still have been kept informed of your whereabouts.'

'I realise that only too well, sir, and I can only once again apologise for the lapse.'

Parkes gave a disparaging grunt. 'And your mismanagement of the press conference? What about that lapse? Do you think a simple "sorry" will suffice there?'

In spite of his depressive mood, Dexter felt a stab of irritation. 'I did not mismanage anything, sir,' he retorted. 'I wasn't even given the opportunity. Mr Moffat insisted on handling the whole thing without consulting me at all.'

'Hardly surprising after your earlier negligent behaviour at Alden House, was it?'

Suddenly conscious of the throbbing pain starting up again in the wound to his temple and thinking how he had come by it, Dexter bit hard at the injustice of the remark. 'There was nothing negligent about my behaviour at Alden House either, sir,' he snapped back. 'Quite the reverse, in fact. I did everything I was supposed to do and a whole lot more besides. But it's not my job, or within my capability, to single-handedly prevent unauthorised access to crime scenes as well. That has to be down to uniform.'

Parkes raised his gaze slightly to study the plaster still attached to Dexter's forehead. 'It's not your job to go chasing people through woods either,' he commented dryly.

Dexter flushed. 'I'm still a police officer, sir.'

'Not while you're the force PRO you're not. You're paid to deal with the press, nothing more.'

Dexter stared at him in disbelief. 'So, when I see an intruder running away from the scene of a murder, I am supposed to walk on by, is that what you're saying, sir?'

Parkes' mouth tightened. 'You're treading on very thin ice, Chief Inspector,' he warned. 'I suggest you moderate your tone.'

Dexter took a deep breath, trying to control his rising frustration. 'Okay, sir,' he said patiently, 'I apologise, but you must see my point. Under the circumstances, there was absolutely nothing else I could have done.'

'Maybe, but you didn't achieve very much by your actions, did you? After all, your man still got away.'

'True, but I am pretty sure I know who he was anyway.'

Parkes' eyes narrowed, but he said nothing and Dexter took that as an invitation to continue, leaning forward almost eagerly. 'Twenty years ago,' he explained, 'a vicious psychopath, named Eddie Challow, was put away for burning a local haulage contractor to death and raping his daughter –'

Parkes cut him off with a dismissive wave of his hand. 'I may only have been in this force five years,' he said tightly, 'but I wasn't exactly shut away in a monastery before that. I am well aware of the case. You married the key witness, I believe?'

Dexter nodded. 'Tania Ferguson, the girl he raped,' he said grimly. 'And since you're familiar with the case, you'll also know that Lionel Berwick was the presiding judge at his trial.'

'So?'

Dexter studied him fixedly. 'As I understand it,' he replied very deliberately, 'Eddie Challow was released from the psychiatric hospital in which he was being held just six weeks before Alden House was torched, and I am convinced that he was also the intruder who attacked me in the grounds.'

Parkes noticeably stiffened. 'And exactly how did *you* find out that Challow had been released?' he said a little too softly, his eyes like gimlets.

'A reporter colleague told me,' he replied.

'A reporter? What reporter?'

Dexter hesitated, surprised by his hostile reaction. 'A freelance. Name of Quentin Fuller. He covered the original trial and probably got wind of Challow's release from someone at the hospital itself. He was bound to smell a connection between the Berwick and Ferguson cases with the MO's being so similar.'

Parkes made a sharp exclamation. 'Which means, I suppose, that the whole damned thing will be plastered all over the nationals by this evening,' he snapped.

Dexter shook his head. 'I wouldn't think so, sir,' he replied. 'Fuller dare not come out with allegations like that without being able to substantiate them and anyway, at present he has an exclusive and he won't want to share his information with anyone else. My guess is he'll ferret around for a while yet until he can dig up enough material for a major story.'

'Or until someone digs that material up for him,' Parkes said pointedly. 'I'm still very curious as to how the press found out about the handcuffs used on Lionel Berwick. I don't suppose you have any idea how that could have happened, do you?'

Dexter's eyes blazed. 'No, I don't, sir,' he threw back angrily. 'And if you're insinuating –'

Parkes silenced him with another wave of his hand. 'I insinuate nothing, Chief Inspector,' he cut in. 'But I do intend finding out, I assure you. As for your theory about Challow being responsible for the murder of Lionel Berwick, it is obviously something Mr Moffat and myself are keeping very much in mind and he will, of course, be interviewed if and when that is considered appropriate. But there must be any number of criminals who would have had a reason for wanting to see the unfortunate man dead and we cannot afford to jump to conclusions this early in the investigation.'

But Dexter was hardly listening to him, for the realisation had begun to dawn on him with amazing clarity. Something you are keeping in mind, sir?' he exclaimed, more or less echoing his words. 'Are you saying you knew all along that Challow had been released?'

Parkes snorted. 'Of course I *knew*,' he retorted. 'Chief officers are automatically informed when a restricted mental patient is released into their area. It's part of normal procedure, I thought you would have known that.'

Dexter's expression was cold. 'And what about the victim, sir?' he breathed. 'Isn't it part of normal procedure to inform them too?'

Parkes shifted uncomfortably in his chair. This wasn't the way he had intended the interview going. 'It is certainly very carefully considered,' he prevaricated, 'but the decision itself is not down to the police to make.'

'Then who is it down to, sir?'

Parkes hesitated under Dexter's uncompromising stare. 'It has to be a matter for the senior member of the professional psychiatric team involved,' he replied carefully. 'In this particular case, it was the view of the Responsible Medical Officer that, for Challow's rehabilitation programme to have any real chance of success, every effort would have to be made to minimise the level of external pressure placed on him as he attempted to acclimatise himself to life outside the institution.'

'You're saying the whole thing had to be kept quiet?'

Parkes grimaced. 'Not quite the way I would have put it at all, but in essence, that's what it amounts to, yes – at least until Challow has managed to settle down, after which the decision will be reviewed.'

He thought a second before continuing, choosing his words carefully. 'As you know only too well, the government had to abandon its very innovative "Care in the Community" programme after one or two unfortunate incidents involving discharged patients resulted in a wave of adverse publicity –'

'You mean when the patients reverted to type and became murdering psychos again?' Dexter interrupted. 'I'd call that a lot more than unfortunate, sir.'

Parkes gave a little embarrassed cough behind one hand. 'Yes, well, the fact remains that the release of restricted mental patients has now become a very emotive issue and it was considered that widespread publicity would not only be detrimental to Challow's recovery, but could actually result in violence against him. I think you'll agree that we've had quite enough problems in the force already from so-called vigilantes targeting paedophiles, without adding to the problem by telling the world that Eddie Challow is back on the streets.' He hesitated. 'Coupled with all this, of course, there was genuine concern over the psychological effect the news of Challow's release might have on your wife, in view of her own psychiatric history.'

'Yeah,' Dexter put in with heavy sarcasm, 'especially as Tania's husband is the force PRO and, if she told him, he might go round blabbing the news to everyone in the media.'

'Now you're being ridiculous.'

'Am I, sir? Am I really? So, when this decision was made, did anyone stop to think what the psychological effect on Tania would be if Challow decided to drop in on her out of the blue, just for old time's sake?'

Parkes shook his head definitely. 'There is absolutely no possibility of that happening. One of the conditions of his release is that he makes no attempt to approach his former victim. If he contravenes that condition, he could find himself back inside PDQ.'

'And does approaching his former victim include sending her an anniversary card?'

'Sending her a what?'

Dexter leaned forward slightly. 'Tania received one from him through the post yesterday morning.'

Parkes stared at him, obviously thrown for a moment. 'From Challow? You're sure about that?'

'Well, it wasn't signed, but it was stamped with the name Bramley Heath, the institution where he was last held.'

Parkes grunted. 'Difficult proving he sent it then, but a bit too much of a coincidence, I agree.' He made a note on a pad on the corner of his desk. 'I will, of course, speak to someone about this. He will need to be advised that this sort of thing is not permissible. Nothing for you to worry about though.'

Dexter gave a short ironic laugh. 'Of course not, sir. The fact that Challow is out, may well have murdered a judge and knows precisely where his former victim is now living is absolutely nothing for me to worry about.'

Parkes made a grimace. 'Once again you are jumping to conclusions, Chief Inspector, but to reassure your wife, I will arrange for the local area beat man to give your house passing attention on the grounds that your wife is being pestered by some anonymous nuisance. In the meantime, you can be reassured that Challow's progress is already being very closely monitored by a professional care team who will ensure that he is returned to the secure unit should there be the slightest suggestion that he is regressing.'

Dexter nodded slowly. 'And how closely is that, sir?' he said. 'Are we talking electronic tagging or is the whole supervision thing being left to the fuzzy-wuzzies in social services?'

Parkes studied him coldly. 'I'll pretend I didn't hear that,' he replied. 'But for your information, it is a joint-agency approach, which is fully supported by the Chief Constable himself. As you know only too well, Mr Pullinger has been making strenuous efforts to forge a much closer working relationship with the other statutory agencies than we've had in the past. Hence the forthcoming launch of his "Working As One" crime reduction initiative which your office has been publicising. In fact, I think it is fair to say that we have a chief constable who has a much more enlightened attitude towards the rehabilitation of offenders than any of his predecessors.'

Dexter's expression was bleak. 'I'm sure Ron Ferguson and Lionel Berwick would rest a lot easier if they knew that, sir,' he retorted bitterly. 'And my wife will certainly be reassured to learn that the Chief Constable has the best interests of Eddie Challow at heart.'

'Now that's enough!' Acutely conscious of the fact that he had been pushed more and more on to the defensive, Parkes was determined to regain the lost ground and reassert his authority. 'I will not tolerate any more of these facetious remarks. Is that clear?'

But he didn't have to, for the telephone came to his aid before he could elaborate further. The call was relatively short and for the most part Parkes simply listened to the speaker at the other end, making just the occasional grunt or other form of acknowledgement, but there was a triumphant gleam in his eyes when he put the receiver down again. 'Control Room,' he explained quietly. 'The body of a local vagrant has been found on the Grazely Bypass. It appears he either fell or jumped off Clifford's Bridge and was hit by a passing articulated lorry. You'd better get down there.'

Dexter looked surprised. 'With respect, sir,' he commented. 'I can't see the press being that interested in a fatal road accident. I'm rather surprised the Control Room bothered you with it in the first place.'

Parkes treated him to a thin smile. 'Oh I think there's likely to be a lot of press interest in this fatal,' he replied. 'As a result of what the Traffic Department found on the body, DCI Lawson was called to the scene and he thinks there is every likelihood that the dead man was Lionel Berwick's killer. Pity about your theory on Eddie Challow, isn't it?'

*

'I think I'm entitled to an explanation, don't you?' Eddie Challow wasn't a very tall man – maybe five foot seven in height – but, with the large knife in his hand, he seemed a lot taller. Quentin Fuller was no coward, but he was not a fool either and although his eyes strayed briefly to the shotgun on the table next to him, he made no move towards it.

Challow seemed to read his mind. 'No point, my friend,' he said with a cold smile. 'It isn't loaded. Now, I asked you a question.'

The pressman nodded. 'Name's Quentin Fuller,' he replied, playing for time. 'I'm a journalist.'

The dark eyes narrowed. 'I am already aware of who you are and what you do, Mr Fuller, but shouldn't I know your name from somewhere?'

Fuller made a grimace. 'Probably. I covered your trial in the local newspaper twenty years ago.'

Challow visibly started and drew in his breath with a sharp hiss. '*Of course*, my unauthorised biographer.' He emitted a short laugh. 'So, twenty years on, and here we are again. Incredible, isn't it? But why the interest in me after all this time?'

'I'm doing a sequel.'

Another laugh. '*Were* doing a sequel, Mr Fuller.' Challow held out his other hand. 'The camera, please. I'll take that, if you don't mind.'

Fuller pulled the strap back over his head. 'Then what?' he queried, still holding on to it.

Challow shrugged. 'Then you get to leave my boat,' he replied. 'I've no interest in you once I have your photographs.'

Fuller nodded slowly, reading the lie in those soulless eyes. 'Help yourself,' he snapped and, before Challow realised his intention, threw the camera straight at him.

Even as the other ducked, Fuller was on top of him, slamming him out of the way as he leaped up the short flight of stairs and burst through the double doors on to the tiny deck. Moments later he was across the towpath and crashing off among the trees, branches clawing at his face and clothes, slimy wet undergrowth snatching at his feet and ankles; running, as he knew full well, for his very life.

He thought bitterly about the loss of his camera as he ran. He'd had the Canon for more years then he could remember. It had become almost a part of him, accompanying him on assignments halfway round the world. Bit of an ignominious end for a trusted friend, he mused grimly, but better that than the loss of his life instead. Anyway, at least he still had the evidence he needed. Challow may have got hold of the film in his camera, but the pictures he had taken before changing the roll were still in his pocket.

Skidding on a mossy hummock, he snatched at a lichen-encrusted branch to stop himself falling and clung to it for a moment, gasping for breath and staring anxiously into the trees behind him.

Silence, but for continued, though muffled, hammering from the boatyard now way over to his left. He frowned, peering among the dripping trees and waist high ferns, listening intently for any sound of pursuit. But there was nothing. The woods seemed still and empty. He didn't like it. A man like Eddie Challow was unlikely to give up that easily, so where the hell was he?

His answer came a split second later, as the unmistakable snarl of a motorcycle engine starting up was followed shortly afterwards by the revving churning noise he had heard so often on television during off-road scrambling events. Hells bells! The little swine was going to ride him down!

In even greater panic, he practically threw himself down the steep slope in front of him, scrambling up the other side on his hands and knees and then into a patch of thorny scrub. The trailing branch of a hawthorn caught on his anorak, ripping through the thin material as well as the shirt underneath and drawing its fiery teeth down his side, while brambles constantly snared his trousers. But he couldn't afford to slacken his pace, for the snarl of the motorcycle was growing ever closer.

A small deer broke cover only yards away, crashing off into the undergrowth to his left, and as he veered sharply in the opposite direction, unnerved by its sudden appearance, he stumbled on to a ragged track that had already been made through the woods. The imprint of shoes, heading away to his right, were clearly visible in the patches of exposed muddy ground and with a sense of relief, he realised that this must have been the way he had come earlier. All he had to do was follow the track in the opposite direction and he would soon be safely behind the wheel of his Mercedes.

Even as this occurred to him, however, the roar of a high revving engine sent him diving back into the undergrowth and, glancing quickly over his shoulder, he saw the motorcycle burst through a tangle of bracken and slither to a stop by the track only feet from where he lay. He could practically feel Eddie Challow's dark eyes boring into him as he kept perfectly still, his head resting on one forearm and his teeth so tightly clenched that he began to wonder whether he would ever be able to unlock his jawbone again.

For what seemed like several minutes, but in reality must only have been a matter of seconds, Challow sat astride his machine, tapping one foot on the ground and revving continuously. He was so close that Fuller was actually enveloped in the poisonous fumes from his exhaust and it was all he could do to stop himself coughing up his insides as each rev produced one choking plume of smoke after another.

Then finally, after a particularly savage twist on the throttle and an unseemly grinding of gears, the motorcycle churned mud in all directions and fish-tailed violently away down the track towards the lane, leaving Fuller coughing and retching in its wake.

It was some time before the pressman could pluck up enough courage to climb to his feet and when he did, the sound of the motorcycle had died away completely and the woods were once more deathly still. Nevertheless, he moved off again with great caution, sticking to the undergrowth at one side of the track rather than using the track itself, very mindful of the possibility that Challow could be concealed somewhere up ahead with the engine of his machine turned off and his shotgun in his hands.

In fact, Fuller's suspicions proved to be groundless and he reached the end of the track without mishap. The lane too appeared to be deserted and he studied it narrowly for some time before venturing from cover. The Mercedes was where he had left it, in a small passing place a hundred yards away, and he breathed a sigh of relief as he dipped into his pocket for his ignition keys. He had feared Challow might have found the car and vandalised it to prevent him getting away, but that had obviously not happened. Maybe someone was watching over him after all.

Jerking open the drivers' door, he stripped off his anorak and tossed it on to the back seat. Moments later he was accelerating along the lane towards the main road, his traumatic flight through the woods pushed to the back of his mind and an expression of jubilation on his face as he thought of what he had accomplished in the last few hours.

Okay, so he had lost his beloved camera, ripped his shirt and anorak and ruined a perfectly good pair of trousers, but the roll of film in his pocket more than compensated for all that. The shots he had taken on Eddie Challow's boat had provided him with the sort of major exclusive most investigative journalists would die for and he knew only too well that when it came to offering the story to the tabloid press, he would be into an auction that would virtually allow him to write his own cheque.

He frowned suddenly. Yeah, but he had some hard thinking to do before that. If he actually went ahead to file copy without first alerting the authorities, not only would he be risking the lives of the innocent people Eddie Challow had already targeted, but he could also find himself on a criminal charge for withholding vital evidence, impeding a murder enquiry or maybe even conspiring to pervert the course of justice. If, however, he told the police before filing copy and Eddie Challow was promptly arrested, he could then end up breaking the law by reporting on a case where proceedings were likely to be considered active under *The Contempt of Court Act*. Catch bloody 22!

He scowled. So what the hell should he do? He couldn't simply chuck in the towel and hand everything over to some hairy-arsed CID wannabe after all the risks he had taken. But what other option did he have? And time was most definitely not on his side.

In fact, it was even more against him than he had appreciated. Suddenly conscious of the loud revving of an engine close behind him, he glanced in the interior rear-view mirror and came face to face with a crash-helmeted motorcyclist staring at him fixedly through the car's rear window as the rider recklessly tail-gated the Mercedes like some leather-clad demon from hell.

For a moment, Fuller seemed to freeze at the wheel, numbed by the awful realisation that Eddie Challow had found him again. But then, as the motorcyclist throttled up and drew alongside his door, slowly turning his black visored face towards him, the pressman's fear was transmitted into blind unreasoning panic and his foot instinctively went for the accelerator.

Within seconds he had launched the Mercedes at the approaching 'T' junction like a cruise missile, flashing past the Give Way sign and across the bold white dotted lines before he even knew they were there. A double-decker bus approaching the mouth of the side road at the head of a long line of impatiently twitching traffic braked heavily and swerved towards the kerb as he cut across its path. But he ignored the blaring horns and his own screeching tyres as he wrestled the car sharply to the right and cut into a convenient gap between a box van and a car transporter crawling up the steep hill towards Heaton.

Hardly conscious of the box van repeatedly flashing its lights behind him as he swung to his offside to see round the transporter, he glimpsed Eddie Challow just a few hundred yards behind him streaking along the offside of the traffic, headlight blazing in hot pursuit. How the motorcycle had managed to get out of the side road so quickly behind him, he just couldn't understand, but Challow obviously had no intention of abandoning the chase.

Fuller made his decision to overtake the transporter more out of desperation than anything else, accelerating hard for the steep incline. It was because of the lorry's bulk that he failed to see the advance warning signs as he crested the hill and when he had finally regained his own side of the road in the face of heavily braking oncoming traffic, he had already begun the steep descent towards Gilstone Crossroads. Under normal circumstances, with firm progressive braking, he would have had just enough time to pull up before reaching the traffic lights, which were showing red against him, but these weren't normal circumstances and when he went for the pedal, he found that there was nothing there. As the lights at the crossroads raced towards him and he futilely stamped on the pedal in a panic-stricken frenzy, it suddenly dawned on him why Eddie Challow had not tried to prevent him driving away. The evil little bastard had already doctored his brakes and his subsequent pursuit had been just a blind, designed solely to force up his victim's speed for the inevitable accident waiting at the crossroads.

*

The body didn't look like that of a human being, just a bundle of rags lying in the coned-off inside lane of the dual-carriageway, partially screened from vehicles passing the scene in the outer lane by a police Traffic Department accident unit. A big continental articulated lorry was parked a hundred yards or so beyond the body on the hard-shoulder and a man in a leather jacket, whom Dexter took to be the lorry driver, was sitting on the rear step of a nearby ambulance, his head in his hands.

'Seems the dead man either fell or jumped from the bridge just before dawn,' Dick Lawson explained, answering Dexter's unspoken question. 'Artic over there carried him for two to three-hundred yards on its bonnet before he fell under its wheels. Driver couldn't stop in time. Poor sod is Polish. Can't speak much English and took a while to find a phone to ring HQ Control.'

'So who is the dead man?'

Lawson nodded towards a police area car parked with the driver's door open behind the articulated lorry. A uniformed woman police sergeant was sitting on the edge of the seat with her feet on the road, talking into the radio handset.'Local nick say he's a vagrant who always passes through the area about this time of year, heading for the *Smoke*. Already known to the police and has form apparently. Name of Walter Leather.' He smiled thinly. 'They call him Shammy.'

'Surprise, surprise,' Dexter commented dryly. 'Positive ID then?'

Lawson shrugged. 'As positive as it can be. Quite a bit of him is still wedged underneath the lorry, but some of his face is still intact and they are sure it's him. We'll do a fingerprint job later, of course, but it'll do for now.'

Dexter shuddered. 'So what was he doing on the bridge?'

Another shrug. 'Out foraging, I suppose. It's possible he jumped. The bridge parapet is a bit high to fall over.'

'And why would he want to kill himself?'

Lawson pursed his lips reflectively. 'Who knows? Maybe he was overcome with remorse for killing Lionel Berwick.'

'So you're quite sure he was the culprit then?'

Lawson inclined his head towards the CID car parked up on the verge. 'Judge for yourself, to coin a phrase. Traffic found some interesting bits and pieces in one of his pockets that certainly point that way.'

Dexter followed him over to the car and waited while he bent inside to pick up something from the front passenger seat. It was an old cardboard box lid and it held four items: a gold pocket watch, complete with chain, a gold cigarette lighter, a strange-looking stubby key and a crumpled business card. Carefully, Lawson inserted a biro into the wide link connecting the chain to the watch and held it up in front of him. 'There's an inscription on the cover,' he explained, 'but as it's difficult to read, I'll read it for you. It says: "To Lionel Berwick, from all his colleagues, on his retirement". Lighter also carries an inscription: "To Lionel on his 60th. Love Lou". Lou was his wife apparently. As for the key –'

'It's for a pair of old-style hand-bolts,' Dexter cut in.

Lawson nodded grimly. 'Of the same type that were used to handcuff the Judge,' he said, 'and when we check, I think we'll find that there's a match. Pretty conclusive evidence, wouldn't you say?'

Dexter frowned. 'Bit unusual for a villain to hang on to identifiable property like this, isn't it? He was taking one hell of a risk.'

'Maybe he wanted some bits as keepsakes.'

Dexter grunted. 'Maybe. And the business card?'

Lawson returned the watch and lighter to the box. 'Ah, now that's where *you* may be able to help. Look at it a little bit closer.'

Dexter bent over the box and studied the card with a frown, then visibly started. 'Quentin Fuller?' he echoed.

'You know him then?'

'Of course I know him. He's a freelance journalist. Actually reported on the Eddie Challow case when he was a local hack up here and he was also the one who told me Challow had been released. But – but why on earth would a tramp have *his* business card in his pocket?'

Lawson studied him fixedly. 'That's exactly what I would like to know, Mike,' he replied. 'And I fully intend asking the gentleman that question just as soon as I can find him!'

Dexter made a wry face. 'And presumably you're not now going to follow up on the Eddie Challow angle?'

Lawson studied him sympathetically. 'I haven't really had a chance to speak to Mr Moffat about that yet, but there's not really much point in the light of all this, is there, old son?' he replied.

Dexter nodded. 'Maybe you should try telling Tania that,' he replied grimly.

Chapter 7

Beldon Hospital Mortuary was a small red brick building, standing on its own at the end of a narrow service road behind the old boiler rooms and laundry block. Mike Dexter compressed his lips into a thin line as he swung his Volvo sharp right inside the car park and pulled up between a police traffic motorcycle and patrol car already parked there.

For a few seconds he stayed in his seat, staring morosely at the mortuary doors and trying to delay the inevitable as long as possible. One corpse before lunch was bad enough, but now to be called to a second within just a couple of hours of the first was a bit beyond the pale, especially as this one was not some anonymous tramp, but a person he had actually known and shared a pint with.

Furthermore, he had always had a thing about mortuaries, ever since, as a young beat bobby, he'd spent much of his duty time in them. Luck of the draw, his wizened old skipper had told him with a lop-sided grin. Some got the crime arrests, some the road accidents (or RTAs), others ended up with the stiffs. He'd just drawn the short straw and got the stiffs. Bad luck, nothing more.

He had seen them all too in his first few traumatic years: from the old-age pensioner who had snuffed it in a favourite armchair after a heavy Sunday lunch, to the road or railway accident victim who had ended up under the wheels of an articulated lorry or the 6.45 express train from Paddington. There were a whole legion of them; grisly ghosts he could never forget. Drownings, gassings, burnings, shootings, stabbings; all marching through his dreams in endless procession, and on the day they had rolled out of the refrigerators for their post-mortems, each one exuding the same sickly sweet smell that had stayed with him for hours afterwards, constantly reminding him of his own mortality.

Small wonder that he hesitated at the mortuary doors now. But it was only momentary and, armed with a packet of extra-strong mints, he then shouldered his way through into the tiny foyer where a police traffic motorcyclist was leaning on the window-sill making up his pocket book. 'Can I help you, sir?' the officer queried, turning sharply to intercept him. For reply, Dexter flashed his warrant card and had the satisfaction of seeing the man tense, then immediately stand aside to indicate the door behind him with a brief nod. 'Sorry, sir. Sergeant Cater's waiting for you.'

Robin Cater was standing beside the slab, his hands thrust into the pockets of his uniform anorak, while a young constable bent over the corpse that was lying there, apparently trying to get a ring off the deceased's finger. At the far end of the cold tiled room the door to one of the three big refrigerators was half-open, revealing the soles of a pair of bare feet projecting from under a sheet on a long metal tray, and over by the window, an elderly man in a green apron and matching green gum-boots sluiced down the ancient Belfast sink with a short hose.

'Good of you to come, sir,' Cater said cheerfully after Dexter had introduced himself. Then noting his interest in the efforts of the young constable, he nodded towards a pile of clothing and other personal effects lying on an adjacent table. 'Trying to get his ring off before we seal up the property bag and stick him in the fridge,' he explained. 'Got to keep the Coroner's Officer happy, after all – when he manages to get here, that is.'

Dexter studied the policeman's lean weathered face sourly. 'I gather from your telephone call that you want me to identify the body?' he said curtly and without preamble.

Cater nodded. 'Only as an informal thing, governor,' he explained. 'So we can satisfy ourselves that he is who the documents he was carrying say he is. We'll have to do a more formal identification when we've managed to trace one of his relatives, of course.' He pursed his lips thoughtfully. 'Actually, it occurred to us that you might have some idea who we could contact in that respect.'

Dexter shook his head and reluctantly moved closer to the corpse. 'I only knew him professionally,' he replied. 'Kept his private life to himself. How did you get my name in the first place?'

Cater grinned. 'We found it in a little black book in his pocket. It sort of jumped out at us.'

Dexter grunted. 'I bet it did,' he said dryly and, forcing himself to look at the corpse, he shuddered. Quentin Fuller had never been the most attractive of men, but he was a whole lot less attractive now. His face and upper torso were heavily lacerated and there was a particularly hideous gash across his throat, which seemed to have all but

106

severed his head from his shoulders. A large piece of his frizzy ginger hair had been sliced away from the scalp and there was a deep rent in one side of his skull from which muscular tissue protruded like congealed whitish jelly. Most gruesome of all were the tiny fragments of what Dexter took to be glass embedded in the mutilated features and they sparkled in the sunlight streaming into the room through the open transom window like an obscene kind of party glitter. He shuddered again. He had not known Fuller all that well, but he still could not help feeling a sense of shock and sadness at the violent death of someone who, just hours before, had been so vibrant and alive. Poor old Quentin, he mused, what a pointless waste.

'He was not wearing a seat-belt,' Cater explained without being asked.

Dexter nodded. 'So I assumed,' he replied, slipping a couple of mints into his mouth before offering the packet to him. 'Well, your stiff is certainly Quentin Fuller, no doubt about that, but how did this happen?'

The other helped himself to an extra-strong. 'Still trying to find that out, sir. We've a few witnesses, but it's a bit early to be sure of anything yet. What we do know is that he went down the steep hill towards Gilstone Crossroads at around seventy mph, without making any attempt to slow down, and jumped a red light at the bottom, burying his car under an army lorry crossing the junction.' The policeman frowned. 'Any chance of suicide, do you think?'

Dexter shook his head firmly. 'No way. This guy was a cynical hard-bitten journalist who lived for the job. And anyway, when I saw him yesterday –' He broke off, for some reason reluctant to tell his colleague about Fuller's interest in Eddie Challow.

Cater studied him fixedly. 'When you saw him yesterday… what, sir?'

Dexter took back his packet of mints and shrugged. 'Full of life. No sign of anything untoward. Maybe there was something wrong with his car.'

The traffic man's eyes narrowed slightly. 'Hardly likely, is it, sir? Car was a brand new Mercedes. Excellent motors normally. Chance is he'd had a skinful, that would explain a lot.'

'What about a vehicle examination?'

Cater nodded. 'Standard practice as it's a fatal. Scheduled for tomorrow morning actually. Same as the PM, in fact. By lunchtime we might be a lot wiser.'

Dexter turned for the door, anxious to be out in the clean fresh air as quickly as possible. 'Call me with the result, won't you?' he said.

Cater sauntered over to the pile of personal property on the table. 'Certainly will, sir. By the way, there was one peculiar thing you may be able to help us with.'

Dexter paused in the doorway. 'Oh?'

The traffic man picked up a roll of 35mm film. 'He had this on him.'

'So? He was a freelance journalist; he took pictures.'

Cater's shrewd grey eyes locked on to his. 'Appreciate that, sir, but when the lads went through his car, they found not only a lot of unused films like this, but photographic equipment too; tripod, camera case, a couple of extra lenses, that sort of thing.'

'As you'd expect,' came the impatient, slightly puzzled retort.

'Exactly, sir, and yet there was no sign of any camera. Now where do you suppose that went, eh?'

'Maybe he lost it or it was stolen at the scene of the accident?'

Cater raised a finger in the air. 'Ah yes, that's probably it.' He gave a tight smile. 'Strange though, wouldn't you agree?'

Dexter didn't answer, but there was a perturbed frown on his face as he left the building and the sharp "*ping*" of the ring suddenly flying off Fuller's finger and hitting the floor seemed to chase after him into the fragile sunlight as if it were trying to tell him something.

*

Detective Superintendent Brian Moffat was in an unusually good mood when he dropped in at Police Headquarters towards the end of the afternoon to see the Assistant Chief Constable Operations. In fact, he could hardly conceal his smug sense of self-satisfaction as Parkes courteously left his desk to wave him towards one of the soft armchairs set before the little mahogany coffee table. 'Sorry to bother you, sir,' the CID man said as he settled into his designated chair, 'but before he went on leave, Detective Chief Superintendent Madden said that, in his absence, you had instructed I was to report directly to you over the Berwick case.'

Parkes nodded. 'Exactly right,' he confirmed. 'Lot of politics involved in this one, Brian,' He sat down opposite. 'Coffee?'

As if by magic, the ever efficient Miss Tensing appeared in the doorway. 'Two coffees please, Laura,' Parkes confirmed. 'You don't take sugar, do you, Brian? No, thought not. One with and one without then, Laura.' He leaned forward in his chair, hands resting on his thighs. 'Now, I gather from your brief phone call earlier that we've about wrapped up the Berwick case?'

Moffat waited for Laura Tensing to close the door quietly behind her before replying. 'Certainly looks that way, sir,' he said. 'Vagrant by the name of Walter Leather, otherwise known as Shammy.'

Parkes gave a faint smile, but said nothing, so Moffat continued. 'Got hit by an artic on the Grazely Bypass during the early hours of this morning. We think he might have jumped or fallen off Clifford's Bridge. Traffic – er – we found heavy deposits of mud and small stones on the bridge parapet which seem to match what he had on the soles of his boots. Body was a bit of a mess unfortunately, but still identifiable. Local uniform knew him well – he had form apparently – and they were able to give us a positive ID.'

'But you will still be following up on that ID with fingerprints?'

Moffat looked affronted. 'Naturally, sir. It's standard practice, as you well know.'

Parkes grunted, insensitive to his reaction. 'So where's the connection with Berwick?'

Moffat forgot his annoyance and allowed his concealed smirk to break free. 'Traffic – er – we found some bits on him which not only link him to the Judge, but to the murder as well. Pocket watch and gold lighter, each inscribed with Berwick's name, and an old-style handcuff key which we're pretty sure Forensic will be able to match to the handcuffs that were used to secure the old boy to the bed. The Lab will also be examining his clothes. The boots he was wearing reek of petrol even now.'

'He could have looted the house after the fire.'

The CID man shook his head. 'Not a chance, sir. The items were completely undamaged – pristine condition, in fact – and besides, we've had twenty-four hour security on the place ever since the crime, so he would have been spotted if he'd tried to get in there.'

Parkes frowned. 'But what about the police handcuffs? How on earth could someone like Leather get hold of them?'

Moffat shrugged. 'We don't know that they were police handcuffs, sir. Could be ex-military. Anyway, they're easy enough to obtain. Ex-army surplus stores are full of things like that. Plenty of sex shops sell them too.' He grinned. 'Maybe he was into some sort of wino bondage?'

The unsavoury joke seemed to fall on deaf ears. 'So why would our man want to murder a crown court judge?' Parkes went on, apparently still not a hundred percent convinced. 'And in such a ghastly manner too?'

Moffat's eyes gleamed. 'Exactly my sentiments, sir. So I had a name check run on him. Turns out he's got quite a record: theft, assault, burglary, even one case of robbery of a petrol filling station.' He licked his lips with evident relish. 'More importantly, he only came out of nick three months ago after doing a six year stretch for aggravated burglary.'

'And it was Berwick who put him away for it, I assume?'

Moffat scowled, plainly irritated by the fact that Parkes had stolen his thunder. 'Not only on that occasion either, sir,' he continued, trying to regain the initiative. 'Berwick also gave him six months for assault three years before that. So Leather had every reason to want to get even.'

'But setting fire to him? Bit of an unusual method, I would have thought. Any previous convictions for arson?'

'None on his record, sir, but maybe he was trying to make a point. You know, handcuffs on a judge, justice fettered, that sort of thing.'

Parkes considered the idea, lips pursed thoughtfully. 'It's certainly possible. So we're just waiting on the Lab now, are we?'

'More or less, sir, but personally I think there's little doubt that Leather's our man.'

Parkes nodded with evident satisfaction. 'Excellent,' he breathed. 'A detection in just two days? It is almost unprecedented in a case like this.'

'There *was* an element of luck in it,' Moffat commented, trying hard to appear humble and failing miserably.

Parkes shook his head sharply. 'Nonsense, man. Good police work, nothing less. You've certainly done yourself a bit of good with this one, Brian, I can tell you.'

Moffat's smirk returned with a vengeance as he thought of his recent application for the chief superintendent's post on the National Crime Squad. The successful resolution of such a high profile murder enquiry could not have come at a better time for him and he was already planning to milk it for all it was worth.

'We shall have to be careful how we play things now though,' Parkes went on. 'There's an opportunity here that must not be missed.'

Moffat looked puzzled. 'An opportunity, sir? I'm sorry, I don't follow you.'

For reply, Parkes quickly raised one hand in warning as a sharp knock on the door heralded the entry of Miss Tensing with their coffee. Only when she had withdrawn and tightly closed the door after her did he elaborate.

'As you will know,' he explained in a low voice, 'this Friday the Chief Constable will be personally launching the force's new "Working As One" joint agency crime reduction strategy, which seeks to target the causes rather than just the effects of crime.' He smiled wryly. 'Another of Mr Pullinger's many visionary initiatives, which is, of course, well in line with the Home Secretary's own thinking.'

'Unfortunately, only last month we released the worst quarterly crime detection figures for the past three years and with the press already saying our policies are soft on crime and hard on the community, our esteemed leader is likely to face stiff opposition to any crime strategy that appears to let the criminal off the hook.'

He leaned forward slightly. 'Now, since Lionel Berwick was a very well respected and connected figure – a personal friend not only of the Home Secretary and the Lord Chief Justice, in fact, but also our own Police Authority Chairman – it occurs to me that a nice speedy detection in this case would give Mr Pullinger something pretty impressive to take along to the launch with him and it might also have the effect of diverting attention from our poor detection record.'

Suddenly Moffat looked a lot less happy. 'We might find it a bit difficult trying to sew everything up by then, sir,' he ventured cautiously. 'Forensic will take more than a few days to come back to us and –'

Parkes cut him short with an impatient wave of one hand. 'I'm sure an SIO of your calibre will have no difficulty chasing them up,' he said cheerfully. 'Mention my name if you have to.'

'Yes, sir,' Moffat persisted hesitantly, wondering what difference Parkes' name would make to anything, 'but there are still quite a few official formalities that have to be dealt with before we can go public and an inquest has yet to be opened into the deaths of both Judge Berwick and the tramp. By rights, we should wait –'

'Minor issues, man,' Parkes dismissed airily. 'Minor issues.' He raised a questioning eyebrow. 'Not beginning to have doubts about Leather being our man now, are we, Brian? I mean, you *are* in charge of the investigation and if you think –'

'No, sir, of course not.'

'I can always tell the Chief Constable it's a no go. I'm sure he'd understand.'

Moffat swallowed hard. 'Absolutely not, sir,' he said hastily, forcing a sickly smile. 'As you say, there are only one or two minor issues to deal with. Shouldn't present too much of a problem if we get our skates on.'

Parkes almost beamed. 'Excellent. That's settled then. I knew I could rely on you, Brian. Now, why don't you drink your coffee before it gets cold?'

★

'Social visit, Dennis?' Chief Constable John Pullinger looked up curiously from the minutes of the last Police Authority meeting he had been studying and pushed his swivel chair back from the desk on its well-oiled casters.

A stocky balding individual in his early forties, his ready smile and engaging manner belied the reputation he had gained among his senior colleagues as a ruthless self-seeking opportunist. He was one of the new brand of chief officers, with an impressive academic background rather than distinguished service in the armed forces and an in-built contempt for the old militaristic style of policing. A radical in every sense of the word, he had adopted an almost evangelistic approach to his role, seeing more visions for the service than *Moses* had seen for the *Israelites* and replacing traditional hard-nosed policing tactics with a myriad of highly publicised community initiatives that did not necessarily reduce crime, but certainly helped to pave the way for his eventual selection to the Home Office Inspectorate.

As a policeman, Pullinger engendered very little respect among the rank and file of the force, who had more faith in a chief with genuine operational credibility (or *street cred*), than one who had walked the beat more as a career formality than anything else. But like many of his kind, Pullinger was not worried about his standing among the rank and file. He was only concerned with the image he presented to those outside the force, particularly those who might have some influence over his future career aspirations, and it was at times when he saw that image coming under threat that he was at his most dangerous.

Parkes knew this only too well and despite his chief's friendly welcome, he was nevertheless very much on his guard as he carefully closed the door behind him. 'Thought you might like to hear the good news, sir,' he replied. 'It looks like we've got the Berwick case in the bag.' He glanced out of the window and glimpsed Detective Superintendent Moffat walking with short quick steps across the front car park to his car. 'It's all down to our Mr Moffat now.'

Pullinger retrieved a half-smoked cigar from a glass ashtray on his desk and made a wry face. 'Well, there's a sobering thought,' he said, lighting up and ignoring Parkes' grimace as the smoke began to reach out towards him. 'I'll never know why my predecessor accepted that man from the Met in the first place, but,' and he shrugged, 'our loss, their gain, I suppose.'

Parkes leaned back against the window sill, drawing comfort from the cold damp afternoon air seeping into the room through the open fanlight. 'Seems we're stuck with him now anyway, sir,' he replied, then added innocently: 'Unless, of course, you'll be recommending him for the chief superintendent's post on the National Crime Squad.'

Pullinger gave him an old-fashioned look. 'Only if I had an axe to grind with the NCS,' he replied wryly. 'I'll see what Heather Rolland thinks of him when she joins us next week as our new Personnel Director. Be an interesting one for her to cut her teeth on.' He sat back in his chair, his eyes watchful. 'Now, you were telling me about the Berwick case. In the bag, I think you said.'

Parkes nodded. 'Exactly that, sir,' he replied. 'You'll see from this morning's incident report that we had a nasty fatal during the early hours. Apparently a local vagrant was hit by an articulated lorry on the Grazely Bypass near Clifford's Bridge and the interesting thing is that everything we have points to him being responsible for the Alden House job.'

Pullinger tensed. 'You're sure about that?'

'Absolutely. He had enough incriminating evidence on him – including identifiable property from the premises and a handcuff key we should be able to tie into the hand-bolts on Berwick's wrists – even for Moffat to see a connection. Furthermore, our man evidently had not long been released from prison and he was put there in the first place by none other than Lionel Berwick.'

Pullinger's eyes gleamed. 'So we're finally off the hook where Eddie Challow is concerned then?'

'It would appear so, yes. Forensic are doing the business now and after some minor investigative formalities, we should be in a position to announce "case closed" very soon.'

'In time for the "Working As One" launch on Friday?'

'That's the general idea, yes.'

'Excellent. But you'll be watching points, of course?'

'You can count on it, sir.'

Pullinger sighed. 'I do hope so, Dennis. The last thing I need at present is to rub the Director of Social Services up the wrong way. It was difficult enough getting her to sign up to our new joint agency approach and it wouldn't take much for her to change her mind.' He studied Parkes fixedly. 'That wouldn't do with my presentation less than forty-eight hours away, Dennis, wouldn't do at all.'

Parkes received the thinly disguised warning loud and clear. 'No fear of that, sir,' he said quickly. 'As I've already intimated, I will be personally monitoring the situation.'

Pullinger nodded several times. 'I would have expected nothing less of you, Dennis,' he replied smoothly. 'Anything else?'

Parkes hesitated. 'There is one other issue you should be aware of.' 'Which is?'

'Chief Inspector Dexter has found out about the release of Eddie Challow and he's pretty miffed about his wife not being told.'

Pullinger's eyes narrowed appreciably. 'How did that happen? I thought I made it perfectly clear when we last discussed this issue that Challow's release was not to be disclosed to anyone?'

'Very clear indeed, sir, but apparently Dexter had this press contact – a man by the name of Quentin Fuller.'

'Press?' The agitation was very evident in Pullinger's tone now. 'Are you saying the press have this information? Gordon Bennett, man, do you realise how sensitive this thing is? Challow is just one of a number of detained patients being unobtrusively released into the community under the government's new "Community Care Programme". If this were to become public knowledge, the world and his wife will be baying for the Home Secretary's blood – especially after the problems we had with the last release programme.'

He ran a finger round the inside of his collar, which seemed to have suddenly become too tight. 'And neither he nor the heads of the other agencies who have signed up to the process will thank me if this force is seen to be the one that let the cat out of the bag.'

Parkes quickly shook his head. 'That isn't a problem, sir,' he said hastily. 'I've since learned that Fuller was killed in an accident at Gilstone Crossroads this morning and apparently he had an exclusive on this thing, so he won't have filed copy.'

Pullinger visibly relaxed. 'Thank heavens,' he breathed involuntarily, then quickly added: 'Well, it's very tragic, of course, but one of those things that happens, I'm afraid, and we can certainly do without the press finding out about Eddie Challow's release and speculating on a link between that and Lionel Berwick's death.'

He stubbed out his cigar in an ornate glass ashtray. 'So, is Dexter aware of the reasons for his wife not being told? As you well know, that particular decision wasn't ours to make. It was down to the Responsible Medical Officer himself – although for operational reasons and in the spirit of our new level of cooperation, I did agree to support that decision.'

Parkes nodded. You agreed to support it all right, he thought cynically, but only to safeguard your own marvellous new initiative and to ingratiate yourself with the Home Secretary in time for the next round of appointments to the HM Inspectorate.

'Indeed, sir,' he said aloud. 'And Chief Inspector Dexter *is* aware of that fact.'

'Do you still anticipate a problem then?'

'Not with him, sir. Loyalty's a pretty big thing where our PRO is concerned and anyway, he's far too ambitious to want to rock the boat. His wife might be a different matter though.'

He hesitated. It was on the tip of his tongue to mention the anniversary card the Dexters had received, but then he thought better of it. No sense winding the boss up and making a rod for his own back. 'With her psychiatric history,' he said carefully, 'she's a bit of an unknown quantity and apparently she's convinced that Eddie Challow was responsible for Lionel Berwick's death and that she is next on his hit list.'

Pullinger frowned heavily. 'So let's get this damned case closed and archived before she has any excuse to start making waves,' he said with renewed irritation. 'Then maybe we'll *both* be able to sleep at night!'

*

Kitty Morrison was sitting in a high-backed swivel chair, with her shoes off and her bare feet on the desk, when Mike Dexter paid a visit to the small office she had been allocated at Bellingham Police

115

Station. She had the telephone receiver cradled in the hollow between her neck and one raised shoulder and was wriggling the chair from side to side as she chatted to someone on the other end of the line, apparently oblivious to the fact that the black leather belt she optimistically called a skirt had ridden halfway up her thighs to expose a lot more than was normally acceptable at a police station.

She jerked her head round quickly when she heard the door creak open and managed a quick: 'Catch you later,' into the receiver before swinging her long legs off the desk and scrabbling round for her shoes.

'Don't mind me?' Dexter said sarcastically, slumping into a moth-eaten easy chair in the corner. 'You just make sure you're comfortable.'

She stood up with a barely concealed grin, thrusting her feet into her shoes and smoothing her skirt down with both hands. 'Sorry, Mike,' she replied. 'I was on my break and it's kinda quiet at the moment.'

He treated her to a wry smile. 'Must be if you've got time to chat to old flames on the telephone.'

Another brief self-conscious grin and she stared at the floor for a second. 'He's no old flame, Michael,' she retorted, eyeing him coquettishly. 'He's my new man and I've got a hot date with him tonight. Cooking him a very special meal at my place.'

Dexter grunted. 'Well, I only hope he treats you a lot better than the last couple did. I can do without my press assistants coming to work with black eyes and covered in bruises.'

She shook her head firmly. 'Uh-uh, not this guy. He's a gentleman – bit like you really – and he knows how to treat a lady.'

'Bit like me, meaning he's nearly old enough to be your father?' Dexter shook his head slowly. 'You certainly pick 'em, Kitty, don't you? The last two were in their forties. Where'd you find this one – the local drop-in centre?'

She pouted. 'Actually, I met him at the gym I go to. We kinda got involved.'

'So he's Mr Universe, is he?'

She grinned again. 'Close, Mike, close. He's certainly got some physique. Takes care of himself, you know. I like that in a man.'

'So there's still some hope for me then?' Dick Lawson poked his head round the door with a broad grin on his face, appraising Kitty quite openly.

Dexter turned his head slightly to stare up at him. 'I was coming to see you in a minute,' he commented.

Lawson nodded, suddenly serious. 'Thought you might be. Shall we adjourn to my office?'

Lawson's office turned out to be a small nine-foot square cubby-hole at the end of the corridor, bearing the sign "Local Intelligence Officer" on the door. Apart from a rickety desk with a single empty filing tray, a couple of green framed canvas chairs and a few exposed cables protruding from the wall, which had no doubt once been connected to a computer, the place was bare, and the musty odour of years of accumulated dust immediately assailed Dexter's nostrils as Lawson threw open the door and ushered him inside.

'Nice,' Dexter said dryly, staring round him and wrinkling his nose in disgust. 'You mean you actually work in here?'

Lawson gave a short laugh and nodded towards the telephone on the desk. 'Not more than I can help,' he replied. 'Just a reporting point really when I'm not out and about. The governor has the old inspector's office and we've put the incident room in what used to be the club room and bar on the top floor.'

He grabbed a khaki haversack from the back of one chair and produced a thermos flask. 'Coffee?' he queried. 'No milk, I'm afraid, but it has an interesting taste.'

Dexter sat down on one of the chairs and sipped his drink from the small plastic cup, tasting the whisky immediately. 'So,' he said suddenly, 'what gives?'

Lawson sat down on a corner of the desk, ignoring its despairing groan, and took a sip from his own cup. 'Not a lot at present,' he replied. 'Governor's gone to see ACC Ops to brief him about the dead vagrant and we're all waiting for him to come back with the result.'

'Then what?'

Lawson shrugged. 'Who knows? We have to wait on Forensic and the PM, of course, and there's still some fingerprinting and local enquiries to be done. Personally, I would also like us to put out a public appeal for sightings of our man in the vicinity of Alden House, just to give us a bit more meat on the bone, but that will be up to Mr Moffat.'

Dexter smiled grimly. 'You don't believe Shammy Leather did the Judge anymore than me, do you?' he said. 'The whole thing is just too pat, too bloody convenient.'

Another shrug. 'Doesn't matter what I think, Mike. All the

evidence we've got so far points to him being the culprit and that's really all that counts, you know that as much as I do.'

'I take it you haven't spoken to Moffat about Eddie Challow since our last conversation then?'

Lawson chuckled. 'Oh I tried, believe me, I tried, but he went completely bananas and wouldn't listen to anything I had to say, probably because I mentioned your name; you seem to be having that sort of effect on him at present. So, I rang a contact of mine at the Criminal Record Bureau and asked him to check Challow's record for me.' He shook his head slowly. 'Usually he's pretty good and comes up with anything I want, but this time he nearly had an aneurysm and refused point blank to pass on any specific detail, apart from confirming that Challow was out. Apparently our little psycho was released on to some kind of very hush-hush experimental rehab programme, which is so politically sensitive at the moment that we can't even fart in his vicinity without approval from the top.'

'Yeah, I gathered much the same thing when I received my last lecture from ACC Ops. It all smacks of something rather nasty.'

Lawson pursed his lips reflectively. 'Oh I don't think it's quite that. Bit of naughty self-interest at the top maybe, but nothing more. If we had some definite evidence to link Challow to the Alden House job, there'd be no question but that we'd have to interview him. Now Walter Leather's firmly in the frame, however, that issue is unlikely to arise.'

'But I bet there were some loud sighs of relief at the *Big House* when certain people heard the news.'

'Highly likely, I should think. But I'm not closing any doors on the investigation just yet.'

'I bet Moffat is though.'

Lawson sighed. 'Mr Moffat has his way of working, Mike, and I have mine.'

Dexter snorted. 'Maybe, but as he's running the investigation, in the final analysis his ways will be your ways.'

'Not entirely. I still have at least one enquiry of my own to follow up.'

Dexter nodded. 'That being the journalist, Quentin Fuller, I suppose,' he replied grimly. 'Well, you've had that one. He was killed in an RTA at Gilstone Crossroads this morning.'

Lawson started. 'Killed?' he exclaimed and closed his eyes briefly in resignation. 'Poor devil. How did it happen?'

Dexter shrugged. 'Damned fool was going too fast down the hill by the sound of it. Overtook an artic, jumped a red light and rammed an army lorry broadside on.'

Lawson frowned. 'But why was he going so fast? Surely he must have seen the signs? They're pretty distinctive on that stretch of road.'

'Who knows? Maybe he had one too many? That was Traffic's theory anyway.'

Lawson sighed. 'Well, whatever, it's all pretty academic now anyway and we'll certainly never know why a vagrant like Shammy Leather was walking around with one of Fuller's business cards in his grubby pocket.'

'So that's it then, is it? Berwick case closed, just like Moffat wants?'

For the first time, there were signs of defeat in Lawson's eyes. 'It's beginning to look that way, unless you've got any other bright ideas?'

Dexter grunted. 'Bright ideas seem to be fresh out of fashion these days,' he said bitterly. 'They cause too many ripples.'

Chapter 8

Tania slipped the last of the computer print-outs into an envelope and tossed it into the post tray for the next morning. Then, stretching experimentally in the high swivel chair, she pushed her reading glasses up on to her forehead. Closing her eyes tightly for a moment, she pinched the bridge of her nose between one finger and thumb before relaxing with a weary sigh.

The laboratory on the other side of the glass partition enclosing her small office was almost empty. Most of the technicians had already gone home and only a couple still worked on under the harsh glare of the strip lights, testing the racks of blood samples Tania had removed from the refrigerator for analysis that morning. It had been a long day, but then every day in the Red Cell Serology Unit at Heaton General Hospital was the same, and her job as Assistant Technical Officer always left her tired and irritable when she went home in the evenings.

She had decided to go back to work in the end, not just because of the row she had had with Mike that morning, though she knew that was what he believed. In fact, she had intended going back all along, seeing it as a sort of therapy; a means of putting Eddie Challow out of her mind by giving herself other problems to think about. It seemed to have worked too and it was only now, as she contemplated walking down to the large staff car park at the back of the building and driving home, that her fears began to return.

'Time you left,' a voice drawled at her elbow and she started involuntarily, swinging round to face the short balding technician who had entered the office behind her, his white lab coat over one arm.

She relaxed again and forced a smile. 'I shall be in a minute, Ray,' she replied. 'Just got to collect some samples from Maternity and put them in the fridge for tomorrow.'

The lab man nodded, his blue eyes smiling through his gold-rimmed spectacles. 'Mind you do,' he said with mock severity. 'Don't want you spending the night here.'

'Perish the thought,' she muttered, as he headed for the locker-room, whistling tunelessly.

The lab lights went out as she was leaving the office and Donald Grey, the other late bird, was close behind her when she went through the doorway into the main corridor. 'Safe journey, Tania,' he called and she heard him clatter off down the stairs to her right as she turned left.

Heaton Hospital was a massive three block complex, linked by a series of tunnels and galleries. It comprised a bewildering maze of corridors, hallways and staircases, giving access to four levels of wards, outpatient clinics, operating theatres, laboratories, waiting areas, consulting rooms and all the other essential services common to any major hospital. Getting lost was not that difficult and Tania remembered only too well her very first day in the building all those years ago when it had taken her nearly half an hour to find her way back from the Blood Bank. Even now, there were parts of the place she had never ever been to, but curiosity was never her thing and she made sure she stuck to familiar well-trodden routes when collecting samples for analysis from the different departments she visited on a daily basis.

She did that now as she headed for the Maternity wing in the next building, pushing through rubber doors, along narrow passages and down short stone staircases with a confidence that would have amazed any uninitiated observer. At first she encountered large numbers of people heading in the opposite direction – other lab technicians, administration staff and nurses – eagerly making their way home after the trials and tribulations of the day. But within a very short time she was almost on her own, passing only the occasional white-coated figure as she cut through the non-public areas of the hospital, her soft-soled shoes squeaking on the vinyl floor.

Then, jerking open a single door at the top of a short stone staircase, she found herself in the Outpatients Clinic and there was no one about at all. The lifts stood silent and the reception desk was closed, with the shutters firmly in place. All but two security lights had been switched off and the rows of plastic chairs in the huge waiting area looked strangely sinister as they marched away from her into the gloom.

She hated this part of the hospital after dark. The deep secret shadows; the baleful orange security lights that created grotesque threatening shapes out of the most ordinary things; the strange noises

121

as windows rattled and doors stirred in sudden draughts; the whole sense of abandon, of being cut off from the rest of the world.

She shivered and, quickening her step, pushed through the first door on the left. She found herself in a short passageway which opened out into another, but much smaller, waiting area. Someone had turned the main lights off here as well, but the glow from a single security light in the Maternity Unit's reception office filtered through the sliding window above the counter and provided a little ghostly illumination of its own. As usual, the office door was closed, but not locked and a dozen or so plastic bags containing the test tubes she had come for were piled in a small heap in a lidless box beside the refrigerator. It seemed that Maternity had had a particularly busy day.

She bent down to pick up the box, then froze, turning her head quickly to stare over her shoulder. The sound had been quite pronounced, like a chair being scraped across the floor, and it seemed to have come from the direction of the Outpatients Clinic. She listened intently for several seconds, but the sound was not repeated. Probably one of the security officers tidying up on his way through, she thought. Shrugging, she finally picked up the box of samples and headed for the door, anxious to get back to the more populated areas of the hospital as soon as possible.

The Outpatients Clinic appeared to be as deserted as before and she studied the waiting area for a moment to make sure. But there were just rows of empty chairs. She realised she had been holding her breath for several seconds and now released it with a relieved sigh, moving off towards the lifts and the staircase.

The soft cough stopped her in her tracks, and she whirled round to stare across at the waiting area. At first nothing, then suddenly a lumpy mass rising from among the chairs; a figure that stood there watching her. 'Who are you?' she gasped, feeling foolish, yet frightened.

No response. The figure remained motionless. She blinked furiously, trying to focus properly in the poor light. The headlights of what sounded like a large van blazed through the far windows of the clinic, briefly illuminating the place from end to end as it trundled noisily past on the hospital's perimeter road. Her stare once more met only empty chairs. The figure had vanished – if it had ever been there at all. She shook her head slowly and took a deep breath. Her imagination was certainly running riot tonight.

She made for the stairs at a much brisker step than usual, keeping close to the right hand wall for reassurance and resisting the temptation to actually break into a run. Once she thought she heard stealthy movement in the shadows just ahead – a soft footfall and the rustle of clothing, followed by what sounded like the swish of the rubber doors on the other side of the lift area – but she saw no one and assumed it was simply her imagination playing tricks on her again.

The *"ding"* of the lift had nothing at all to do with her imagination, however, and in the act of reaching for the handle of the door to the stairs, she turned sharply again, her gaze riveted on the orange indicator button on the far wall. A second later the large double doors slid back, spilling ghostly light across the floor. She waited, but no one stepped into view and, craning her neck to study the lift's interior, she saw that it was completely empty.

There was a soft chuckle from somewhere close at hand and she swallowed hard, darting a frightened glance into the shadows pressing in on her from all sides. Someone was playing a nasty little game with her, she realised that now, but after the events of the last two days and the suspicions now chilling her mind, she had no desire to find out who that might be.

Wrenching the door open, she made for the stairs in a panic-stricken rush, almost dropping her box of samples in the process. As she reached the lower floor, she heard the bang of the door at the top of the stairs she had just left and the sound of footsteps coming down after her; not in the eager hurried way she would have expected, but with a confident measured tread that was all the more unnerving.

Pulling open another door in front of her, she took off at a run along the narrow passageway that lay beyond, hoping to lose her pursuer in the basement labyrinth she had now learned to negotiate so well. Ducking through doorways, along more narrow passages and across a number of small square hallways, she finally reached the foot of a further flight of stone stairs. Hauling herself up breathlessly to the next landing, she paused for a few moments to peer down into the gloomy depths, listening intently. There wasn't a sound and she leaned back against the wall for a second or two, her eyes closed and her heart still pounding as if it were trying to tear itself free. Her tactic had succeeded; she had lost him, thank God.

Minutes later, she was back in the brightly lit central corridor of the main hospital building, still shaking slightly, but gradually recovering her composure now that she was in a busier part of the complex again. There were not as many people about as before, but enough to give her the reassurance she needed; a female cleaner, bent over her trolley a short distance away, a couple of young nurses smiling in her direction as they marched past, talking and laughing, and a white-coated doctor, with his stethoscope dangling from his neck like a badge of office, emerging from a doorway directly opposite and following briskly in their wake. Normality at last.

The light had been left on in the short passageway leading to her office, so she didn't bother to switch on the main lights in the lab, but opened the refrigerator door and deposited the box of samples inside. They would do there until the morning.

She heard the faint sound as she straightened up and a cold shiver ran down her spine. Hardly daring to look, yet unable to stop herself, she turned to stare into the shadowy depths of the lab. There was a familiar soft chuckle and she glimpsed the fiery red spot of a cigarette butt.

'Who the hell *are* you?' she whispered. 'What do you want?'

'You mean you don't know, Tania?' a hard voice mocked. 'You really don't know?'

She forced back the acid in her throat and clenched her fists fiercely by her sides. 'Get out or I'll call Security.'

There was a soft tutting sound. 'Now, that's not very friendly, is it? And anyway, I can always find you again.'

She backed towards the passageway and the exit door, ready to run if he came after her, but before he had any opportunity to do so, the door behind her was suddenly thrown open and, as she spun round with an involuntary gasp, a heavy uniformed figure strode through, then stopped short in astonishment. 'Sorry, miss. Didn't know you was still working in 'ere.'

For a second Tania simply stared at the big security man in a daze, her mouth working silently. He strode over to her and peered into her face. 'You okay, miss?'

'In there,' she gasped, waving an arm in the direction of the lab and falling back against the wall. 'A man.'

She heard another door slam as he went for the light switch and when the fluorescent tubes fizzed and sparked into life, she wasn't surprised to see that the place was completely empty.

'No one 'ere, miss,' the security man announced after a brief tour.

She nodded weakly. 'Must have left by the other door,' she whispered, waving again towards the opposite end of the lab.

While he went off to check, she walked slowly across the room to the corner where she had seen the glowing cigarette butt. A swivel chair had been pulled away from the workbench and turned towards the centre of the room. The smell of the cigarette was still noticeable and a thin wisp of smoke curled from the abandoned butt almost hidden under the circular metal foot-rest of the chair. She bent down to pick up the butt and instinctively stubbed it out on the workbench.

'Nothing there, miss,' the security man growled as he marched back into the lab. 'You sure someone was in 'ere?'

She held up the cigarette butt. 'Proof enough for you?'

He took it from her and frowned. 'It ain't even smoking.'

'That's because I just put it out,' she said tightly.

He studied her dubiously. 'Now why would you want to do that, miss?'

She shook her head wearily. She didn't even know that herself, but it was too late now anyway. 'It's still warm. Feel it for yourself.'

He seemed not to have heard her. 'Funny places these labs, y'know. Play tricks on you in the dark. Many's the time I've thought –'

She glared at him. 'There *was* a man in here, Mr…?'

'Tom, miss.' He patted her arm like a Dutch uncle. 'I'm sure there was, miss. Good job I was on me rounds then, weren't it? I'll report it, of course, an' keep an eye out for anyone suspicious rest of the night, if it makes you feel any better. Er – couldn't describe this feller, I suppose?'

'It was dark,' she replied patiently. 'But he did speak to me.'

Tom raised his eyebrows. 'Did he now? What did he say?'

She studied his rough kindly face for a moment, then shook her head. She could see he didn't believe her, could practically read the word *neurotic* stamped indelibly in his expression. He probably knew all about her history already; most of the other staff she worked with seemed to know about it anyway. Good old Tom had no doubt discussed it with the other security officers. 'That one in the RCS lab has been in the nuthouse, you know. Long time ago, but they never fully recover, do they? Sandwich short of a picnic, if you ask me.' She shook her head and gave a tight smile. 'It doesn't matter, Tom. Could you just see me to my car?'

The security man brightened. 'Certainly, miss. No problem at all.'

Tom's escort, however, proved to be more embarrassing than helpful. He walked very close to her through the corridors, dwarfing

125

her slim figure, and attracting strange looks from passing staff who probably thought she was being taken into custody. In the end she politely explained that she could 'manage now' and left him to continue on his rounds.

The car park was almost empty of cars, its black tarmac surface, now wet from recent rain, reflecting the cold yellow glare of the tall security lights. She studied every inch of it before venturing out of the hospital entrance, then crossed the service road and covered the couple of hundred yards between the entrance and her car with short quick steps that could quite easily have turned into another run.

She fumbled for her keys in her handbag and swore when she couldn't find them. 'Silly bitch,' she breathed, knowing full well that she should have got them out before leaving the hospital, not left it until now. She had another search and this time succeeded in spilling half the contents of the bag on the ground. Her heart was thudding heavily again as she bent down to pick the bits up. Lipstick, diary, mascara, tissue, yes, but it looked like her compact had rolled beneath the car. She stretched under the vehicle, hanging on to the door handle with her other hand, but though her trailing fingers touched something solid, she couldn't quite grab hold of it. In the end, tears welling in her eyes, she had to get down on her hands and knees to reach for it – and it was then that she saw the shoes. Someone was standing on the other side of the vehicle...

*

Kitty Morrison was furious. Her new boyfriend, Alan, was late. He had promised faithfully that he would be on her doorstep by eight-thirty and it was now twenty minutes past nine. As a result, the *boeuf bourguignonne* she had prepared for him was already burning in the oven, the lettuce leaves of the seafood starter were beginning to curl up at the edges and the crushed ice in the fancy wine cooler was starting to melt, partially lifting the label on the bottle of Chardonnay she had selected to accompany the starter. The only thing that looked like surviving was the Australian red and it had been standing on the hearth so long that she had had to remove it to the kitchen before the bottle cracked open with the heat of the open fire.

Staring at the clock on the mantelpiece, she swore several times with frustration. It seemed that all the effort she had made to create the right sort of atmosphere for a romantic evening had been for nothing and to think she had actually put her job at risk by closing the temporary press office at Bellingham Police Station half an hour earlier than scheduled, just to give herself enough time to drive home and get everything ready.

Maybe Mike Dexter was right about her choice of men after all, she thought bitterly, but then she couldn't help herself. Her sexual appetite had been insatiable from her early teens and older guys with the right sort of physique had always attracted her. It had something to do with their experience and staying power. The younger set were usually just looking for a quick jump and it was all over for them even before her first orgasm, but the more mature men liked to prolong things as much as possible and they were often less inhibited in the way they made love. In short, sex for her came down to the difference between going for a starter or a four-course banquet and tonight, with her special dinner well on the way to being ruined, she thought that maybe Alan Salter couldn't manage either. Yeah, maybe the ungrateful arsehole was not worth seducing after all.

In fact, she had almost given up on him completely and was seriously thinking about turning off the oven and taking both bottles of wine to bed with her instead, when she heard the sound of an approaching motorcycle.

Seconds later he was with her in the tiny living-room, removing his black crash helmet and handing her a large box of chocolates with a disarming smile. 'Sorry I'm late, Kitty,' he said and sniffed appreciatively. 'Something smells good. Better watch it doesn't burn.'

'You bastard,' she choked, throwing the chocolates at him. 'You said eight-thirty and it's now –'

'I know, I know, nearly half-past nine,' he acknowledged, dropping the chocolates on to a chair before unzipping his leather jacket, 'and I said I was sorry, but I couldn't get the damned bike to start.'

He studied the long black dress she was wearing and raised his eyebrows as he noted the shapely thigh protruding through the provocative slit up the side. 'You look better to eat than your dinner smells,' he observed. 'Perhaps we should simply skip the meal, eh?'

'Like hell,' she snapped back, trying hard to remain angry, but delighted with his compliment nevertheless. 'Not after all the trouble I've gone to – *and* you might like to know that I also risked getting fired by shutting up shop at Bellingham nick half an hour early.'

'Naughty girl,' he murmured, shaking his head in mock reproof. 'And how *is* the old murder enquiry going, eh? Any arrests imminent?'

She glared at him. 'Can we just forget about bloody police work for one night?' she snapped. 'You've been going on about it since we first met and I've already told you a lot more than I should.'

'Can you blame me, my love?' he said, moving closer and trapping her against the edge of the table. 'Ordinary people like me find it so fascinating. That's why there's such a lot of it on TV.'

She felt her heart beginning to pound with excitement as she read the blatant message in his eyes. 'I – I know,' she faltered, 'but – but it's almost as though you're more interested in it than in me.'

He slipped one hand through the split in her skirt and she felt it travel slowly up her bare thigh. 'Now how could anything be more interesting than you?' he breathed. 'Especially dressed the way you are.'

She drew in her breath sharply at his hard caress. 'The dinner,' she gasped, half-heartedly trying to pull away from him. 'It will be ruined.'

His other hand gently unzipped the back of her dress. 'Do you know?' Eddie Challow said with a predatory smile, 'Suddenly I don't feel at all hungry.'

*

The young Sergeant looked embarrassed and he threw Mike Dexter a brief helpless glance before turning back to Tania.

'It's not that I don't believe you, Mrs. Dexter,' he explained, 'but look at it from my point of view. You've given me absolutely nothing to go on. You say you were followed through the hospital and that a man threatened you in the laboratory –'

'No, Sergeant,' she cut in, shaking her head several times. 'That's the whole point. It wasn't just a man; it was Eddie Challow.'

The policeman sighed heavily. 'But it was dark, Mrs Dexter, and you say you didn't see his face.'

She stared at him incredulously. 'But he spoke to me, for crying out loud. Don't you think I'd know Eddie Challow's voice when I heard it?'

The Sergeant nodded and tried to choose his words carefully. 'But according to what you say, Mrs Dexter, he was put away twenty years ago, and you haven't seen or spoken to him since.'

Tania glanced quickly at her husband's tense face and swallowed hard. 'Sergeant Kitts,' she said, clenching her fists tightly in her lap, 'I was stalked by Eddie Challow through the hospital. He then reappeared in the lab and taunted me.'

'Yet the security guard ,' Kitts consulted his notebook, 'Tom Johnson, saw no one at all.'

She took a deep breath. 'Of course he didn't. Challow left by the other door the moment he heard him coming in.'

'Must have moved pretty quickly, Mrs Dexter – *and* known his way around the hospital well enough – to get to your car before you.'

Anger flared in her eyes, but she controlled herself. 'Naturally he knew the hospital well, Sergeant,' she replied tersely. 'His mother used to work there and he's probably been following me about the place ever since he got out.'

Kitts thought for a second. 'And you say he must have taken your car keys from your handbag while it was left in the lab?'

'How else would they have ended up back in the ignition? And it wasn't me that found them either.'

The policeman nodded. 'No, I gather they were found by another security guard when he came to your assistance.'

She grimaced. 'You mean when I screamed the place down? I did get rather hysterical, didn't I? And I'm sorry if I upset the resident patients, but I – I just flipped.'

'Hardly surprising,' her husband commented reassuringly, 'and at least it sent Challow packing.'

Kitts nodded again, but was careful not to commit himself one way or the other. 'But why would Challow want to go to all the trouble of stealing your keys and then leave them in the car?' he queried.

Tania took a sip of her coffee, which was now almost cold. 'Because it's all part of his nasty little game of revenge, that's why,' she said bitterly. 'He's letting me know he can get to me at any time anywhere and when he tires of the game, that's when he'll come for me.'

Kitt's expression was even more dubious, but he hesitated before coming out with the question Tania had been waiting for all along. 'Are you sure you didn't just leave the car keys in the ignition yourself?' he asked. 'We all do that from time to time.'

She glared at him and he reddened appreciably. 'Well I *don't*, Sergeant,' she snapped, then stood up quickly, rubbing her hands up and down both arms in a gesture of irritation. 'You think I've made all this up, don't you?'

Mike Dexter stepped quickly to her side and put his arm round her shoulders. 'It's not that at all, love,' he soothed. 'Peter is only doing his job. We haven't any evidence for him, that's the trouble, and he can't arrest someone without evidence.'

129

She pulled away from him. 'So, what about the anniversary card he sent us, Sergeant?' she snapped. 'You didn't say a lot about that when I mentioned it earlier.'

'It's not a crime to send someone a card, Mrs Dexter,' the policeman replied quietly. 'It could be that he was technically in breach of the conditions of his release, but that's all, and even if we could prove he actually sent it, which we can't, he could always say he did it as a goodwill gesture.'

Shaking her head in disgust, she went over to the kitchen window and stared out into the darkness. 'So we just wait until he actually murders me, is that it?' she said in a low weary voice. 'Then you'll have all the evidence you need, won't you?'

Her husband threw Kitts a warning glance and the latter stood up and put his pocket book away. 'I'll keep in touch, Mrs Dexter,' he promised. 'Meantime, if you need to speak to me again, just ring Elvington Police Station.' Then to Dexter himself: 'I'll see myself out, sir.'

As the front door closed behind him, Tania burst into tears.

Chapter 9

Mike Dexter was late for work for the second day running and he was in a particularly grouchy mood when he got to Police Headquarters. Tania's ordeal at the hospital the previous afternoon had affected her badly and as a result, he had spent another sleepless night desperately trying to comfort and reassure her; checking and double-checking that all doors and windows were securely locked and investigating every little sound she heard, from the creak of the roof timbers contracting to the cry of a vixen in the woods behind the house. Not surprisingly, he felt like a wrung-out dishcloth when he finally stomped into the Headquarters Press Office and headed for his own inner sanctum at the far end, only vaguely aware that Carol Layton, his other press liaison assistant, was back from her two week holiday in Cyprus and smiling at him from her desk in the corner.

John Durrell was attending to the kettle when he arrived and the balding ex-policeman followed him through into his office with a steaming mug of coffee, a concerned look on his craggy face. 'You look like a dog's breakfast, governor,' he commented.

'Thanks,' Dexter retorted sourly. 'So would you if you'd been up all night.'

Durrell raised one eyebrow and set the mug on the corner of his desk. 'Tania?' he said, hazarding a guess.

Dexter nodded. 'She was harassed by a stalker at the hospital yesterday afternoon. Upset her a lot.'

Durrell's jaw hardened. 'The bastard. Do we know who he was?'

Dexter tossed his car keys on to his desk and contemplated the mountain of paper waiting for him. 'We've a pretty good idea, but it's a long story, so I won't bore you with the details. Suffice to say, he put the wind up her to such an extent that she couldn't sleep last night and was in no fit state to return to work this morning.'

Durrell suddenly looked very concerned. 'You mean she's been left on her own today?' he exclaimed.

Dexter's eyes narrowed at the censure in his tone. 'No, she hasn't, as it happens,' he retorted defensively, resenting the question. 'I dropped her off at her aunt's place in Chilbury on my way here and if a day with Aunt Mildred doesn't cure her of a craving for company, nothing will.'

He glanced back into the main office. 'I see Carol's back, but where's Sarah?'

Durrell hesitated. Ever the diplomat, he didn't like dropping other people in the mire. 'She – she had to go out.'

Dexter frowned. 'Out? Out where?'

Durrell sighed. 'To Bellingham nick, to look after the press.'

'What on earth for? Kitty's there.'

Durrell made a face. 'She didn't turn in this morning, governor. Moffat's doing his crust again.'

Dexter raised his eyes to the grubby office ceiling, focusing for a moment on the remains of one of the previous year's Christmas decorations someone had neglected to pull down. 'I might have known it,' he breathed. 'Hot date, new hangover. I take it you've phoned her home?'

Durrell nodded, turning back into the main office to answer the buzz of the mini switchboard on his desk. 'Mobile as well as home number, gov,' he replied, lifting the telephone and pausing for a second with one finger poised to flick down the switch beneath the flashing yellow light. 'Sarah went round there on her way to the incident room too, but couldn't get any response, even though Kitty's sports car was still parked outside.'

As Durrell answered the incoming call, Dexter slumped into his swivel chair and idly flicked through the topmost papers on his desk. Damn Kitty, he mused. This was about the third time her craving for men and booze had put him on the spot in just as many months and he was fed up covering for her. She was probably still under the sheets with some bloody muscle head, sleeping it off.

'Morning, Mike.' Carol Layton cut in on his thoughts as she popped her head round the door, a telephone message form in one hand. 'Took a call for you just before you came in. Some traffic sergeant.' She consulted the message. 'Oh yes, Sergeant Cater. Says he's got some news for you, whatever that means.'

Dexter took the message from her, but made no effort to satisfy her obvious curiosity. 'Good holiday?' he queried, studying the diminutive little brunette's healthy colour with envy.

She flashed her studded navel and a large expanse of midriff. 'All over tan,' she replied with a cheeky grin.

'I'll take your word for it,' he returned dryly and reached for the telephone as she returned to her desk.

He was still thinking about the stud in her navel, and wondering how on earth she managed to soap over it in the shower, when a curt voice answered him on the end of the telephone. 'Traffic.'

'Sergeant Cater please?' he said, not exactly impressed by the manner of response.

'Not here.'

Dexter's mouth tightened. 'Chief Inspector Dexter, Press Office,' he snapped. 'He wanted to speak to me, if that's not too much trouble for you.'

There was a change in tone immediately. 'Er – sorry, sir, he's out on enquiries at the moment; the fatal yesterday. Likely to be away some time.'

Dexter grunted. 'Just tell him I called,' he said. 'And try answering the telephone properly next time!' Then he slammed the receiver down with such force that he bounced a tin of pins off his desk on to the floor.

For the next few minutes he tried to concentrate on the paperwork in front of him. But after approving a couple of press releases and trying unsuccessfully to draft a carefully worded response to an MP's enquiry for the Chief Constable's signature, he gave up. Kitty's absence was bugging him and he was more than a little curious about the call from Sergeant Cater. In the end, downing the remains of his cold coffee, he grabbed his mobile telephone and headed for the door. 'Out for a couple of hours, John,' he said. 'Can you manage?'

Durrell was on the telephone, apparently dealing with a press call, and he covered the mouthpiece for a second. 'Tell Kitty Panadol might be the best remedy,' he grinned, guessing where his boss was going.

'Or a boot up the arse,' Dexter growled, throwing the office door wide.

*

Kitty Morrison lived on the south side of Bellingham, in a rented cottage close to the lower end of the Mid-Shires Canal. The place looked deserted when Dexter pulled up behind the yellow sports car parked in the lane outside and he frowned as he crunched his way up the gravel drive to the porch. Things certainly didn't look promising.

Seizing the wrought iron knocker, he hammered several times on the front door and waited for a response. There was none. He hammered again, twice shouting Kitty's name at the top of his voice before stepping back out of the porch to study the windows. They were tightly closed and the curtains were drawn right back.

A glider from the nearby aerodrome sang its way across the grey sky as the small aircraft that had towed it into the air banked steeply to return to base, its tow-wire trailing behind it, but it was the only sound that disturbed the heavy stillness and nothing moved inside the house.

Strangely uneasy, though he couldn't think why on Kitty's past form, he followed the gravel drive down the side of the house and crossed the lawn to the canal towpath. The water was black and motionless, not even a single ripple stirring its surface. He turned round to face the rear of the house and studied the upstairs windows in the same way as he had those at the front. Both were tightly closed, but this time the curtains were drawn across the one at the far end, suggesting the room was occupied. His jaw hardened and he would have investigated further, but at this point his mobile shrilled and he stopped short, fumbling for the telephone in his pocket. 'Dexter,' he snapped.

'Sergeant Cater, governor,' came back immediately. 'It seems like we keep missing each other. Press Office gave me your number.'

Dexter nodded unnecessarily. 'Yes, I gather you've got some news for me about the fatal. I suppose Quentin was pissed, was he?'

Cater cleared his throat noisily. Dexter guessed he was smoking while talking. 'Couldn't say, governor. PM's been put back to this afternoon; they've got rather a lot of meat down there today, I hear. Anyway, I doubt whether we could tell exactly what state he was in without a proper analysis of his blood. No, actually I rang about something else.'

'Which is?'

Cater seemed to hesitate. 'I'd rather not go into details over your mobile, sir, if you don't mind. Bit insecure, I think you'll agree. Thought perhaps you might like to drop by Slade's Garage at Bellingham instead. I'll be here for another half hour, if that's okay with you.'

Dexter glanced at his watch. 'Give me ten minutes,' he replied and he had switched off the telephone and was already striding back along the gravel path towards his car before Cater had a chance to respond.

Delia Sullivan got off the bus from the centre of Bellingham just before midday and walked the few yards from the bus stop to the mouth of Canal Close with the brisk step of someone who had a job to do. She made a face as she turned into the close, negotiating the deep ruts and potholes as if they concealed anti-personnel mines and studying with some envy the quaint cottages on both sides. As a single parent, with a boy of just under five, Delia always had difficulty hiding her bitterness when she saw how the other half lived. She knew she would never be able to afford even renting one of the cottages herself, let alone buying one. Still, at least cleaning up the mess of those that could enabled her to keep her head above water and that was the main thing. The job had its compensations too. She'd made a lot of friends in the twelve months she had been doing it and Kitty Morrison was one of her favourite clients.

An ordinary girl with a real zest for life, Kitty filled Delia with admiration. Okay, so she was promiscuous, but so what? At least she didn't try to pretend she was something she was not and as well as always paying on time, she often gave Delia a little bit extra for her young son. Every time she did it, she made it seem like the most natural thing in the world. No patronising comment or high and mighty attitude, just a broad grin and a fiver or a tenner stuck in the top pocket of Delia's blouse. A real diamond, that was Kitty Morrison, and Delia would have done anything for her.

Small wonder that when she turned into the driveway of Kitty's rented cottage and saw her yellow sports car parked outside, that she smiled with anticipation. Kitty was obviously at home this morning, which meant that they would have a nice little chat and a cup of tea or coffee as she cleaned round.

She called Kitty's name (they had long dispensed with formalities) as she turned her key in the front door, but was not unduly surprised by the lack of response when she smelled the stale odour of spicy cooking wafting through from the kitchen and saw the half-empty brandy bottle on the sideboard. She recognised the signs only too well; Kitty had scored again.

'I know what *you've* been up to, madam—' she called as she walked through to the kitchen, then abruptly broke off, surprised to find everything so neat and tidy, with no left-overs on the work surface, no unwashed dishes piled in the sink and no characteristic grease stains on the cooker hob. Kitty *always* left the place in a mess after one of

135

her do's, so this was pretty unusual; maybe things hadn't gone quite according to plan.

She grinned as she climbed the steep wood-panelled staircase. 'You up there, Kitty?' she queried, visualising her lying flat out on the double bed, with her head buried in the pillow as she tried to escape the light. 'Maybe you'd like some coffee, eh?'

But Kitty was beyond coffee and carefully pushing open her bedroom door and peering inside, it took Delia a few moments to grasp what she was seeing.

Kitty was there all right, lying naked and face-downwards on the bed, one arm trapped beneath her and the other trailing the floor inches from a broken glass tumbler. Her beautiful ebony skin had long since lost its glossy lustre and, when Delia forced herself to approach the bed, open-mouthed and trembling, to take the slightly stiff wrist in one hand, she found no sign of a pulse. Kitty Morrison had evidently been dead for several hours.

*

Slade's Garage was a boon to the police Traffic Department. In the first place, it had a secure two-acre yard where badly damaged vehicles could be taken by Dan Slade's fleet of tow-trucks, which relieved traffic bases and operational police stations of what had become an onerous storage responsibility. But more importantly as far as the bobbies themselves were concerned, *The Slade*, as they called it, had a unique asset that was revered throughout the entire force area, drawing patrol officers to the shabby ramshackle premises from miles around. That asset was an unremarkable looking sixty-two year old woman with a foul tongue and peroxide dyed blonde hair, called Lena Joyce, for Lena made the best hotdogs in the business and in the eyes of tired street weary police officers, that single fact elevated her to sainthood.

Robin Cater had his crooked teeth into one of her large greasy creations when Mike Dexter stepped into the tiny café. Gulping down a sizeable chunk, he returned the roll to the plate on the counter and pivoted round on the barstool to face him. 'Morning, governor,' he grinned, wiping the leaking juices off his fingers with a paper napkin. 'Can I treat you to one?'

Dexter made a grimace. 'No thanks, Robin,' he returned, 'I've too much respect for my guts. You said you had something to tell me.'

Cater sighed and, with a last regretful look at his roll, he quit the barstool and waved Dexter towards the door. 'Show you more like, governor,' he corrected.

Dexter followed him out of the café and across a concrete hardstanding to the big corrugated iron shed that housed the garage workshops. 'Alf Settle, the civvy Vehicle Examiner, did his examination of your man Fuller's car first thing this morning,' Cater explained over his shoulder, 'and he got a bit of a shock, I can tell you.'

The double doors of the workshops were half-open and when Dexter followed Cater inside, he saw the big silver coloured Mercedes up on one of the ramps at eye level. Even from the side, he could see that the front of the car was very badly crushed, with the engine block forced up through the bonnet and the offside wheel bent under the chassis at an unnatural angle.

Dexter grunted. 'I'm not surprised,' he agreed. 'Like me, he probably thought Mercs were supposed to be safety cars.'

Cater ducked under the ramp with a loud snort. 'Nothing short of a tank could have withstood the sort of impact this motor suffered,' he commented. 'But come and look at something – and mind yourself.'

Carefully lowering his head, Dexter joined him under the remains of the front axle. An inspection lamp had been attached to the ramp, its powerful beam directed upwards. 'See?' Cater said, pointing with one gnarled finger.

Dexter squinted, but couldn't see anything of any significance. 'See what?' he queried a little testily.

Cater chuckled. 'Obviously not a car man, are we, sir? Look at the brake pipe.'

Dexter tried to peer closer, but gave up and Cater tapped him on the shoulder. 'Let's get out from under it and I'll explain,' he said.

Away from the car, the traffic man took a half-smoked cigarette from behind his ear and lit up. 'It seems that our fatal accident may not have been an accident after all,' he went on grimly. 'Alf found a nice cut in the offside brake pipe.'

Dexter started. 'What are you saying? That someone did it deliberately?'

Cater nodded. 'Alf thinks so anyway, but we'll have to get an expert opinion from the lab before we can be sure. I've already arranged for local CID and Scenes of Crime to attend and I'm expecting them here any minute. Thought you might like a preview before they all arrived.'

'But surely the damage could have been caused by the impact itself? I mean, look at the state of the car.'

Cater drew slowly on his cigarette and shook his head. 'Unlikely. Surprisingly, the linkage is still intact and Alf is adamant that it is a cut as opposed to a split or a rent caused by the collision. He reckons the fluid had probably been squirting out all the way down the hill and by the time Fuller got to the crossroads, there would have been no pressure on the brakes at all.'

Dexter pursed his lips thoughtfully. 'If what you're saying is true, he couldn't have come far then, otherwise he would have noticed the problem well before his descent towards Gilstone Crossroads.'

'True, but that still leaves a lot of country within spitting distance of Gilstone to check.'

'But why would anyone want to cut the brake pipe on his car? It doesn't make sense.'

'Maybe he obstructed a farm entrance or something.'

'Oh come on!'

'Or it could just have been some sort of warped prank.'

'A *prank*?'

Cater nodded. 'Takes all types, you know that as well as I do. And according to the local nick, there's been quite a bit of vandalism to cars in the area over the last few months. Bored kids from Gilstone apparently, mainly from the gypo site in Honey Lane. They get out to the surrounding villages on their bikes and cause all sorts of problems.'

Dexter shook his head firmly. 'Sorry, that doesn't hold water and you know it. Scratch the bodywork, break off a mirror or a windscreen wiper – maybe even slit a tyre – but to get down under a car and cut one of the brake pipes? No way, I can't see kids doing that. They're more likely to try nicking the car altogether.'

Cater sighed. 'You're probably right. Trouble is, we don't have anything else to go on at present.' He studied Dexter for a moment, then added pointedly: 'You got any ideas of your own, sir?'

Once again, Dexter made no effort to enlighten him about Eddie Challow and he was spared further questions by the blast of the garage tannoy, which put paid to any further conversation. 'Sergeant Cater, could you please go to the office. Someone to see you.'

Cater grunted. 'Probably Scenes of Crime or CID,' he said. 'Maybe they'll have some bright ideas, eh?'

After he had gone, Dexter wandered over to the Mercedes again and ducked under the ramp. He could just make out the brake pipe now in the glare of the inspection lamp, but he still couldn't see the cut Cater had spoken about, so for the second time he gave up looking. Leave it to the experts, he decided, coming out from under the ramp and wandering round to the front of the car. The Mercedes was an even bigger mess when viewed head on than from the side and he shook his head sadly as he slowly completed the circuit. Poor old Quentin, he mused. The car had been his pride and joy. Maybe in a peculiar way it was best he couldn't see it.

'Excuse me, mate.' The voice at Dexter's elbow made him jump and he turned quickly to study the long-haired youngster standing right behind him. The lad was wearing the dirty green overalls and heavy black boots of the car mechanic and Dexter noted with a humourless smile that there seemed to be more oil stains on his face than anywhere else. Maybe that's how he earned his credibility, he thought uncharitably.

'Yes, what is it?' he retorted a little sharper than he had intended.

The mechanic hesitated. 'You're a copper, ain't you?'

'I'm a policeman, yes.'

The lad nodded and delving into a pocket, produced a cartridge of exposed 35 mm film. 'When we was bringing the car in, I found this stuck under one of the seats. Thought I should hand it in.'

'Why didn't you give it to Sergeant Cater?' Dexter snapped, taking the film from him.

The lad grinned. 'I got form, mate,' he replied. 'He don't like me. Nicked me for drink driving a few years back, so I keep out of his way. Can you give it to him. Say Jamie Reeves found it.'

'That's your name, is it?'

Another grin. 'No, it's me mate's name, but we brought the motor in together on the tow-truck so it don't matter.'

Dexter was still trying to work that one out when the lad strode off across the workshop and out through a side door. He was on the point of going after him, when the mobile phone in his pocket shrilled excitedly. It was John Durrell and his voice was grave. 'Better brace yourself, governor,' he said. 'I've got some pretty awful news.'

Dexter's heart lurched violently. 'Tania –?' he began.

Durrell cut him off. 'Nothing to do with Tania, sir,' he replied, quick to allay his fears. 'It's Kitty.'

'Kitty?' Dexter queried with a deep frown. 'What the hell has she done now?'

Durrell hesitated. 'Seems her cleaning lady found her dead in bed this morning, gov,' he said quietly. 'Suspected overdose by all accounts.'

★

'Hey, what you doin', Len?' Jimmy Scott stared across at his twelve-year old friend and grinned broadly. Lenny Walsh had never been fishing before and it showed. He had made at least half a dozen attempts at casting his line across the placid water before managing to drop his float somewhere near the middle of the canal. Now, only twenty minutes later, he had succeeded in tangling the whole lot up as he tried to reel it in. What a plonker, he mused.

Carefully laying his own fishing rod on the bank of the canal, Jimmy climbed to his feet and sauntered over to his friend, shaking his head with the weary resignation of a sixty year old.

'Got caught up, that's all,' Lenny snapped, his face beetroot red as he remembered all the earlier boasts he had made about his angling expertise. 'Soon clear it.'

Jimmy chortled. 'Yeah, you'll clear it, all right,' he agreed, watching him as he knelt on the wet grass and yanked on the trapped line. 'You'll more likely snap it first. You really are a prize wally.'

Lenny glared at him venomously and, throwing his rod to one side, jumped to his feet. 'Okay, big head,' he snarled. 'Then *you* do it!'

Jimmy grinned again. 'Easy when you know how,' he replied. 'You just need the right touch.'

Getting down on to both knees, he rolled up one sleeve of his heavy sweater, then turned his face away from Lenny so that his friend wouldn't see him wince as he slid his arm into the ice-cold water.

'Well?' Lenny sneered, as Jimmy ran his fingers down the line into a mass of slimy roots thrusting their way out of the bank from a nearby tree stump. 'I thought you said you had the right touch?'

Jimmy gritted his teeth against the cold, conscious of the fact that his arm was already going numb. 'Give me a chance, will you?' he threw back over his shoulder, tugging desperately at the thin strand of nylon and beginning to wish he had not been so ready to show off.

'Water cold, is it?' Lenny chortled, bending over him to study his face. 'Not so clever as you thought, are you?'

Jimmy made one last big effort, pushing the line outwards,

140

away from the bank, instead of trying to wiggle it free. But the next second the worst possible thing happened. It snapped completely.

'You dipstick!' Lenny howled, grabbing the severed line. 'Now I'll have to buy a new hook and float.'

But suddenly Jimmy wasn't listening. 'It isn't just the roots of the tree,' he exclaimed, forcing his hand back into the water. 'There's something else down here that it kept catching on, something heavy.'

Lenny's howls abruptly ceased. 'Maybe it's a body,' he breathed, his eyes now lit up with excitement. 'Or it could be a safe from a robbery.'

Jimmy snorted. 'Don't be so stupid,' he panted. 'You've been watching too many cop stories on TV. Anyway, it isn't *that* heavy –'

He failed to finish the sentence, for the next moment the object broke loose from whatever was holding it and he was able to pull it right out of the water and drop it on to the bank. For a moment the two boys simply stared at his find in open-mouthed astonishment.

'It's – it's a camera,' Lenny gasped, stating the obvious.

'Yeah, and an expensive one by the look off it,' Jimmy returned, picking it up curiously.

'But what's something like that doing in the canal?'

Jimmy shrugged. 'Dunno. Less some bloke dropped it off a boat by accident. Looks as though the lens bit has been bashed by something.'

'Maybe it was dumped there by burglars after a raid? Or – or by a secret agent after –'

'Now you're being stupid again.'

Lenny's freckled face reddened for the second time at the put down. 'So what do we do with it then?' he muttered. 'Join a friggin'-camera club?'

Jimmy stood up and began wiping the mud off the camera with his handkerchief. 'Not likely. We should be able to get quite a bit for something like this.' He stared at his friend thoughtfully. 'There's that second-hand shop in Bellingham. It will only take us half an hour to get there along the towpath. We can clean it up on the way.'

'And what if someone sees us? We've already bunked off school.'

Jimmy snorted. 'Don't be such a wimp, Len. Who's to see us at Bellingham when the school's at Gilstone?'

'You forget, the camera's not ours to sell.'

Jimmy grinned even more broadly. 'It is now,' he declared. 'Finders keepers, I say.'

But as it turned out, he was wrong about that, for they had only gone about twenty yards when a dark thickset figure stepped out from among the trees to bar their way.

Chapter 10

A woman police constable was standing at the front door of Kitty Morrison's canal-side cottage when Mike Dexter arrived and she insisted on seeing his warrant card and radioing to someone inside before allowing him access.

Upstairs, the curtains had been drawn back in the tiny bedroom overlooking the canal and a weak ray of sunlight filtered through the cracked window pane, lightly brushing the exposed thigh of the naked woman who was lying crosswise on the bed, partially covered by a sheet.

A portly grey-haired man in a rumpled grey suit straightened up from the bed as Dexter entered the room, throwing a brief inquisitive glance in his direction before turning to a uniformed sergeant standing just behind him. 'So that's it then,' he declared, lifting a bulging briefcase from the floor and resting it on a nearby chair to snap it shut with an air of finality. 'Straightforward overdose. Benzodiazepines and malt whisky never make an ideal combination, I'm afraid.'

'Straightforward overdose?' Dexter queried a little sharper than he had intended. 'What makes you say that?'

The man in the grey suit stared at him again, frowning irritably. 'Because I happen to be a doctor, that's why, Mr… whoever you are.'

The Sergeant gave a discreet cough. 'This is Chief Inspector Dexter, Dr Watson,' he cut in hastily, obviously the recipient of the radio call made by the policewoman on duty at the front door. 'Mr Dexter is head of the department where the deceased lady was working.'

The Doctor grunted, apparently unimpressed. 'Is he indeed? Well, Chief Inspector, as my literary namesake might have concluded, it wouldn't take the skill of *Sherlock Holmes* to deduce cause of death in this particular circumstance and my examination of the unfortunate young lady rather confirms the obvious.'

'Nothing is ever obvious where a sudden death is concerned, Doctor,' Dexter said dryly. 'There's always the possibility of something else.'

Watson's mouth tightened. 'As a police surgeon, I hardly need reminding of that fact, Chief Inspector,' he snapped. 'And in this case, I am satisfied that there *is* nothing else.'

He held up a small plastic bottle. 'She had this clutched in one hand and a bottle of Glenfiddich beside her on the bed – both empty, I would add.'

Dexter took the plastic bottle from him and peered closely at the label. 'Temazepam?' he queried.

Watson nodded curtly. 'Tranquillizers,' he said. 'They were no doubt prescribed to her by her own doctor, since Miss Morrison's name is on the label, and it looks as though she has taken the whole bottleful. If you want to kill yourself, this is probably the nicest way to do it.'

Dexter handed the bottle back. 'And why should she want to do that, Doctor? She told me she had a hot date last night and she was a lot happier than I'd seen her for a long time.'

'Maybe her date didn't turn up?' the Sergeant suggested helpfully.

'And she killed herself just because of that?' Dexter shook his head slowly. 'Doesn't make sense.' He hesitated. 'You probably don't know it, skipper, but Kitty had a pretty lousy taste in men. She suffered more than a few bruises as a result and even ended up in hospital once.'

The Sergeant raised his eyebrows slightly. 'Well, there's no sign of anything untoward on this occasion, sir. No marks on the body or anything like that.'

'But no suicide note either, eh?'

'Not so far as we can find, sir, no. But that doesn't mean she didn't – well – top herself.'

Dexter studied Kitty's lifeless body for a moment, as if mesmerised.

'Tragic, sir,' the Sergeant went on, following the direction of his gaze. 'And such a young woman too.'

'Unbelievable,' Dexter replied grimly. 'Any idea as to time of death?'

'Around three, maybe four o'clock in the morning,' Dr. Watson cut in tersely. 'PM should establish things a little more precisely, I think.'

Dexter shuddered at the thought of the razor-sharp scalpel slicing through that beautiful ebony skin.

'Obviously I can't issue the usual death certificate under the circumstances,' Watson went on, 'but naturally there'll be an inquest.'

'Difficult case for the coroner though, don't you think?' Dexter put in. 'No note or any positive evidence of suicide.'

Watson shrugged. 'Probably go down as misadventure or something,' he replied. 'Not really my problem.'

Dexter studied him coldly. 'No,' he agreed. 'Just another stiff to you, I suppose.'

Watson glared at him. 'What did you say your name was?'

'*I* didn't, but as the Sergeant has already said, it's Dexter, Chief Inspector Mike Dexter.'

Watson nodded. 'Thank you, Mr Dexter,' he replied, stalking from the room. 'I shall remember that.'

'He will too, gov,' another voice commented from the doorway as Watson's footsteps clattered away down the wooden staircase. 'He's a personal friend of ACC Ops.'

Dexter turned quickly to find a very tall thin blonde in a black leather coat and slacks standing in the doorway, both hands raised above her head to grip the lintel and vivid green eyes studying him fixedly.

'Hello, Mary,' he said with a faint smile, recognising one of his former Crime Squad protégés. 'It *is* a long time no see. What on earth brings you here?'

Detective Sergeant Mary Lane, nicknamed *Bean* (or beanpole) due to her height and pencil-like figure, let go of the lintel and ducked through the low doorway. 'Nothing sinister, gov,' she said with a grin. 'I've been looking into that fatal over at Gilstone Crossroads, that's all. Control needed a local CID officer to check this job out and I was the only one in the area at the time.'

Dexter nodded, glancing at the bed again. 'And?'

She shrugged. 'I've had a good look round, but I can't see anything here for us. No marks on the body, no sign of a forced entry; in fact, no suggestion of anyone else being here when she died.'

Dexter frowned. 'I just don't get it. When I spoke to Kitty yesterday afternoon, she led me to believe that her new boyfriend was coming over to her place for a special home cooked meal after she'd finished work.'

'Well, if he was, there's no evidence of it. Kitchen's spotless; not so much as a dirty glass anywhere.'

'Which is pretty surprising in itself. Kitty was not the tidiest of people.'

She gave a short humourless laugh. 'You can say that again. Rest of the place is like a tip. I don't know how she ever found anything.'

'Exactly my point.'

She snorted. 'Oh come on, gov, I can't go around shouting "foul" just because a girl dies and leaves a clean kitchen. I'd be laughed out of the department.'

'Straightforward suicide in your book then?'

'Or accident maybe. Have to wait and see what the Coroner says at the inquest.'

'And meanwhile?'

'Few local enquiries, speak to her GP, that sort of thing. What else is there?'

'You could try and trace her boyfriend. I believe she met him at the local gym.'

'Okay, so I'll do that too. Anything else?'

Dexter smiled faintly, realising only too well that he was treading on professional corns. 'I'll let you know if there is.'

She nodded coldly. '*Thank you*, sir. Now if you've got a moment, I'd like to have a word about something else.'

'Be my guest.'

She threw a quick glance in the direction of the uniformed Sergeant hovering in the background and grimaced. 'Can we talk outside?'

Guessing what was on her mind, he followed her downstairs and across the small garden to the canal, where she turned to face him, her eyes sharply focused.

'So, what gives with Quentin Fuller, Mike?' she demanded, dropping the formality of rank now that they were on their own.

'I don't follow you.'

'Oh yes you do. You're holding back on something; it's bloody obvious.'

'Who says?'

'Sergeant Cater, and he's a pretty shrewd cookie.'

He nodded. 'Yeah, I'd formed the same impression of him myself. Went on about a missing camera, if I remember, though what that has to do with anything, I fail to see.'

She took a deep breath. 'Can we forget about the camera for a moment? What was Fuller doing in this neck of the woods?'

'How the hell should I know?'

She swore. 'Oh please, Mike, it's me you're talking to. The man was following up on something and he had your name and the Press Office telephone number written in his notebook.'

Dexter shrugged. 'As a journalist, I would expect him to have the names and telephone numbers of every police PRO in the country listed somewhere. Nothing significant in that.'

'I'm not talking about his address book, but a plain notebook he was carrying – a new one by the look of it – in which he had scrawled your name and the name of a certain pub not a million miles from here called The Trout.'

'So we had a drink together. Nothing wrong with that, is there?'

'And he told you what?'

Dexter sighed wearily, not really sure why he had been giving her the run around in the first place or why he had adopted the same tactic with Sergeant Cater earlier. Maybe it was a hang-up from all his years on CID and the natural reluctance of the professional detective to part with information. On the other hand, perhaps it was simply because he was tired of covering the same ground again and again, knowing full well that if he couldn't influence events at the top of the tree, he was hardly likely to be able to achieve much of a result at sergeant level.

'Okay, okay,' he said finally, 'he was chasing a story about a local psycho being released from the nuthouse.'

Her eyes narrowed. 'What local psycho?'

'Eddie Challow.'

'What *the* Eddie Challow? The one who –'

'The same,' he cut in quickly to save her the embarrassment of going into further detail. 'You still remember the name then?'

Her expression softened. 'How could I ever forget?' Her eyes studied his face a little too intently, as if searching for something. 'You certainly bent my ear enough about the case when we were on the Squad.'

He nodded slowly, thinking of the long hot nights they had spent together in the Crime Squad surveillance car, watching a "target" criminal who did nothing more extraordinary than play poker, empty bottles of whisky and bonk half a dozen different women in a variety of different positions. It had been just after Tania's second period of regression when he had desperately needed someone to talk to. *Bean* had been the perfect listener – too perfect, in fact, for the pair of them had been drawn a lot closer together than was healthy for two colleagues in the same department. Only Mary's selfless restraint and his own devotion to Tania had ended the carnal attraction before it

147

had started, but the guilt over what might have happened was still with him – even more so now he was close to her again and could feel the same old urges surfacing that he thought had been buried years ago.

The sudden unexpected intensity of his feelings – the accelerating heart beat, the dryness in his throat and the uncomfortable hardness in his loins – confused and frightened him and he turned away quickly to study the murky water of the canal.

'So Challow's out again, is he?' she went on, her voice strangely husky.

He moved away from her and, bending to pick up a pebble from the towpath, sent it skating across the canal. 'Several weeks ago apparently. Fuller thought he might have been the one who torched Judge Lionel Berwick's place at Bellingham.'

She cleared her throat. 'I thought some dead tramp was in the frame for that job?'

'So it would appear.'

'But you think otherwise?'

He laughed harshly and faced her again. 'Doesn't matter what I think, Mary. Minds have been made up. Convenient result, you see. We get a nice detection in our crime book and the Chief avoids upsetting social services at a time when he needs them to support his "Working As One" initiative.'

She emitted a low whistle. 'That's a pretty cynical statement, even for you.'

He laughed again. 'Fact of life, Mary, fact of life. Police work is all to do with politics now, especially at the top. It has sod all to do with fighting crime.' He raised one hand before she could interject. 'Do you know, I often think about the young coppers walking the streets at night, shaking door handles. Poor devils bust a gut to get a good arrest and naïvely think that someone at the top appreciates what they've done. But in reality, the powers that be know nothing about it and if they did, they wouldn't give a toss anyway; they're too busy playing their own stupid one-upmanship games.'

She made a wry grimace. 'You have got it bad today, haven't you, Mike? What's brought all this on? Tania going through another bad patch, is she?'

He grunted. 'Can you wonder at it with Eddie Challow on the loose again?'

'But she must have realised he was bound to be released sooner or later?'

He scowled. 'Yeah, but it would have been nice if someone could have warned her about it in advance. First she knew was when Quentin Fuller contacted me with the glad tidings.'

'Not the best way to find out, I agree, but it's unlikely that Challow will have any interest in Tania after all these years anyway.'

'Is it? In that case, why did he send us both a wedding anniversary card and then start stalking her at the hospital where she works?'

Mary's eyes widened. 'He did *what?*' she breathed, then stared at him with sudden excitement. 'But – but that means he can be pulled in again. There are bound to be conditions attached to his release, like keeping away from his former victim; there always are. Breaching them means he goes back to the funny farm.'

He nodded grimly. 'Yeah, but first you've got to prove he breached them and it's Tania's word against his. He didn't even sign the damned card, just made sure we'd know where it came from.'

'But why would he risk going back inside by harassing her in such an obvious way? If he meant her real harm, he's had plenty of opportunity to do it.'

The anxiety in Dexter's eyes was plain to see. 'Who knows what makes a psycho tick, Mary? Maybe this sort of cat and mouse game appeals to his twisted mind and Tania is convinced that when he tires of the game, he will come after her, in the same way as he did Lionel Berwick.'

'Except that we now know Lionel Berwick's killer was someone else.'

Dexter shook his head vehemently. 'We know nothing of the sort.'

'Mike, be reasonable,' she said patiently. 'Identifiable property from the torched house, together with the key to the handcuffs used on the Judge, were actually found in the dead tramp's pockets and his shoes were saturated in petrol. What more evidence do you want?'

He treated her to a keen stare. 'And how do *you* know all this?'

'Word soon gets round, especially with such a high profile case as the murder of a crown court judge. From my perspective, it seems a pretty conclusive result too, so what's the point in starting another hare running?'

Dexter shook his head again. 'You don't understand. It's not that at all. The whole thing is just too pat – and there's something else too.'

'I thought perhaps there might be.'

He studied her fixedly again. 'When I was called to the murder scene, I disturbed someone hiding in the woods; a guy in leathers and

149

a crash hat.' He touched the plaster still attached to his forehead. 'He made off on a trials motorcycle after clobbering me with a piece of wood.'

'And you think it was Eddie Challow.'

'I'm convinced it was.'

'Then you saw his face?'

He shook his head. 'I've already said he had a lid on, full visor, the lot.'

'So how could you possibly know it was Eddie Challow?'

'Believe me, I know.'

She sighed heavily. 'Mike, you just *want* it to be Eddie Challow. It could have been anyone.'

'It was him all right and the more I think about it, the more certain I am.'

She pursed her lips, nodding slowly. 'Okay, so if Challow was the culprit, how come the tramp had so much incriminating evidence in his pockets?'

'Maybe it was planted on him as a way of throwing the intrepid *Super Plod* off the scent.'

'Now you *are* in the realms of fantasy.'

'Perhaps I am, but I just can't buy the tramp as the killer.'

'Can't or won't?'

'Okay, so I won't and Quentin Fuller wouldn't have done either if he'd still been alive.'

She visibly tensed. 'You reckon Fuller was on to something then?'

'If he was, he didn't tell me about it, but yes, I think he may have had a lead of some sort.'

'He didn't mention a guy called Alan Salter, did he?'

'Not to me, why?'

'Or *Water Gypsy*?'

Dexter raised his eyebrows. 'Sounds like the name of a boat.'

'Exactly my thoughts.'

'So what have Salter and a boat got to do with anything?'

'Both names were written in Fuller's notebook just below yours and, after what you've just told me about his interest in Eddie Challow, it's logical to assume that they must be connected with the same enquiry.'

Dexter pursed his lips thoughtfully. 'Sounds very much like it,' he agreed, 'which means Salter could be a friend of Challow's or at the very least, someone who knows where he's gone to ground.'

'A someone who is living on a boat somewhere perhaps?' she added meaningfully.

His gaze quickly flicked to the canal. 'On the Mid-Shires, you mean?'

'Well, it's certainly possible'

'That's one hell of a lot of waterway to check.'

'Not necessarily. We already have the name of the boat Salter may be living on. Bit of old-fashioned legwork should do the trick.'

His eyes gleamed. 'Especially if we got stuck in now. It would be just like old times –'

'No way, Mike,' she cut in hastily. 'You are much too close to this thing and anyway, you're no longer on CID, just in case you had forgotten.'

'But what if you turn up Eddie Challow as a result? I know what he looks like, you don't.'

She smiled grimly. 'You might be wrong there.' Fishing in her coat pocket, she produced a small black and white photograph from her wallet. 'This was found in the back of Fuller's notebook. It looks like an official mug shot, so he must have half-inched it from somewhere.'

Staring into Eddie Challow's cold expressionless face after so many years gave Dexter a chilling sense of déjà vu and he shivered. 'Yeah, that's him,' he confirmed. 'It's a face I'll never forget, in this life or the next.'

She gave a triumphant smile. 'Excellent. Another jigsaw piece in place. All I've got to do now then is find Mr Salter.'

'All *we've* got to do, you mean.'

Her smile faded. 'I've already told you, no, Mike. I think you're in big enough trouble with *Super Plod* at the moment – not to mention the hassle you've created for yourself with Dr Watson – without adding to it.'

Dexter scowled. 'And how did you know about my run-in with *Super Plod*?'

She shrugged. 'As I said just now, word soon gets around.' She hesitated, then went on quickly. 'Look, Mike, you're the force PRO and PROs are expected to be polished tactful people, able to smooth over ripples and keep everyone happy.'

'And I'm not, I suppose?'

Her mouth tightened and she glanced away for a moment before meeting his gaze levelly. 'The word is out that you're losing it, Mike,' she said simply. 'You're treading on too many toes and upsetting all the wrong people. You don't seem to realise you're not a hairy-arsed DI anymore, who's able to say what he thinks regardless of the consequences; you're in a whole different ball game now.'

'I think I've already touched on the sort of game I'm in, Mary,' he replied dryly. 'As for treading on toes, I don't give a damn about that while Tania's life is at stake.'

'Don't you think you're being just a little bit melodramatic?'

He gave a short cynical laugh. 'I doubt whether Lionel Berwick would see it that way if he were in a position to give an opinion.'

She gave an exasperated sigh. 'Just leave this investigation to me, will you, Mike?' she said heavily, turning away from him to head back to her car in the lane. 'Don't foul things up for both of us, eh?'

Her scornful parting shot stung him more than he cared to admit, especially in view of his reawakened, though guilt-ridden, feelings towards her, and he watched her go with a sense of angry frustration; furious that he had allowed himself to be put down by a DS with half his service, yet acutely conscious of the fact that he had asked for all he'd got by stepping over the line between his personal and professional life.

He was so wrapped up in his own sour mood that at first he didn't hear his name being called and when it finally dawned on him that someone was trying to attract his attention, it took him a couple of seconds to work out where the voice was coming from.

The woman police constable who had been manning the front door of the cottage came across the lawn towards him, waving her radio. 'Mr Dexter,' she said again. 'Sergeant Mahoney upstairs needs to speak to you urgently. Can you pop up to see him, sir?'

Dexter got a grip on himself and nodded quickly. 'Problem?' he queried, following her round the cottage to the front door.

She shrugged. 'Dunno, sir. Something about a telephone call, I think.'

Douglas Mahoney met him on the stairs, looking perplexed. 'Just had a call from the guy who runs the Bellingham Keep Fit Centre, sir,' he explained, leaning against the banister rail. 'A Mr Keith Everett. He wanted to speak to Miss Morrison.'

'And?'

The Sergeant looked down at his feet, his face reddening. 'I sort of let the cat out of the bag that she was deceased, sir. I know we would not normally do this until any relatives have been traced and formal

ID gone through, but he was obviously suspicious when I answered the phone and I had to tell him who I was.'

Anxious to get to the point, Dexter nodded quickly. 'Don't worry about it, skipper. People will find out soon enough anyway. So, what did Mr Everett want?'

Mahoney breathed a perceptible sigh of relief. 'It seems that Miss Morrison's locker at the centre has been screwed, sir, and he wanted her to go over and check to see if anything had been taken.'

Dexter's eyes narrowed. 'Screwed, you say?'

'Yes, sir. I thought it a bit peculiar – you know, in view of her death and that. I've already asked Control to send one of our lads over there, but I thought you'd want to know as well.'

'Damned right I do, skipper,' Dexter breathed. 'Give Mr Everett a ring back, will you? Tell him I'll be there in ten minutes.'

*

Detective Chief Inspector Dick Lawson was uneasy and it showed. As he left the incident room at Bellingham Police Station and strode purposefully down the stairs to the first floor, his face wore a heavy frown instead of the usual relaxed easy-going expression he habitually adopted and his eyes looked strangely troubled.

Detective Superintendent Brian Moffat noticed the change as soon as his deputy stepped into his temporary office and he eyed the single sheet of paper in Lawson's hand suspiciously.

'Well?' he snapped, sitting back in the comfortable swivel chair he had purloined from the area beat sergeant's office on the ground floor.

Lawson reached across his desk and set the piece of paper on top of the incident report Moffat had been studying. 'I've just been reading your press release, sir,' he said, dropping into an adjacent armchair.

Moffat glanced at it and frowned. 'Yes, it was drafted for me by the press girl upstairs – Sarah someone or other. What's wrong with it?'

'Nothing as far as press releases go, but I think it would be a big mistake putting it out at present.'

Moffat's frown deepened. 'But if there's nothing wrong with it, why shouldn't it go out?'

Lawson hesitated, knowing that there was no easy way of saying what he had to say. 'I'm not convinced Walter Leather did the Alden House job in the first place,' he said simply.

153

Moffat gaped at him. 'You're not *what*?' he breathed. 'Is this some kind of a joke? If it is, I don't find it in the least bit funny.'

Lawson shook his head. 'No joke, sir, I assure you. I've never felt that comfortable with Leather as the culprit, you know that. That's why I suggested we needed to make a lot more enquiries before coming to any definite conclusions.'

Moffat's face flushed a delicate shade of pink. 'More enquiries?' he exclaimed. 'More enquiries? Bloody hell, man, are you mad? The tramp's pockets were full of Lionel Berwick's property, he reeked of petrol and he even had the key to the handcuffs on him. What more evidence do you want?'

'I'm sorry, sir, but I feel things have been moving much too fast on this investigation; at an unprecedented rate for a murder enquiry, in fact. '

Moffat glared at him. 'Oh you do, do you?' he grated.

Lawson didn't bat an eyelid. 'Very much so, sir,' he replied coolly, 'and from the information I received in your absence this afternoon, I think that we would be ill-advised to go public with a result at present.'

'Information? What information?'

Lawson hesitated again before replying. 'Apparently the fingerprint examination of the identifiable property found on the tramp has turned up something rather surprising. Leather's dabs were found all over the watch and the lighter, but there were no other marks at all.'

'What's so surprising about that?'

Lawson studied his flushed face. 'Well, you'd expect to find some prints belonging to Berwick on his own gear, wouldn't you? But there was not a trace, not even inside the watch cover.'

'Maybe Leather wiped them off.'

Lawson shook his head. 'And why would he bother to do that, sir? The property was engraved with Berwick's name, so rubbing off the prints would have achieved nothing if he had been stopped and searched by police.'

'So, what are you suggesting? That someone planted the stuff on him?'

'It's certainly possible.'

Moffat snorted disparagingly. 'Then, I suppose, that same someone just picked him up – all twelve stone of him – carried him to the bridge over the bypass and chucked him off the top, eh?' He made a dismissive gesture with one hand. 'What absolute rubbish. You're getting as paranoid as that fool, Dexter.'

Lawson's mouth tightened. 'Maybe I am, sir, but there's something else you should know too.'

'Oh? And what is that exactly?'

'DS Robbins, in charge of the house search team, came to see me a short time ago and it seems that Judge Berwick was a bit of a shooting man. Liked to blast the odd pigeon or two when he got the opportunity.'

'So?'

'Well, he apparently used a twelve-bore shotgun, which, according to his cleaning lady, was kept in a gun cabinet in his study. The point is, when Robbins' team carried out a search of the house, they found the gun cabinet buried under a pile of debris, but the weapon was missing and there were signs that the cabinet had been deliberately forced open.'

'You're saying the gun's been stolen?'

'Dead right I am, and whoever nicked the weapon took the trouble to reduce it in size first. Robbins found a good twelve inches of sawn-off twin barrels lying with a broken hacksaw blade in a corner of the garage.'

'Sawn-off?'

'Exactly, and since the tramp didn't have the weapon on him and no trace of it was found at the old Ferguson house in Tulse End where he was apparently dossing, who does have it?'

Moffat grunted. 'Is all this leading to something?' he snapped.

Lawson mentally counted to ten. 'Oh, it's leading to something all right, sir,' he retorted, 'and it's this: in my opinion, we should take another look at the Berwick case before we jump in at the deep end, maybe consider other options,' and he paused deliberately before ending the sentence, 'like a certain psycho, called Eddie Challow, for instance?'

Moffat stiffened, his eyes widening and his colour rising again. 'I thought I'd already made the position about this case abundantly clear to you?' he said, his tone soft, but menacing. 'The Lionel Berwick murder investigation is over, solved, do you understand? We know who committed the crime and we're not going to waste time and resources looking for someone else, just to please that idiot, Michael Dexter. Now have you finally got that?'

Lawson nodded grimly. 'Oh, I've got it all right, sir, and it stinks to high heaven, but as I don't know where to find Challow and no one is prepared to divulge that information anyway, I can't do much about it.'

Moffat half rose in his chair. 'You won't try to do anything about it anyway,' he snarled, 'not unless you want to finish your promotion prospects for good and put on a funny hat again.'

Lawson's eyes narrowed. 'That sounds like a threat to me, sir,' he said. 'I could take that further.'

There was a flicker of alarm in Moffat's eyes. He could see by the expression on his DCI's face that he had gone too far by suggesting he could be returned to uniform and he quickly changed his approach. 'Look, Richard,' he patronised, 'you know how important this detection is for the force and as I've already told ACC Ops that we have a result, he will almost certainly have passed that on to the Chief. There can be no going back now.'

Lawson's stare was icy. 'Not even if we've got the wrong man, sir?' he said quietly.

Moffat raised his eyes to the ceiling in a gesture of frustration. 'Walter Leather is *dead*,' he expostulated.

'And that makes it all right, does it, sir? He's dead, so he can't complain?'

Moffat lost his cool again and slammed his fist on the table. 'That's not what I mean and you damned well know it! You're just twisting my words. Leather did that job and, had he still been alive, I'm confident that we'd have had enough evidence to charge him with it. So let's put an end to all this crap, shall we?'

'Fine, sir,' Lawson rapped, jumping to his feet, 'but just think on this. That shotgun was taken by someone for a specific reason – you don't shorten the barrels of a twelve bore for the sheer fun of it – and if the tramp didn't nick it, then there's an even chance that someone like Eddie Challow did.' He strode towards the door, but turned briefly with his hand on the handle. 'Maybe that so-called idiot, Mike Dexter, was right after all,' he added. 'Maybe Challow *is* waging some sort of vendetta against those who put him away, which means we could have a few more victims to go yet. If you can sleep at night with that thought on your conscience, I certainly can't.' And he stalked from the office without even waiting for a reply.

Chapter 11

Mary Lane had only just left Mike Dexter at Kitty Morrison's cottage when she received the call on her personal radio from the Area Control Room. Within fifteen minutes she had pulled into the rear yard at Gilstone Police Station and was climbing the stairs.

'So, what gives, Dennis?' she demanded curtly as she strode into the large almost empty CID office and tossed her car keys on to her desk. 'Control said something about a camera being found.'

Detective Constable Dennis Skinner glanced quickly over one shoulder, a cigarette protruding from the corner of his mouth as he finished pouring himself a cup of coffee from the machine in the corner. '*The* camera more like, Mary,' he replied. 'Want some coffee?'

She nodded and settled on the edge of her desk. 'Black please. So what have you got to tell me?'

The stout bearded DC tapped the appropriate buttons and waited for the second plastic cup to fill, the characteristic rasp of his breathing from years of smoking competing with the hiss of the machine. 'Area Four, Jim Staples, checked two kids – twelve, thirteen year olds, something like that – on the Mid-Shires towpath. They should have been at school, but had apparently bunked off to go fishing.'

He turned away from the machine to hand her an overfull cup of coffee, then leaned against the lip of the opposite desk to slowly sip his own. 'They did have fishing rods with them, but they also had an expensive looking camera they claimed to have hooked out of the canal.'

'What sort of camera?'

'Canon 35mm SLR.' His heavy-lidded eyes gleamed. 'And one with a nice little metal plate riveted to the base, engraved with the name of our man, Quentin Fuller.'

She drew in her breath sharply. 'Fuller? You're sure about that?'

He waved an arm towards the windows. 'See for yourself. It was a bit damp, so I put it on a towel on the window-sill to dry off.'

She followed the direction of his gaze and nodded. 'No hurry. I'll take a look once Scenes Of Crime have done the business.'

He shook his head. 'Unlikely SOCO will find anything of value. As well as dripping water, it's still plastered with mud and there are bits of weed tangled up in the mechanism.' He frowned. 'No film in it though, which struck me as rather strange in view of all the photographic kit Fuller had in his car.'

'Maybe the kids took the film out and slung it?'

'Not according to them. They say they didn't even open the thing when they recovered it.'

'They would say that, wouldn't they?'

'Why should they lie? We've already got them in possession of the camera anyway. The film's not going to make much difference, is it?'

'So, you reckon the kids' story about hooking it from the canal could be true?'

He shrugged. 'Can't see anyone nicking a camera, then throwing it in the canal, can you?'

'Not unless it was the film they were after.'

He raised his eyebrows slightly. 'You mean our late pressman could have been taking naughty pictures of someone who didn't want to be photographed?'

'Well, it's certainly possible, isn't it? So where are the kids now?'

'Interview room. Sergeant Halton in Custody was reluctant to bang them up in the detention room, in view of their ages and the fact that they seemed to have a plausible reason for being in possession of the camera.'

'You mean they've been left on their own together? That was a bit daft, wasn't it? They'll certainly have got their story straight by now.'

He shook his head. 'Not a chance. Jim Staples has been keeping them company. We thought you would want to interview them personally when their parents finally decided to arrive.'

She took a sip of her coffee, studying him over the rim of the cup. 'And presumably Staples already knows why we have an interest in the camera?'

Skinner emitted a short cynical laugh. 'What do you think?' he retorted. 'Whole bloody nick knows about the Fuller case. News travels pretty fast around here.'

She screwed up her face in disapproval. 'Damned bush telegraph.'

Another laugh. 'You can blame the *Black Rats* on Traffic for that.

Poor old Robin Cater will never forgive CID for muscling in on what was originally their job.'

She grunted and took another sip of coffee. 'Our wily old sergeant still bleating about it, is he?'

'You know Robin, bit of an old woman at times. But his heart's in the right place. Actually rang me ten minutes ago to say he had some more information and would be over later to deliver it in person.'

'What sort of information?'

Skinner shrugged. 'No idea. Wouldn't tell me. Probably hoping he can barter for a slice of the investigation. But he asked me to let you know he was coming.'

She set her coffee cup on the edge of the desk and stood up, smoothing the creases out of her trousers. 'Well, while he's playing silly games, I suppose I'd better look in on our two hardened criminals downstairs, eh?'

Skinner hesitated. 'You don't want me with you, do you?'

She raised her eyebrows. 'Oh, I think I can manage this one on my tod, Dennis. Why?'

He suddenly looked very uncomfortable. 'Well, I'm due to finish in half an hour and as it's the missus' birthday, I sort of said –'

She grinned. 'On to a promise then, are you, Dennis?'

He snorted. 'You've got to be joking. More like a bloody threat.'

She laughed outright and headed for the door. 'You clutter off,' she said, mischief in her eyes, 'but tell that lady of yours to be gentle with you, eh? I don't want you pulling any of your important muscles.'

★

The two boys looked up expectantly when Mary entered the interview room, but their faces fell the moment she said who she was. The pair of them were mud up to the eyeballs and the smaller of the two, a weedy looking lad with protruding teeth she later found to be called Lenny Walsh, looked as though he had been crying. A short thickset constable with a neat military moustache and penetrating grey eyes was sitting on the opposite side of the interview desk and he stood up sharply as she came into the room. 'Skipper,' he acknowledged. 'Just waiting for their parents.'

'So I gather. Got a minute?'

Staples nodded, then eyed the boys severely. 'Just sit there, and no talking. Understand? I'll only be outside this door.'

'Yes, Mr Staples,' they both whispered as one.

In spite of the seriousness of the situation, Mary had difficulty keeping a straight face. 'You've got them well trained, Jim,' she said once they were outside in the passage.

He grinned. 'Been on this area for fifteen years, skip. Known 'em since they were babies.'

'So which one had the camera?'

'The dark-haired lad, Jimmy Scott, was carrying it when I stopped them. Looks like an expensive bit of kit too. There's some damage to the lens hood, as if the thing has been dropped or knocked against something pretty forcibly, but it's still worth a few bob, I would think.'

'And you reckon their story about finding the camera in the canal is legit?'

'Don't really think it can be anything else, judging by the state of it.' He chuckled. 'I'm not too sure about their claim that they were on their way to hand it in though. Flog it to a bent dealer more like.'

'Whereabouts did you stop them?'

'About half a mile from Curling Lock, near the village of Maple Bucksters.'

She hesitated for a moment. 'I gather you know what this investigation is all about?'

'Something to do with a brake pipe being cut on the Mercedes that was involved in the Gilstone fatal?'

She nodded slowly, her mind sifting through the possibilities. 'It could be that the Merc was actually parked somewhere near the village before the accident. If it was, any chance of these two lads having had anything to do with the cutting, do you think?'

He laughed outright. 'No way. They're a couple of little tea-leafers, yes, but that's all. I doubt whether they'd even have known where the brake pipes were. Anyway, it couldn't have been them. I've already been on to their school to check their attendance record. Seems they were all present and correct yesterday. Young Scottie, as they call him, even managed to get himself put on detention for late homework.'

She frowned. 'So, we're still looking for someone else then. Any ideas?'

He pursed his lips reflectively. 'Not really. We get a fair bit of damage to boats along the canal – gypsy kids usually from the Honey Lane site – but nothing like this.'

'You mentioned boats.'

He nodded. 'Yes, canal boats, mainly used by tourists in the holiday season and moored up during the winter. There's a boat building and repair yard at Maple Bucksters, run by an eccentric character named Tommy Lee. Most of the craft are his.'

'Ever heard of a boat called *Water Gypsy*?'

'Not specifically, but it sounds like one of Tommy's.' He grinned. 'He was a gypo himself once – until he got religion, that is. Most of his boats would have names to do with his days on the road; you know, *Water Gypsy*, *Gypsy Rose*, *Gypsy Queen* – that sort of thing.'

'And what about a man named Alan Salter? Ring any bells?'

He thought for a minute. 'Not with me, but Tommy does employ quite a bit of casual labour, particularly in the holiday season. So it could be someone he took on in the summer.'

She grunted. 'Then maybe I should pay your Mr Tommy Lee a little visit when we're finished here, eh?'

'Might be worthwhile.' He jerked a thumb towards the interview room door. 'And our two *felons* in there?'

She shrugged. 'Well, we'll have to go through the motions before kicking them out, but any interview looks like being a complete waste of time to me.'

He chuckled again. 'Oh, I don't know. At least you'll get to meet Scottie's parents and that's an experience in itself, I can tell you.' He half-turned as high-pitched incoherent shouting suddenly erupted from the direction of the station duty office. 'In fact, it sounds like Mrs Scott has just this minute arrived. I'll introduce you, if you like?'

*

The Keep Fit Centre in Bellingham was a large yellow brick building occupying a corner of the only public pay and display car park in the town. The foyer, with its rubber plants and spinners displaying healthy lifestyle literature, smelled of old trainers and sweat, which wafted through from the workout rooms whenever the inner door was opened.

Dexter had never been into physical punishment as a way of looking good and the strong odour brought back unpleasant memories of compulsory PE as a child and, much later, the rigorous fitness regime of the Police Training School. He had a lot of difficulty concealing his feelings as he waited for the pretty brunette on reception to buzz her manager, but fortunately he didn't have to wait long.

Keith Everett was the archetypal PTI. Short and muscular, with close-cropped black hair and restless brown eyes, he was dressed in a sweatshirt, tracksuit bottoms and trainers when he appeared in the foyer within minutes of being called. Extending a sinewy tattooed arm in welcome, he gripped Dexter's hand hard, as if trying to make a point. 'Good of you to come, Chief Inspector,' he said, ushering him through another door behind the reception desk. 'We'll go this way, if you don't mind. Less conspicuous, I think.'

The door gave access to what appeared to be some sort of administration office, complete with a flashy looking computer and workstation, a row of filing cabinets and a photocopier. But they passed right on through this into a much plusher inner sanctum, with sporting certificates on the walls and a glass-fronted bookcase containing an assortment of silver cups and medals.

'Do have a seat, Chief Inspector,' Everett said, indicating an armchair in front of a smart mahogany desk. 'Tea? Coffee?'

'No thanks, sir,' Dexter replied firmly, flexing the muscles in his hand. 'I'd just like to see the locker, if you don't mind.'

Everett nodded. 'Understand perfectly.' He hesitated. 'It *is* true about Kitty then?'

'You mean that she's dead? Very much so, I'm afraid.'

The other sighed. 'So tragic. I can still hardly believe it. How on earth did it happen?'

'That's for the Coroner to decide.'

Everett's curiosity refused to allow him to leave it there. 'Yes, I know, but was it just…?'

Dexter studied him grimly. 'Was it what?'

'Well, you know – er – natural causes?'

Dexter grunted. 'There's nothing natural about death, Mr Everett,' he replied coldly, 'nothing natural at all. Now, can I see this locker?'

Everett suddenly looked uncomfortable. 'Yes, yes, of course,' he said quickly, turning towards another door. 'Not a lot to see though, I'm afraid, apart from twisted metal.'

The female changing room lay at the end of a short passageway and Everett entered confidently without knocking. Dexter spotted Kitty's locker almost immediately. It was at the start of the second row and had a photograph of her favourite film star, *Sean Connery*, taped to the partially open door. Everett was right about the twisted metal; someone had really put some force into springing the lock

162

and the door edge was almost bent back on itself. 'No chance Kitty forgot her key last time she was here, I suppose?' Dexter queried dryly.

Everett shook his head. 'It's a rule of the centre that all members hand in their locker keys before they go home,' he explained. 'These are then locked in our admin office safe until they are signed out again.' He smiled smugly. 'I introduced the policy myself when I first came here as a means of improving our approach to security.'

'Worked too, didn't it?' Dexter commented sarcastically, eyeing the buckled door.

Everett scowled. 'Nothing is foolproof, Chief Inspector,' he snapped. 'You should know that better than anyone.'

Dexter carefully opened the locker door wide, using his handkerchief and the top corner of the door. Apart from a couple of sweatshirts and a pair of tracksuit bottoms on hangars, the locker contained nothing more interesting than the usual female paraphernalia of hairsprays, bottles of perfume and makeup. 'When was this job done, do you think?' he queried sharply.

Everett shrugged. 'One of my personal trainers, Kim Talbot, checks the place every night before we lock up. She swears the lockers were all secure yesterday evening, but she noticed the damage to this one when she came in here this afternoon, looking for some missing kit.'

'So the locker must have been screwed this morning?'

'As the place is alarmed at night and there are no signs of a break-in, that must be it, yes, though why Kitty's locker was selected, I can't imagine.'

Dexter let the door swing back into place again and turned to face him. 'So, you've no idea who might have been responsible then?'

Everett hesitated. 'Not exactly.'

'What do you mean by that?'

'I'd rather not say – at least not here anyway.'

Dexter nodded, easily seeing through the flimsy façade to a man who, despite his outward show of reluctance, had every intention of verballing someone. 'In that case, sir, why don't we adjourn to somewhere more private?' he suggested politely.

Back in his plush office, Everett kept up the pretence for a little longer. 'I don't make a habit of gossiping about members of the centre, if I can avoid it,' he said, leaning against the glass-fronted bookcase and affecting a suitably worried expression. 'Their private lives are none of my business, you understand.'

Dexter dropped into an armchair in front of his desk. 'Can we just get on with it, Mr Everett?' he said, irritation creeping into his tone. 'Exactly who are we talking about?'

Everett flushed, then nodded quickly. 'Er – yes, of course. Well, there was this guy who joined us a couple of weeks back. Just moved into the area apparently. Proper fitness fanatic too, with the physique to prove it. Certainly caught Kitty's eye anyway.'

'How do you know that?'

Everett gave a short bitter laugh. 'Only a blind man would have missed it, Chief Inspector,' he said with feeling. 'She was all over him from day one and it wasn't long before the pair of them were into some kind of relationship, though what she saw in a weirdo like that, I'll never understand.'

Dexter's eyes narrowed. 'Weirdo?' he queried, sensing the jealousy festering only just below the surface. 'What do you mean by weirdo?'

Everett emitted a disparaging snort. 'Precisely that. Had to be well into his fifties – almost old enough to be Kitty's father, in fact – but liked to put himself about as the strong silent type. Rarely smiled or spoke to anyone except her and seemed to have some kind of chip on his shoulder.'

'But what makes you think he could have been the one who broke into Kitty's locker?'

'Seemed like the type, I suppose, and shortly after he turned up here this morning for an early workout, Kim actually caught him coming out of the female changing room. Fortunately it was a men only day today, so there were no female customers using the room at the time, otherwise it could have been pretty awkward. Some of our lady members are a bit funny about that sort of thing.'

'What reason did your man give for going in there?'

'Said he'd made a mistake and gone through the wrong door.'

'Maybe he had?'

'No way. Not only are the male and female changing rooms clearly marked and at opposite ends of the corridor, but he'd been to the centre on enough occasions to know where everything was. Unfortunately Kim was very busy at the time and didn't give the matter too much thought. She just assumed he'd made a genuine mistake. It wasn't until she found the damaged locker later that she put two and two together and reported the incident to me.'

'And did you try following things up yourself ?'

He shook his head. 'I wasn't given the chance. By the time Kim told me about the locker, the guy had already resigned his membership.'

'Resigned?'

'Yes, and that was strangest thing of all. He simply went to reception less than an hour after he had signed in and said he no longer wanted to be a member. Gave no reason for his decision and made no enquiries about a refund. Just handed in his key and left.'

Dexter grunted. 'Certainly all rather suspicious, I must admit. But why on earth would he want to break into Kitty's locker in the first place, especially as you say he and Kitty had become an item?'

Everett shrugged again. 'You're the policeman,' he retorted sourly. 'Why don't you ask him?'

'Maybe I will, but it might help to have his name and address first.'

'That's easy enough.' Everett stepped through the connecting door to the adjoining office and returned a few minutes later with a small index card. 'Salter,' he said, reading from the card. 'His name was Alan Salter –'

'Salter?' Dexter cut in sharply, remembering his conversation with Mary Lane. 'Did you say Salter?'

Everett was plainly surprised by his reaction. 'Well, that's the name I have here. Why, do you know him?'

Dexter's face was grim. 'Not exactly. Does he have an address?'

'Of course. All members are required to supply their home details.'

'His home wouldn't be a boat by any chance, would it?'

Everett raised his eyebrows. 'As matter of fact, it would. I said he was weird, didn't I? Apparently the thing's called *Water Gypsy* and it's moored on the Mid-Shires Canal near some place called Maple Bucksters.'

Dexter felt his heart miss a beat under a sudden adrenalin surge. 'And this Alan Salter,' he said in a carefully controlled voice, 'what does he look like?'

Everett thought for a second. 'As I've already said, well into his fifties. Not very tall, but quite muscular. Curly black hair, greying a bit.' He hesitated. 'Face almost corpse-like though, with the coldest eyes I've ever seen. Would give anyone the creeps.' He gave another short, but slightly uneasy laugh as he latched on to something less disturbing. 'Oh yes, and he always turned up at the centre in a black crash helmet and leathers, like some bloody Sixties greaser. Helped his hard man image, I suppose, but I thought he looked totally ridiculous.'

Dexter stared at him fixedly. 'Leathers?' he breathed. 'Are you saying he rode a motorcycle?'

Everett nodded. 'If you could call it that. It was one of those off-road machines they use for scrambling.'

*

There was a traffic car cheekily parked in the detective inspector's parking bay when Mike Dexter pulled into the rear yard at Gilstone Police Station. He found out why when he bumped into Sergeant Cater on the stairs as he headed up to the CID office. 'No point going up there, gov,' Cater commented. 'Ain't no one in.'

Dexter frowned. 'So where are they all then?'

Cater shrugged. 'Duty Inspector says there's only been two of them about this afternoon anyway. Mary Lane and some DC – er – Skinner I think she said his name was. The others must either be day off or seconded to the Berwick investigation. Apparently Mary was interviewing a couple of kids earlier about a theft and was last seen heading out of the nick about fifteen minutes ago.'

'So what are you doing here? Time you were off duty, isn't it?'

Cater nodded. 'Never did bother about clocks, gov,' he replied with a grin, 'not when there's a job to be done.'

Dexter followed him back down the stairs. 'Wouldn't have anything to do with the Fuller case by any chance, would it?'

The traffic man chuckled. 'Like your visit you mean?' he queried.

Dexter smiled faintly. 'Okay, okay, let's stop playing games, shall we? What have you got?'

Cater faced him, selecting a cigarette from a crumpled packet and lighting up, in direct contravention of the force's ban on smoking in police stations. 'With respect, gov,' he said cannily, 'I seem to be doing all the telling lately while you do all the listening.'

'RHP,' Dexter said bluntly. 'Rank has privileges.'

'I know what RHP means, sir,' Cater replied dryly, 'but it don't cut no ice with me. You shouldn't even be involved in this case as the force PRO and you know that.'

Dexter scowled and, taking him by the elbow, led him into an adjacent office. 'Okay, I wanted to see Mary Lane about the sudden death of one of my staff,' he said, revealing half the story. 'She was found dead in bed this morning and I don't believe it was an accident. In fact, I have reason to believe her boyfriend might have had something to do with it.'

Cater raised his eyebrows. 'If you don't mind my saying, gov,' he exclaimed, 'death certainly seems to follow you around.'

'So it would seem. Anyway, I've told you why I'm here. Now it's your turn.'

Cater nodded. 'It *is* to do with the Fuller case,' he admitted reluctantly. 'We had a witness come forward after he heard about the fatal on local radio and I felt Mary should know about it.'

'A witness?'

'Yeah, a local bus driver. Seems that just before the accident your mate, Fuller, drove out of a side turning in front of his bus and he had to slam on his brakes to avoid hitting him. He didn't bother to report the incident at the time, as there was no actual collision and this sort of thing is a regular hazard in his particular job. Then he heard about the fatal.'

'And where did all this happen?'

'Road called Bottom Lane at the foot of Gilstone Hill, on the other side of the crossroads.'

'So what's at Bottom Lane?'

'Nothing special. Dead end actually. Leads to a hamlet called Maple Bucksters close to the Mid-Shires Canal. Place has a small church and half a dozen cottages, that's all. Oh yeah, and there's some kind of boatyard that rents out canal boats for the tourist trade at Curling Lock. Nothing else to speak of.'

The mention of canal boats and Maple Bucksters had set Dexter's heart racing again as all the bits of information he had digested over the past few hours began to slot into place, but he made a determined effort to conceal his excitement.

'So what the hell would someone like Fuller be doing in a backwater like that?'

Cater took a long pull on his cigarette. 'Taking a leak maybe. There's a pile of woodland between the lane and the canal. Perhaps he was shy.' Cater hesitated. 'There is one other interesting thing though.'

'What do you mean?'

'Well, when Fuller came out of Bottom Lane, he was apparently going like the proverbial and he seemed to be in some sort of race with a motorcycle. Damned thing was right up his arse.'

Dexter's guard slipped. 'Motorcycle?' he exclaimed. 'What kind of motorcycle?'

Cater's eyes narrowed. 'Bus driver couldn't say exactly,' he replied slowly, 'but he thought it was some kind of scrambler.' He studied

Dexter with a thoughtful frown. 'There's more to this than you're telling me, isn't there, sir?'

Before Dexter could answer, a middle-aged uniformed bobby with a small military moustache poked his head round the door. 'I hear from the governor that you're looking for DS Lane, skipper,' he said.

Cater half-turned towards him. 'Hi, Jim,' he acknowledged. 'Yeah, we just missed her.'

Jim Staples nodded. 'Well, she's gone over to Tommy Lee's Boatyard at Maple Bucksters.'

'Maple Bucksters?' Dexter snapped. 'What took her there?'

Staples stared at him curiously for a moment, then glanced back at Cater.

The traffic man waved his hand dismissively, spilling ash from his cigarette down his tunic. 'Chief Inspector Dexter, Headquarters,' he said, answering the other's unspoken question.

Staples relaxed. 'Sorry, sir, I wasn't sure who you were.'

Dexter nodded impatiently, his excitement almost boiling over. 'You said she went to Maple Bucksters,' he reminded him, 'and I asked you why.'

Staples nodded back. 'I nicked a couple of kids earlier today on the Mid-Shires towpath not far from there. They had an empty camera with them which they said they had pulled out the canal –'

'A camera?' Cater cut in, suddenly very focused.

His sharp reaction seemed to surprise the area beat man and he hesitated a moment before replying. 'Er – yes, that's right; an expensive looking Canon SLR. Mary and I interviewed them with their parents, but it was obvious that their story was legit, so we kicked them out.'

'And this camera,' Cater persisted, 'no idea who it belongs to, I suppose?'

'As a matter of fact we do. The name was engraved on the bottom of the case – Quentin Fuller, the stiff from the Gilstone fatal.'

'So what has an SLR camera to do with Tommy Lee's Boatyard?'

Staples shrugged. 'Not entirely sure, skip, to be honest. Mary had a bit of info about some guy living at Maple Bucksters on a canal boat called *Water Gypsy*. I said it was likely that the boat belonged to Tommy Lee and she seemed to think that there could be a connection between the guy on the boat and the camera.'

Dexter's jigsaw was complete. 'Eddie Challow,' he breathed without thinking.

Staples frowned. 'No, sir,' he corrected, 'That wasn't the name she mentioned. It was someone called Salter – Alan Salter.'

Dexter's face was a grim mask. 'Take my word for it,' he rasped, 'they're one and the same person and you've just let that damn fool woman go to see a serious pickle-head on her own.'

Staples flushed. '*I* haven't let her do anything, sir,' he retorted indignantly. 'She's the DS, not me, and anyway, I had to stay here to deal with the release of the two kids.'

'What the hell is all this about, governor?' Cater demanded, turning on Dexter quickly and forgetting himself in his rising frustration.

Dexter pushed him towards the door. 'I'll tell you on the way, Sergeant,' he rapped. 'We'll go in your car – it's a damned sight faster than mine.'

Chapter 12

Mary Lane reversed the CID car into a corner of the floodlit car park between what appeared to be an ex-army Land Rover, still complete with its distinctive camouflage colours, and a long uncoupled trailer. Fingers on the door handle, she sat there for a moment studying the big boat shed through the windscreen. She hated to admit it even to herself, but in the gathering dusk the place looked pretty spooky and despite her years of police experience on hard unforgiving streets, she almost found herself wishing she had left this particular job until daylight. But, as a detective sergeant on a potential murder enquiry, she hadn't the luxury of choice and time was always the enemy of any investigation. Flicking back the door catch with a wry grimace, she stepped out into the chilly dank air and carefully locked the door behind her.

A couple of workmen in overalls passed her on the way to their own cars as she approached a side door to the building. 'Doing anything tonight, darling?' one shouted after her.

'You couldn't afford me anyway, *sweetheart*,' she responded over her shoulder and grinned at the guffaw that followed her inside.

A heady mixture of odours – new paint, wet varnish and diesel oil – greeted her on the other side of the door and in the shadowy gut of the building, lit only by a couple of strip lights high in the vaulted roof, a small square of concrete floor, littered with steel drums, coils of rope and other debris, stood out like a spotlighted stage. In the gloom beyond, the fierce blue light of an acetylene torch blazed coldly and somewhere over to her right she could hear tuneless whistling.

'What you doing here?' The voice barked at her from a few feet away, making her jump, and she turned to face a lean bearded man in overalls and a hard hat who had appeared from the shadows with hardly a sound.

She held up her warrant card in front of him. 'Detective Sergeant Lane, Gilstone nick,' she snapped back, annoyed that she had been caught unawares.

The man nodded, appraising her coldly. 'So?'

'I'm here on an enquiry.'

'Bit late, ain't you? It's knocking off time. Most of the lads have already gone and I shall be shutting up shop in a minute or two.'

'And you are?'

He tilted his protective helmet back on his head. 'Tommy Lee. I just happen to own this place.'

'Good, then you'll know Alan Salter?'

'What if I do? What's he done?'

'Nothing as far as I know. I just want a word in his shell-like.'

He grunted. 'I thought your lot had agreed to leave him alone?'

She frowned. 'Sorry? Are you saying he's been in trouble with us?'

He gave a short disbelieving laugh. 'You really don't know, do you?'

'Perhaps you'll tell me?'

He stabbed a finger in her direction. 'Listen, love, I suggest you ring your boss or whoever pulls your strings. Seems you need educating.'

She felt the anger bite. 'I'm ringing no one, mister. Just tell me where I can find Alan Salter, will you.'

He muttered something under his breath, then turned on his heel. 'The guy with the torch, that's Alan,' he threw back over his shoulder. 'You're lucky. He's only just come back.'

'Back from where?'

'How should I know? He never seems to be here half the time anyway and now you lot are sniffing round him again, he'll be no use to me at all.'

'Only doing my job, Mr Lee,' she replied.

He snorted. 'Yeah, that's as maybe, but this is well out of order and I'm going to speak to someone about it.'

The cold blue light of the acetylene torch seemed to bore into Mary's skull and the bizarre figure in the grotesque mask crouched behind it looked like something out of a bad dream.

She hesitated, feeling a stab of apprehension as she approached the man. 'Mr Salter?'

There was no response above the flare of the torch as the flame hungrily licked a dome-shaped metal casing in front of him.

'Mr Salter!'

The iron-clad head turned towards her and the figure straightened slowly.

171

'Would you turn it off please?'

The man simply stared at her, the torch missing its target and lancing blue fire into the gloom beyond the metal casing.

For some unaccountable reason, a shiver ran down her spine. 'Turn the bloody thing off!' she shouted.

Abruptly the flame died and the figure removed his mask. 'No need to shout,' he said quietly. 'I'm not deaf.'

Mary cleared her throat. 'Er – Mr Salter?' she queried, suddenly feeling foolish.

'Might be. Who's asking?'

'DS Mary Lane, Gilstone CID.'

There was a hard chuckle and the other laid the torch carefully on the ground. 'Lady cop. *Nice.*'

Something about the way he spoke set the alarm bells jangling inside her head and she stepped back a couple of paces as he came towards her. 'I – I want to ask you some questions,' she stammered.

'Do you now?' he replied, stepping fully into the pool of light cast by one of the overhead strip lights. 'Well, here I am, so ask away.'

But Mary was too surprised to ask anything at first, for she knew at once that she had seen this particular face before – in a photograph found in Quentin Fuller's wallet – and, according to Mike Dexter, the name that went with it was certainly not Salter, but Eddie Challow.

*

With the firm sensitive touch of the police advanced driver, Sergeant Cater negotiated a seemingly impossible route through Gilstone's grid-locked rush-hour traffic, the pulsing roof strobe and shrieking siren of the big BMW clearing a narrow path through the jam as effectively as *Moses'* staff had parted the waters of the Red Sea.

As he drove, the traffic man took in all that Dexter had to say about the Eddie Challow affair, making only the occasional grunt of acknowledgement and showing little real surprise, apart from a slight tightening of the lean jaw-line.

By the time Dexter had finished his promised explanation, they had left the main Heaton – Gilstone road and were racing towards Maple Bucksters along Bottom Lane, the branches of the trees that crowded to the edge of the road reaching out towards them like spectral claws in the powerful headlights.

Curling Lock was sign-posted from Maple Bucksters and they

found Tommy Lee's Boatyard without any difficulty. The Gilstone CID car was clearly visible in the corner of the floodlit car park, sandwiched between a Land Rover and trailer, but there was no sign of Mary Lane or anyone else for that matter.

The boat shed itself appeared to be shut up, but lights still burned in a couple of the windows, suggesting that at least someone was working late. Cater checked the CID car and put his hand in front of the radiator grill. 'Still warm,' he commented, following Dexter across the car park to the double doors at the front of the building. 'Can't have been here long.'

The doors were tightly closed and padlocked, and a chain-link fence prevented access to the yard on the far side of the shed. 'So where the hell *is* she?' Dexter exclaimed, a brittle edge to his voice.

Cater shrugged and returned to the car park, a second later poking his head back round the corner of the building. 'Governor?' he called. 'Another way in here.'

The traffic man had already disappeared through the side door when Dexter got to the spot and he turned up his nose as he followed him into the foul-smelling gloom. Two strip lights had been left on in the vaulted roof space, but much of the shed remained in darkness and Cater came a cropper almost immediately, walking into a heavy steel drum only feet inside the door and cursing angrily under his breath as he bent over to rub his knee furiously with both hands. 'Damned thing,' he snarled. 'Fancy leaving it there.'

But Dexter was not in the least bit interested in his predicament or in his views on health and safety. Alerted by the sound of raised voices, he was already pushing past him towards the lighted area where two figures seemed to be locked in some sort of heated argument. As he got closer, he recognised Mary Lane's distinctive profile and it wasn't difficult to guess the identity of the person she was arguing with.

'Well, well, well,' Eddie Challow sneered as he suddenly caught sight of Dexter striding towards him with Sergeant Cater hobbling along painfully in his wake, 'if it isn't the heavy mob.'

Turning quickly in the direction of his gaze, Mary Lane glared venomously at her two colleagues. 'What the hell are you doing here?' she demanded in a tone that was pure ice.

Challow gave a short hard laugh. 'Now that *isn't* the way to talk to a chief inspector, my dear,' he mocked. 'It could seriously jeopardise your promotion prospects.'

173

'And how did you know I was a chief inspector, Challow?' Dexter grated. 'Was that one of the little titbits you got from Kitty Morrison before you murdered her?'

'*Murdered* her?' the little psychopath echoed. '*Moi?* Now that's a very serious allegation, Mr Dexter.'

'Don't play games with me, you little shit,' Dexter snarled, while Cater hovered uneasily in the background. 'I know you killed her, the same as I know you killed Judge Lionel Berwick and Quentin Fuller.'

Mary grabbed Dexter's arm. 'What the hell is all this about?' she exclaimed. 'What has *he* got to do with Kitty Morrison?'

Dexter kept his eyes fixed firmly on Challow's face. 'Alan Salter, alias Eddie Challow, was the man Kitty was dating,' he replied grimly. 'That's what I came here to tell you. Somehow he found out that Kitty used the Bellingham Keep-Fit Centre and he joined the centre himself with the sole object of pulling her. Once he'd done that, it wasn't difficult to subtly pump her for information about me and – more importantly – Tania.' Pulling his arm free from Mary's grip, he thrust his face closer to Challow's, his fists clenched tightly by his sides. 'That's how you found out where we lived and where Tania worked, wasn't it, you crazy little pervert? And when you had got all you wanted, you simply gave Kitty a nice little cocktail to blow her mind, just in case she blabbed about you to someone.'

Challow smiled, and slowly shook his head. 'Oh dear, Mr Dexter, you are in a state tonight, aren't you?' he mocked, standing his ground. 'Delusions like that could get you put away, you know.'

Dexter grabbed the front of his overalls tightly. 'The only one who's going to get put away is you, Challow,' he snarled. 'And this time there'll be no reprieve, I'll make bloody sure of it!'

'That's enough, Mike,' Mary snapped, grabbing his arm again and pulling his hand away. 'I think you had better go.'

Cater stepped forward quickly, his anxiety about the situation clearly apparent. 'Come on, sir,' he said. 'I'll drop you back to your car at the nick.'

Challow laughed again. 'Yes, Michael, and while you're about it, why not make an appointment to see a psychiatrist?' he goaded. 'The strain of being married to a screwball like Tania is getting to you.'

The force of Dexter's fist in his face sent Challow stumbling backwards and a loud gasp exploded from his lungs as he slammed into a stack of wooden pallets a few feet behind him. But there was a

174

triumphant smirk on his face, despite the blood spurting from one nostril, as he groggily straightened up again. 'That will cost you, *Mr Dexter*,' he gasped, pulling out a handkerchief and holding it to his nose, 'that will cost you dearly.'

As if to reinforce his point, two more figures chose that moment to arrive on the scene at a run. One of them was Tommy Lee and the other a thin hatchet-faced woman with straggly black hair and horn-rimmed spectacles who had the stamp of social worker all over her.

'What on earth is going on here?' the woman rapped, rushing straight to Challow's side and putting her arm round his shoulders. 'You okay, Alan? I was on my way home when Tommy rang me. It's a dammed good job he did.'

'Absolute disgrace,' Tommy Lee exclaimed, glaring at Dexter. 'Totally unprovoked assault, that was. You're for the high jump over this, mate, you know that, don't you?'

Dexter came to his senses with a cold feeling in the pit of his stomach as his anger subsided and the enormity of what he had just done dawned on him. 'Just keep him away from my wife,' he muttered, 'or I won't be responsible for the consequences.'

'Time to be going, Mike,' Mary hissed in his ear, 'and I mean *now*!'

'Come on, governor,' Cater growled. 'Let's get you back.'

'Governor?' Tommy Lee echoed. 'Do you mean to say this man is a senior police officer?'

Challow gave another hard laugh. 'Oh he's senior all right,' he retorted. 'Very senior, in fact. This is Chief Inspector Mike Dexter, Tommy, the force's PRO. He and I go back a long way, don't we, Michael?'

'Ignore him,' Mary warned softly as Dexter's fists clenched a second time and she pushed him roughly in the general direction of the door. 'Just walk.'

For once Dexter didn't argue. He could feel the fury once more rising inside him and knew he was in enough trouble already, without adding to it.

'Give my regards to the lovely Tania, won't you, Michael?' Challow called after him.

'Walk!' Mary repeated grimly.

'Flagrant police brutality,' the social worker added. 'Your chief constable will be hearing from my director over this.'

'I bet he will,' Mary snapped as she pushed Dexter through the

175

door and out into the car park. 'Congratulations, Mike, you've really done it this time, haven't you?'

'Sorry, Mary,' Dexter muttered, half-turning. 'I just lost it.'

She snorted. 'Oh you lost it all right, big time.' She nodded towards the BMW traffic car, which was just pulling away again with a grim-faced Robin Cater back behind the wheel. 'And it looks like you've lost your lift as well.'

He sighed heavily. 'Can't say as I blame him. He did me a favour bringing me here and I let him down badly.'

'You let us *both* down badly,' she corrected, heading for her own car. 'What you just did in there was inexcusable and I hope they hang you out to dry for it.'

He nodded grimly. 'Oh I'm sure they'll manage that, Mary. But in the meantime, can you run me back to Gilstone nick?'

She threw open the door of the CID car and ducked inside. 'Why don't you try walking?' she retorted, slamming the door shut again and starting the engine. 'It might clear your head.'

He stepped back quickly as she pulled away with a crunching of gears and a swirl of gravel, but then, a few yards further on, her brake lights came on again and she poked her head out of the window. 'Okay, so get in. I've carried enough arseholes in this car in the past, so I suppose one more won't make any difference.'

The journey back to Gilstone was completed in absolute silence. Neither of the two old colleagues could think of anything worthwhile to say. Both were well aware of the gravity of the situation and they knew that no amount of conversation would improve things. But pulling into the back yard of the police station, Dexter felt compelled to make one final point. 'Don't stick your neck out on my account, Mary,' he said quietly, staring at a couple of uniformed bobbies going in the back door of the building. 'I hit him and you're going to have to say that when you're interviewed.'

She didn't answer, but simply sat there, staring straight ahead. Frowning, he peered into her face and saw that her cheeks were wet and glistening in the car park lights.

'Tears, Mary?' he queried softly. 'Not you, surely?'

She turned her head towards him. 'You bloody fool, Mike,' she whispered. 'You must be looking at a charge of assault occasioning actual bodily harm at the very least and if Challow's nose turns out to be broken, it could be grievous bodily harm. They could throw the key away on this one.'

'Don't you think I realise that?'

'Then why the hell did you do it? You must have seen that he was deliberately trying to goad you.'

He fell back in his seat, shaking his head. 'I don't know,' he said wearily, 'really I don't. Maybe after all that's happened in the last few days something just snapped.'

In her frustration she hammered the steering wheel several times with her closed fists. 'But he's won now, don't you see that?' she blazed. 'If you had just kept out of things, I might have been able to get somewhere with him, but after this little episode, I'll be lucky if I'm still on the investigation in twenty-four hours.'

He grunted. 'I doubt whether they'll take you off the investigation just because of what *I've* done, especially as you've been doing so well on it up until now.'

She stared at him for a moment, then gave an incredulous laugh. 'Doing so well? You've got to be joking. I've got a stiff who might or might not have been murdered, a car that might or might not have had its brake pipe cut and a psycho who might or might not be involved somewhere along the line. I haven't got a single solid fact to go on. My governor's really going to appreciate my efforts when I dump this little lot in his lap and recommend a full murder enquiry, isn't he?'

'I think you'll find you've got a lot more than you appreciate?'

'Like what for instance?'

'Well, to start with, Eddie Challow's photograph and the name of the boat he's living on were in the back of Fuller's notebook. That in itself suggests Quentin was following up an enquiry on him.'

'So I arrest him on the strength of that, do I?'

Dexter scowled. 'Just listen, will you. There's some other bits you may not know about. Robin Cater tells me that a bus driver has come forward to say that immediately before the fatal at Gilstone, he saw Fuller's Merc race out of Bottom Lane from the direction of Maple Bucksters with some sort of scrambler type motorcycle chasing after it.'

Mary's eyes narrowed. 'Go on.'

'Eddie Challow's boat is moored near Maple Bucksters. That's too much of a coincidence.'

'And you're suggesting Challow may have been the motorcyclist?'

'I'm positive he was.'

'But we don't know if Challow even has a motorcycle?'

He nodded firmly. 'After my enquiries this afternoon, we do. The manager of Kitty Morrison's gym told me that Salter, alias Eddie Challow, who was evidently the current man in her life, rode a scrambler type motorcycle. It all fits, Mary, and don't forget that the biker who clobbered me at Berwick's house was riding a trials machine, which is quite similar to a scrambler. This indicates a link between Challow and the murders, not only of Quentin Fuller and Kitty Morrison, but Lionel Berwick as well.'

'So, do we have an index number?'

He frowned. 'Well, no, not as far as I'm aware, but it's still an important link, and a quick visit to Challow's boat will soon establish whether he has a bike parked nearby.'

'And what if he has? That still doesn't put him in the frame. Lots of people have scrambler or trials bikes.'

He gave a short exasperated sigh. 'Okay, so what about the camera that's been recovered? I gather two kids hoicked Fuller's SLR out of the Mid-Shires Canal this afternoon and where they found it wasn't a million miles from Maple Bucksters either?'

'That's true enough, but again, what does it prove? So someone nicked it from his car, then panicked and tossed it into the canal? That sort of thing happens to stolen property every day.'

'But I understand there was no film in it?'

'So?'

'Doesn't that strike you as strange?'

'Of course it does. I've never known a pressman carry an empty camera around before.'

'And what have you deduced from that?'

She snorted. 'Deduced? Who do you think you are? *Sherlock Holmes*?'

His mouth tightened. 'I'm trying to help you, Mary.'

'Help?' she echoed ruefully. 'Well, after the sort of help you've given me this afternoon, forgive me if I don't take up the offer.'

'Concentrate!' he snapped. 'If the film was missing, then it suggests that someone could have removed it and if they did that, then maybe, just maybe, there was something on it that they didn't want anyone else to see.'

She sighed. 'Don't you think that that thought has already occurred to me? But since I don't actually have the film, it's all pretty academic anyway.'

He dug into his pocket. 'Well, maybe I *do*.'

For a moment she simply stared at the little spool in the palm of his hand without saying a word. Then very gingerly she took it from him and held it up in the interior light. 'Where did you get this?' she breathed.

He hesitated. 'It was found under one of the seats of the Merc by the mechanic who collected the car after the smash. He gave it to me to hand in.'

'And you've hung on to it ever since, without saying anything to anyone?'

He shrugged. 'I only got it when I went to see Fuller's car at the garage this afternoon. I meant to put it with all his other property, but I've been rather preoccupied in the last few hours, in case you hadn't noticed.'

She shook her head in disbelief. 'But it could contain vital evidence.'

He nodded. 'Or maybe just wedding photographs, who knows? I'll leave it with you anyway.'

She pocketed the film, still shaking her head. 'I'll have to put it in the internal despatch bag for Headquarters Photographic before I go home. Maybe they can do a quick developing job for me when they get in tomorrow morning.' She studied him critically. 'But you really are a prat for not producing this sooner. What do I say to the boss about how I came by it?'

'Tell him the truth.'

'That will do you a power of good on top of everything else, won't it?'

He opened the car door and climbed out into the chilly night air. 'In for a penny, as they say,' he replied, leaning momentarily on the door frame to stare in at her. Maybe when my prosecution file goes to CPS, I'll have this taken into consideration with that GBH you mentioned, eh?'

She ignored the dig. 'Call me when you get home,' she said firmly, also getting out of the car. 'Will you do that?'

He didn't answer, but instead, turned towards his battered Volvo parked a couple of empty bays away. 'Thanks for the lift, Mary,' he said as he slipped behind the wheel. 'Don't forget to put that film in.'

Then he was reversing from his parking space and swinging out through the exit with a double flash of his brake-lights, leaving her standing in the middle of the car park staring after him. 'At least you'll be home before me,' she murmured ruefully, finally heading for the back door of the police station.

But she was wrong about that, for Dexter had only driven a few hundred yards down the road before the shrill of his mobile forced him to pull into a convenient lay-by to answer it. According to the illuminated display, the caller was someone in the Headquarters Press Office and he felt more than a twinge of apprehension as he grunted a reluctant acknowledgement.

'That you, governor?' John Durrell's familiar voice queried sharply.

Dexter felt his stomach drop with the force of a runaway lift. There was something in the ex-skipper's tone that warned him to expect the worst.

'Who else would it be?' he snapped back.

Durrell sighed heavily down the phone. 'Sorry, gov, but there's big *trouble at mill.* 'I was just about to go home and was told to get hold of you pronto.'

'ACC Ops again?' he hazarded a guess.

There was an affirmative grunt. 'Not a happy man, gov,' he went on. 'And he wants to see you – like yesterday.'

'That's our Mr Parkes.'

'There was a pause and Durrell's breathing faded for a moment. Dexter visualised the old sweat peering cautiously behind him. Then he was back. 'Listen, Mike,' he said, suddenly getting personal, 'some really heavy shit is going down, I can tell, and Sarah's just come out of the boss's office with a grin on her chops that looks like it might decapitate her.'

Dexter scowled. If Sarah's grin had anything to do with him, that really was bad news. 'On my way, John,' he said wearily, 'and thanks.'

'Best of luck, gov,' came back softly. 'I hate to say it, but I think you'll need plenty this time.'

★

There was a white mask-like expression on Dick Lawson's face when he returned to his office shortly after his run-in with Brian Moffat. As a rule, he was not the type of person who sought confrontation or easily lost his temper, preferring to settle disagreement through reasoned discussion and persuasion rather than resorting to anger. In fact, it was often a source of wonder to him how someone with his quiet reserved nature had actually managed to get as far as he had in an organisation like the police, where confrontation was such an integral part of the culture. But if he was normally slow to anger, he was certainly angry now – though more so with himself for his weakness in not speaking out sooner than with his boss for his usual pig-headed arrogance.

To be honest, he had known right from the start that the Berwick murder investigation was not being handled properly; that the machinations of internal politics had already compromised the investigative process. But for what he now recognised as selfish career reasons, he had avoided making waves, keeping his feelings of unease to himself and ignoring people like Mike Dexter, who had tried to get him to stand up and be counted.

Well, things were about to change dramatically. With or without Moffat's approval, he was going to do some investigations of his own. In fact, he was determined to get to the truth, even if that did mean he wouldn't make superintendent before he retired, and he was still trying to decide the best way to go about it when the telephone rang and made the decision for him.

'Dick?' the deep rasping voice queried at the other end of the line. 'It's Eric Carnell.'

Lawson grimaced, visualising the force's fat little Welfare Officer shoe-horned behind his desk, one podgy hand no doubt dipping into a paper bag of fudge or cream toffees as per usual. The last thing he needed now was a protracted conversation with the garrulous Yorkshireman about the death of some police pensioner who had retired from the force when he was still at school. 'Yes, Eric,' he said wearily 'So who's gone to the angels this time?'

There was a throaty chuckle and almost immediately afterwards, the distinctive tell-tale rustle of a paper bag. Lawson couldn't stop himself smiling in spite of the unwelcome call. 'Ey, lad,' Carnell retorted, apparently with his mouth full. 'That's a bit unkind. I'm not always the bearer of bad news.'

Lawson leaned back in his chair and lit a cigarette, knowing from past experience that this could be a long call. 'Okay, so you're ringing up to tell me I've won the Force Lottery, eh?' he replied. 'If that's it, then the answer is no, you can't have any of it, okay?'

Another chuckle, which ended abruptly, and then Eric was serious again. 'Andy Pollard,' he said, digesting whatever it was he had been eating.

Lawson raised his eyebrows, remembering his old boss with affection. He'd had great times working with him on CID, probably the best he'd had in his whole career, and he didn't really want to hear what he felt sure Carnell was about to tell him. 'So he's popped his clogs too, has he?' he said, deciding to get it over with.

Carnell seemed surprised at his question. 'Not unless you know more than me, Dick,' he replied. 'Last time I went to see him was about a week ago and he was well enough then.'

Lawson breathed a sigh of relief, then abruptly frowned. 'So why the call? I haven't seen Andy since his retirement do which has to be around twenty years ago.'

Carnell grunted. 'Aye, he told me he'd sort of lost contact with everyone. That's why I was a mite curious about your call today.'

'*My* call?'

'Yes, a couple of hours ago, when you rang Debbie Carrington.'

'Debbie who?'

'Debbie Carrington, my secretary.'

Lawson started to say something, but, true to form, Carnell was already off at a gallop and didn't give him a chance. 'When she mentioned it to me,' he went on loudly, 'I thought, 'ey, lad, better have a word with old Dick Lawson, see what's to do. Andy's had a bit of a rough time lately, see. Ginny, his wife, left him for a younger model about two months ago and he's also had, well, a few financial difficulties. Been trying to help him over it all. You know, providing a shoulder and all that –'

'Eric!' In desperation, Lawson shouted down the phone, cutting him off in mid flow. 'Will you please let me get a word in? I haven't phoned your secretary today or any other day. Got it?'

'But you rang her not an hour since, asking for his address.'

'And why would I do that? I already know where Andy Pollard lives. He wrote to several of his old team a few weeks back, suggesting we had a reunion, and I've still got his address and telephone number.'

There was a short stunned silence. Lawson could practically hear Carnell's heart doing cart-wheels and when the welfare man spoke again, his voice was anxious and hesitant 'But – but, Dick, Debbie says that, in line with normal procedure, she rang you back on your own Headquarters extension to confirm your ID before giving out the information, and you were there in your office waiting for the call.'

'In my office?' Lawson frowned again. 'But that's impossible. I've been at Bellingham nick on the Berwick murder enquiry all day.'

There was a sharp intake of breath down the phone. 'Bloody Nora, Dick, if it wasn't you, then who the hell –'

'*Shit!*' The truth hit Lawson with almost physical force and he left his chair as if propelled from an ejector seat. Heedless of Carnell's voice calling after him from the telephone, which he left swinging on its cord over the edge of the desk, he sprinted off down the corridor, heading for the stairs, one hand trying to free the car ignition keys trapped in the lining of his pocket as he ran and a taut sick feeling deep in the pit of his stomach.

Detective Superintendent Andy Pollard had retired from the force just weeks after successfully wrapping up the last major crime investigation of his career and he had left the job a contented man. But what he hadn't known at the time, and Lawson knew now, was that the ghost of that last investigation would follow him deep into retirement and re-surface with a vengeance twenty years later, for the man he had been responsible for sending down was none other than Eddie Challow.

Incredible as it seemed, Challow must not only have had the audacity to walk straight into Police Headquarters and phone the Welfare Department from Lawson's own office, but also the balls to actually remain there until Debbie Carrington had rung him back with the information he wanted – and it didn't take the brain of *Hercule Poirot* to deduce what he wanted that information for. Lawson could only pray that he got to his old governor first.

*

Assistant Chief Constable Dennis Stanford Parkes should have been angry, very angry, but from the look of him, he could no longer muster the energy and he waved an arm towards the chair in front of his desk with the weary gesture of someone twenty years his senior. 'You damned fool, Michael,' he murmured as Dexter sat down. 'You stupid damned fool!'

Dexter was surprised to detect a fleeting expression of what looked very much like sympathy in those normally cold blue eyes. 'You've heard then, have you, sir?' he said quietly.

Parkes grunted and sat forward in his chair, his elbows resting on the desk as he studied him over steepled fingers. 'When I told John Durrell to get you in here, it was as a result of a complaint I'd received from a certain Dr Watson,' he went on without answering the question, 'and after all the previous complaints I'd had about you from Detective Superintendent Moffat, I fully intended posting you to Headquarters Control Room where you could do no more harm. But that was before a certain Tommy Lee rang the Control Room regarding your latest exploits.'

'Sorry, sir,' Dexter replied lamely. 'I'm afraid I lost my rag.'

Parkes stared at him. 'You lost your *what*?' he exclaimed. 'For heavens sake, man, you shouldn't even have been talking to Eddie Challow, let alone losing your rag with him. Beats me how you managed to find out where he was living in the first place.'

Dexter's face hardened. 'I can answer that, sir,' he said quietly.

Parkes straightened up in the chair and waved him to silence. 'I don't want to hear it,' he snapped. 'There's an official investigation into the business now and I shouldn't be discussing this with you at all.'

Dexter leaned forward. 'You don't understand, sir,' he went on earnestly. 'My late press assistant, Kitty Morrison, was supposed to have committed suicide, but –'

'Enough!' Parkes blazed, snatching off his spectacles to glare at him. 'I said I didn't want to hear anymore about it and I meant it. If you have anything to say, you can save it for the investigating officer, is that clear?'

He took a deep breath, plainly annoyed with himself for losing control. 'Take some leave, Michael,' he muttered, replacing his glasses and pulling some papers out of a filing tray to hide his discomfort. 'Sort yourself out, eh? I've appointed Sarah Hamilton-Lancing to deputise for you while you're away.'

Dexter grimaced. 'Are you suspending me then, sir?' he queried.

Parkes shuffled his papers and shook his head. 'It's not my place at this stage,' he said, avoiding his stare. 'Detective Superintendent, Les Angel, has already been appointed to investigate this sorry affair and doubtless he will be interviewing you once he has seen the complainant and assessed his injuries. A decision will be made about your future when the full facts are known.'

Dexter smiled bitterly. 'You mean suspension comes later?' he commented.

Parkes' face darkened and the spark of anger was back in his eyes. 'No, Chief Inspector,' he snapped, glaring at him again. '*Prison* probably comes later. Now just – just get out!'

Dexter felt strangely numb as he left the office and closed the door behind him. None of what was happening seemed to be real. It was all like a bad dream and as he tramped down the stone staircase to the lower floor, all he could think of was what he was going to tell Tania.

The Press Office was in darkness when he walked through to his own inner sanctum – everyone had gone home, which was hardly surprising considering the time – but the electronic news monitor still churned out its never-ending stream of messages with its familiar irritating metallic chatter, drowning even the sound of the small television behind his desk, which someone had inadvertently left on. Turning the television off, Dexter slumped into his chair and sat there for a few moments, staring into space.

'Prison comes later.' Parkes' parting words mocked him from inside his head. 'They could throw the key away on this one,' Mary Lane's voice joined in. He shuddered, seeing in his mind's eye the grey cell, with its narrow bunk bed and tiny reinforced glass window; hearing the booming crash of heavy iron doors closing one after the other along a narrow corridor; smelling the sickly-sweet odour of stale cooking and the overpowering stench of male sweat and unflushed toilets. An involuntary gasp escaped his lips and, jerking open the right-hand drawer of his desk, he reached for the whisky bottle he had earlier shared with Dick Lawson. But even as his fingers closed round the slender neck, the mobile in his pocket shrilled.

'Michael?' a woman's voice at the other end exclaimed.

He frowned. 'Aunt Mildred?'

'Yes, dear. I'm sorry to ring you, but you did give me this number in case –'

'Yes, yes,' he snapped, closing his eyes tightly for a second in an involuntary gesture of irritation. 'What is it?'

'Well, it's Tania, dear. I'm afraid she's had a bit of an accident.'

His blood ran cold. 'An accident?' he repeated hoarsely.

'Yes dear. She's been taken to Heaton General Hospital.'

Chapter 13

It was a good hour before Dick Lawson turned on to the brilliantly lit promenade of the small seaside town where Andy Pollard had made his home and headed in the direction of the pier. He should have alerted the local police, he realised that now, especially as he was in another police force's area. But his natural copper's reticence had won the day and he had decided to follow up his hunch on his own, rather than send the balloon up and feel a fool afterwards.

He found the place he was looking for more by accident than anything else. It was one of a long terrace of Victorian-style tenements that someone had had the bright idea of turning into hotels and the sign in the single window said "Vacancies". The front door was not locked and there were lights on in the foyer as he stepped inside, but no one responded when he struck the bell on the counter with the palm of his hand. 'Andy?' he called, turning to peer along the empty corridor which struck off into the darkness to his right. Silence, but for the muffled sound of the sea on the other side of the promenade.

He frowned and, beginning to regret his decision to go it alone, he lifted the flap on the counter and went through into the tiny lighted office at the back. It was empty, but a lukewarm cup of coffee on the desk and the *Windows* design on the computer screen beside it suggested that someone had been there not too long ago.

He returned to the corridor and listened intently. A coach lumbered noisily past on the promenade and as its engine faded into the distance, the rumble of the sea returned, but otherwise there wasn't a sound. 'Andy?' he called again, but there was still no response.

His frown deepened and, locating a switch, he flooded the corridor in front of him with pale opalescent light. For the first time he glimpsed a low archway with stairs dropping away into the darkness. He approached the stairs and peered into the gloom, immediately detecting a strong stale beer smell, mixed with the odour of yesterday's fries. A sign on the wall beside his head, bearing the

186

words "Restaurant & Bar", pointed downwards, but he turned back into the foyer, his instinct persuading him to take the ascending staircase to the right of the reception counter instead.

He found himself in a fully carpeted corridor with solid white numbered doors opening off on both sides and a single glass door at the far end, equipped with a horizontal metal bar and the familiar illuminated "Emergency Exit" sign. There was not a soul to be seen and, after calling Andy's name again and receiving no response, he tried one or two of the doors. They all proved to be unlocked, but he discovered only empty bedrooms on the other side, with beds neatly made up for the guests who had never arrived. The whole place had an air of neglect about it and he could now detect an unpleasant smell that grew stronger and stronger as he headed along the corridor towards the emergency exit door.

At first he couldn't put his finger on what it was, for there were so many different odours wafting about the old building that separating one from another was almost impossible and his initial thought was that it came from some sort of powerful cleaning fluid, maybe used to clean the carpets or de-scale the toilets. In fact, it wasn't until he reached the end of the corridor and started up a third and final staircase, ignoring the "Private" sign screwed to the banister post, that realisation suddenly dawned on him. It wasn't carpet or toilet cleaner that he could smell, but petrol!

In a second his cautious ascent had turned into a panic-driven rush, as he went for the stairs two at a time, powering himself up the steep incline towards the small brown door at the top with the stamina of an athlete in the final stages of a pentathlon.

His last recollection was of jerking the door wide and staring for just a micro of a second into the fiery seething maw of hell as an enormous blast simultaneously lifted him off his feet and propelled him back down the stairs engulfed in flames.

*

It took Mike Dexter nearly forty-five minutes in heavy slow-moving traffic to get to Heaton Hospital, only to find on his arrival that the big pay and display public car park was completely full and that he had to drive all the way round the hospital's meandering one-way system simply to return to his starting point. In desperation he abandoned his Volvo in a clearly marked prohibited waiting area close to the main entrance and sprinted the few yards to A & E.

His problems didn't end once he was through the big double doors, however. Half the population of Heaton seemed to be milling about in the large reception area and each time he found a member of staff to speak to, someone else caught their eye first. Near to exploding with frustration, he finally managed to buttonhole a harassed looking staff nurse, which resulted in him being immediately whisked to the head of the reception desk queue, but even then he was simply directed to a seat with the words 'Dr Jamieson will be with you shortly.'

Predictably, the estimate 'shortly' stretched to over half an hour and when the diminutive little Scotsman finally appeared in his rumpled white coat, his bland smile only served to inflame Dexter even more. 'What the hell's going on?' Dexter blazed, jumping to his feet the moment Jamieson introduced himself. 'My wife –'

'Your wife is fine, Mr Dexter,' the other said quickly, raising both hands in front of him in a calming gesture. 'She had a bit of a fall, that's all, but I'm sure she'll be okay.'

'A fall?'

Jamieson nodded. 'Yes, it seems she experienced some sort of blackout whilst at the home of a Mrs Harptree – her aunt, I believe – and hit her head on the corner of a stone hearth.'

'A blackout? What kind of a blackout?'

Jamieson pursed his lips and shrugged. 'Difficult to say at this stage, Mr Dexter. All we know is that she was brought in here with a head injury after a fall.'

'But you say she's going to be okay?'

'As far as we can tell, yes. Bit of concussion there and she's obviously in a state of shock, but I don't think there are any bones broken.'

Dexter thrust out his jaw aggressively. 'Where is she? I want to see her.'

Jamieson shook his head. 'I would rather you didn't at present,' he replied firmly. 'She's in X-ray just now and we'd like to do a few other tests on her first, just to make sure everything is okay.'

'And then?'

'Well, it's likely that we'll be keeping her in overnight for observation, just as a precaution, you understand, nothing more than that. So why don't you grab yourself a cup of tea and a sandwich from somewhere, then come back again in' (and he consulted his wrist-watch) 'say, a couple of hours? You can leave a contact telephone number with us if that eases your mind.'

'I don't want a bloody cup of tea, doctor,' Dexter rasped, controlling himself with an effort. 'I want to see my wife and find out what happened to her.'

Jamieson sighed. 'Believe me, I can understand that, Mr Dexter, but since it's not possible for you to see her just now, maybe you should try and find out from her aunt what happened.'

Dexter nodded grimly. 'Don't worry, Doctor, I fully intend doing that,' he snapped. 'But I shall be back here in an hour and a half anyway, so don't think you've got rid of me for the rest of the night.'

Jamieson gave another bland smile. 'The thought never occurred to me, Mr Dexter,' he replied.

*

Aunt Mildred was a tiny bird-like woman who always put Dexter in mind of Agatha Christie's *Miss Marple* and she hurried down the garden path of her dilapidated cottage to meet him the moment his car drew up outside. 'Oh Michael, thank goodness,' she breathed anxiously. 'How is she?'

'Still undergoing tests,' he replied tightly. 'I wasn't allowed in to see her.' Then suddenly his anger surfaced in a rush. 'What on earth happened here, Aunt Mildred? You said you would look after her.'

She nodded unhappily. 'I know, dear, and I feel awful, but it was the flowers, you see.'

His anger quickly subsided and he frowned. 'Flowers? What are you talking about?'

She sighed and patted him gently on the arm. 'Let's go inside, Michael,' she suggested. 'I'm sure you could do with a nice cup of tea.'

The familiar smell of damp stonework and pot-pourri greeted him as he followed her through the low doorway and the grandmother clock in the living-room beyond immediately chimed its welcome from the shadows beside the fireplace.

'Forget the tea, Aunt Mildred,' he called after her as she headed for the back kitchen. 'Just tell me about these flowers.'

She was gone only briefly, returning with a large bouquet in her hands, which she thrust out towards him as if she thought the flowers were contaminated. He took the bouquet from her curiously, surprised that the flowers had not been removed from their plastic wrapping. She watched him intently. 'White lilies,' she said finally.

'I can see that. So what?'

189

'Tied with black ribbon,' she added. 'It's the sort of thing you send to a funeral.'

He felt his skin prickle unpleasantly. 'And it was addressed to Tania?' he finished for her.

She shook her head and held out a small white card. 'Worse than that,' she said.

'Worse?' He took the card and scanned the message. 'To my dearest Rebecca. RIP,' he read aloud. 'Who the hell's Rebecca?'

'She was Tania's sister,' she answered quietly.

His eyes widened. 'Her *sister*? I never knew she even had a sister.'

She took a deep breath and settled on the edge of an adjacent chair. 'I think you'd better sit down too, Michael,' she replied, indicating a deep armchair opposite. 'There's something you should have been told a long time ago.'

For some reason – perhaps due to the look on her face or the tone of her voice – he didn't argue and sat down immediately.

She fidgeted in her own chair for a moment or two, plucking at her skirt with one tiny hand and staring at the floor, as if she didn't know where to begin.

'You said Tania had a sister?' he encouraged.

She threw him a quick worried glance and nodded. 'Rebecca,' she said again, then hesitated, returning to her skirt plucking.

'And judging by the flowers and your use of the past tense, I take it she's now dead?'

Another sigh. 'Oh yes, she's dead all right, poor little waif. It all happened so long ago, you know.' She raised her head to stare in his direction, but he could see by the look in her eyes that she was not really looking at him, instead focusing on something far more distant, something he wouldn't have been able to see even if he'd turned his head to stare in the same direction. 'They were all living in Essex then,' she went on dreamily. 'Ron, Katherine and the two girls. They had a very expensive Tudor house in the country, not far from Brentwood, and Ron was earning a lot of money on the stock market.'

Dexter grunted several times, impatiently glancing at his watch. 'Can we just get to the point, Aunt Mildred? I've got to get back to the hospital.'

She started and the dreamy look left her face immediately, to be replaced once more by a troubled frown. 'Tania would have been about seven when it happened,' she explained. 'She was five years younger than Rebecca –'

'When what happened?' he cut in. 'When Rebecca died, you mean?'

She nodded again. 'Everyone said it was the convent school that made her do it. Stress, they said. Too much discipline, too much old-style religion. You know, fire and brimstone, that sort of thing. She was a bit of a live wire, you see – always fighting against authority – so, I suppose, they had to hold her on a short leash.'

'Are you saying the kid took her own life?'

She stared at him levelly. 'Hung herself, Michael, that's what she did. Hung herself from a beam in the old barn at the back of the house. It was Tania who found her.'

'Tania *found her*?' He closed his eyes for a second. 'At seven years old? Good grief, that's obscene.'

Mildred eased herself back into her chair, gripping both arms tightly. 'She doted on Rebecca,' she went on. 'Finding her like that nearly destroyed her. She lost the power of speech for almost a year and, but for the care and support of the Holy Sisters, I dread to think what would have become of her.'

'Holy Sisters?' he echoed. 'Do you mean to tell me that her mother had her shut away in a convent?'

Mildred pressed her lips together tightly. 'You have to understand that Katherine was very religious,' she said finally. 'Tania was already going to the convent's day school and Katherine thought that by boarding her there, she would be able to ensure that she got the care and religious direction she needed.'

Dexter thought of the cold stone walls and echoing corridors of a monastery he had once visited in France and shuddered. 'What, you mean like Rebecca?' he said with heavy sarcasm. 'The convent did her a *lot* of good, didn't it?'

The old lady frowned again. 'That wasn't a very kind thing to say, Michael,' she reproved.

'You're probably right, Aunt Mildred,' he said acidly, 'but it so happens that I don't feel particularly kind at the moment, not after the bombshell you've just dropped in my lap. I mean, I may only be Tania's *husband*, but to be kept in the dark about all this for almost twenty years…'

Mildred flinched slightly. 'I didn't like keeping things from you, Michael,' she replied, 'but it wasn't my place to tell. That was up to Tania and as she seemed to have blanked the whole thing from her mind, I didn't see the point in raking it all up again.'

He grunted. 'And if she hadn't ended up in hospital because of those flowers, would you have told me even now?'

She made a wry face. 'Probably not. Some things are best left unsaid. And anyway, even if you had been told, what good would it have done? The flowers would still have been delivered and Tania would still have ended up in hospital.'

He scowled, reluctant to admit that she had a valid argument, but seeing no point in pursuing things any further. 'And the flowers themselves, did you see who delivered them?'

She shook her head. 'Local florist, I believe, but only Tania could tell you that. She answered the door, you see and she'd only just closed it again when she read the card and collapsed.' She hesitated, then added carefully: 'Do you think it could be this man who she says has been hounding her?'

He made a sour grimace. 'I can't see it being anyone else, but heaven knows how he found out about Rebecca when I didn't even know about her myself.' He glanced quickly at his watch, anxious to avoid getting into a lengthy discussion with the old lady about Eddie Challow. 'Anyway, I'd best be off if I'm to get to see Tania at the hospital.'

She stood up, smoothing her skirt with both hands. 'Give her my love, won't you, Michael?' she said.

He nodded, softening a little and studying her carefully. 'Will you be all right here on your own?'

She gave a short laugh. 'I've had to be all right for the past ten years, ever since poor Henry died,' she reminded him, patting him gently on the arm. 'I don't think one more night is going to make that much difference, do you?'

He gave her a quick peck on the cheek. 'You're an inspiration to us all, Aunt Mildred,' he said as he ducked his head through the low doorway, 'an inspiration to us all.'

An inspiration, she may have been, but for all her outward resilience, Mildred Harptree nevertheless made a point of checking that all the doors and windows of her cottage were securely locked before she went to bed that night. Then as she lay on the small double bed and caressed the sheets where her beloved Henry had once lain beside her, she thought of Tania, alone and vulnerable in her hospital bed, and whispered a soft prayer to the dark beamed ceiling.

*

Tania had been given a sedative of some sort and was fast asleep by the time Mike Dexter made it back to Heaton General Hospital. The stern looking staff nurse only reluctantly allowed him in to see her 'for five minutes', but as it turned out, he sat beside her bed for much longer than that, his anxious gaze focused on her drawn white face while his fingers gently stroked the back of her hand.

The scenario gave him a strong sense of déjà vu and his mind flashed back to that other occasion just over twenty years ago when he had sat beside Tania's bed in exactly the same hospital, studying her face as he was studying it now. She had opened her eyes then; deep misty pools that locked on to his for a few brief moments before closing again as she drifted back into her shadow world. Now though, her eyes remained closed as her breasts gently rose and fell with the rhythmic action of deep slumber and it wasn't long before his own eyes started to close as his chin dropped on to his chest.

He awoke two hours later when another staff nurse shook him firmly by the shoulder and politely but firmly sent him on his way. 'Go home and get your head down,' she advised. 'She'll be quite safe with us.'

Reassured, he left the hospital almost with a feeling of relief, gulping down great lungfuls of cold fresh air as he stepped out into the lamplit night.

The air seemed to revive him, but he was still very tired and he found himself continually blinking to clear his vision as he climbed behind the wheel of his Volvo and headed in the direction of home, promising himself a stiff whisky and the biggest cheese sandwich he could put together when he got there. To keep himself awake, he switched on the radio and tuned into the local station, but the dulcet tones of the female presenter, coupled with the snatches of soft mood music she insisted on playing, soon had exactly the opposite effect. The fatal fixed stare that all motorists come to know and dread at some stage in their driving experience preceded short bouts of head nodding, until finally his chin dropped on to his chest again as he drifted off into the deceptively comfortable world of all embracing velvet shadows.

Pulsing blue lights in his face, loud shouts and the screech of tyres on the wet road as his foot instinctively slammed the brake pedal to the floor, brought him back to reality with a panic-stricken infusion of burning adrenalin and he spun the steering wheel hard right to avoid the police Land Rover slewed halfway across the road in front of him.

The Volvo narrowly missed the front of the vehicle and came to an abrupt halt with its front wheels embedded in the soft verge on the opposite side of the road.

Then the drivers door was being yanked open and rough hands were hauling him out of the vehicle as the powerful beams of at least three flashlights blazed through the windscreen with the force of space-age lasers. 'You bastard,' a voice yelled in his face, 'You filthy drunken bastard!'

Then he was on his back in the grass and something (maybe a closed fist or a hand-lamp) had hit him hard in the face, sending his senses reeling.

'Get off him,' an authoritative voice barked. 'Get off him *now!*'

The heavy press of bodies fell back and someone helped him to his feet as another flashlight played on his face. 'Bugger me!' a familiar voice exclaimed. 'It's Chief Inspector Dexter.'

Dexter fell back against the wing of his car and felt his cheekbone tenderly, conscious of the blue light pulsing in the darkness behind him. 'You dickheads,' he grated, angrily pushing one of the flashlights down with his other hand so that the beam was directed at his feet instead of into his face.

'For Pete's sake, governor,' the same familiar voice exclaimed, 'what were you at? You nearly mowed us down.'

Dexter shielded his eyes and snatching the flashlight from the dark figure in front of him, directed the beam on the face of the speaker. In the harsh cold glare Sergeant Cater's face looked like that of a corpse.

'Sorry, skipper,' Dexter mumbled, 'I – er – must have nodded off.'

'You did that all right, sir,' Cater growled. 'By rights I should get you to give us a blow.'

Dexter leant his head back against the roof of the car. 'Go ahead,' he replied weakly. 'You won't find anything. I haven't been drinking; I'm just worn out, that's all.'

Cater hesitated, then abruptly turned on the uniforms behind him. 'Okay you lot, show's over. Back to where you were – and I mean like *today!*'

Dexter felt the perspiration mixing with the steady drizzle streaming down his face into his shirt collar. For a few seconds he closed his eyes and just let it soak into him. Cater's hand was on his arm now. 'Come on, governor,' he said gently. 'Nice cup of coffee would do you good. My car's just over there.'

Slumped in the passenger seat of the big traffic car, Dexter took the cup of the flask in both hands and gulped down the hot sweet liquid as if he were dying of thirst. 'Don't worry, governor,' Cater said with a dry chuckle, 'you won't catch anything from my cup. I ain't got AIDS no more.'

Dexter managed a faint smile. 'You must think I'm a prize prat,' he said bitterly. 'First an ABH on Eddie Challow and now this.'

'Not my place to make judgements, governor,' Cater replied. 'I just hate to see a good man destroying himself bit by bit like he's got some sort of self-inflicted cancer.'

Dexter nodded and returned the cup to him. 'Wife's in hospital,' he replied. 'Just come from there –' He broke off and cast the traffic man a sidelong glance. 'Ever felt like there's a gremlin on your back, Robin, turning the screw tighter and tighter and laughing at you as he does it?'

Cater shrugged. 'You know what they say, gov,' he replied. 'Life's a bitch and then you die. Now, I think we'd better get you home, eh? One of my lads will run you there.'

Dexter shook his head firmly and straightened his shoulders. 'No need, skip,' he replied. 'I'm okay now.' He peered through the windscreen as the two white-capped traffic officers in front of the bonnet flagged down a heavy lorry and strolled across to speak to the driver. For the first time he saw that the road he had been following was coned off and a police accident unit was parked just beyond the cones, its retractable mast erect and its powerful floodlights creating a huge white circle in the road. 'So, what's going on here?' he queried, as the traffic men talking to the lorry driver stepped back and watched the big artic swing hard right into the mouth of another road with the hiss of airbrakes and the protesting groan of its trailer coupling. 'You should have been off hours ago.'

Cater grunted. 'Yeah, well that'll teach me to *go* home next time, won't it?' he replied. 'Decided to finish off some paperwork, see, and then it was too late. Two fatals tied up the night skippers and then this happened.'

Dexter glanced around him. 'And what exactly is *this*?' he queried.

There was the rasp of a match and Cater's gaunt face was briefly illuminated as the car began to fill up with smoke. 'Stag's Corner Filling Station,' he growled. 'Poor buggers got hit about two hours ago.'

'Hit?'

Cater briefly turned on the ignition and operated the buttons in his armrest to open the electric windows. 'Yeah, but not your normal blagging,' he replied, throwing him a sideways glance. 'They were taking a delivery of fuel at the time – big ERF tanker fresh out of TQ International's Grange Depot near Heaton on a multiple delivery. Thirty-five thousand litres on board. Some bastard with a shotgun blasted the attendant in the kiosk and nicked the tanker before it could unload.'

'Nicked it?'

'I said it wasn't your normal blagging, didn't I? Driver was pitched out the cab as it drove off and ended up under the trailer wheels. He was spread along the road for around a quarter of a mile, I gather. That's why we've closed this section off. SOCO are all over the place.'

Dexter shuddered at the vivid image his description had conjured up. 'Poor devil,' he muttered. 'But what about the garage man?'

'ICU at Heaton Hospital. Only a fifty-fifty chance apparently.'

'And the tanker?'

Cater shrugged. 'Disappeared.'

'You're joking?'

'I know it sounds daft, but that's the strength of it. Trouble is, we were a bit slow off the mark. Roadblocks weren't all in place until forty minutes after the garage was hit, so the damned thing could have gone anywhere.'

'But a flaming tanker? It's not exactly inconspicuous, is it? What about X-ray One-Four?'

'What, the force chopper? They got it up in twenty minutes, which has to be a record for the Air Support Unit, but it didn't even get a sniff.'

Dexter was fully awake now. 'So why wasn't I told about this? Bloody hell, man, the press will be all over you soon.'

Cater stubbed out his cigarette in the ashtray, avoiding his gaze. 'Sorry, gov,' he muttered gruffly, his embarrassment almost tangible. 'ACC Ops' instructions. Sarah – er – Hamilton-Lancing has been called out instead.'

'Sarah?' For a moment Dexter gaped at him, his mind sluggishly trying to come to terms with what he had just been told. 'They've moved Sarah in over me?' Then abruptly his shoulders sagged and he fell back in his seat, totally deflated. 'I might have known it,' he said bitterly. 'They just couldn't wait, could they?'

Cater didn't answer him, but retrieved his flat cap from the top of the instrument console and pushed his door open, wearily climbing out of the car. Then, almost as an afterthought, he turned to poke his head back inside. 'Go home, gov,' he said quietly. 'There's nothing you can do here and I'd feel a lot happier if you were on your way.'

Dexter swung his own door wide and joined him on the roadside. 'A lot happier if I was out of your hair, you mean?' he sniped across the roof. 'Anyway, thanks, Robin, I owe you one.'

The traffic man gave a grim smile. 'Just don't fall asleep at the wheel this time, gov,' he said. 'The next *Black Rat* you meet may not be quite so understanding, eh?'

In fact, sleep was the last thing on Dexter's mind as he drove back through the twisting moonlit lanes. Having suffered the ultimate in wake-up calls after his near collision with the police Land Rover, he couldn't have felt more wide-awake. Furthermore, the double humiliation of losing control of his car in front of half a dozen of his more junior colleagues, then finding out third-hand that Assistant Chief Constable Operations had already made good his threat and replaced him as force PRO with his own conniving deputy, gave his tortured brain all the unwelcome stimulation that was necessary.

He arrived home in a state of high tension; desperately worried about Tania, fearful for his future and nursing not only a deep resentment towards everyone and everything around him, but, most of all, a sense of absolute self-loathing.

His outlook on life didn't improve when he finally swung in through his gateway either. The tall chimneys and ornate crown of the house's steep tiled roof were back-lit by a mushrooming red glare, as if a fiery hole had been punched in the night sky. At first sight, it looked as though the woods behind the house were ablaze, but as he threw the car door open and scrambled out on to the shingled driveway that was already filling up with curious neighbours, the truth dawned on him with sickening clarity. The fire wasn't among the trees at all, but well beyond them on the far side of the two-acre field.

'My God, Gwenda,' he shouted hoarsely at the figures milling around his car. 'That filthy psycho's torched the barn!'

Then he had shouldered them aside and was charging recklessly down the track at the side of the house, skidding and sliding in the same mud he had ploughed through once before, knowing that this time the emergency was for real, but the likelihood was that he was already too late.

Chapter 14

'Seems like some kind of timed incendiary device was used, governor,' Detective Sergeant Jim Chalmers growled. 'Fire service found some bits of what looked like a clock in the debris and we're just waiting for Scenes of Crime to turn up to do the necessary.'

Dexter stared at the blackened remains of the barn in the early dawn light, but said nothing. The cold rising from the frost-hardened ground had already numbed his legs and feet, and he could now feel it creeping insidiously up his insides, despite the heavy uniform overcoat one of the bobbies had draped over his shoulders. It was time to be heading back to the house, time to be thinking about what he was going to tell Tania when he collected her from the hospital; the job he dreaded most of all. Somehow though, he just couldn't tear himself away. He could still smell that awful stench of burning horse flesh. Gwenda hadn't stood a chance. She must have been cremated where she stood and within minutes of the blaze erupting amongst the bales of straw stacked against the wall; cremated like Lionel Berwick and Ron Ferguson all those years before, cremated by a sadistic pyromaniac to whom the torching of live flesh was the greatest aphrodisiac of all.

'This geezer you told me about, gov,' the slight bushy-haired DS said suddenly, half-turning towards him. 'Eddie Challow, wasn't it? You reckon he's a psycho and that he done this?'

Dexter nodded absently, his gaze still focused on the burned-out shell in front of him, shocked and sickened by this latest senseless atrocity and too tired even to reply.

The CID man stuffed some gum into his mouth and began chewing furiously, his eyes moving restlessly as he talked. 'Trouble is, you don't have no real evidence to – like – connect him with the job, do you?'

Dexter's expression was bleak 'He did it all right, you can count on that. Evidence or no evidence.'

The Sergeant's chewing slowed to almost a stop, but his eyes continued to move. 'Yeah, well, as you say, sir,' he said slowly, 'but we can't just go accusing people with nothin' to go on, can we?'

Dexter shook his head. 'Same old long-playing record, eh, Sergeant?' he said, tearing his gaze away from the remains of the barn to cast him a critical sideways glance. 'Was a time when we would feel someone's collar on a lot less than you've got here.'

The other frowned, his gum briefly despatched to the side of his mouth. 'Yeah, well, them time's have changed, gov, you know that. Sus ain't enough anymore.'

Dexter turned away from the barn and headed slowly across the field towards the house. 'Seems to me, Sergeant, that nothing is enough anymore,' he threw back over his shoulder. 'The law's a villain's charter nowadays. Maybe we should go back to the old days of *hue and cry*. At least that got results.'

The detective hurried after him. 'I hope you're not going to do anything you shouldn't, gov,' he cautioned breathlessly. 'That could get you into a whole lot of trouble.'

Dexter gave a short cynical laugh. 'No more than I'm in already, believe me,' he retorted.

Chalmers spat his gum into the frozen grass. 'Listen, gov, if you'll just stop a minute and tell me a bit more about this Eddie Challow geezer, maybe there'll be something in there we could follow up.'

Dexter stopped so suddenly that the other nearly collided with him. 'Just leave it, skipper, will you?' he said testily. 'You won't get anywhere with this thing – you won't be allowed to, believe me – and it's way out of your league anyway. So why don't you go and catch a bike thief or something, along with the rest of the so-called Criminal Investigation Department?'

'That wasn't very fair.' Detective Sergeant Mary Lane confronted Dexter with a reproving frown as Chalmers stormed past her along the woodland track leading to the house.

Dexter was unrepentant. 'Tough,' he retorted, his face darkening appreciably as the anger boiled up inside him. 'You know as well as I do that this is another job that has Eddie Challow's mark all over it. No one will do anything about it, though, will they? Anymore than they've done anything about all the other things that that perverted little swine's done since he got out.'

'You're missing the point. Jim Chalmers was only trying to do his job. You had no right to treat him the way you did.'

Dexter glared at her. 'Right? You talk about right? Think of the people who have been murdered by Challow so far, Mary.' He extended one hand and tapped each finger in turn with his other hand. 'Lionel Berwick, Quentin Fuller, Kitty Morrison, maybe even that poor sod of a vagrant, Shammy Leather. What about their rights, eh? Then there's all the intimidation Tania's been subjected to, not to mention this latest atrocity and the rights of poor old Gwenda, who was literally burned alive.'

He seemed to sag suddenly and slumped back against a split pine, once more overcome by intense weariness.

Mary stepped forward anxiously, but he waved her back. 'And despite all this, not once has Challow been pulled in for questioning. It's – it's as if he's immune from any sort of police investigation; as if he can do anything he wants, knowing full well that our esteemed leader has his nose so far up the arse of the Director of Social Services that he won't lift a finger to stop him.' He took another deep breath. 'Okay, so maybe I did behave like a dickhead, but you'd have acted in exactly the same way if you'd been in my shoes.'

She bit her lip, nodding quickly. 'Yes, I know, and I'm sorry I ran out on you the way I did.'

He sighed. 'No need to feel sorry, Mary. I'm just grateful you're here now.'

She glanced quickly at her feet. 'I dropped everything as soon as I heard. It was on local radio. Sort of a newsflash. You know the kind of thing: "Mystery fire at police chief's home". I'm just surprised they got it out so soon.'

He shrugged. 'Probably a stringer. There were enough people outside when I arrived. Could have been any one of them.'

She nodded and stared at him again. 'How's Tania taken it?'

He straightened up with a grimace. 'Tania doesn't know yet.'

She followed him as he moved off along the track. 'Doesn't know? But how –?'

'Tania's in hospital,' he cut in sharply. 'I've just got back from there. Some swine – I wonder who – sent her an RIP message attached to a funeral bouquet yesterday afternoon.'

She drew in her breath sharply. 'Eddie Challow?'

He grunted. 'You'll make a detective yet.' They had reached the back door of the house now and he turned slightly. 'You coming in?'

She didn't answer, simply waiting for him to unlock the door. The kitchen was cold and unwelcoming. He flicked the light on and

200

walked straight through to the hallway, then into the small square sitting-room at the front of the house. Mary followed him, unzipping her leather jacket as she watched him jerk open a walnut cabinet and reach for a bottle of whisky. 'Like a pick-me-up?' he said.

She shook her head firmly. 'I don't need a pick-me-up, Mike, and neither do you – especially with Tania in the hospital.' Her eyes narrowed. 'When did you last eat?'

He slopped some spirit into a glass and downed it in one gulp before reaching for the bottle again. 'Can't remember. I'm not hungry anyway and besides, I've got to pick Tania up from Heaton General soon.'

She studied him critically. 'All the more reason you should get something inside you. And scotch isn't it. Now go and get a shower. I'll see what's in the fridge and rustle you up something.'

He glared at her defiantly, the neck of the bottle poised over his glass. 'It's my bloody house, you know.'

'Please, Mike,' she said softly, stepping forward to place a hand on his arm. 'Tania needs you in one piece, not shot to blazes.'

He hesitated and she made the most of the opportunity, firmly taking the bottle from him and screwing the top back on. 'Shower,' she said again and prised the glass from his hand. 'I'll bring you up a coffee.'

Dexter was still in the shower when Mary finally knocked on the bedroom door with a steaming mug in one hand, and the smell of fried bacon wafting up from the kitchen followed her into the room. The door of the en suite bathroom was ajar and she could hear the rush of water from the shower as she placed the mug of coffee on the bedside cabinet. 'Bacon sarnie downstairs,' she called. 'Don't let it get cold.'

There was no reply and she tapped on the bathroom door itself. 'Mike, coffee's here.'

Still no answer and she frowned, remembering his pale drawn face and the haunted look in his eyes. 'You okay in there?'

Nothing but the sound of rushing water. Suddenly very anxious, she pushed the door open and peered inside. The shower jets seemed to be full on and within the clouds of steam that filled the large cubicle and smoked over the glass panels, she glimpsed the naked figure hunched up on the floor.

★

201

A slight breeze was stirring the curtains framing the open window when Dick Lawson awoke in a small room off one of the main wards of Worton Hospital and the cool air fanning his badly blistered face seemed like the caress of an angel.

He moved one leg experimentally and felt the pain immediately shoot up into his thigh. The pain-killing injections he vaguely remembered being given when he was brought in the previous night were obviously wearing off. Movement was difficult enough anyway, for some sort of cage had been erected over him from his chest to his feet, apparently to keep the bedclothes off his body, and he didn't actually need to see himself to know that he must have suffered pretty extensive burns as a result of the fire at the hotel.

Even now he could scarcely credit the fact that he had got out of the place with his life and the peculiar irony was that he owed his salvation to the very blast that had blown him off his feet. If the force of the explosion had not hurled him back down the stairs, he would have been barbecued to a crisp where he was standing. As it was, he still had vivid recollections of staggering to his feet in the midst of a gigantic ball of fire; of hearing the flames roaring around him and the sound of someone screaming from somewhere above his head; of smashing through a door at the foot of the staircase on to an iron fire-escape as the staircase and corridor behind him burst into flames; and of throwing himself down the slippery iron steps in the rain as sticky fiery fingers tried to hold him back and a couple of burly passers-by leaped on him to extinguish the flames by rolling him in the sodden grass. Thank God for bad weather and the local council's failure to cut the grass before the autumn, he thought grimly. He would never query his council tax again.

Then abruptly his reverie was interrupted by the sound of a door opening and the next moment a young raven-haired nurse smiled down at him. 'So we're awake now, are we, Chief Inspector Lawson?' she said.

'Know who I am then?' he said weakly.

She checked the drip attached to his arm. 'Not that difficult considering you had your warrant card in your back pocket,' she replied. 'How are you feeling?'

He tried to smile back, but stopped when it started to feel as though his face was going to split in half. 'Top of the world,' he whispered. 'How bad is the damage?'

She studied him for a moment with pursed lips and a quizzical frown. 'Oh, you'll live all right, but you've got some nasty burns and quite a bit of smoke inhalation, so you won't be going anywhere for a while, I'm afraid. That's just as well too, for the local police urgently want to talk to you. They've been pestering us all night. They think some sort of bomb was used, I believe.'

He swallowed carefully several times to try to relieve the rawness of his throat. 'So do I – incendiary device, triggered when I opened the door. Anyone else hurt?'

She smiled again. 'Now, there's no need for you to worry about things like that. Dr Kumari will be in to see you shortly.'

His chest contracted and he went into a spasm of violent coughing. 'Never mind Kumari. Anyone else hurt?'

Her mouth tightened in disapproval. 'Another man *was* brought in, yes; the hotelier, I believe. But listen, you must try not to talk.' She reached for a plastic mask attached to a cylinder at the head of the bed. 'Would you like some more oxygen?'

He shook his head weakly. 'Man's name Andy Pollard?'

She frowned. 'I think so, yes. The fire service got to the hotel in record time, but he was already dreadfully burned and there was really nothing anyone could do for him. He died shortly afterwards, I'm afraid.'

'Cuffed to the bed, was he?'

She looked shocked. 'How on earth did you know that?'

He swallowed several times again. 'Clever guess.'

She nodded, then shuddered. 'How anyone could do a thing like that, I just can't understand. The fire crews had to lower him out of the window on the frame apparently.'

'Did he say anything before he died?'

She replaced the oxygen mask, then turned away from him to raise the sheet covering the cage that had been erected over his body, studying him for a few moments with critical interest. 'Nothing that made any sense, no.'

Lawson closed his eyes in a gesture of frustration. 'So what *did* he say?' he said, trying to control his laboured breathing and fight the overwhelming desire to cough up his insides.

She let the sheet fall back into place and reaching towards the end of the bed, produced what looked like a chart attached to a clipboard. 'Something about a girl,' she replied, jerking a biro from her top pocket to scribble an entry.

'A girl?'

She looked up with a perplexed frown, her pen poised. 'Yes, Rod's girl, Rob's girl, some name like that.' She brightened. 'No, I know what it was: Ron's girl. He said, "Tell Ron's girl", that was it. The police are very concerned as to what he could have meant, but they have no idea who this girl could be, so they are up a gum tree.'

Lawson grabbed her wrist with surprising strength and raised himself up off the pillows. 'My God, Tania,' he said hoarsely, as she desperately tried to pull herself free. 'For heaven's sake, get me a phone!'

★

'Mike?' Springing across the bathroom, Mary Lane wrenched the shower doors back and, heedless of the water now drenching her as well, she bent over Dexter's hunched form. 'Mike!'

To her astonishment, he scrambled to his feet, reaching across to turn the shower off while futilely attempting to cover himself at the same time. 'What the hell are you at?' he exclaimed over his shoulder.

Mary stepped back quickly, one hand flying to her mouth as she convulsed into giggles. 'Oh Mike, I'm so sorry. I – I thought you had collapsed.'

'Collapsed?' he gasped, half-turning towards her, his hands cupped in front of him. 'I dropped the blasted soap, that's all. I was trying to find it.'

'The soap?' she echoed, leaning back against the wall, shrieking with laughter. 'The *soap*?'

He snatched a towel from the rail beside the shower and hastily covered himself. 'Do you mind? I would like to get dressed, if that's at all possible.'

Her laughter died and suddenly there was a different expression on her face as she straightened up off the wall and appraised him quite openly. 'You're not bad for your age, I'll give you that, Mike,' she said softly. 'Not bad at all. Tania's a lucky woman.'

He swallowed hard, reading the blatant message in her eyes and feeling a familiar guilt creeping out of the closet in his mind, because he knew there was an identical message in his own. 'Look, Mary –' he blurted, trying to find the right words to cover his embarrassment.

She moved closer to the cubicle and her finger traced an imaginary line down his chest. 'Don't say anything,' she whispered. 'We both want the same thing, you know that.'

'That's not true,' he lied desperately. His throat was dry despite the

204

water still streaming down his body, and he could feel an uncomfortable hardness developing beneath the towel that he was unable to control. 'Please, Mary, don't –'

But she had already kicked off her shoes and pulled her sodden tee-shirt up over her head. Her body was lean and well toned from regular exercise and her eyes shone with excitement as she undid the zip of her tight blue jeans and peeled them off like a second skin. Dressed only in the skimpiest of underwear, she pressed against him and slipped one hand under his towel. 'Let's take a shower together,' she whispered and, with the speed and dexterity of a stage magician, she whipped the towel away.

Within seconds she was also naked and with him in the cubicle, one hand reaching across to turn on the shower as her free arm encircled his neck. Then, as the hot water streamed down their bodies and the clouds of steam rose around them like a soft white mist, her long fingers seized his hair, jerking his head back, and her open mouth and questing tongue found his own.

Mary's need was urgent and she pressed him hard, all her pent-up emotions rising to the fore in a wild exultant rush. At first he responded in kind, lost in the ecstasy of the moment and in the desperate need to achieve the sexual fulfilment he had been denied in all those loyal but frustrating years with Tania. But then another even stronger feeling took over and he tore both her arms from around his neck and pushed her away. 'No, this is all wrong,' he gasped, fumbling behind him to turn off the shower. 'I – I can't do it, not here, not now.'

She slumped back against the tiled wall, panting heavily and watching him with a sense of despair as he scrambled out of the cubicle and snatched up his towel. 'Mike, please,' she pleaded, 'You're all I've ever wanted.'

He shook his head vigorously, as if trying to shake his own impure thoughts out of his head. 'For heaven's sake, Mary, I'm married and Tania's in hospital. How can you expect me to –?'

'But you don't *love* her,' she shouted as he pushed through the door into the bedroom. 'You never have.'

She left the shower cubicle in a rush and followed him into the bedroom where he was towelling himself down vigorously. 'Mike, listen to me. You married Tania because of what had happened to her, not because you loved her. She was vulnerable and you felt protective towards her. You convinced yourself it was love, but instead, it was... '

She tailed off and he glared at her. 'Pity? Is that what you're trying to say? I married her out of pity? That's an awful thing to come out with.'

She shook her head miserably, staring down at her toes. 'I know, Mike, but it's true,' she choked. 'Why can't you admit it? You forget how much you unloaded on me in the Crime Squad car all those years ago. I know how you felt then and nothing's changed just because a few years have passed.'

He began to pull on his clothes, trying desperately not to look at the slender body glistening wetly in the light of the two bedside lamps. 'Just get dressed, will you?' he grated, forcing himself to turn away from her. 'I don't want to hear anymore about it.'

'I love you, Mike,' she said suddenly in a low voice, 'I always have. Why do you think I transferred off the Squad and went on secondment to the Drugs Intelligence Unit for three years? I needed to get away from you because it was tearing me apart. I – I thought I was over it too. Then right out of the blue you turned up at Kitty Morrison's and I knew I couldn't let you go again.'

'Bloody hell, will you *stop it!*' he shouted, tears in his own eyes as he sank on to a corner of the bed. 'Do you think this is easy for me?'

She went over to the bed and bent down in front of him, one hand caressing his hair as she stared into his tortured face. 'Oh Mike,' she said, her own tears streaming from her eyes, 'what are we going to do?'

He took her other hand in his and squeezed it tightly. 'What *can* we do?' he croaked. 'I can't leave Tania. We've been together for all these years. She needs me. I'm her rock and she'd fall apart without me.' He took a deep breath and pulled his hand away. 'We have to forget this ever happened.'

'No,' she sobbed, bending her head to touch his chest with her forehead. 'I can't.'

'You have to,' he said sharply, regaining control of his emotions and firmly pushing her away as he climbed to his feet. 'There's no other alternative.'

She clung to his legs. 'And what if she regresses?' she sobbed. 'What are you going to do then?'

He returned her stare bleakly. 'Look after her as I've done before,' he said simply.

'You mean carry on the pretence?'

'If that's what it takes, yes. What would you have me do? Abandon her?'

She was spared an answer, for it was at this point that the telephone rang and when Dexter picked up the extension receiver and rapped out his number, Dick Lawson's strangled voice immediately responded. 'Mike, that you?'

Dexter visibly started. 'Dick?' he queried uncertainly. 'What's happened? You sound dreadful.'

There was a fit of violent coughing. 'Smoke damage, that's all,' the voice croaked back. 'Got caught in the draught.'

'Smoke damage? What are you on about? Where are you?'

There was a heavy pause. 'Worton Hospital.'

'Worton? But that's way off our patch.'

'Tell me about it.' More coughing, then with sudden urgency: 'Mike, Andy Pollard's dead. Torched in his own place, like Lionel Berwick'

'Andy Pollard?' Dexter echoed, staring blankly at Mary who must have caught the gist of the conversation, for she raised one hand to her mouth with a sharp gasp.

'Challow's coming after Tania,' Lawson croaked. 'For God's sake, get her away somewhere!'

*

It was almost completely light when Mary Lane pulled up in front of Heaton General Hospital. Nevertheless, the security lights lining the service roads and footpaths that criss-crossed the extensive wooded campus in an elaborate geometric pattern still glittered coldly in the gloom and the partially-lit twin tower blocks housing the hospital's principal departments stood out like giant electrical circuit boards against the expanding grey bar of the horizon.

Dexter might well have left Mary behind had a newly arrived Scenes of Crime van not parked right across the gateway of the house, effectively blocking his Volvo in. This had given her the precious few minutes delay she'd needed to pull on some clothes, and even as the errant SOCO shifted his vehicle to allow Dexter to swing out into the lane, Mary was jumping into her feisty Golf GTI and racing after him, gravel showering from under her spinning front wheels.

Dexter took some real chances on the way to the hospital, driving like a man possessed, and despite the superior speed of Mary's Golf, she just couldn't keep up with him. By the time she reached Heaton General, he had already abandoned his car and raced into the building, leaving the driver's door wide open and the headlights full on.

She almost caught up with him again in the Reception area, but then lost precious seconds dodging round the burly security officer he had only just shouldered aside. When she finally reached the stairs leading up to the wards, she was left with just the fading echo of his footsteps.

Fortunately, her long legs were soon able to narrow the distance between them, but she was still a floor behind him when she heard his footsteps stop and a door slam on the landing above. She reached the landing only seconds later, but by the time she was through the door and into the corridor beyond, he had completely disappeared.

She hesitated. The sign on the wall facing her indicated Aspen Ward to the left and Sycamore to the right and the trouble was, she had no idea which one was Tania's. With a resigned shrug, she plumped for Aspen, once more breaking into a run and calling on her last reserves of energy as she prayed that the gut feeling she had relied upon for so many years was not about to let her down.

It wasn't and when she got to Aspen's deserted duty desk, she was relieved to see Dexter coming out of a doorway to the right of the main ward. But her relief was short-lived when she saw the ashen look on his face. 'We're too late,' he panted, panic in his eyes. 'Challow's already been here and he's got Tania.'

Staring over his shoulder, she saw that the single bed in the room behind him was empty, the sheets thrown back untidily on one side.

'You don't know anything of the sort,' she exclaimed. 'Maybe she's just wandered off somewhere?' She glanced quickly about her. 'Where's the night nurse? Surely someone's on duty here?'

He shook his head slowly as he tried to get his breath back. 'You don't understand,' he said weakly, moving to one side of the doorway and leaning back against the wall with his eyes partially closed. 'Check the toilet.'

Throwing him a swift puzzled glance, she stepped into the room and gingerly pushed the door of the little en suite wide – only to step back with a shocked exclamation, one hand flying to her mouth.

The nurse had been dumped unceremoniously in the shower cubicle and her killer had not even bothered to pull the curtain across. Instead, he had left her in a grotesque heap on the basin floor like a broken rag doll, her tongue protruding from her swollen lips and the ligature that had cut her young life so short still twisted tightly round her neck.

Chapter 15

'So that's how the swine got in past Security.' Mike Dexter stared at the smashed lock on the heavy glass door, his face set into a tight mask and his fists clenching and unclenching in repeated spasms of barely controlled emotion.

Wilf Martin, the early turn Inspector, studied him for a moment, his broad bearded face registering an expression in which sympathy and apprehension were strangely mixed. With just a sergeant and three uniformed constables available to respond to the hospital incident and one of those assigned to guard the murder scene until CID arrived, he had enough problems on his hands without having to deal with a chief inspector on the verge of throwing a wobbly. 'PC Digby here found the break-in when he – er – checked the back of the building, sir,' he said uneasily.

'So much for hospital security,' Mary Lane commented dryly, throwing a contemptuous glance in the direction of the thin chinless security supervisor hovering in the background.

The security man flushed angrily. 'Can't be everywhere at once,' he muttered. 'There's only me and George as it is.'

The uniformed constable standing beside him gave a discreet cough and carefully stepped through the open doorway into the yard outside. 'I also found this, sir,' he added, trying to control his excitement.

Dexter followed him and stared at the wheelchair lying on its side among the bushes. 'Your man must have had a wagon of some sort parked here,' Digby explained, pointing triumphantly at the tyre marks still visible in the thin layer of frost coating the tarmac surface. 'Seems like it leaked a bit too. If you look closer, you'll see some fresh oil stains.'

'Okay, *super sleuth*, you've made your point,' Martin said gruffly. 'The DCI will be here in a minute and I don't think he'll be very pleased if he finds people have trampled all over everything before the SOCO team can do their stuff. As a matter of fact, you can stay here now and make sure that no one does.'

'What sort of vehicle do you reckon it was?' Mary said sharply, for once indifferent to the obvious need to preserve the scene, in spite of her CID training.

Digby bent down and stared more closely at the marks. 'Something biggish anyway,' he replied. 'These are from wide tyres with heavy treads. Maybe a Land Rover or some sort of truck.'

'Like one used to tow a bloody boat trailer, for instance,' Dexter put in harshly as he lurched back through the doorway.

Mary stepped quickly in front of him, placing a cautionary hand against his chest. 'You don't know that,' she said, reading his mind. 'And anyway, Challow's not likely to go back home if he's responsible for all this. He may be a psychopath, but he's not stupid.'

Dexter glared at her, an unreasoning madness of his own smouldering in his eyes. 'No?' he snarled. 'But at least it's somewhere to start, isn't it? And this time I'll do my *own* kind of investigation.'

Before she could stop him he had pushed her roughly aside and was striding back along the corridor towards Reception, leaving Wilf Martin gaping after him in astonishment.

'Quick, Wilf, your radio,' Mary shouted over her shoulder as she stumbled off in pursuit. 'Get some backup down to Tommy Lee's Boatyard at Maple Bucksters, and tell Control they'd better make it like yesterday!'

*

Assistant Chief Constable Dennis Stanford Parkes had not had a very good night and it showed. His boyish face wore a drawn pasty expression and there were the sort of dark smudges under his dull heavy-lidded eyes that were usually associated with a patient suffering from kidney disease.

As Assistant Chief Constable Operations, being woken by his bedside telephone in the middle of the night was an occupational hazard that pretty well went with the territory and since taking over the post, he had got used to the bad news that invariably came down the phone line in the early hours of the morning from Headquarters Control Room or one of the "on-call" superintendents. This time, however, it had been the bad news night to beat all bad news nights.

A tanker driver dismembered under the wheels of his lorry during the hijacking of his load of thirty-five thousand litres of unleaded petrol and a garage attendant near death's door in the local hospital after being blasted with a shotgun; a vicious arson attack on a barn at

Mike Dexter's home, resulting in the horrific destruction of his horse; and finally, to cap it all, a suspicious fire at a hotel in a neighbouring police area which had not only claimed the life of one of the force's own retired detective superintendents, but had resulted in the hospitalisation of a senior DCI, who shouldn't have been there in the first place.

No wonder his phone had been clamouring for attention all night and it had certainly made sure he was denied the opportunity of sleeping for more than an hour at a time. More to the point, it had had the same effect on his domineering sharp-tongued wife, Angela, and that was the worst part of it, for although Dennis Stanford Parkes BA may have wielded considerable power and authority at work, at home it was an entirely different story.

Worn to a frazzle and still feeling the sting of Angela's tongue in his ears, he found himself almost looking forward to the Chief Constable's boring presentation at the morning's launch of his "Working As One" initiative when he stomped into his office half an hour later than usual and dropped heavily into his swivel chair. His troubles were far from over, however, and when John Pullinger suddenly swept into the room just as his secretary was in the process of making him a very welcome cup of coffee, he knew instinctively that the rest of the day was going to be downhill all the way.

'I wondered when you'd think of popping in, Dennis,' Pullinger said acidly, trailing a long sheet of printer paper in one hand like the last few sheets of a very wide toilet roll. 'Decide to have a lay in, did you?'

As a mark of respect, Parkes hauled himself to his feet, but it was only a grudging acknowledgement of the rank, more automatic than anything else, and his expression was cold and hostile. 'As a matter of fact, sir,' he said tightly, 'I've been up since the early hours.'

Pullinger raised his eyebrows. 'Have you indeed?' he replied, draping the print-out over the corner of the desk. 'Bit of a busy night, was it?'

Parkes recognised the morning's incident report with a sense of apprehension. 'You could say that, sir,' he replied.

Pullinger scowled, a tic throbbing in one florid temple. 'Oh, I believe you, Dennis,' he snapped. 'I believe you. This damned report says it all. Murders, shootings, hijackings, arson attacks, not to mention AWOL DCIs – Just what I needed before the launch of a controversial new crime reduction strategy to a couple of hundred hostile sceptics.' He consulted his wrist watch. 'Which, incidentally, is in just over twenty minutes time.'

'Everything is under control, sir,' Parkes said hastily. 'I've got a full investigation team down at the murder scene and X-ray One-Four has been carrying out an aerial sweep of the area. They've already found a burned-out car in a field near the attacked garage, which was apparently stolen earlier in the evening from one of the villages. It's almost certainly connected with the armed robbery and SOCO are going over it as we speak. I've also got CID on the ground at Dexter's home and Brian Moffat's looking into the Lawson incident for me, so –'

Pullinger cut him short. 'Spare me the trivia, Dennis,' he said irritably. 'I'll leave that for you to sort out. My main concern at the moment is with one particular person.'

Parkes grimaced, easily reading his mind. 'Dexter,' he said heavily.

'Dexter,' Pullinger confirmed, his voice rising an octave. 'My bloody loose cannon of a PRO.' He stabbed a finger at the incident report lying across the desk. 'Why wasn't I told about this assault business last night?'

Parkes cleared his throat nervously. 'I did try, sir, but the complaint wasn't made until the evening and by then you had left for the day and couldn't be contacted by Control Room.'

Not surprisingly, Pullinger didn't pursue that particular aspect any further. 'Well, the whole thing's gone much too far already in my opinion,' he went on quickly, 'though I'm pleased to see our man's still not been suspended.'

Parkes shook his head. 'We can't suspend him, sir, not until Challow's been interviewed and confirms he wants to take things further. All we've got at the moment is Tommy Lee's telephone complaint and that's not enough on its own. I have told Dexter to take some leave though, which should keep him out of our hair for awhile.'

'And the Police Complaints Authority? Anything gone to them yet?'

'I've issued instructions that we hang fire where they're concerned until we've got more positive information to give them.'

'Well, you've done something right anyway. We don't want that lot jumping up and down before we've had time to think things out properly.' Pullinger's mouth tightened as he brooded over the situation. 'Damn Mike Dexter!' he jerked through clenched teeth.

'Man's an absolute liability. All I seem to hear lately is his dratted name. Not satisfied with bringing the force into disrepute by attacking a man at his place of work, he goes and grabs prime time on local radio with a story about his barn being burned down.'

For some inexplicable reason Parkes found himself rushing to Dexter's defence. 'We can hardly blame him because someone chose to set his barn on fire, sir,' he pointed out, 'or that the media have shown an interest in the job. They were bound to home in on it in view of his position and the fact that a horse was destroyed. It's the sort of emotive stuff that makes a good story.'

Pullinger was unrepentant. 'Man's a damned *Jonah*, whatever you say,' he growled, then added almost as an afterthought: 'Any more news on the barn fire?'

'Not yet, apart from the fact that it *was* arson; probably caused by a timed incendiary device. Trouble is, it only occurred a few hours ago, and I'm still waiting for more information to come in.'

Pullinger threw him an uneasy glance. 'Timed incendiary, you say? I don't like the sound of that one little bit.' He hesitated, then almost too casually voiced the previously unspoken thought that was on both their minds. 'No chance that – er – Challow might have been involved, is there? I mean, bearing in mind his past history.'

Parkes' gaze locked on to his and each read the fear in the other's eyes. 'Nothing to suggest that so far, sir,' he replied with as much confidence as he could muster. 'Could have been anyone with a grudge.'

Pullinger grunted. 'As long as Dexter doesn't come to his own conclusions,' he said grimly. 'He already seems to have a hang-up about the man because of his wife's paranoia and we certainly don't want a repeat performance of what happened yesterday.'

Parkes nodded. 'I've already covered that exigency, sir. One of the local officers was sent down to Tommy Lee's as a precaution first thing and I've also spoken to Detective Superintendent Les Angel from Complaints & Discipline. He's due to re-visit Challow this morning; he couldn't get hold of him last night.'

'Yes, I know.'

'Oh?'

'Yes, I spoke to Angel myself about an hour ago. '

'*You* spoke to him, sir?'

Pullinger nodded, plainly irritated by the implied criticism in the other's tone. 'I *did* – and to Jane Morgan, the Director of Social

Services, in fact. Someone had to before this thing was blown out of all proportion.'

'But – but with respect, sir, in your role as chief officer, you should not be involved in the enquiry at all. You will have to adjudicate at any future discipline hearing and your impartiality has to be beyond question.'

Pullinger studied him with an expression of undisguised contempt. 'It's about time you joined the real world, Dennis,' he retorted. 'Dexter's for the chop however you look at it. What I say and do behind the scenes won't change things one iota, but I can at least try and save the force some embarrassment by going for a low key approach that will keep things out of the press.'

Parkes' eyes narrowed warily. 'Low key, sir? I'm not sure I follow you?'

Pullinger turned quickly towards the secretary's office, treating Laura Tensing to a hostile glance as she shuffled papers on her desk. Reddening, she stepped forward and firmly closed the door between the two offices. 'Jane Morgan agrees with me,' Pullinger went on in a low voice. 'We must avoid a criminal prosecution at all costs. As I've said before, the press would have a field day if they found out about Eddie Challow being released and it would completely wreck the government's new softly softly mental health initiative, putting the Home Secretary in an impossible position.'

'That's hardly our problem, sir.'

Pullinger made a grimace. 'Maybe not directly,' he replied grimly, 'but being seen as the whistle-blowers where Eddie Challow is concerned could turn out to be a bit career limiting for you and I in the future. Not only that, but in the eyes of the other agencies, our commitment to the partnership approach would immediately be brought into question, almost certainly resulting in a withdrawal of all cooperation for our new initiative.' He shook his head slowly. 'The very prospect just doesn't bear thinking about.'

Parkes allowed himself a brief cynical smile at the generous way he had been included in things now that there was a possible problem. 'So Les Angel has been told to lean on Challow, is that it, sir?' he said quietly.

'Nothing so unsubtle, Dennis.'

Parkes shrugged. 'I don't see how you're going to cuff a criminal complaint any other way.'

Pullinger scowled again. 'We're not going to *cuff* anything, Dennis.

As you yourself have already pointed out, Challow hasn't actually made a complaint yet and it may be that he won't want to when it comes down to it. After all, he has even more reason than us not to want his release plastered all over the newspapers. Les Angel is a good man and I'm sure he'll be able to reach some sort of accommodation with our psychopathic friend, especially as Challow's social worker will be present at the interview and will be looking for a similar result.'

'I can't see any accommodation, as you call it, that would be acceptable to someone like Eddie Challow?'

Pullinger selected a cigar from a silver case. 'Listen Dennis,' he said, staring at him fixedly as he lit up. 'Eddie Challow will want just one thing out of this business – Michael Dexter's head – and I am quite sure we can oblige him. All we have to do is to persuade Dexter to resign and I am assured by Jane Morgan that Challow will forget the whole thing.'

Parkes' jaw dropped. 'Persuade him to what? You've got to be joking, sir. He'll never –'

'Think about it, man,' Pullinger interrupted again. 'Challow gets his own back by wrecking Dexter's career and Dexter gets to leave the force voluntarily without a stain on his character. No court case, no discipline hearing, just a quiet departure into obscurity. It's the ideal solution.'

'It won't work.'

Pullinger treated him to a watery smile. 'I have every confidence in your ability to *make* it work, Dennis.'

'Me?' Parkes laughed outright. 'Dexter won't listen to me. Why should he?'

'Because you'll tell him what the alternative is, Dennis, and I don't think he would care too much for a spell inside at his age.'

Parkes sat down heavily. 'I can't believe I'm hearing this,' he breathed. 'It's tantamount to a conspiracy.'

'Don't be absurd.'

'Well, I don't know what else you'd call it. Dexter is being hung out to dry for the sole purpose of suppressing a possible criminal complaint.'

Pullinger snorted his objection. 'Dexter has hung himself out to dry, Dennis,' he retorted, deliberately ignoring the reference to a criminal complaint. 'That's all there is to it. It's his own damned fault. Actually we'll be doing him a favour by offering him a way out.'

Parkes' jaw hardened. 'I'm sure he'll be eternally grateful for that, sir.'

Pullinger chose to overlook the sarcasm. 'Whatever you like, man,' he went on briskly, 'whatever you like. Just sort things out, eh? A nice tactful approach should do it – and keep me posted on developments. The press will be aching to quiz me after the night we've had. Thank heavens I've got a major detection to announce in the Lionel Berwick case.' He started as something else occurred to him. 'Now that Dexter's out of things, I trust someone else from the Press Office will actually be at the launch to keep those hyenas off my back?'

'Hopefully, you won't have that many. If you remember, that's why we arranged the event for a Friday, which is traditionally a dead day for news stories, because of the weekend.'

'That's as maybe, but there are bound to be one or two seasoned campaigners who will turn up.'

'I realise that and I've already arranged for John Durrell to be there to keep them in check. He's very experienced and should do a good job.'

Pullinger nodded doubtfully. 'He'd better. There's a lot riding on this. Now, I must be making tracks. I've got a brief pre-launch chat with the Police Authority Chairman in two or three minutes. Hopefully, I can get him on-side with the news about the Berwick case before the rest of the pack arrives.'

'I take it my attendance will not now be required then?'

Pullinger shook his head. 'Hardly – not with all that you've got to do.' On his way to the door, he half-turned and studied Parkes narrowly for a second. 'Just don't let me down, Dennis. I need your very best shot where this business is concerned.'

Parkes continued to stare at the doorway for several minutes after Pullinger had gone, his gaze focused on the gradually dispersing cloud of smoke his chief's big cigar had left behind and his mind struggling to come to terms with the despicable nature of the job that had been thrust upon him.

Dexter wasn't his favourite chief inspector and the man had certainly developed the knack of winding him up – driving him to distraction even. But he had no real animosity towards him as a person. In fact, if he was honest with himself, he rather respected him for his honest up-front attitude, even if it did have a tendency to cause tidal waves on occasions. The thought of taking on the mantle of a new-style *Brutus* and stabbing him in the back, didn't appeal to him one little bit, but what was the alternative?

He was still agonising over the issue when the smell of freshly ground coffee re-focused his mind as well as his gaze and he contemplated the steaming cup that had just been placed on his desk with a wry grimace. 'I'd much prefer a brandy, Laura,' he commented, straightening in the chair and reaching for the cup.

Laura Tensing made a disapproving clucking sound. 'That will do you a lot more good, Mr Parkes,' she replied severely. 'Put a spring in your step.'

'It needs to put a spring in something, Laura,' he complained with another grimace and returned the cup to its saucer. 'No sugar.'

'Sugar's bad for you, Mr Parkes,' she admonished. 'You should try and do without it.'

He shook his head wearily. He wasn't in the mood for another of Laura's lectures about the body being a temple. 'Will you just try and get hold of Chief Inspector Dexter on his mobile,' he said. 'I need him to come and see me.'

She nodded and, lowering her voice, inclined her head towards the door behind her. 'Would you like to speak to Mr Moffat first? He's just come into my office and he says it's urgent.'

Parkes stared past her and saw part of an arm and shoulder projecting beyond the door frame. 'Brian?' he queried sharply. 'What are you skulking about out there for?'

Moffat immediately appeared through the doorway, his face flushed and twitching with evident apprehension. 'I need a word, sir,' he blurted. 'Something's come up.'

'Another coffee please, Laura,' Parkes said with a heavy sigh and waved the CID man to a nearby chair. 'So, what's the problem this time?'

Moffat hesitated, adjusting the gold-tinted spectacles on the bridge of his nose. 'Could be a big one, sir,' he replied, waiting a moment while Miss Tensing shut the connecting door behind her. 'I've just been in touch with my opposite number over the border about the Lawson job.'

'As I asked you to. And?'

Moffat took out a big handkerchief and blew his nose loudly. 'Seems Dick Lawson actually went there to warn Andy Pollard that he was in some kind of danger, but when he got to Pollard's hotel and tried to find him, he inadvertently triggered an incendiary device rigged up in the poor devil's flat; hence his burns.'

Parkes frowned. 'But how did he know Pollard was in danger?'

Laura Tensing returned with the extra coffee before Moffat could reply and even as she disappeared again, closing the door discreetly behind her, he took a gulp from the cup before answering the question. 'Apparently Lawson mentioned Eddie Challow's name,' he said finally.

Parkes felt his insides begin to stir unpleasantly. 'Challow?' he echoed.

'Pollard was the SIO when he was put away,' Moffat explained quickly. 'Lawson seems to share Dexter's view that Challow might be waging some kind of vendetta against everyone involved in the case. We had a stack-up about it yesterday and Dick seems to have gone off on some enquiry of his own.'

Parkes remembered the incendiary device that was said to have been used at Dexter's home and suddenly felt very sick. 'Then Berwick –?' he began.

Moffat swallowed hard and gave a brief nod. 'Lawson reckons we've fingered the wrong man.'

Parkes drained his coffee cup despite the absence of sugar, desperately trying to hold down his rising panic as he thought of the Chief Constable and the imminent launch of his prized initiative. 'Didn't you speak to Lawson personally?'

Moffat shook his head. 'Hospital said he was too ill to be interviewed. They won't even let the local CID near him anymore either.'

'But where's the evidence for all this?'

'We haven't any that actually ties Challow into anything.'

'Well, there you are then.'

'But we *do* have something that seems to link Pollard's death to that of Judge Berwick's.'

'A link? What sort of a link?'

Moffat looked really unhappy now and beads of perspiration had broken out on his forehead. 'Pollard was anchored to his bed when they found him,' he went on huskily, 'and whoever did the job used old style police handcuffs.'

Parkes closed his eyes tightly for a second. 'Just like Berwick,' he breathed.

'*Exactly* like Berwick, sir.'

Parkes re-opened his eyes very slowly and focused on Moffat's sweating face, his initial shock suddenly replaced by an inbuilt survival instinct. 'The press will tear us to pieces when they make the connection on this,' he said grimly, 'and the Chief will be looking for someone to nail to the wall, you know that, don't you? We had better do some quick thinking if we are to save your bacon.'

Moffat gaped at him. '*My* bacon?' he exclaimed. 'With respect, sir, it was you who said –'

'*I* said?' Parkes raised his eyebrows. 'Excuse me, Brian, but I seem to remember that when you telephoned me, you claimed to have the case against the tramp "all wrapped up", as you put it. You said you were completely satisfied he was our man. It now seems you were a bit hasty in coming to that conclusion, doesn't it?'

Moffat shook his head quickly. 'That's not fair, sir,' he choked. 'I only did what you told me to do.'

'Told you to do, Brian? Exactly what did I tell you to do?'

'Well, you didn't actually tell me, but you implied –'

'Implied, Brian? You are a senior investigating officer. Are you saying you're not prepared to accept responsibility for your own decisions? I don't think that would go down too well with the Chief Constable when he's considering your application for the National Crime Squad.'

Moffat shook his head again. 'That – that's not what I meant at all, sir,' he said hastily. 'But I did get the impression that you wanted a quick detection in time for the big crime reduction launch, so I was under a lot of pressure.'

'Nonsense, Brian. I merely said that it would be nice to be able to make the announcement at the event, that's all. You obviously misunderstood my point.'

'Maybe I did, sir, but I don't see why I should be pilloried as a result.'

Parkes forced a smile. 'Nothing was further from my mind, Brian,' he reassured. 'We just need a little time to come up with a plan of action, that's all. Trust me.'

But time turned out to be one commodity that was in very short supply and when the telephone on Parkes' desk suddenly shrilled, he somehow guessed, even before he lifted the receiver to his ear, that another problem was about to be unloaded on him. He wasn't disappointed either.

'Control Room for you, Mr Parkes,' Laura Tensing announced and almost at once another woman's business-like voice came on to the line. 'Mr Parkes? Inspector Morton. We have a serious incident in progress, sir. Detective Chief Inspector Alloway has just arrived at the scene and asked that you be notified.'

'An incident?'

'Yes, sir. A nurse has been found strangled in a shower at Heaton General Hospital and one of the female patients snatched from her bed.'

'Good grief, when did all this happen?'

There was an uncomfortable pause. 'The body was discovered about six-thirty this morning, sir.'

'Six-thirty, and you're only telling me now?'

'Sorry, sir, but the incident wasn't reported immediately.'

'Not reported? So who found the body?'

'Chief Inspector Dexter, sir, and a Detective Sergeant – er – Lane.'

'Dexter? What the hell was he doing there?'

'Visiting his wife, I believe, sir. She's the missing patient. And there's something else too.'

Parkes' hand was gripping the receiver so tightly that the whites of his knuckles were showing through the skin. 'What sort of something else?'

'We've been asked to get some back-up to a boatyard owned by a Tommy Lee in the village of Maple Bucksters. Something to do with Mr Dexter being on his way there from the murder scene.'

Parkes slowly lowered the telephone receiver and held it against his shoulder for a few moments, staring past Moffat at the far wall as he tried to marshal his thoughts.

'Sir?' the Inspector's voice queried faintly.

Taking a deep breath, he raised the receiver again. 'Is X-ray One-Four still up?'

'Yes, sir. We diverted them from the Stag's Corner incident to carry out an area sweep re the kidnapping.'

'Then instruct them to break off from that and pick me up here. I will be at the heli-pad in ten minutes.'

Without waiting for an acknowledgement, he cut the caller off and dialled an internal number. The Chief Constable's secretary answered immediately. 'Miss Chance?' he queried sharply. 'ACC Ops. Can I speak to the Chief urgently please?'

'I'm sorry, Mr Parkes,' came the brisk reply. 'Mr Pullinger is now at the multi-agency forum.'

'Can you get a message to him?'

'I'm afraid not, Mr Parkes. He's already started giving his presentation. I can contact him when he's finished, if you wish?'

Parkes closed his eyes tightly for a second. 'No, leave it, thank you, Jackie. It's – er – not that important.'

'Damn and blast!' Parkes grated as he slammed the receiver back in place. 'Now we are in the cart.'

'Dexter again?' Moffat ventured nervously. 'I couldn't help hearing you mention his name just now.'

Parkes nodded grimly. 'As always,' he retorted, jumping to his feet. 'Seems that the wife of our meddling PRO has been kidnapped from her bed at Heaton General Hospital and some poor devil of a nurse found strangled in the shower.'

'Dexter's wife? But who on earth would want to kidnap her?'

Parkes ducked into the small dressing room on the other side of his office and returned with his uniform anorak and peaked cap. 'That'll be your job to find out when you get over there.'

'*Me*, sir?' Moffat vacated his chair as if it had suddenly become electrified.

Parkes nodded curtly. 'I want you to take command of the investigation. The local DCI, Jim Alloway, is already at the scene and he can fill you in on the details when you arrive.'

Moffat gaped at him. 'But what about the Berwick enquiry? After the fire at Worton, I'll have no option but to re-open the case and I can hardly run different major enquiries at the same time.'

Parkes grunted. 'I don't think they'll turn out to be different enquiries, Brian. In fact, I reckon this is going to be one of the biggest multiple crime enquiries we have ever dealt with. You've already identified a possible connection between the Berwick case and the job at Worton, which means that at the very least we're going to have to set up a cross-border conference to combine both investigations, and I've a horrible feeling that there's a further connection between those two incidents and this latest crime – possibly even the torching of Mike Dexter's barn as well.' His thin lips twisted into a wry grimace. 'Maybe Mike Dexter and Dick Lawson weren't so far off the mark with their vendetta theory after all.'

Moffat ran his tongue along his lower lip. 'Eddie Challow,' he breathed.

Parkes donned his cap and shrugged into his anorak. 'It's certainly starting to look that way,' he agreed, 'and as you're already the SIO on the Berwick enquiry, you're the obvious person to pull everything together. It's a golden opportunity for you to redeem yourself.'

'But – but what will the Chief say if Challow is brought in for questioning?'

Parkes emitted a hollow laugh. 'I think he'll be pretty pissed off!'

'So what do we do then?'

Parkes frowned. '*We* don't do anything, Brian; *you* do. And the sooner you get to the hospital in that flashy BM of yours, the sooner you can get started on the job.'

Moffat looked bewildered. 'But I thought we were both going over there in the force chopper?'

Parkes grabbed a personal radio from his drawer and fitted it with a new battery from a small charger on the bookcase behind his desk. 'Then you thought wrong,' he snapped. 'I've got a much more urgent commitment for X-ray One-Four.'

Moffat scowled. 'I can't see what could be more urgent than investigating a murder, sir?' he said sullenly.

Parkes threw him an old-fashioned look. 'Can't you, Brian?' he retorted coldly as he headed for the door. 'How about trying to prevent one being committed in the first place?'

*

A green and white emergency ambulance was parked behind Mary Lane's car when she burst through the hospital's main entrance on to the forecourt. Whether it had been parked there deliberately because she had left her Golf in a prohibited "Ambulances Only" area or because a casualty had needed off-loading quickly, she had no idea, but it meant that she was completely blocked in and she could only watch helplessly as Mike Dexter raced off down the drive in his Volvo. It was only a matter of minutes before the ambulance crew returned to their vehicle and drove away, casting her dark hostile looks as they did so, but by then she knew that her chances of catching up with him before he got to Maple Bucksters were virtually nil.

Nevertheless, she did her best, abandoning the main road for a shorter cross-country route and pushing her powerful little car to its limits through a labyrinth of narrow winding lanes. But a big surprise awaited her when she finally swung into the car park of Tommy Lee's Boatyard, for although there were plenty of other vehicles already there – most of them with police markings – Dexter's distinctive blue Volvo was conspicuous by its absence.

A traffic car was parked close to the building on the far side of the car park, a uniformed sergeant standing by the vehicle trailing the radio handset on its long cord out through the window as he held a conversation with someone. Recognising the traffic man as Robin

Cater, she drove across the car park and pulled into a space beside his car, staying in her seat until he had finished his conversation and replaced the handset in the car.

'Hi, Mary,' he said, concern etched into his weathered face as he opened her door for her. 'So, where's our man then? Control said he was on his way here.'

Climbing out of the car, she stared around the car park again and frowned. 'He was.'

'Well, I haven't seen him and I was the first to arrive.'

'But he left Heaton Hospital at least ten minutes before me and there was no sign of his car en route.'

Cater grunted. 'That's as maybe, but he hasn't appeared yet. Just as well really, since Control didn't happen to tell us exactly what we were supposed to do when he did. All a bit confusing.'

'He could have been and gone before you got here.'

The traffic man shook his head. 'No chance. I was already in the village when the call came through.'

She continued to peer round the car park. 'What, visiting a nice little tea spot, Robin, or just using your natural clairvoyant skills?'

He grinned and pulling a half-smoked cigarette from behind his ear, firmed it up with deft fingers before slipping it into the corner of his mouth. 'Sadly, neither. I was following up an enquiry on a nicked car.'

She sighed heavily. 'Well, at least we seem to have got here before him, which is something anyway.'

'Wouldn't have made any difference if we hadn't.'

Mary stared at him curiously. 'What do you mean?'

Cater lit his cigarette. 'If it was Challow he was after, he would have been disappointed. Arsehole's gone – done a bunk apparently.'

'Are you positive?'

'Absolutely. Poor old Tommy Lee's doing his crust. There's also a pretty pissed-off detective superintendent on site too – Les Angel – with that weird looking bird from social services in tow.'

Mary grimaced, glancing around her uneasily. 'I can guess what that's about. So where are they now?'

Cater waved an arm in the direction of the towpath. 'Heading for Challow's boat with a spare key Tommy's given them, though I don't know what they expect to find there.'

'Our boatyard owner's being very cooperative all of a sudden.'

'Not surprising really. When Challow disappeared, so did Tommy's Land Rover.'

'His Land Rover?' Mary's heart lurched as she thought about the tyre marks at the back of the hospital.

'Yeah, ex-army wagon. Camouflage markings, big front grill – you know the sort of thing. Tommy uses it mainly to tow his boat trailer.'

'What makes him think Challow took it?'

Cater shrugged. 'Apparently one of his workers lives in the village and is a bit of an insomniac. He was out walking his dog in the early hours when he saw Challow drive past at the wheel. He didn't think anything of it at the time. Thought that Tommy must have given him permission. Only mentioned it when he turned up for work several hours later and heard the motor was missing.'

'So Tommy's not turning the other cheek on this one then?'

Cater gave a dry chuckle. 'Hardly. Seems he'd already had a go at Challow for borrowing the wagon without his permission. This is like the last straw – especially as he hasn't brought it back this time. One of the local lads is taking a statement off him now and I don't reckon he'll be preaching too much Christian forgiveness.'

'One of the local lads? But I thought you said you were dealing with the job?'

He shook his head. 'Not this one. Mine is a car that was nicked from outside the local pub yesterday evening and found burned out near the scene of the tanker heist.'

She nodded. 'The blagging. Oh yes, I heard about that on local radio.'

'Not just a blagging, Mary, a bloody murder as well, and as CID reckon the stolen car was connected with the job, they asked me to pop over and speak to the registered owner.'

She frowned. 'So two vehicles have been taken from the same village the same night then? Doesn't that strike you as a bit odd?'

Cater shrugged again. 'Not really. This sort of thing is pretty common these days, you should know that.'

'Maybe, but we shouldn't rule out a possible connection either.'

Cater laughed outright. 'A connection? You mean Eddie Challow could have nicked both motors? Oh come on, Mary, I know you lot like to improve the crime clear-up rate, but you'd need a bit of a leap of the imagination to tie these two jobs in together.'

'Imagination or not, we still can't afford to dismiss the idea.'

'Point taken, but I reckon even Eddie Challow would have had a job nicking two cars and a petrol tanker within hours of each other – I mean, what would he want with a tanker anyway?'

Mary stared at him in disbelief. 'Robin, he's a bloody arsonist,' she exclaimed. 'What do you *think* he would want with a petrol tanker? If Mike Dexter is right and Challow does have a vendetta against those who put him away, he'd have a ready-made bomb to use wherever he wanted.'

She snapped her fingers excitedly. 'Hell's bells, the news flash on local radio said the tanker belonged to TQ International. I seem to remember Mike Dexter once telling me that Challow used to work for them, but he got the sack. That's when he went to work for Tania Ferguson's old man.'

Cater looked confused. 'Mary, what are you on about?'

Mary's eyes widened. 'Robin, TQ International has a huge depot at Grange. My God, what if that twisted little pervert wants to get his own back on them as well and intends doing it with one of their own tankers?'

Robin Cater, removed the still smoking cigarette from his mouth and stared at her in open-mouthed astonishment, staggered by the enormity of what she was suggesting. 'Mary,' he protested, 'you've got absolutely no evidence of any of this.'

'Evidence or not, we have to get Control to alert the depot, just in case.'

He snorted, dropping his cigarette on the ground and treading it underfoot. 'Oh yeah, great idea. Then some mercenary security officer will drop a word in the ear of the press and before we know it, we'll have a full-scale panic on our hands.'

'So we just forget about it, is that what you're saying?'

He frowned irritably. 'No, that's not what I'm saying at all, but we can't just go over the head of the SIO and send everybody charging around like chickens with their heads cut off. Someone much higher up than us has to make that sort of decision.'

'And meanwhile, Challow could already be heading for the depot in the tanker with a nicely primed explosive device on board. Do you want that on your conscience?'

Cater mentally counted to ten. 'Use your head, Mary,' he said tersely. 'If he had intended doing that, he'd have done it by now. He's hardly going to drive around in a stolen ten-wheel petrol tanker all night, waiting for the right moment, is he? Anyway, what would someone like him know about bomb making?'

Mary was not given the chance to reply, for the sudden violent explosion that ripped through the still air, rattling all the windows in

the adjacent building, dramatically put paid to any further conversation. Spinning round in the direction of the sound, the pair stared
aghast at the tongues of flame and column of thick black smoke that
rose above the trees beyond the sharp bend in the towpath and, as a
mix of boatyard workers and uniformed police officers burst through
the doors of the boat shed into the car park, Mary sprinted for the
entrance. 'Challow's boat, Robin,' she shouted over her shoulder.
'God help us, but I think he's just answered your question!'

Chapter 16

Mike Dexter fully expected his mobile telephone to ring as he raced away from the hospital and when it did, he was pretty sure that the caller would be Mary Lane trying to persuade him to turn back. 'It's no good, Mary,' he shouted before she could say anything. 'I'm doing this my way now.'

The masculine chuckle that responded was completely unexpected and he swerved slightly, glancing at the telephone in its hands-free cradle, as if he expected to see the caller's face there. 'So glad to hear that, Michael,' a hard metallic voice replied. 'We don't want anyone else in on our little game, do we?'

'Challow!' Dexter almost spat the name as he recognised the hateful voice. 'Where are you, you filthy scumbag?'

Challow clicked his tongue reprovingly. 'Now, now, Michael, no need to get abusive – especially as I have a lady with me.'

Dexter hit the brakes hard and the car fishtailed for several yards before its nearside wheels mounted the left-hand verge and slithered to a halt in the soft grass. Ignoring the blaring horn from behind as a large van swung out to pass him, he grabbed the telephone from its cradle. 'What the hell have you done with my wife?' he snarled.

There was a heavy sigh. 'Nothing yet, my dear Chief Inspector, but I am known to be unpredictable, so who's to say what could happen if my mood were to change?'

Dexter swallowed several times. 'Now you listen to me, Challow,' he said hoarsely. 'You harm Tania in any way –'

'And you'll do what exactly?' came the sneering reply. 'Kill me perhaps? Oh very Hollywood, Michael; very *James Cagney*. Bit cliché though, don't you think? And you forget, *I* hold all the aces.'

Dexter got a grip on himself with difficulty. 'So what do you want, you little sicko?' he grated through clenched teeth.

There was an exaggerated sigh. 'You really have got out of bed the wrong side today, haven't you, Michael? And there was me ringing you up to invite you to a nice party I'm throwing. I'm not sure you'd fit in if you're in that sort of mood.'

'Why don't you just cut the crap and get on with it.'

'Oh it's no crap, Michael, I have a real extravaganza planned and Tania has pride of place.'

Dexter leaned back in his seat and closed his eyes tightly for a moment, desperately trying to keep his cool. 'Okay,' he said heavily, 'what's all this leading up to?'

'Why, the party, of course.'

'Which is where?'

'All in good time, Michael, all in good time, but if you're heading towards Tommy Lee's, you are getting colder by the mile.'

'So how do I get warmer?'

'By following the directions I will give you, simple as that. But before we start your little mystery drive, a word of warning.' The naked menace in Challow's voice was unmistakable now. 'This party invitation is strictly limited. Try to bring along a single guest, like one of your friends in blue for example, and I promise you, I'll turn Tania into a fireball brighter than the sun!'

Dexter felt his skin crawl, for he knew that that was one promise Eddie Challow would be sure to keep.

*

A pall of black smoke hung over the canal where *Water Gypsy* had once been moored and beneath it the half-submerged broken skeleton of the boat was just visible, still blazing fiercely in the shallow water. The force of the explosion had quite literally ripped the boat apart, hurling pieces in all directions, and the towpath was littered with the debris: wood panelling, broken spars, cooking utensils, the remains of interior furnishings, even part of what looked like a calor gas cooker. Fanned by a strengthening breeze, some of the more combustible material continued to burn, both on the towpath itself and among the trees that bordered it, flaring eerily in the smoky gloom like scattered napalm, and crackling and hissing with all the obscene enthusiasm of a satanic barbecue.

Mary Lane's long legs had got her to the scene first, outstripping Robin Cater and his smoker's lungs by several yards, but she quickly realised that there was nothing she could do and she was already turning on her heel to head back down the towpath when the traffic man finally caught up with her. 'Convinced now?' she choked through her handkerchief as the smoke thickened around them. 'Challow must have rigged up the boat before he fled.'

Cater peered past her into the gloom. 'Maybe it was just an accident,' he wheezed. 'Gas bottles are always exploding on these damned things. He could actually still be in there.'

Mary moved to one side as other police officers and workers from the boatyard pushed past her, a couple of the latter carrying small fire extinguishers which they began to spray around them ineffectually. 'Do me a favour, Robin,' she exclaimed. 'That was a bomb and you know it, which means that the only people you're going to find in there are Les Angel and that poor devil of a social worker, who will both be well beyond help now. We've got to get on to the Control Room before that madman hits the TQI depot.'

Cater was given no chance to argue, for the next moment she was gone and with a despairing groan he stumbled after her fast retreating figure, unable to summon the energy to move any faster. By the time he reached the car park, she was already sitting sideways in the driver's seat of the traffic car with the door open and her feet resting on the ground as she spoke rapidly into the radio handset.

'They're sending the Operations Support Unit to the TQI depot now,' she said a few moments later and pushed him back with the car door as she climbed out. 'And the fire and ambulance services have also been alerted as a precaution.'

Cater shook his head slowly. 'I still think we should have reported this to someone higher up the ladder,' he said with a frown.

Mary nodded skywards as the police helicopter suddenly thudded in low over the trees. 'Well, maybe we're about to be given the chance,' she replied grimly. 'Control said ACC Ops was already on his way here when I called in and, if I'm not mistaken, that will be our Mr Parkes arriving now.'

*

The village of Tulse End was about to have its annual "Winter Fair & Barbecue", according to the billboards lining the approach road, and a large blue and white marquee had already been erected in the middle of the village green, with stalls and fairground rides in the process of being constructed around it. The whole place had a festive atmosphere to it and The Goose Inn, mini mart, garage and encircling cottages were all bedecked with Union Jack flags and coloured ribbons.

Mike Dexter hardly noticed what was going on. He had far more important things to think about than a village fair and he steered his way round the road closure signs and steel barriers stacked in readiness beside the green as if in a trance. It was years since he had visited Tulse End, the last time being just before Eddie Challow was put away, and sight of the place immediately evoked the horrific memories that had been the stuff of his nightmares for two decades.

As part of his nasty little game, Challow had taken him on a long roundabout route to the village, forcing him to stay connected on his mobile phone the whole time as the necessary directions were given – no doubt to prevent any assistance call being made and to ensure that Challow knew precisely where he was at every stage of the journey. Dexter cursed his own blindness for failing to see at once that the old Ferguson house on Quarry Wood Hill was precisely the place the little psychopath would choose for his final bolt-hole. It was there that the awful business had started and there that Challow would want to finish things, and he shuddered uncontrollably at the thought. Heaven alone knew what sort of fate that warped calculating brain had reserved for Tania and himself, but whatever it was, he knew full well that the chances of either of them seeing another day were virtually nil.

'Still trying to think of a way out, Michael?' Challow's voice cut in on his thoughts.

Dexter turned into Quarry Wood Road, as he had already been told to do, and accelerated up the hill, his mind working overtime. There was no way he could let himself go like a lamb meekly to the slaughter, but at the same time, he dare not do anything that would jeopardise Tania.

'Speak to me, Michael,' Challow said softly. 'I get worried when I can't hear your voice and a worried psychopath is nothing to want, believe me.'

'I'm still here,' Dexter said quickly, swinging right in front of the quarry gates and continuing up the hill towards the old haulage yard. 'Where would I go?'

A short laugh. 'Well, you could turn tail and run, but then, of course, I would have no option but to waste the lovely Tania.'

Dexter's mouth was dry and his heart was in overdrive. There had to be some way, but right that moment he just couldn't think of one.

The road ahead now ended in a wide turning area enclosed by a high brick wall and he braked to a stop, his gaze focused on the partially overgrown entrance gaping at him a few yards away. The stone pillars that flanked it on either side looked as though they should have supported heavy iron gates, but these were no longer in evidence and beyond, a narrow driveway seemed to burrow its way into the undergrowth like the tunnel of a giant worm.

Almost immediately, Challow's voice was in the car with him again. 'I assume you've arrived,' he said, more as a statement than a question. 'Now all you have to do is drive straight through the entrance and follow the road to the end. I will meet you there. And no tricks please.'

Dexter's mouth tightened, his lips compressing into a thin line. The swine was certainly on the ball this time. It was as if he had an all-seeing eye. In reality though, it was more likely that he had already worked out the distance from the village to the site and was carefully timing his approach.

'I'm waiting, Michael,' Challow's voice mocked from the mobile.

Dexter studied the trees intently, considering his chances of outwitting his tormentor by abandoning the car and going ahead on foot to surprise and overpower him. But he dismissed the idea as a non-starter even as it occurred to him. He hadn't a clue where Challow would be waiting for him or where he was holding Tania and he knew from past experience that the heavily wooded site went back a long way and accommodated a number of large buildings, which would take hours to search. No, his only real option was to play along with Challow in the hope that an opportunity to turn the tables on him would present itself at a later stage. The thought of doing nothing now, however, filled him with a seething frustration, which he found very difficult to control and he rammed the Volvo into first gear with savage disregard for the protesting gearbox before launching the powerful car at the gateway as if it were a target.

Seconds later he was bumping across a broken concrete hardstanding among empty derelict buildings, his wheels scraping against scrub and brambles and his mind back with the ghosts of twenty odd years ago.

Pulling up alongside a pair of derelict fuel pumps, he switched off and stared around him apprehensively. A rabbit bounded across the open space in front of his car, disappearing into one of the former warehouse buildings to his left, and directly opposite, a loose corrugated iron sheet flapped with a hollow clanking noise on the roof of the derelict lorry garage. Otherwise nothing moved. The placed appeared to be deserted.

He waited for further instructions to issue from the still connected mobile, but there were none and, losing what little patience he had left, he reached for the door handle – only to freeze when he spied the long-handled screwdriver projecting from among the wodge of maps and insurance documents jammed in the door pocket. His heart began to beat a little faster. It was like a gift from the gods. Conscious that Challow could be watching him from somewhere, he lowered his right arm very carefully and pulled the screwdriver free, sliding it up the sleeve of his jacket with the blade pointing downwards and resting in the cupped palm of his hand, ready for immediate use. Then, unhooking his mobile, he eased open the car door and carefully climbed out, his feet crunching on broken glass as he turned towards the old staff canteen a few yards back on his right.

Straightaway he heard noises from the mobile clutched in his other hand and quickly raised it to his ear. 'I said you're getting colder, Michael,' Challow repeated.

Dexter stopped dead. 'Getting what?' he echoed. 'This isn't a game, you arsehole.'

A mirthless laugh. 'Oh, but that's exactly what it is, Michael, and you really should enter into the spirit of things.'

'Just tell me where you are so we can get it over with.'

'But that's all part of the game, Michael, don't you see?'

Gritting his teeth, Dexter did an abrupt about-turn and headed across the hardstanding in the direction of the pair of roofless warehouses.

'Oh dear, now you're getting even colder, Michael. Actually you'll soon be freezing to death.'

Dexter nodded grimly, studying the lorry garage with narrowed eyes. 'So you're in there, are you?' he breathed and turning on his heel, he marched briskly towards the building.

Challow laughed again. 'Ah, now that's it, Michael, you're starting to get warmer this time. You could even be on fire before you know it.'

The menacing double meaning was not lost on Dexter and he gave a brief involuntary shudder as he approached the big steel doors. He resisted the temptation to reply, however. Challow obviously had a vantage point or a spy-hole somewhere in the garage itself, which gave him a clear view of the derelict site in front of him, but the chances were that his view of anyone approaching the building would progressively diminish as the subject got closer. This meant that for the first time the little psychopath was at a disadvantage, because he would have no idea exactly where his intended victim was and that was a disadvantage Dexter intended exploiting to the full.

Switching off his mobile completely so that any further calls would not give his position away, he shook the screwdriver out of his sleeve and gripped its bulbous handle tightly in his right hand, smiling with satisfaction as he ran the index finger of his other hand along the sharp tip. Then, turning his attention to the steel doors, he frowned heavily. It was evident that they were only just pulled to, with the padlock hasp, that seemed to have been recently fitted, open and projecting towards him, minus the padlock itself. The invitation could not have been plainer and he rejected it with contempt. He had no intention of going in the front way. There had to be another entrance somewhere. All he had to do was find it.

Moving swiftly along the wall, and sticking to a strip of rough grass that had forced its way up through the concrete, he ducked down the side of the building. He found the small single door about halfway along and tried the rusted handle. It was unlocked. Sensing a possible trap, but presented with no alternative other than to continue, he held the screwdriver out in front of him as he carefully eased the door open and stepped through.

He saw the huge petrol tanker first, parked in the middle of the rubbish-strewn concrete floor, the cylinder on its long trailer emblazoned with the name "TQ International". Beside it was an old Land Rover with army style camouflage markings that looked very much like the one he'd seen parked at Tommy Lee's Boatyard, it's tailboard now down to accommodate a large trials motorcycle. Then he saw Tania. She was sitting on what looked like a blanket, dressed in jeans and a sweater, her hands behind her and her back against one of the massive front wheels of the tanker, looking tiny and doll-like in the vastness of the otherwise empty building. And finally he saw Eddie Challow, staring at him along the twin barrels of a sawn-off shotgun levelled at his chest from just a few paces away. 'Good try, Michael,' Challow said softly, his dark eyes boring into him like those of a deadly snake. 'But I'm afraid you lose the game.'

*

The press were everywhere, like an invasion of cockroaches. How they had found out about the incident at Curling Lock – whether via a local stringer or from information picked up off Mary Lane's radio call to Headquarters Control Room – mattered little. The plain fact was that they were all over the scene and it was only a question of time before they discovered the true identity of Tommy Lee's missing boat tenant. Then the whatnot would really hit the fan.

Staring out of the window at the two uniformed bobbies standing in front of the blue and white tape cordoning off the towpath, Assistant Chief Constable Dennis Stanford Parkes watched the assortment of down-at-heel newshounds pleading with Sarah Hamilton-Lancing to be let through. It was ironic. A few hours ago he had been desperate to get rid of Mike Dexter, but now saddled with his deputy, fresh from the scene of the tanker heist and panicking like some newly assigned work-experience student, he would have given anything to have seen him turn up in his battered Volvo to take charge of the press.

'So, we have two dead then?' Parkes queried, turning away from the window of Tommy Lee's little office and fastening his gaze on Mary Lane's taut white face.

She nodded. 'I understand that the fire service have found the remains of two people, sir; a man and a woman. They were both in a bit of a mess apparently and – er – not entirely complete, so identification will be difficult, but we think one of the bodies might be that of Detective Superintendent Angel.'

Parkes closed his eyes briefly. 'Poor devils,' he breathed. 'And we're sure it's murder?'

'Well, I hardly think it was an accident, sir.'

Parkes' eyes narrowed, as he tried to make up his mind whether or not she was being facetious. In the end, he decided to give her the benefit of the doubt. 'Neither do I, Sergeant,' he agreed. 'But why should Challow want to booby-trap the boat? He doesn't appear to have a grievance against Mr Lee and he'd hardly want to murder his own social worker.'

She shrugged. 'I can't answer that, sir, but maybe he has a grudge against humanity as a whole.'

Parkes grunted, finding that prospect too frightening to contemplate. 'And you think he was responsible for the Stag's Corner Filling Station job as well and now intends to target the TQI depot?'

Sergeant Cater, sitting quietly in the corner, fidgeted uneasily. Mary threw him a critical glance. 'I think it's a distinct possibility, sir.'

Parkes waved a hand towards the window. 'Your distinct possibility could result in mass panic if our media friends out there get hold of it.'

Her mouth tightened. 'It will be a lot worse if we do nothing and my hunch is proven right, sir,' she said boldly.

He treated her to a cobra-like stare. 'Well, we have enough units down there if he tries it,' he replied, 'and I've sent X-ray One-Four on an area sweep just in case. If our man is en route, they should soon spot him.' He transferred his cold gaze to Cater. 'And as I am now left without any means of transport, Sergeant, you win the raffle and get to run me back to HQ.' He smiled thinly. 'Our resourceful detective sergeant here can remain on site to assist the local DI with the investigation and brief Detective Superintendent Moffat when he arrives.'

Mary raised her eyebrows, her expression betraying the fact that she was not too impressed with her lot or with his choice of SIO. 'But I thought Mr Moffat was dealing with the Judge Berwick case?' she said tactfully.

He grunted. '*And* the hospital incident,' he replied. 'Busy man at the moment is our Mr Moffat. But if all these cases are suspected to be the work of the same villain, then it's right that they should be investigated by the same SIO – and that could ultimately mean the Stags Corner job too.' He raised his eyebrows a fraction as he caught her glancing quickly at her watch. 'Sorry, Sergeant, are we keeping you from something?'

She reddened. 'No, sir, but I'm still rather concerned about Chief Inspector Dexter. As I explained when you arrived, he hasn't been seen since he left Heaton General Hospital and we know he was on his way here.'

Parkes gave a disparaging snort. 'Why, are you suggesting he may have been kidnapped too?'

'I don't know, sir.'

'Well, have you rung his home?'

She nodded. 'I telephoned there on my mobile a few moments ago. No reply.'

'And his mobile?'

'Permanently engaged, sir.'

'Then he must be alive and kicking, I would have thought.'

'I don't know, sir.'

Parkes studied her for a moment. 'You don't know a lot, do you, Sergeant? Try that mobile number again.'

Both Cater and Parkes watched her intently as she dialled and moments later, they heard the high-pitched unobtainable tone, followed by the tail-end of the recorded message: 'The mobile telephone may be switched off.'

Parkes released his breath with a loud exasperated hiss. 'Brilliant!' he exclaimed. 'So now, as well as five murders, a lorry hijacking and a kidnapping, we also have a missing police officer. In the last few hours this force area has begun to look like a damned war zone.'

'There could be another two stiffs to add to the list, sir,' Cater commented for the first time.

Parkes cast him a baleful look. 'What?'

Mary nodded. 'Yes, sir. We think that Eddie Challow could have been responsible for a fatal TA involving a journalist by the name of Quentin Fuller, who was investigating Judge Berwick's murder. It seems that one of the brake pipes on his car may have been deliberately cut. Chief Inspector Dexter is also convinced that his press liaison assistant, Kitty Morrison, who was found dead in bed from a suspected drugs overdose, was in fact another of his victims. Apparently Challow was dating her at the time and probably pumping Kitty for information about the force.'

Parkes ran the palm of one hand down his face with a despairing sigh. 'Which is no doubt how he got hold of Andy Pollard's address,' he said bleakly.

Cater frowned. 'Andy Pollard? He queried.

Mary nodded. 'The man who put Challow away,' she said.

Parkes threw her a keen glance. 'Exactly,' he said dryly, 'and it seems he was torched in his hotel over the border yesterday evening. Identical MO to Judge Berwick. One of our senior detectives, DCI Dick Lawson, was also badly burned in the fire and is currently in the local hospital.'

Mary took a deep breath, but didn't let on that she knew this already. 'Which means Challow must have already murdered eight people,' she summarised, 'probably nine if he used the tramp as a red herring. We have to nail him before he kills again.'

Parkes nodded grimly, his mind concentrated on his own ruthless agenda. 'Or before the press manage to find out who he really is,' he snapped.

'We might have a problem there, sir,' Robin Cater said quietly.

Parkes turned on him sharply. 'A problem? What sort of a problem?'

Cater shrugged. 'A Tommy Lee sort of a problem, sir. According to the local lads, he was pretty bitter about things when he discovered

Challow had nicked his Land Rover. Kept mouthing about how badly his Christian generosity had been repaid and demanding to know what the authorities were going to do to compensate him. I reckon he'll be feeling even less charitable now that he's lost his boat as well. The chances are he'll spill the beans in the first available ear – especially if there's a nice fat wad at the end of it.'

'Then we must get hold of him quickly.'

'Bit late for that, sir,' Cater replied with just a hint of malicious satisfaction. 'Last time I saw him, he was being ushered in the direction of the George & Dragon by some woman with a radio mic and pack-set. I reckon we could be looking at a national front page story by six o'clock.' He gave a crooked smile. 'You never know, sir, even the Chief Constable could be on the telly tonight.'

*

John Pullinger was a very relieved man. Despite his earlier concerns, the launch of his controversial initiative to the packed multi-agency forum seemed to have gone extremely well, and he knew he owed a lot to his enthusiastic young staff officer for the way the whole event had been organised and managed. The smart professionally produced information packs placed on every chair; the eye-catching coloured posters, shouting their key crime prevention messages from the walls; and, most impressive of all, the superb audio-visual programme supporting the speech with cinema sound and the projection of top quality video images on to the huge screen behind the podium he was sharing with the heads of the other principal statutory agencies.

Without a doubt, the whole thing had been a PR triumph and when the meeting finally broke up for coffee, even the pallid and usually sour-baked face of the Social Services Director, Jane Morgan, betrayed the suggestion of a smile. 'An excellent performance, Chief Constable,' she murmured without enthusiasm, pouring herself a black coffee. 'And your reference to the early detection of the Berwick murder was a real master stroke.' She studied him over the rim of her cup as she took a tiny sip. 'I think you've managed to convince most of the would-be doubters.'

Pullinger glanced cautiously around him before replying. 'I sincerely hope so,' he replied. 'But I'm quite sure the press will do their best in the question and answer session to find something they can home in on.'

She nodded grimly. 'Well at least we seem to be safe in relation to the Eddie Challow connection – despite the best destructive efforts of your meddling press officer.' She drew him to one side, away from the coffee and the throng of delegates standing together in their tight clan-like circles. 'Any news on that front yet?'

He shook his head. 'There's not likely to be until this event is over. I left word with my secretary that I was not to be disturbed. I can only assume that the interview with your man went ahead as planned.' He frowned. 'I just hope he has agreed to cooperate.'

She took another sip of coffee. 'There won't be a problem there, provided your Mr Dexter agrees to turn in his badge – or whatever it is you people do in such circumstances. A media story on the incident is the last thing either of us wants under the circumstances and it would, of course, be quite impossible for me to continue supporting this new partnership initiative if I did not have complete confidence in your commitment to deliver your end of the – ah – agreement.'

Pullinger gave an uncomfortable little cough behind one hand. 'Dexter is history, I assure you,' he said hastily. 'I expect to have his resignation on my desk by this afternoon.'

She gave another brief smile. 'Then we have nothing to worry about, have we, Chief Constable?' she replied, turning back into the room. 'Everything seems to have been neatly sewn up.'

In fact, nothing could have been further from the truth and it was unfortunate that they failed to notice the young reporter by the conference room doors, taking a call on his mobile telephone and throwing excited, almost ravenous glances in their direction as they returned to the podium. Had they been aware of the man and his agitated body language, they might well have been alerted to the fact that something nasty was going down and been prepared for it when it surfaced. Instead, when they finally took their seats with the other members of the partnership, it was with a false sense of security that soon became apparent.

'Chief Constable,' the reporter said, springing to his feet when John Durrell invited questions, 'you talked a lot this morning about the importance of a multi-agency partnership to tackle the causes rather than just the effects of crime, but surely the most important job of the police is the protection of the public?'

Pullinger treated him to his most benign smile. 'So it is,' he replied smugly, 'so it is. And by working more closely with our partners, we will be in a much better position to challenge criminal behaviour and prevent re-offending.'

The reporter nodded slowly, but he remained on his feet, a disconcerting gleam in his eyes. 'Very commendable, Chief Constable,' he went on smoothly. 'And does working with your partners include conspiring together to cover up the government's back-door release of dangerous mental patients?'

The question hit the podium with all the numbing force of a stun grenade and for a moment Pullinger seemed to lose it completely, swaying unsteadily in front of the flashing cameras, his jaw working silently as an excited murmur ran through the astonished audience and the other agency heads seated on either side of him froze into wax-like effigies.

'Absolute nonsense,' he blustered, recovering with difficulty and desperately trying to bluff things out. 'Don't know where you reporters get these stories from. Now, any other questions please?'

'Nonsense, is it, Chief Constable?' the pressman persisted, ignoring the peremptory dismissal of his allegation and conscious of a sudden expectant hush around him. 'So are you saying you know nothing about the secret release of a psychopath named Eddie Challow or that he has been living on a canal boat at Curling Lock under an assumed name?'

Pullinger's normally ruddy complexion was chalk white and beads of perspiration had broken out on his forehead. 'I am not responsible for parole issues concerning restricted mental patients,' he retorted , his right hand travelling to his chest where he was conscious of a sudden sharp stabbing pain that seemed to be forcing itself up into his throat and down his left arm. 'They are a matter for the Home Secretary.'

'Maybe so, Chief Constable,' the reporter agreed. 'But I have reliable information that you and your *partners* here were fully aware he had been released and that you went out of your way to conceal the fact, despite the obvious risk to the community.'

'These are very serious allegations,' Pullinger countered harshly, his face twisted into a savage grimace as his hand continued to press tightly against his chest in an effort to shut off the pain, 'and I must warn you –'

The pressman's eyes narrowed. 'Oh they're serious all right,' he cut in. 'Especially since the maniac you have shielded so effectively is now on the run after a suspected bomb blast this morning claimed the lives of both a social worker and one of your own senior officers?' His face hardened. 'Under the circumstances, Chief Constable, don't you think you should do the decent thing and resign?'

But Pullinger was no longer listening, for as his fingers clawed frantically at his chest, his legs buckled under him and he pitched straight off the podium into the first row of chairs below.

Chapter 17

'Lose the screwdriver, Michael,' Eddie Challow ordered without raising his voice. 'I don't think it would be much use against a twelve-bore.'

Dexter hesitated, then let it drop to the floor at his feet.

'Excellent. Now kick it over towards me.'

The policeman reluctantly complied. 'What have you done to Tania?' he breathed, staring at the pathetic figure apparently tied to the massive tanker wheel just yards away, legs thrust out in front of her and head lolling forward on to her chest.

Challow chuckled. 'She's a bit out of it at the moment, Michael, I'm afraid,' he replied, making sure he kept his eyes on him as he bent down to pick up the screwdriver and carefully push it into his belt. 'Still getting over the effects of the little injection I had to give her, you see.'

'You bastard!'

'Now that's rather unfair, Michael, especially as I took all the trouble to make sure she was dressed in some nice warm clothes from her locker before we left the hospital.' Another chuckle. 'You know, I almost enjoyed dressing her as much as I did *un*dressing her all those years ago.'

He broke off, raising the shotgun sharply as Dexter's body tensed. 'Uh-uh, no silly moves please, Michael. We don't want any stray shotgun pellets hitting the tanker, do we? Could be a tad risky with all that petrol on board – especially for Tania.'

Dexter visibly relaxed and the other smiled his approval. 'That's better. We don't want any nasty accidents, do we? Bit of a waste after all the planning and effort that's gone into getting the tanker up here. Not easy driving one of those monsters after twenty years off the road, you know, particularly as I had to come in by the back door across the old MOD firing range to avoid attracting attention in the village. That old quarry track obviously hasn't been used for quite a while and it left a few dents and scratches in the bodywork, I'm afraid, but –'

Dexter cut him short. 'Never mind the garbage, Challow,' he snarled. 'I want to see my wife – like *now*.'

The other inclined his head in a conciliatory gesture, though he kept the shotgun firmly trained on the policeman's chest. 'Be my guest, Michael, but no tricks please.'

Dexter needed no second invitation and in three short strides he was down on one knee beside his wife, one hand under her chin gently raising her head as he stared into the half-closed eyes. There was a momentary flicker of recognition and a soft moan escaped the pale lips, but her hands remained behind her back and he saw that they were indeed tied to the wheel of the lorry. 'What the hell have you pumped into her?' he said hoarsely without taking his eyes off her.

Holding the shotgun with one hand, Challow carefully withdrew a thin glass tube from his coat pocket with the other. 'Oh just a little something I borrowed from the hospital before I left,' he murmured, turning the tube round in his palm with deft fingers. 'The shrinks give it to their stressed patients all the time, so I thought Tania might like some to calm her down.' His voice hardened. 'In fact, I thought you might like some too.' And even as Dexter pivoted round to face him in a futile defensive gesture, the hypodermic needle was plunged into the back of his neck.

★

It was mid-afternoon before Mary Lane was able to extricate herself from the double murder enquiry at Curling Lock on the pretext of a violent headache. Detective Superintendent Moffat had not been too happy at her departure, seeing her as a key member of his now massively expanded team, but noting her white face and haunted sunken eyes, her own boss, DI John Robinson, had firmly insisted that she be allowed to go home and rest.

'See you in the morning,' Robinson said as she climbed behind the wheel of her car. 'And get some shut-eye in the meantime, eh?'

But shut-eye was the last thing on Mary's mind. All afternoon she had been trying to contact Mike Dexter, but without success. According to the dull recorded voice of the operator, his mobile was now switched off and his home number had responded each time she had called with a similar answer phone message, telling her to leave her name and number. Even the Headquarters Press Office had no idea where he was and despite a force-wide radio circulation of his car details, his Volvo had not been sighted since leaving the hospital.

As a last resort, she dropped into Gilstone Police Station on the outside chance that he had been trying to contact her and had left a message on her voice mail. But again, there was nothing and, setting the telephone down with an irritable grimace, she stared around the empty CID office, desperately trying to decide what to do next, one hand still resting on the telephone as the long fingers of the other drummed noisily on the polished desk top.

It was then that she caught sight of the bulky brown envelope, marked "urgent" which had been left propped up against the nest of overfull filing trays. It had obviously been put there by Dennis Skinner before he had left the office on whatever job it was that had forced him out of his comfortable swivel chair, for there was a note attached to it in his distinctive bold handwriting:

Civvy from HQ dropped this in for you on his way home. Said you wanted it PDQ. Not naughty poses, I hope.

In a second Mary had pushed her concerns about Mike Dexter to the back of her mind. She knew the envelope could only contain the prints from the film found in Quentin Fuller's car and she felt a little flutter of excitement as she slit open the flap with her paperknife and emptied the contents on to the desk.

There were four of the familiar photograph portfolios inside, each one bearing the force crest in the centre, plus a reference number in the top right-hand corner, and it soon became apparent that, contrary to Mike Dexter's cynical suggestion a few hours before, Fuller had been doing a whole lot more than taking wedding pictures. In fact, he had managed to obtain the sort of photographic evidence that an experienced police surveillance team would have given anything for.

The first two portfolios contained mostly photographs, taken at various angles, of a burned-out and still smoking building, with fire appliances and police vehicles parked in the foreground, and she instantly recognised the place from the newspaper pictures she had seen of Judge Berwick's house. Then came the shots of a narrow boat, the name *Water Gypsy* clearly visible on the bow, which had evidently been taken from woodland cover as some of the prints were framed by branches and leaves.

Eddie Challow featured almost entirely in the third portfolio, a series of tele-photo shots capturing his cold expressionless face staring directly at the camera as he left the boat and walked off along the towpath, his dark eyes boring into the lens as if he actually knew the camera was there. But it was the last portfolio that gave her the biggest shock, her eyes widening and her mouth drying up as she stared in horror at the things that had been assembled on what appeared to be some sort of table top, like a crude still life composition.

The sawn-off shotgun and half dozen or so loose cartridges were frightening enough in themselves, but the sausage-shaped substance in the cardboard box, which had been positioned on the table top among a tell-tale assortment of strapless watches, batteries, electrical wiring and what looked suspiciously like detonators, added a whole new dimension to the term *frightening*. She didn't need to be an expert in ordnance to know what she was looking at and for a few seconds she found it almost impossible to tear her gaze away. When she finally did, however, turning her attention to the last two prints in the portfolio, everything abruptly jerked into place – like an out of focus camera lens snapping into shot on a thought in her brain.

The prints themselves were photographs of a detailed ordnance survey map of the force area's Grazely Moor District, weighted down at the corners by ashtrays and an empty vase, and just south of Grazely itself, the village of Tulse End, with its derelict quarry workings and warning MOD sign, had been ringed by someone in thick black ink. Suddenly it dawned on her that she had made the most terrible mistake of her life and she snatched up the telephone in a panic.

The female communications operator in the Area Control Room at Heaton Police Station answered almost immediately.

'DS Lane, Gilstone CID,' Mary blurted. 'Get me the duty inspector – and fast.'

There was a brief pause before a brisk male voice answered. 'Inspector Whitley. What is it, skipper?'

'The TQI containment at Grange, gov,' she said quickly. 'I think we've got the wrong target.'

There was a sharp intake of breath. 'Wrong target? But you were the one who put it up in the first place.'

She swallowed hard, nodding quickly to herself. 'I know and I've made one hell of a mistake. Eddie Challow is not interested in the depot at all. He's going after Tulse End village.'

'Tulse End? And how on earth do you know that?'

She took a deep breath. 'Look, governor, with respect, this isn't the time to go into all the whys and wherefores. We have to redeploy the

244

Armed Response Unit and Operations Support Unit at the TQI depot immediately.'

'You mean pull them off? I can't do that. That's a Headquarters operation. I'd have to get the authority of ACC Operations first'

'Then we need to get that authority PDQ.'

There was an incredulous snort. 'You've got to be joking. Have you any idea what's been going on up at the *Big House?* The Chief collapsed with a suspected heart attack this afternoon and he is on the critical list at County Hospital. Now, on top of that, we've got the press running a major sleaze story about a conspiracy between the top brass of this force and the Home Office. The shit really has hit the fan this time and I'm told that ACC Ops has been closeted with the Police Authority Chairman for the past two hours trying to sort out the mess.'

'There'll be an even bigger mess if we don't get to Tulse End before Eddie Challow.'

'And what if you're wrong and he hits the TQI depot, as expected, after the troops have been taken off?'

'He won't. I told you he's after Tulse End.'

'Yes, and earlier on today you said he was after TQI. Why should what you're telling me now be any more reliable than what you said before?'

Mary controlled her frustration with an effort. 'Look, gov,' she said with brittle patience, 'we're wasting time. You *must* get to Mr Parkes, no matter what.'

'And you expect me to contact HQ and get someone to march into the ACC's office, busting up a critical meeting, on the strength of what you've just told me? Be your age, Mary. He'll want chapter and verse before he'll even consider making the sort of decision you're after, and so far you've given me zilch.' He sighed. 'Look, the local ABO, Ted Street, is on duty at Tulse End this evening; they've got some kind of a pig roast and fair there tonight. I'll call him up and ask him to keep his eyes open. I'll also get one of the local area cars to pop over there when one is free. That's the best I can do until ACC Ops is contacted and before that can be done, you have to give me a lot more information.'

But Mary was fresh out of patience, and she had already slammed down the telephone in disgust and was heading for the door at a run.

★

Mike Dexter surfaced very slowly. Someone was urgently calling his name. 'Michael, wake up, will you. You have to wake up!' Reluctantly he opened his eyes and tried to focus properly. Two lights bobbing up and down in a black void. Now doubling to four. He squeezed his eyes shut, then opened them again. Back to two lights; fuzzy, indistinct. Part of a wall materialising, then vanishing again as the lights started to dwindle. He wanted to go with them, drift back into comforting oblivion.

'Michael, *please*!' He focused with difficulty and the lights steadied, smoky yet intense. He was conscious of the strong sickly-sweet smell of paraffin, mixed with the distinctive urine-like odour of damp wood and stonework. 'Oh Michael, thank God!'

He turned his head to one side, choking back the surge of vomit in his throat. Tania's face was inches from his own. She was white and ghost-like, her hair dishevelled and her eyes sunken but unnaturally bright in the harsh undiluted glare of the two hurricane lamps suspended a few feet above their heads. He tried to move, but realised his wrists were tightly bound and lashed to something behind his back.

He was sitting beside Tania on what appeared to be some sort of mattress, legs thrust out in front of him, back against the wall, and he could feel the mattress quivering under him every time he moved, as if it were perched on something none too stable. 'Where the hell are we?' he demanded hoarsely, conscious of the distant sound of music, punctuated by the muffled shrieks and whistles normally associated with fairground rides.

'The house,' Tania whispered. 'My father's old bedroom.'

'What?'

'Keep still, Michael,' she pleaded in a frightened sob. 'It's not safe up here. There's – there's no proper floor, only a few planks Challow's laid across the bits that survived the fire. They could give way at any moment.'

He peered over the edge of the mattress and immediately spotted several wide gaps in the floor where the light from the lamps haemorrhaged away into stygian darkness. 'But how the hell –?' he began.

'He – he forced me to help him carry you up here when I came round from the injection he'd given me at the hospital,' she blurted before he could finish the question. 'There's a ladder sticking up through the floor just in front of the mattress.'

He leaned forward as far as his bonds would allow and glimpsed the shafts and the topmost rung. 'So, where's the little swine now?'

She shook her head miserably. 'I have no idea where he's gone. He put me out with another needle soon after dumping me up here.'

He grunted. 'And how long ago was that?'

She shrugged, desperately trying to hold back her tears. 'Has to be several hours, I just don't know. But it's dark outside – you can see the moon through that hole in the roof – and the fair in Tulse End is in full swing.'

He strained his neck and part of a pale misty disc stared back at him, cold and disinterested. 'So why can't we see through the balcony window?'

She took a deep breath, still fighting to keep control. 'He blocked it up with something before he left.'

'Playing games as usual, is he?' he muttered, then studied her face narrowly. 'Are you all right? He hasn't touched you, has he?'

She hesitated, looking away from him. 'I – I don't think so, but I only came round about half an hour before you…'

Her voice trailed away and he made a tight grimace, turning his attention to his bonds in a futile attempt to take his mind off what they were both thinking, then abruptly cursing as something cut sharply into his wrist.

'Don't,' Tania said quickly. 'You'll only injure yourself. He – he used chicken wire to tie us up. The more you pull on it, the tighter it gets.'

'Chicken wire?'

She nodded, her tongue darting along her lower lip. 'Just like my father.' Her eyes locked on to his and he saw her throat convulse in a hard swallow. 'Michael, we're lying on Daddy's old iron bed,' she said tremulously, 'the same one he was tied to when – when it happened. It's been up here all these years, clinging to the remains of the floor.'

He felt his skin crawl. 'The same bed?' he rasped. 'After twenty odd years? How the hell could that be?'

'Because your lot left it up here afterwards, that's why,' she sobbed, finally breaking down. 'You should have taken it away. Now he's going to fry us on it, just like my father!'

'Oh you would have to go and spoil it all,' a hard mocking voice commented from the gloom and Eddie Challow's face appeared above the mattress at the foot of the bed like that of a disembodied phantom as he hoisted himself slowly up the ladder into the room.

★

The Tulse End Winter Fair seemed to be well underway when Mary Lane drove into the narrow lane leading to the village and she found herself at the back of a long queue of cars creeping towards the signed car parks. Revving the engine of the powerful little car as her frustration got the better of her, she eventually spotted a slight widening of the road and pulled out to overtake – stopping with a sudden jolt as a marshal in a yellow coat jumped in front of her bonnet, one hand thrust out in front of him as if he thought he was *Superman*. 'No queue jumpin',' he shouted. 'You get back in line, Miss.'

Ignoring the blasting horns of the other cars, she lowered the window and thrust her warrant card under his nose. 'Police,' she snapped. 'Now get out of the way before I run you over!'

'Got your number,' she heard him yell after her as she nosed her way past him. 'I know your chief constable.'

'Bully for you,' she muttered, swinging sharply across the nose of a flashy looking Jaguar and continuing down the lane on the inside of the traffic queue as it swung into an open gateway, signed "Free Car Park".

She actually ploughed through the red and white plastic bollards coning off the lane just beyond the car park entrance, sending a blue and white police sign crashing to the ground on its metal stand, but was forced to reduce her speed to a crawl as she threaded her way through the crowds thronging the last few yards of the lane. Seemingly oblivious to the abusive shouts that followed her and the fists that slammed into the side of the car, she finally reached the edge of the village green, but was forced to stop again when a young uniformed policeman stepped in front of her. 'Can't you read?' he shouted, jerking the drivers door open.

'DS Lane,' she responded, climbing out of the car. 'Did Control call you?'

Ted Street, the local beat officer, straightened and nodded. 'Something about a nutter with a petrol tanker. I'm keeping an eye open, don't worry.'

She emitted a short unamused laugh. 'Keeping an eye open?' she exclaimed, raising her voice to make herself heard above the noise around her. 'You'll need a damned sight more than that if Eddie Challow turns up here, I can tell you.'

He stiffened. 'Eddie Challow? Control didn't tell me about him. Didn't even know he was out again. I was just told to keep my eyes peeled for a stolen petrol tanker and to radio in the moment I saw it.'

She closed her eyes briefly in resignation. 'That idiot inspector,' she muttered under her breath, then added in a louder voice: 'So what do *you* know about Eddie Challow?'

The policeman shrugged. 'Not a lot, except he was put away for murder and rape at the Ferguson place.' He grinned 'And I happen to be living in his old house.'

She studied the crowds milling among the brightly lit stalls and sideshows that covered the village green, crinkling her nose at the mix of rich appetising smells – barbecuing meat, frying onions and candyfloss – that embraced her senses on the chilly night air, as strategically placed speakers tried desperately to do justice to an old *Beatles'* number, while competing with the organ music of the adjoining fair.

'So you have no idea what he looks like?' she queried, instinctively raising her voice even more.

He shook his head. 'Funny thing though, there was another guy asking questions about him the other day.'

She jerked her head round to stare at him, ignoring some catcalls from one of a group of leather-jacketed youths slouching past. 'What other guy?'

Another shrug. 'Some journalist – or at least that's what he said he was. Checked him outside my house. He told me he covered the original story twenty years ago. Seemed to find it amusing that a copper was living in Challow's old cottage.'

'What did he look like?'

He frowned. 'Can't really remember now. Think he had a ginger beard. I do remember his car though. Big white Merc.'

Mary started. A bearded man in a white Mercedes? It had to be Quentin Fuller. 'Where did he go after he left you?' she snapped.

'No idea. Maybe up to the old Ferguson place if he was on some sort of follow-up story. Seemed very interested when I mentioned Quarry Wood Hill.'

She snapped her fingers. 'But that's it; the old Ferguson place. That's where Challow will be, not down here in the village. I should have sussed that out straightaway.'

He frowned again. 'Why would he want to go up there? Place is derelict. Only a few old empty buildings.'

'Exactly. The ideal place to conceal a stolen petrol tanker until it's needed – *and* hide a couple of hostages. How do you get to it?'

He pointed across the green. 'Quarry Wood Road is over there, between the vicarage and the cemetery. What's all this about hostages though? No one said anything –'

But she was already ducking back into her car. 'Get on to Control. Tell them to send the cavalry down here *now*.'

'But you can't go up there on your own.'

'Someone's got to before it's too late.'

She was pulling away before he could do anything to stop her and it was only as her tail-lights disappeared among the revellers crowding the road that the awful realisation dawned on him. He had left his personal radio in the police Land Rover parked on the other side of the green.

*

'Comfy then?' Eddie Challow deposited a large oblong can on the floor to one side of the ladder and, straightening up inside the room, propped himself on a wooden box in the corner, studying his two captives with evident relish. 'You should be grateful, you know,' he added. 'I went to a lot of trouble getting hold of that mattress and persuading one of our knights of the road to help me lug it up here.' He chuckled. 'Unfortunately Ron Ferguson rather soiled the original with barbecued body juices and I gather the forensic team had a bit of a job separating him from what was left of it.'

'You filthy heap of shit!' Dexter breathed.

Challow shook his head. 'You really do have a most foul tongue, don't you, Michael?' he admonished. 'Mind you, poor old Lionel Berwick wasn't much better, I have to say. Came out with some quite choice expletives, he did – and him a judge too. Don't know what the world is coming to. Now, Shammy Leather, he was completely different. Never stopped pleading right up to the last moment. But in the end he preferred to take his chance jumping off the bridge than being opened up by a twelve-bore at two feet.'

'But why kill a harmless tramp? He was no threat to you.'

'I'm afraid he got greedy, Michael. I paid him good money to help me. Then some interfering journalist poked his nose in here and he was ready to do a deal with him for a little bit extra. So I'm afraid he had to go – and the journalist a bit later too. He was getting much too close, you see. Could have ruined everything.'

'And you planted some of your keepsakes from Judge Berwick's house on the tramp to throw the police off the scent?'

Challow shrugged. 'All part of the game, Michael, and it did increase my lead time, so it was well worth it.'

'You see slaughtering helpless people as a game then, do you?'

Challow made no effort to deny it. 'Well, I must admit that in the Judge's case it did rather satisfy an inner longing. I enjoyed throttling that nurse too, of course, but that was more sexual than anything else, whereas old Berwick was strictly a personal thing.'

'You mean revenge.'

'Okay, so it was revenge. I don't have any trouble with that word. But Berwick was anything but helpless, I assure you. Put up quite a fight actually. Still, he burned well, a bit like a piece of dry wood, in fact. Most wizened old men are the same, I suppose; just sinew and bone. I should think Andy Pollard was different though. Quite a lot of weight there, more grease to fry. But sadly, because of my tight schedule and the need to be miles away when the hotel went up, I had to use a trigger device, so I wasn't around for the result. I did have a chat with Andy before I left though – straightened out a few misconceptions.'

Dexter stared at him with undisguised revulsion. 'And Kitty Morrison?' he grated. 'You must have been really proud of yourself there?'

Challow sighed. 'Oh yes, the lovely Kitty. Bit of a waste that was, but I had to do it, you see. I'd got all I wanted out of her and she was becoming a liability. Still, I did the job as humanely as possible, you have to give me credit for that.'

'And you forced her locker at the gym just in case she had put anything in there about you?'

Challow nodded. 'Very romantic girl, young Kitty. Didn't want some diary left for prying eyes, did I?' He chuckled again. 'This is a bit like one of those "Whodunit" type round-ups, Michael. You know, the clever detective getting the villain to confess everything just before the end. If I hadn't searched you thoroughly while you were out for the count, I'd suspect you of being wired.'

'You murdered all those poor innocent people just to get at me?' Tania whispered in disbelief.

'And not just people either,' Dexter added harshly before Challow could answer. 'He also torched our barn, and Gwenda with it.'

'Gwenda?' Tania seemed to shrink into the mattress. 'You killed my Gwenda?'

Challow sighed again. 'And I'm so sorry you weren't there to see it, my dear. But when I had those flowers delivered to you at your aunt's home, I didn't realise they would have such a dramatic impact and that you would end up in hospital. I'd planned on you being back home to see the show, you see. Still, at least it proved one thing, I haven't lost my touch.'

'Your touch?' Dexter echoed.

'Oh yes, Michael. You see, handling explosives is quite an art and timers in particular can be very temperamental things. Fortunately I had a good teacher. My father was in army ordnance before he became a quarry blaster. He taught me all he knew. Couldn't resist it, you see. Liked to impress his little boy. Big mistake though, because his little boy eventually used all that expertise on him.'

Dexter nodded slowly, not really surprised by this latest admission. 'So you murdered him as well then?'

Even in the gloom he could see Challow's face change, the thin veneer of cold indifference vanishing to reveal the rabid beast beneath. 'He deserved it,' he said with sudden venom. 'He was a violent drunken animal. Always knocking my mother and me about. Put her in hospital once, you know. But I fixed him in the end – and for good too.'

'The original child psycho, eh?' Dexter retorted with heavy sarcasm.

Challow recovered his composure and smiled again, refusing to be goaded. 'Everyone has to start somewhere, Michael,' he replied, 'and, ironically, I was able to build on my earlier education by studying electronics when I was put away. Innocent enough interest in itself, but particularly useful when you're making sophisticated detonator triggers and timers. In fact, the most sophisticated trigger I've used so far was the one I set up on my canal boat as a present for Tommy Lee. Hopefully, he's found it by now.'

Dexter did look surprised this time. 'Tommy Lee? But why would you want to kill him? He took you in, gave you somewhere to stay.'

Challow leaned forward slightly. 'Yes, Michael, but he also bled my mother of her only savings in her last years of life, thinking I would never find out. But I did and it's payback time.'

'So, it's you against the world, is it?'

Another chuckle. 'Only those who owe me, Michael.'

'Yeah, as well as anyone else who happens to get in the way – like the tanker driver and the garage assistant, for example.'

Challow shrugged again. 'What is it our American cousins call

252

that, "collateral damage", isn't it? Can't be helped in a war, Michael; it's an inevitable consequence.'

'This isn't a war, Challow, this is multiple murder.'

The other laughed loudly. 'With the best yet to come, Michael, I promise you,' he replied, 'and you will have a grandstand view of the event, of that you can be certain.'

Carefully picking his way across the room, he fumbled with what looked like a heavy blanket hanging from the wall in front of them and as it crumpled to the floor, cool damp air seeped through the empty frame of the balcony window, bringing with it the strange smells of the night and allowing a flood of moonlight into the room.

'See what I mean about a grandstand view?' Challow mocked.

Perched as it was on the highest point of Quarry Wood Hill, the house might well have afforded a spectacular view of the surrounding countryside had it been a bright sunny day. Now, illuminated only by the pale opalescent light of the moon, the world it surveyed was for the most part a secret hidden place, buried in a silver-traced blue-black sea, from which, far below, the lights of Tulse End erupted in a fusion of colour, like a miniature Las Vegas.

'The village makes a wonderful sight lit up like that, doesn't it?' Challow went on. 'But if you think that's impressive, just wait until I deliver my nice shiny present from TQ International. It will be like the Fourth of July – especially with the amount of gelly I've packed around the tank.'

Dexter's eyes widened in horror as he suddenly thought of something Sarah Hamilton-Lancing had told him a few days before. 'The explosive store at Littleton Camp,' he exclaimed. 'You did that as well.'

Challow sighed. 'One man crime wave, that's me, Michael,' he replied. 'But they did ask to be hit, you know. Very poor security there and so many goodies on offer.'

Dexter felt physically sick. 'But you can't mean to target Tulse End? For pity's sake, there are hundreds of people down there.'

'Why do you think I picked this particular night? It's the one occasion when most of the village will be at home.'

'But those people have done nothing to you.'

'Nothing?' Challow almost spat the word and, lurching towards the bed, he gripped the iron rail at the foot of the mattress and thrust his face towards his two captives, trembling with emotion. 'Nothing, you say? Do you call hounding a frail old lady out of her home and into her grave *nothing*? Because that's what the worthy upright citizens of Tulse End did to my mother while I was inside. Judged her, condemned her and executed her – without evidence, without charge and without trial. And why? Not for anything she had done, but because she happened to be the mother of a convicted psychopath. Well, Mister Chief Inspector, now I am going to do the same to them, and you and the lovely Tania can sit here and watch while they burn.'

'And you're prepared to massacre scores of innocent children in the process?'

Challow straightened up, regaining control with an effort, and in the strengthening moonlight streaming in through the window, his expression was suddenly cold and bleak, like that of a cemetery statue. 'What is it the *Good Book* says, Michael?' he said. 'Something about the sins of the fathers being visited on the third and fourth generations?'

Dexter swore savagely. 'And what about your sins, Challow? All the lives you've taken and still intend to take? You think you have a God-given right to murder who you like?'

'No, but I have a right to justice,' Challow said softly. 'I was locked up in a mental hospital for twenty years for a murder I didn't commit. Have you any idea what that was like? Twenty years of my life spent behind bars with a load of crazies and my own mother sent to an early grave, believing I was guilty. I can't change the past, but I can at least ensure that those responsible don't have a future.'

'Oh come on, Challow, you're not still banging that same old drum, are you? You got what you deserved, so don't try using injustice as an excuse for revenge.'

Challow shook his head slowly. 'Do you know what's really ironic, Michael? Most of the crimes I committed in my youth – the fires I started in Tulse End, the young girls I assaulted in different parts of the country when I was out on the road – I got away with. Yet the one crime I did not commit, the murder of Ron Ferguson, got me twenty years.'

Dexter snorted his contempt. 'How very unfair,' he retorted. 'My heart bleeds for you. And I suppose you didn't rape Tania either? Which, in case you've forgotten, also contributed to your sentence.'

Challow turned to look at Dexter's wife. 'I never denied I had sex with Tania,' he replied, 'only that I didn't take her against her will. But as far as Ron Ferguson is concerned, I had nothing at all to do with his death – even if I have to admire the panache of the person who actually put him to the torch.'

'Okay, so, if *you* didn't kill him, who did?'

'*I* did,' Tania said in a soft tremulous voice. 'I killed my father.'

Chapter 18

'Are you crazy?' Mike Dexter stared at his wife in stunned disbelief, his sense of shock rendering him totally insensitive to his choice of words. 'What the hell possessed you to come out with a statement like that?'

Tania turned her face towards him, putty white and glistening with freshly shed tears. 'Because it's true, Michael,' she said brokenly. 'I – I killed my father – me, no one else – and it's time to admit to what I've done.'

Eddie Challow clapped his hands very slowly. 'Oh, bravo, Tania,' he sneered. 'A confession to be proud of. Pity it's come twenty years too late.'

She hung her head, staring at the mattress. 'I'm so sorry, Michael,' she whispered. 'You're the last person I would want to hurt after all you've done for me, but I just can't keep it to myself any longer. It's been haunting me all these long years.'

Dexter shook his head wildly. 'You're – you're not well, Tania,' he blurted, a look of panic on his face. 'You don't know what you're saying. For heaven's sake, listen to me. *He's* the murderer. You haven't killed anyone. It's all part of your illness.'

She looked up at him again and the agony in her eyes was clearly visible in the bright moonlight. 'Please, Michael,' she pleaded. 'You must believe me. It's got nothing to do with my illness. That was just a convenient place for me to hide; my refuge from the truth. But you can't hide from things forever. Eventually you have to deal with the ghosts – and they come to me every single night to remind me of what I've done.'

'But this is total rubbish Tania. What possible reason would you have for killing your own father?'

She took a deep ragged breath. 'Because of Rebecca,' she said quietly. 'Because of what he did to my beautiful sister.'

'Your sister?' Dexter echoed. 'Tania, sweetheart, you're all mixed up. Aunt Mildred told me about Rebecca yesterday. Ron didn't do anything to her. She committed suicide because of the stress she had suffered at the convent school.'

She shook her head slowly. 'Oh Michael,' she whispered, 'don't you see? It had nothing to do with the convent school. That was just the excuse my mother came up with to hide the family's terrible secret. Rebecca hung herself for one reason and one reason alone: my father. For month after month she'd had to suffer the degrading sexual abuse he'd inflicted on her, until finally, she couldn't stand the shame of it anymore and ended her life with a rope!'

He gaped at her. 'You're saying Ron Ferguson was a *paedophile*?'

She didn't answer him directly, but went on speaking in a halting distant voice, her eyes strangely unfocused, as if her mind were elsewhere. 'When it all began, I was too young to understand what my father was doing, you see, and my mother made sure the truth was kept from me as I got older, sending me away to the convent school soon after Rebecca's death so that I would be protected from him. I stayed there until I went on to university, so I never suffered at his hands the way poor Rebecca did and I wouldn't have known anything about it even now, but for the letter.'

'Letter? What letter?'

She carried on in the same slow distant tone, as if unaware of the question. 'I suppose it was by way of being my mother's own confession really. All those years she had kept it to herself for the sake of the family's reputation, but in the end, when she knew her time was coming, she had to set the record straight; to unburden herself before she died, just as I have to. Father O'Malley must have known what was in her letter when he handed it to me after the funeral. Mum would have confessed to him first, of course, but as a priest, he would never have breached the sanctity of the confessional – not even to Dad – and when he himself died just days later, I realised I was the only one who knew the truth. That's when I decided to make my father pay for what he had done and burn the sin out of him with God's all-cleansing fire.'

Dexter closed his eyes tightly as he tried to keep control of his emotions. 'No!' he gasped, the bile rising in his throat and almost choking him. 'You couldn't do something like that. Challow must have pumped some stuff into you to make you say these things.'

Her eyes refocused and once more began to brim with tears. 'Oh Michael,' she whispered. 'Loyal, trusting Michael. You have to understand? Nothing can help me now. It's done. Finished. All I can do is pray for forgiveness before I die.'

Dexter opened his mouth to say something, but this time no sound came out and as he desperately tried to find the words, Tania seemed to sink into the mattress, her head bent forward on her breast as if she had withdrawn into herself in some sort of catatonic trance.

'Difficult to believe, isn't it?' Challow mocked, taking advantage of Dexter's shocked silence to chime in. 'It was a while before I tumbled to the truth too, you know. Thing was, I realised I had been set up, but what was missing was a tangible motive, so I thought it had to be down to the village who hated my guts or the police who needed a rapid detection. Never dreamed the lovely Tania was behind it all – not until a few years after I had been put away, in fact, when a new inmate at the hospital put me wise. By then though it was too late to do anything about it.'

Dexter recovered suddenly, straining at the wire securing his wrists to the head of the bed. 'You lying, twisting bastard!' he snarled. 'What crap are you coming out with now?'

Challow watched his futile struggles for a moment, then smiled grimly. 'No crap, Michael, just fact. Remember Gilbert Trench, the internet paedophile the press nicknamed *The Pornbroker*? You should. It was quite a colourful case and he got sent away for at least as long as me. Well, Trench was put on the same hospital wing as me and, since we had similar pursuits (if you know what I mean), we soon got talking. And guess what? He knew Ron Ferguson very well, though certainly not because of his haulage business – more as a fully paid-up member of his own thriving little paedophile club.

'That in itself was interesting enough, but when Trench told me that Ron had actually hit on his own daughter, I suddenly realised that the motive for the Ferguson murder was staring me straight in the face and the moment I had that, everything else just fell into place.' He emitted a short cynical laugh. 'To think that at the start I actually believed dear little Tania had persuaded her father to employ me out of the goodness of her heart. I must have been really stupid. It was all part of the frame, you see. Get me in the firm, lead me on until I made the wrong move that got me the sack and bingo! With my form for arson and sexual assault, I was the perfect suspect in waiting.'

Dexter moistened dry lips. 'You're completely off your head,' he said harshly, but the bricks in the wall he had erected in his mind were already beginning to crumble and his tone lacked any real conviction.

Challow nodded. 'Maybe I am, Michael, maybe I am, but not

about this and if you think on it, everything underpins Tania's own confession. For instance, the way I was lured to the Ferguson house by a phone call from Ron, offering to pay me off. Why didn't he just send me a cheque? I shouldn't think he wanted to see my ugly face on his doorstep anyway. But the thing was, Tania did, didn't she? She needed to get me to visit the site at the critical time as part of her elaborate stitch-up. That's obviously why she persuaded her old man to make the phone call in the first place. The fact that no one answered the door when I rang the bell was hardly surprising under the circumstances, for no one was in any position to answer doors, were they? Ron was no doubt already pissed out of his mind and tightly gagged and lashed to the bed with chicken wire, ready for the barbecue, while Tania herself would have quit the premises altogether well before the pre-arranged appointment time. She couldn't afford to be at home when I turned up, could she? She needed to be seen in the village at the critical time and she made sure the locals would remember her being there by stopping off at the local pub, wearing as little as possible, before heading back to the house.'

Dexter swallowed hard several times and glanced uneasily at his wife's hunched figure. 'That's a load of balls,' he said desperately. 'She was out jogging, as she did most evenings.'

'Oh she was out jogging all right, Michael, but she made sure she was sitting in the middle of Quarry Wood Road when I drove back down the hill, claiming to have twisted her ankle and giving me the very clearest of come-ons. She told the court I dragged her into the bushes, but actually it was she who led the way, wiggling her bum in her tight shorts and skimpy top.'

Dexter snorted. 'Oh yeah, she was obviously up for it. That's why she left nail marks in your face.'

Challow chuckled. 'All part of the plan, Michael. See, she'd already gone through my unlocked van when it was parked on site a few days earlier, planting the stolen property from Ron's study amongst the rubbish in the back where I wouldn't see it. She'd also helped herself to some of my chicken wire, which she later used to lash her old man to the bed, and nicked my spare petrol can, with my fingerprints all over it, which was to be so conveniently left at the murder scene. But she felt she needed something extra; something that would not only physically tie me into the vicinity of the crime, but also put the court against me even before they had heard all the evidence.

'The solution was to have a nice little rape scene. Properly played out at the trial, she knew that this would ensure righteous indignation among the jury and also enable the prosecution to produce irrefutable forensic evidence of my guilt. You know the sort of thing: hair and clothing fibres left in the flattened undergrowth, traces of my juices left inside her body, the skin from my face under her fingernails. All good stuff, I'm sure you'll agree, which, coupled with both the chicken wire and petrol can and the presence of the all important motive, would ensure that I was sewn up like a kipper.'

Dexter made one last effort. 'If you're so bloody clever, why did you fall for it then?'

Challow shrugged. 'Because at the time I saw Tania as nothing more than an over sexed little prick-teaser, who had already led me on for weeks and had finally got me the sack. So, when she turned on me in the woods after first offering herself to me on a plate, I thought she was just playing silly games again. That got me mad and I decided to give her exactly what she'd been asking for all along. No one was more surprised than me when she shouted "rape", but I just put her complaint down to sour grapes and the fear most slappers have of becoming pregnant, thinking she would withdraw it after she'd thought about it later.' His voice hardened. 'But she didn't did she? I had been specially selected to carry the can for murder and the rape was an essential part of the evidence. So instead, she just stood by and watched them send me down for a crime I didn't commit.'

Tania stirred suddenly, raising her head to stare at him. 'Think of it as poetic justice, Eddie,' she said bitterly. 'Retribution for all the other crimes you *did* commit and got away with – like the murder of the runaway teenager they found in the quarry, for instance.'

'Yeah, but they couldn't prove that one, could they?' he sneered. 'Police had me in for hours, but in the end they had to let me walk.' He gave a short contemptuous laugh. 'Unlike you and another little hot arse I picked up on the road and dumped down a mine shaft a few months earlier, she didn't get the full treatment, so there was no forensic evidence for the *Old Bill* to go on. I admit I had intended giving the little bitch one when I spotted her hiding out in an old quarry shed, but fortunately for me she laughed in my face, so I settled for a little rough foreplay before throttling the life out of her instead.'

Tania didn't take her eyes off him. 'I'm glad you told me that, Eddie,' she said quietly, her voice strangely cold and hard. 'It eases my conscience. You're the same sort of scum as my father was and you should have been erased from the face of the earth just like him.'

Challow lurched forward again and, gripping the iron rail at the foot of the bed with both hands, he thrust his face towards her as before. 'Erased, eh?' he sneered. 'Now there's an imaginative word. Well, let me tell you something, my love. Tonight, it's me who's going to be doing the erasing, starting with Tulse End, and it's fitting that TQI should be the instrument of my revenge.'

He swung away from the bed once more, staring out of the window and breathing heavily. 'Have you any idea what 35,000 litres of exploding fuel will do to a village like that? It will create a fire-ball that will be seen for miles, even without the boost provided by the petrol pumps at the filling station. And all I have to do is to roll my mobile bomb down the last few yards of Quarry Wood Hill and detonate it when it hits the village green.'

He reached in the pocket of his leather jacket and held up something in one hand. 'You haven't seen my new toy, have you? It looks a bit like a TV monitor actually, but it has a much better range and once armed, it only requires one little button to be pressed, then "*BOOM*"! No tanker and no Tulse End.'

He faced them again, his dark eyes gleaming. 'But don't worry, I haven't left the pair of you out of things. In fact, I thought we'd finish our party with another much smaller barbecue once the main event has kicked off. I don't think you'll be disappointed with the result either, for when the timed incendiary device I've rigged up under your bed sets off all the inflammable material I've packed around it, a first-class cooking temperature can be guaranteed.' Pulling a small clock from his other pocket, he placed it carefully on a stool on Dexter's side of the bed. 'I thought I'd leave this for you so you can keep track of the time, which now stands at' – and he peered at the luminous face – 'exactly 1933 hours. Only twenty-seven minutes to zero hour, so you haven't long to wait.'

'The authorities will hunt you down, you know that, don't you?' Dexter put in abruptly. 'You won't be able to hide from them forever.'

Challow chuckled. 'Don't you believe it, Michael,' he retorted. 'By the time they start looking, I will already be on a plane to Australia with my nice new passport and identity. See, the thing is, you come across people with some interesting connections when you're inside and one little man I befriended had a nephew on the outside with particularly useful artwork skills. Did an excellent job for me too.' He manufactured a sigh. 'Sadly, he had to have an unfortunate accident afterwards, but life is full of these little tragedies, isn't it? Talking of which, it's time I was getting on with my job.'

Bending down beside the bed, he produced a reel of sticky tape and a couple of balls of soft spongy material. 'Can't have you calling out to some stray passer-by once I've left, can we?' he explained, expertly gagging them both, despite their protests. 'And I think we've said about all there is to be said, don't you?'

Extinguishing the two hurricane lamps, he picked up the large square can he had brought with him and unscrewed the cap, sniggering inanely as his captives shrank away from him when they smelled the petrol. 'Just time for the marinade before I go,' he said.

*

Driving through the moonlight without lights at just over a crawl to avoid advertising her presence, Mary Lane thought she would never actually get to the old Ferguson place and it didn't help her frustration when she eventually reached the T junction halfway up Quarry Wood Road and turned left towards the quarry entrance by mistake. Jerking to a halt at the last moment when she spotted the half-open gates, she aimed her torch through the windscreen to read the warning notice, then reversed back into the junction with a muttered curse and headed in the opposite direction.

Broken glass glittered in the turning area at the top of the hill and she pulled up on to the grass verge opposite the tunnel-like entrance to the old haulage site and sat there for a moment with the engine running, gnawing her lip. Even this far up the hill, she could hear the muted sounds of the fair in Tulse End, but there was not a murmur or a glimmer of light from among the closely packed trees on the other side of the wall in front of her and she felt a stab of apprehension.

Maybe she had been a bit too hasty coming up here on her own. Once in the depths of those woods, how the hell would anyone be able to find her? And what did she expect to achieve against a psychopath armed with a shotgun anyway?

Pulling her mobile telephone from her pocket, more as a reflex action than anything else, she checked the illuminated window and saw that the battery indicator was registering almost nil. Suddenly she wished she had not left Gilstone Police Station in such a hurry. Then perhaps she might have thought to grab a police radio on the way.

But it was too late now and with so little charge remaining in the battery of her phone, she was left with no option but to switch it off, just in case she needed it for an emergency call later.

So, what to do now? Carry on regardless in the hope that she could find a way of outwitting Challow or simply jack it all in and wait for the heavy mob to arrive – if they ever came at all? Common sense dictated the latter, but she had never been a quitter in her life and something told her that Tania and Mike Dexter were in big trouble and needed her like yesterday.

Carefully engaging gear, she drove across the turning area and nosed her way through the entranceway, feeling the darkness close around her like a shroud as the foliage shut out all but the tiniest traces of moonlight. That almost non-existent trickle of light was all that she had to drive by and it was an unnerving experience heading into an almost solid wall of blackness, trusting to luck and the occasional glimpse of a tree trunk to guide her way.

She abandoned the car the moment the trees began to thin out, and the returning moonlight suddenly illuminated a large building directly ahead. Driving the vehicle right off the road through a small gap in the undergrowth, she winced as the nearside wing made a horrible scraping sound when it rubbed up against something hard, like a projecting branch or concealed tree stump.

Her door also caught on something as she pushed it open and immediately the interior light blazed in her eyes. 'Damn,' she muttered, closing it to before fumbling for the switch to flick the light off altogether. 'Why don't I just hit the horn to announce my arrival!'

Feeling inadequate and vulnerable, but determined to press on, she grabbed her torch off the front seat and forced herself out of the car, zipping up her leather jacket as she gently closed the door behind her for a second time. The air that greeted her was cold and damp, laden with the strong smell of fungus and rotting leaves like a recently opened grave, and she was unable to repress a shudder as she picked her way back to the track through the clinging wet undergrowth.

In the blaze of moonlight, the ruined buildings that were gathered round the broad concrete hardstanding looked even more sinister than the dark secret woods from which she had emerged and she stood for a few moments, looking for any signs of life. But there were none and, taking a deep breath, she set off along the line of trees at a run, trying to keep in their shadow as much as possible.

The first two buildings she came to were worth no more than a cursory glance. Little more than roofless shells, with several gaping holes in their half-corrugated iron walls, they were incapable of concealing anything. The big hangar-like building beyond was a different story, however, and, squeezing through the gap between the steel doors, she found exactly what she was looking for.

Even against the massive dimensions of the old lorry garage, the stolen petrol tanker still looked enormous and in the moonlight pouring through a hole in the vaulted roof, it certainly dwarfed Tommy Lee's Land Rover and the distinctive blue Volvo parked beside it. Her heart lurched when she recognised Dexter's car and she practically ran towards it, dreading what she might find as she jerked open the driver's door and peered inside. But it was empty and, breathing a heavy sigh of relief, she advanced cautiously through the moonlight towards the opposite end of the garage, determined to check out the rest of the building.

A few yards beyond the tanker she was once more plunged into darkness, leaving her no choice but to risk using her torch, partially masking its light with the fingers of one hand. A few yards more and the probing pencil-like beam caught the dull glint of metal as an iron staircase reared up in front of her, apparently accessing the office block which abutted on to the garage at this end of the building. Raising the torch briefly, she glimpsed the rectangular gash of a doorway, flanked by a row of large windows just above the landing of the staircase, glass shards glittering in the yawning window frames.

The staircase trembled the moment she put her weight on the first step, swaying slightly, its plates and bolts creaking in protest as she began the climb, but she reached the top without mishap and ducked through the low doorway. Broken glass crunched under her feet and naked cables festooned with cobwebs brushed against her face as she made a cursory search of the three cramped floors. But she found nothing of interest, save a few pieces of broken furniture and a rusted filing cabinet, and she returned to the upper floor where she had entered the office block feeling frustrated, yet relieved.

She caught a glimpse of the light when she reached the top of the internal wooden staircase. It was visible through the open door of one of the back offices. Striding through, she leaned out over the window sill and peered intently into the night. For the first time she noticed the ruined house on the hill above the garage, silhouetted against the face of the moon and looking for all like the set of an elaborate horror movie. The light appeared to be emanating from some sort of flickering lamp in one of the top floor windows and, even as she studied the spot, it was abruptly extinguished.

Of course! The Ferguson house itself. The scene of the original crime was exactly where Eddie Challow would have chosen to take Mike and Tania, exactly the place his warped mind would have selected for... She shuddered, trying not to think about what the little psychopath might have planned, concentrating instead on getting out of the building and up to the house as quickly as possible without being detected.

The moon had taken refuge inside its invisible envelope by the time she stepped out into the cool night air and the headlights approaching the site along the concrete road were therefore more obvious, flickering eerily among the trees as the vehicle rattled and bumped its way over the broken surface. There was no mistaking the big white Land Rover with its illuminated "Police" roof sign as it raced into view, swerving diagonally across the hardstanding towards her as its headlights picked out her motionless figure by the garage doors, and she swore savagely under her breath. So much for the covert approach. Ted Street had certainly put paid to that.

As the Land Rover slid to a stop a few feet away, she ran towards it, waving her arms frantically to tell him to switch off his lights. But Street was already too late and, as he threw open his door and started to climb out into the re-emerging moonlight, the shotgun blast slammed into his chest from no more than ten feet away, hurling him back into the vehicle. Frozen to the spot in horror, Mary watched Eddie Challow pivot round towards her, the shotgun springing up in his hands like a live thing to give her the other barrel.

*

Harry Lynch was no friend of the police. In fact, as a professional criminal, he naturally saw the *Old Bill* as the main obstacle between him and his dream of an unearned cushy existence. It was therefore particularly ironic that Lynch should become indirectly responsible for saving the life of the very detective who had given him so much grief in the past few months.

Lynch had always been an opportunist and when he heard about the Tulse End pig roast and fair, he knew that, with so many houses in the village left unoccupied for the evening, he could be in for some easy pickings.

Exactly three minutes before Mary stepped out into the moonlight from the office block of the old Ferguson haulage site, Lynch smashed the toilet window of a large Georgian house off the village green and immediately activated the burglar alarm. Even as he bolted, the central station call centre to which the alarm was remotely connected had identified the location of the property and had dialled the police Area Control Room at Heaton.

The luckless Ted Street was blasted in the chest four seconds before the Area Control Room called him up and that time was of critical importance to Mary Lane, for the metallic voice of the Control Room operator barked from the radio pack-set in the Land Rover at precisely the moment that Eddie Challow turned his shotgun on her.

The sudden burst of sound completely threw him and the weapon jerked in his hand when he pulled the trigger, blasting a hole in the corrugated iron roof above Mary's head and galvanising her frozen body into immediate action.

As Challow broke the shotgun to reload, Mary ducked into the narrow passageway between the office block and the steep bank which bordered it, charging into the dense scrub that tumbled down the slope at the back of the building. Moments later she heard footsteps pounding after her and another shotgun blast ripped through the bushes to her right. Instinctively she threw herself sideways and pitched headlong down the slope, finally slamming to a halt against the trunk of a tree with an agonised gasp, convinced she must have at least cracked a rib. Heavy feet stumbled around her in the undergrowth, but she forced herself to lie perfectly still, trying to ignore the pain in her side and hold back her tears as she thought of Ted Street.

It was her fault that he was dead and she knew she would never forgive herself for that. She should have known he would come after her to back her up – no self-respecting bobby would let a colleague go it alone in such a risky situation – and if she hadn't been so pig-headed in the first place, he would still be alive now. What a horrible mess.

More clumsy movement around her and the next moment the barrel of the shotgun was thrust into the patch of scrub in which she was hiding, missing her head by inches. Further probing around her body, but miraculously the barrel missed her each time. There was a pause and the sound of heavy breathing. Then a sharp ex-clamation as if Challow had suddenly thought of something, followed immediately by his feet crashing off through the scrub. Turning over on to her uninjured side and using the bole of the tree to pull herself up on to her knees, she risked a quick glance and saw his leather-jacketed figure disappear at a run into the gloom down the side of the lorry shed.

For a moment she hesitated. His sudden departure could have been a ruse to flush her out, but she couldn't stay hidden for ever. She had to do what she had come here to do – find Mike and Tania, hopefully before it was too late – otherwise Ted Street's ultimate sacrifice would have all been for nothing. But there was something else she had to do first and that was to get some armed backup on site. With this in mind, she felt for the mobile phone she had slipped into her pocket earlier – which, though low on battery, was at least worth a try – only to find her pocket was empty. She tried the other pocket without success, then closed her eyes in despair. The telephone must have fallen out during her tumble down the slope and it could be anywhere now. For a few moments she scrabbled around her in the undergrowth, wincing as each movement sent a sharp stabbing pain through her ribcage, but it was a pointless exercise. There was no sign of the phone anywhere.

Standing up cautiously, she studied the spot where Challow had disappeared, wondering if he was standing just out of sight in the gloom, watching her and waiting for the moment she was close enough for him to have a good clear shot. She took a chance and, with one hand pressed against her ribcage to try and shut off the pain, she moved awkwardly towards the back of the building, turning to her right at the last minute to head along a strip of concrete to the opposite end. Nothing happened and she followed the path down the other side of the shed to the front.

The moon was full and the hardstanding in front of the building was bathed in its brilliance. She studied it for a moment. The drivers door of the Land Rover was still wide open and she could see a foot and the lower part of a leg protruding from under it. She shuddered, then gritted her teeth and stepped out into the open, walking quickly towards the vehicle and throwing frequent apprehensive glances to the left and right as she did so.

She got to the Land Rover without a problem and carefully reached for the handle of the front passenger door to pull it open, closing her eyes tightly for a second as she tried to prepare herself for what she knew she was going to find inside. But nothing can prepare anyone for the sight of another human being blasted at close range with a twelve-bore shotgun and she physically retched when she saw the mutilated remains of the young bobby stretched across the drivers seat on his back, with his head and shoulders partially overlapping the front passenger seat.

Ted Street had taken the full force of the blast from a distance of about ten feet and he would have died instantly – but that had to be the only saving grace, for his torso had been ripped wide open, exposing ruptured organs, which had forced themselves out through the horrendous gash in a black glutinous mass and now glistened obscenely in the moonlight. One arm was thrown up in a vertical position, trapped between his side and the back of the seat, while the other dangled over the edge of the cushion, still clutching his personal radio.

Her first thought, once she had torn her gaze away from the grisly sight, was to call for assistance on the Land Rover's main VHF radio, which was slotted into the instrument panel and would have connected her directly to Headquarters rather than to the Area Control Room. But when she unclipped the handset and tried to transmit, she found that the radio was completely dead and closer examination revealed severe damage to the fascia, almost certainly caused by stray shotgun pellets.

For what seemed like several minutes, but in reality must have been a fraction of that time, her gaze was drawn to the lifeless hand clutching the UHF personal radio and she released a long uncontrollable shudder. 'Oh my God,' she choked, clutching at the edge of the door for support as her senses swam and perspiration began to trickle down her face in tiny rivulets, 'I can't do this.'

But she had to and she knew it. With half-closed eyes and gritted teeth, she knelt on the door sill and leaned forward across the passenger foot-well, thrusting an arm into the semi-gloom below the drivers seat. The floor felt wet and sticky and something dripped on to the back of her hand as she brushed against the seat, but she forced herself to stay with the task and, finally locating the limp arm, she carefully prized the pack-set free of Ted Street's death grip.

But the strain of what she had had to do, coming as it did on top of her firsthand witness to the horrific murder of one of her own colleagues, was almost too much for her and the emotional shock hit home with debilitating effect even as she scrambled out of the car. Sinking on to the door sill with her back towards the corpse, she leaned weakly against the door pillar and stared up at the moon, grateful for the faint breeze that now caressed her hot clammy face as she desperately tried to pull herself together.

How long she would have remained in that state if she had been left to her own devices, it is impossible to say, but as it was, the initiative was taken right out of her hands when the pack-set in her lap suddenly burst into life. 'Charlie-Alpha Four-Six, PC Street, this is Inspector Whitley. Please respond. Charlie-Alpha Four-Six, advise your location immediately.'

It was obvious from the involvement of Whitley that the Area Control Room at Heaton had called Ted Street a number of times already and there was a sharp edge to the Inspector's tone. Quickly turning down the volume of the set, Mary depressed the transmit button, her years of police service abruptly overcoming her emotional shock as she did exactly what she had been trained to do and tremulously transmitted her own radio call-sign, 'Two-Four,' followed by her location and the police code for emergency assistance.

The Control Room operator's metallic voice responded immediately: 'All other mobiles wait. Go ahead Charlie-Alpha Two-Four.'

Repeating her location, she provided a terse account of what had happened, asking for immediate armed backup and the complete evacuation of Tulse End.

She had the satisfaction of hearing the Control Room operator hesitate a fraction and when he continued, there was a sharper note to his usual monotone delivery. 'Understood Two-Four. X-ray One-Four already en route re earlier request from Four-Six. Further backup in hand. Please define your exact location on site.'

But Mary had no intention of defining anything. She couldn't, for Eddie Challow had at that moment stepped through the partially open doors of the lorry shed just yards from the Land Rover and through the side window of her open door she could see that he was staring straight at the vehicle.

*

X-ray One-Four had returned to its operating base at Lex Drove Flying Club for refuelling and stand-down when the call came through from Headquarters Control Room. After a frustrating non-eventful afternoon – first patrolling the skies above TQ

International's Depot looking for a stolen petrol tanker and then carrying out sweep after sweep of the Heaton General Hospital site searching for a missing patient – the two-man crew had jumped at the chance of a more active role. They were even more keyed-up when shortly after receiving the initial call from the Control Room, a further radio message came through just as they were about to get airborne, telling them to wait for passengers. Fifteen minutes later they were joined by two fully armed officers from the force's Tactical Firearms Unit, bearing news of Ted Street's reported death.

The 180 mph EC135 Eurocopter, with its powerful strobe lights and thermal imager, took off minutes later and as it thudded through the darkness towards Tulse End, the young freckle-faced police sniper in the back carefully removed the Heckler & Koch automatic sniper rifle from its case and carried out a few last minute checks.

At the same moment, twenty miles away, Assistant Chief Constable Dennis Stanford Parkes, who had reluctantly authorised the deployment of armed officers in the police helicopter, backed up by a further team in one of the force's armed response vehicles, leaned on one of the communication consoles in the Headquarters Control Room. White-faced and chewing his lower lip, he waited tensely for confirmation from the Superintendent in command of the Operations Support Unit that the evacuation of Tulse End was underway. Instead, he heard only the helicopter observer's sharp matter-of-fact transmission slicing through his borrowed headphones: 'X-ray One-Four now Ten-One (Mobile). ETA Tango Echo seven minutes.' Despite all the staff manning the consoles around him, Parkes had never felt so alone in all his life.

*

The first shotgun blast peppered the front passenger door of the Land Rover and shattered the window. Fortunately Mary had already anticipated what Challow would do and had thrown herself to the ground before crawling right under the vehicle, but she also managed to drop Street's personal radio in the process. The next blast at much closer range took out most of the windscreen and the back window, some pellets exiting through the bodywork and roof.

He was playing with her, she realised that, but she also knew that the third shot was likely to be even closer and that this time it would almost certainly find her, so she took the only real option she had left. Scrambling out from under the vehicle while Challow was in the process of reloading, she ran towards the steep driveway leading up to the house, putting as much confidence as she could in the claim made by a police firearms instructor friend a few years before that shortening a shotgun's barrel not only spread the shot, but also reduced its effective range and accuracy.

Whether he was right or not was of less interest to her than the fact that the next shot once more missed her completely – either falling short because she *was* effectively out of range or going wide because Challow's aim was poor – and then she was forcing herself up the slope towards the house as fast as her injured ribcage would allow.

But Challow was not about to give up that easily and, turning her head to glance behind her as she staggered across the waste-ground in front of the house, she saw he was not only in hot pursuit, the shotgun held loosely in one hand, but actually appeared to be gaining on her. Had it not been for her injury, she would have outstripped him without difficulty, but running with one hand pressed into her side to try and shut off the pain reduced her speed by at least half and she knew that it was only a matter of seconds before he either caught up with her or was close enough to use his shotgun again.

Then, quite suddenly, she had reached the house and was stumbling through the front door, conscious that Challow was only yards behind her. Clawing herself free of the coils of electric flex that reached down from the ceiling to ensnare her, she ducked into a doorway on her right, freezing behind the splintered panelling of the door as footsteps pounded the floor of the hallway she had just left.

The footsteps ran on past her and she heard the crunch of broken glass, followed by a dull thud, as if someone had jumped on to soft ground. The back garden? Then silence. Very carefully she retreated further into the comforting darkness of the room, one hand behind her to feel for any obstructions. There were none and within a few paces her back was up against the external wall of the house, where tiny slivers of moonlight were visible through hairline chinks in the boarded-up window.

The footsteps returned, advancing slowly along the hall from the other direction. She peered desperately into the darkness, looking for another way out or somewhere to hide, but she could only pick out vague angular shapes that could have been anything, from boxes to pieces of furniture. Hardly able to breathe and with her heart pounding fit to burst, she edged her way along the wall past the window and bumped into something soft. Running her hand along it, she identified a padded chair arm. She moved away from the wall and round to the other side of what her trailing hand found to be a big settee, its cushions apparently gone and naked springs exposed. There was a gap between the end of the settee and the far wall and she forced herself into it, hunching her shoulders to enable her to push herself back as far as possible and biting her lip as the crippling pain lanced through her ribs.

The footsteps were outside the door now and her skin crawled at the sound of Challow's soft menacing voice. 'I know you're around here somewhere, Sergeant Lane,' he said. 'I've just checked the kitchen and garden, so it's the only place you could be.'

She held her breath, remaining rigidly still, her fists clenched into tight balls.

He chuckled, almost as if he sensed her terrified presence in the room. 'Come on, Mary, let's get it over with, shall we? You can't hide from me for long.'

She closed her eyes, waiting for the hail of pellets as the shotgun blasted the settee and ripped her apart like poor Ted Street, but for some reason the shot never came and she heard the sudden scrape of his feet on the floor as he turned sharply and stumbled back down the hallway, snarling a curse as he went.

At first she thought he was simply employing another ruse to draw her out and she made no attempt to move, but then she heard the sound too and her heart leaped with excitement. The rhythmic heavy thud of approaching rotor blades was unmistakable and at this time of the night it could mean only one thing: X-ray One-Four. The troops were coming.

Chapter 19

Mike Dexter recognised the distinctive *"crack"* of the shotgun, soon after Challow had left the room, but although there was an uninterrupted view of the lights of Tulse End from the window, nothing of the immediate foreground was visible and he had no idea what had actually happened or whether that shot, and those which followed it shortly afterwards, amounted to good or bad news for Tania and himself. Not that it made much difference either way. Gagged and securely tied to the bed, they were unable to summon help even if help were available and by the time anyone did find them it would be too late anyway.

Tania was his main worry. In her fragile mental state, the petrol dousing she had received at the hands of Eddie Challow had been the last straw. Aside from the physical distress caused by its overpowering toxic fumes, the shock of that lethal soaking on top of the mental stress she had suffered over the past few hours, seemed to have finally snapped something in her mind, shutting down her outward consciousness as an automatic timer can shut down the lights of a building. Only her rasping breath indicated that she was still alive, for otherwise she sat there as rigid as a statue, her eyes wide and staring as she contemplated the depths of some nightmare world of her own.

Still reeling from the shock of her terrible confession and now forced to be an impotent witness to the destruction of her mind, it was all Dexter could do to keep hold of his own sanity. Only the thought of the incendiary timer relentlessly ticking away beneath the bed kept him focused as he continued to struggle frantically with the vicious strands of chicken wire binding him to the iron frame; retching and choking on the fumes from the petrol saturating both the mattress and his own clothing, and crying out in pain as the spirit ran down his arms in rivulets and collected in the savage cuts the wire had inflicted on his wrists.

The sound of two sets of pounding feet in the hallway below

encouraged him to redouble his efforts and he was still struggling when he heard the unmistakable thud of rotor blades. Staring quickly through the balcony window, he saw the helicopter sweep out of the darkness and freeze to a hover over the site, its sinister black shell silhouetted against the face of the moon like a giant predatory bug as its powerful spotlights pin-pointed something he couldn't see directly below.

Then Challow was scrambling up the ladder into the room, making straight for Tania. 'Change of plan, Michael,' he said breathlessly. Laying his shotgun temptingly on the edge of the mattress, he produced something from his pocket and, bending over her, snapped through the wire binding her wrists. 'We appear to have gatecrashers and I need some insurance.'

Jerking her to her feet, he retrieved the shotgun from the bed and heedless of her sharp cry of pain, ripped the gag from her mouth. Then, fumbling with his wire cutters as he made to slip them back into his pocket, he prodded her forward with the barrel of the shotgun held loosely in his other hand. 'Down the ladder,' he grated, 'and no tricks or I'll blow your head off.'

Whether it was the pain of having the sticky tape ripped off her mouth that triggered some fading spark in her brain or the sudden realisation that she was free, it is impossible to say, but while he was temporarily distracted by the wire-cutters, Tania suddenly spun on her heel with a high-pitched scream and went for him, using the only weapons she had at her disposal.

Caught temporarily off guard, Challow reeled backwards with a sharp agonised cry as her long fingernails raked his face, drawing blood and tearing part of his right eye. But despite the pain, he recovered quickly and as she threw herself at him again, the barrel of the shotgun jerked upwards smashing into the side of her head and crumpling her into an inert heap on the floor.

Holding a handkerchief to his face, he savagely slammed one booted foot into her side as she lay there, then turned his good eye on Dexter as the policeman writhed on the bed like a trussed animal, choking his rage through the gag as he tried to snap his bonds by sheer brute force. 'Don't go getting yourself all excited Michael,' he mocked, peering at the clock on the stool by the bed. 'You've only got seven minutes to wait. Pity you won't be around to see the Tulse End extravaganza, but the main thing is that Tania will. In fact, she'll actually be part of it all now.'

With blood dripping from his wounds, he bent down and grabbed hold of her by the hair, dragging her towards the ladder. Then, laying the shotgun on the floor beside him and crouching down over the hole, he manoeuvred her into a legs first position over the edge and pushed her through, showing considerable strength by grabbing her hair at the last minute and reaching into the hole to slide her still inert body down the ladder as far as he could before letting go.

'*Au revoir*, Michael,' he said as he retrieved his shotgun and began to climb through the hole himself. 'Enjoy the barbecue.' Then he paused for a second to deliver his parting shot in just above a whisper. 'Oh by the way, that nice Mary Lane is hiding downstairs somewhere and I'm quite sure she'll be up to see you as soon as I've gone.' He consulted the bedside clock again. 'She'd better hurry though. There's only five minutes visiting time left!'

*

A convoy of flashing blue lights was heading at speed along the dual carriageway below Quarry Wood Hill when X-ray One-Four swooped out of the darkness and homed in on Tulse End village. 'So much for the covert approach,' Sergeant Paul Grey, the Air Support Unit observer, commented dryly. Commercial pilot, Dave Cornish, nodded as they thudded low over the rooftops that encircled the blaze of lights marking the village green. 'They'll have a job getting through that lot anyway,' he said, flicking his head back to indicate the queue of cars and vans choking the narrow approach road, 'and that's even before they try evacuating the fair.'

'It's up to us then, isn't it?' Grey replied grimly, throwing a quick glance at the two armed policemen sitting quietly in the back. 'I just hope it's a false alarm.'

But they realised it wasn't when they reached the old Ferguson haulage site near the top of Quarry Wood Hill and saw the police Land Rover stationary in front of the huge corrugated roofed shed, with its doors wide open. 'Take her down,' Grey ordered and switched on the powerful spotlights. Hovering just thirty feet above the vehicle, the bullet shattered windscreen was plain to see. Grey motioned the pilot to swing the aircraft a few feet to the right of the vehicle. 'Can you take her down further?' he queried and the other nodded, caressing the controls with the practised ease that had once enabled him to land Sea Kings on the pitching deck of a Royal Navy aircraft carrier in the North Sea.

Grey saw the leg projecting out of the car door immediately and his stomach tightened as he snapped into his radio mic. 'Control from X-ray One-Four, Charlie-Alpha Four-Six located. Appears to be a casualty inside. Unable to assess condition. Evidence of severe damage to vehicle. No sign of offender.'

But he was wrong about that and even as he spoke, shotgun pellets hammered into the underside of the helicopter like deadly rain. Reacting instantly, Cornish sent his charge soaring skywards, where it pivoted on its axis well out of range as the young police sniper slid open the door of the machine and partially leaned out, held only by his supportive harness.

The man with the shotgun was clearly visible, standing at the bottom of a steep track that climbed the hill towards a large derelict house. His face was directed upwards towards the helicopter, the shotgun raised threateningly in one hand and his other arm encircling what looked like a body slumped over one shoulder.

'Armed police!' Grey's voice boomed out over the machine's public address system. 'Drop your weapon and stand still!' But Eddie Challow had no intention of doing any such thing and as the sniper's finger slowly tightened on the trigger of his carefully aimed rifle, he broke into a stumbling run towards the lorry shed, knowing full well that Tania's inert body draped over his shoulder formed the perfect shield against the bullet of any police marksman. And as he ducked through the half-open door into the comforting blackness of the shed, he grinned with delight at the sound of a violent explosion. Turning awkwardly in the doorway, he saw the flames of the old Ferguson house reflected in the polished bodywork of the still hovering helicopter.

*

It was Tania's scream that forced Mary Lane out of her hiding-place. Unlike anything she had ever heard before, it cut through her very being like an invisible scalpel, embodying all the anguish and frustration of a soul in torment. Crouched in the narrow gap between the wall and one end of the settee, she had felt reasonably secure following Eddie Challow's rapid departure; reluctant to move until she was positive he had left the house altogether. But the scream changed all that and she was actually at the door and about to step into the hallway when she glimpsed shadowy movement in the moonlit room opposite. Shrinking back into the gloom, she peered round the door frame and, her eyes now well adjusted to the darkness, she saw a dark figure emerge and head off down the hallway, burdened with some bulky object. Only when he got to the front door and was framed in the moonlight for a few seconds were her suspicions confirmed. He was actually carrying a body over one shoulder and just before he disappeared into the night, she caught the gleam of tousled fair hair. Tania, she thought with a shudder. But where the hell was Mike?

Crossing the hallway into the room Challow had just left, she almost blundered into a wooden ladder climbing a narrow shaft of moonlight to the upper floor. She paused a moment to listen, but could hear only the thudding blades of the helicopter, which seemed to be hovering directly over the site. Carefully testing the stability of the ladder, she climbed slowly towards the ragged patch of light above her head, gritting her teeth against the reawakened pain in her ribs and acutely conscious of her vulnerability if Challow decided to double back to the house. But he didn't and a few moments later she was clambering up into a blaze of moonlight, her nose wrinkling at the stench of petrol, which enveloped her in an invisible cloud, and her prickling eyes trying to adjust to the unreal glare as, with a feeling of relief, she peered at the figure on the big double bed.

'Oh Mike,' she exclaimed rushing to his side and bending over him. 'I thought he had killed you.'

To her surprise he pulled away from her, his eyes wide and staring as if he were contemplating some grisly apparition, and she could hear him grunting and choking behind the tape that had been stuck across his mouth.

Unaware that time was rapidly running out for both of them, she gripped his shoulder tightly. 'Michael, it's me – Mary,' she exclaimed. 'Just hang in there for a moment while I try and get you free.'

She felt behind him and found the wire securing him to the bed, then winced as she also discovered the sticky wetness of his wrists. 'Michael, you're cut to blazes,' she exclaimed, holding her hand up in the moonlight to inspect her fingers.

For reply, he shook his head frantically from side to side, his eyes literally bulging in their sockets as he hauled desperately on the wire, lifting the heels of his feet and slamming them into the mattress like a madman.

'Okay, steady on,' she said quickly. 'I'll see if I can get the gag off first. The stench in here must be choking you.'

She winced as she gently pulled a corner of the tape away from his cheek. 'This is really going to hurt, you know,' she went on, then jumped as he suddenly jerked his head to one side while she was trying to peel the stuff back, so that one side of it came away completely and he was able to spit out the gag. 'Bomb!' he gasped, nodding towards the luminous face of the clock on the stool beside him. 'Under the bed. Going to blow in two and a half minutes!'

She stared at him in horror and, ripping off the rest of the tape, glanced about the room wildly. 'But I need something to cut the wire with,' she exclaimed. 'I've got nothing on me.'

He took a quick gasping breath. 'Wire cutter,' he gasped. He brought it up here with him to cut Tania loose. Think he dropped it when she went for him.'

'Dropped it?' she echoed, darting more panicky glances around the room. 'But where?'

He raised his eyes to the ceiling in a gesture of frustration. 'For Pete's sake, Mary! Other side of the bed – and hurry!'

Her foot struck something hard as she followed the frame round and she heard the object skate away from her across the floor. In a moment she was on her knees, searching for it with one hand as she held her ribs with the other. The mechanism of the clock gave a loud click as its approached the last minute. 'Mary, hurry!' he yelled. 'There's no time!'

Her fingers touched something with the cold feel of steel and she snatched it up, dropped it and snatched it up again. The hand of the clock was a fraction away from the hour and Dexter studied it with a horrible fascination as Mary jerked him forward and began to clip away at the tough strands of chicken wire. She had nearly finished the task when the wire cutters slipped from her fingers and dropped down the back of the bed. Their eyes met briefly and each could read the terror there.

Taking a deep breath, Dexter literally threw himself forward, parting the last strands of wire with sheer brute force and pitching over the side of the bed on to the floor. He regained his feet in an instant, but even as he grabbed Mary round the waist and propelled them both through the balcony window in a wild dive, the minute hand of the clock made its last sickening lurch towards the hour and the whole room exploded in flames.

★

The thunder of Eddie Challow's shotgun as he fired at the police helicopter restored Tania to consciousness with brutal suddenness, drawing a long moaning cry from deep inside her as her body went into a quivering muscular spasm and her concussed brain tried to work out what was happening. There was a sense of jolting movement, accompanied by a heavy rhythmic thudding in her ears and a searing white light, which blinded her every time she tried to open her eyes. It dawned on her then that she was being carried over someone's shoulder like a sack of potatoes, with her head and upper body trailing down his back, and as her memory returned, she realised that that someone had to be Eddie Challow.

The arm gripping her round the legs tightened as a metallic voice, distorted and unintelligible to her in her muzzy state, suddenly boomed out from somewhere above her head. Challow immediately broke into a half run and the jolting movement became much more pronounced, shaking her injured head from side to side with cruel force and producing an icy numbness, which swept through her skull like an anaesthetizing drug, making her want to vomit.

Sudden blackness again and she thought at first that she was drifting back into oblivion, but then there was what sounded like a distant explosion and she heard Challow's unpleasant laugh. More jerky motion and a loud cracking noise, like the hinges of a door being opened. The grip round her legs relaxed and she felt herself falling backwards on to something firm but soft, like a bed or a chair. A single light blazed in her eyes and she glimpsed a large elongated mirror, a massive windscreen and part of a steering wheel. 'Sit up, bitch!' a voice menaced and Eddie Challow's face leered down at her.

She shrank away from him, clawing herself upright against the back of the seat on which she had been dumped. Her eyes adjusted to the light and she realised she was in the cab of a big lorry. Of course, the tanker. Challow was sitting behind the steering wheel, the sawn-off shotgun across his lap, with the twin barrels pointing in her direction. The left side of his face was torn and bloodied, the eye closed over and twitching spasmodically as he stared at her. 'Pull another trick like you did just now,' he snarled, the fingers of one hand travelling briefly to the wound, 'and I'll blow both your legs off!'

She screwed up her face, clutching at her own head, now wet and sticky on one side, as the chill in her skull gave way to agonising knife-like stabs of pain, which penetrated her eyes from the inside with coordinating flashes of light that had the intensity of an acetylene torch flame.

'Head hurt, does it?' Challow sneered, the lorry's powerful engine thundering into life as he flicked the key in the ignition. 'Well, it won't for much longer, I promise you that.' Reaching into his pocket, he opened his hand to reveal the small radio transmitter he had produced earlier and pressed a button. Immediately a red light began to flash in the tiny display. He grinned and held the transmitter in front of her eyes. 'Fully armed now, see? All I have to do is press this other button and all your aches and pains will be gone in a flash.' He placed the transmitter very carefully on the dashboard in front of him. 'Then you can join dear old hubby in eternity, eh?'

She made no effort to reply, but watched him as he edged the lorry towards the now wide open doors of the shed, only to stop just short of the entrance, twisting his neck to peer upwards through the windscreen. The helicopter was no longer visible from inside the shed, since the moon was once more obscured by clouds, but the thud of its rotor blades could clearly be heard even above the sound of the tanker's engine and its powerful spotlights continued to probe the concrete hardstanding immediately outside.

With an angry snarl, Challow jerked a mobile telephone from his inside pocket and quickly dialled a number. Even as the call was answered, he responded with a sneering: 'Good evening, Police Headquarters. This is Eddie Challow at Tulse End. Tell that chopper of yours to back off. I've a nice little lady called Tania Dexter in the cab with me. Try anything silly and she gets it. Savvy?'

Without waiting for a reply, he switched off the interior light, revved the engine and sent the tanker lumbering out into the path of the spotlights, accelerating hard towards the exit opposite. As Tania clung to the shaking pitching seat, her gaze was riveted, not on the helicopter hovering some thirty feet above them, but on the flames that once more devoured the gaunt shell of the house on the hill – including the bedroom where her beloved Mike had been left tied to the wrought iron bed.

*

At precisely the same moment that Eddie Challow headed for the site exit, the police convoy, comprising the Operations Support Unit and the fully-equipped Armed Response Vehicle redeployed from the

TQI stake-out, turned into the approach lane to Tulse End – only to be greeted by the worst possible scenario.

The hot dog van had broken down at an acute angle in the narrowest part of the lane and the roadway had ended up as an extension of the official car park, jammed with vehicles that had attempted to edge past the obstruction and got themselves into a hopeless tangle. Superintendent Anne Jackson, leading the half dozen Transit vans, closed her eyes briefly in despair as she stood on the road beside her 4 x 4 in a blaze of flashing blue lights. She had known from the start that this particular job was going to be difficult – it came with the territory – but she had never anticipated that it would prove to be virtually impossible. With the road blocked as it was, the entrance to Tulse End might as well have been sealed off by tightly closed steel doors, for there was absolutely no way through for anything wider than a handcart.

'So what do we do now, ma'am?' her inspector shouted above the blare of horns.

'Get the lads out of their vehicles,' she snapped. 'We'll have to go forward on foot.'

'No time, ma'am,' he threw back grimly. 'Just came through on the radio. That nicked tanker's already on its way down Quarry Wood Hill and we're still a quarter of a mile from the village centre.'

She shuddered. 'Then we'd better advise Headquarters Control that X-ray One-Four is Tulse End's only hope,' she said grimly.

★

Assistant Chief Constable Operations visibly jumped as Sergeant Grey's voice blasted into his borrowed headphones. 'Building on haulage site has just exploded,' the helicopter observer shouted excitedly. 'Tanker's now on the move. Awaiting instructions?'

The civilian operator glanced over his shoulder at the ACC's tense white face. 'What do I tell them, sir?' he ventured anxiously.

Parkes' mouth tightened. 'Tell them to follow. Nothing more,' he snapped. 'We've just been told he has a hostage on board and we can't risk taking out the driver and turning the tanker over.'

The Control Room Inspector standing on the other side of the console stared at him incredulously. 'But he's going after the village, sir,' he exclaimed. 'He's got to be stopped. There are hundreds of people down there.'

'We can't say for certain what he's after,' Parkes prevaricated sharply. 'We've only got DS Lane's assumption that Tulse End is the target. He could still be making for TQI for all we know.'

'Then why did he take the tanker all the way up on to Quarry Wood Hill, sir?'

Parkes ignored the blatant insolence in his subordinate's tone, acutely conscious that all eyes in the Control Room were on him. 'Could have been just a convenient hiding place,' he retorted, moistening dry lips. 'One he would have known about from his original crimes. I can't see why he would want to destroy a nondescript village like Tulse End anyway? It doesn't make sense.'

'Sir, with respect, we can't afford to take a chance on it.'

Parkes nodded, a vein twitching high on his temple. 'I'm well aware of that, Inspector, but I'm not going to sacrifice the life of a hostage on the hunch of one detective whom we can't now even raise on the radio. Find out what's happening with the OSU and ARV I redeployed to Tulse End. They should already be in a position to set up their roadblock in Quarry Wood Road.'

But even as he spoke, Superintendent Anne Jackson's strained voice called up from the scene, with news that he could easily have done without . 'Approach lane to village jammed with cars... Impossible for ARV and rest of team to get through... Making on foot as best we can.'

'Now what, sir?' the operator queried, his eyes wide and staring.

Before Parkes could reply, Grey's voice once more blasted through the headphones. 'X-ray One-Four. Tanker just turning out of old haulage site. Good visual coming up. Permission to take out target if opportunity presents?'

'What do I say, sir?' the Control Room operator persisted, perspiration glistening on his forehead.

Parkes stared back at him, fear and uncertainty etched deeply in his drawn white face. 'There must be some other way,' he breathed.

'X-ray One-Four,' Grey's voice yelled again. 'We have clear shot. Permission to fire?'

'There *is* no other way, sir,' the Inspector put in desperately. 'It's the life of one hostage against the lives of several hundred other people. It *has to be done!*'

'Does it?' Parkes retorted harshly. 'And if you were that hostage, Inspector, would you think your life was a fair trade?'

The Inspector didn't answer. For all his bullishness, he was just glad that he was not the one who had to make the decision.

X-ray One-Four had easily overtaken the tanker as it made for the site exit, the helicopter's spotlights tracing the line of Quarry Wood Road as it thudded towards the junction where the road turned sharp left at the quarry entrance to drop steeply towards Tulse End. None of those on board needed to be reminded of the fact that once the massive artic got on to that steep slope, nothing would be able to stop it until it ploughed into the village green at the bottom. That meant they had just seconds to act.

Slowing a couple of hundred yards from the intersection, Dave Cornish took the helicopter down to a point some fifteen feet from the ground, straddling the road and skilfully holding it there.

At the same moment the young sniper steadied himself in his harness at the open door and lined up his rifle on the windscreen of the approaching tanker. The driver should soon be clearly visible in his night-sight, but he knew that the opportunity was going to be a very brief one. After what had seemed like initial hesitation, the tanker was now bearing down on them at a speed that was far from comfortable and it seemed to have little intention of slowing down. What was more, the moon had started to reappear and although as yet only part of its sickle-like rim was showing in the heavy black sky, it would soon be fully visible, flooding his night-sight with excess light and destroying the clarity of his target.

He didn't allow such concerns to distract him from his purpose, however, concentrating clinically on the task in hand, his finger tensing on the trigger as he waited patiently for Sergeant Grey to receive the green light from Headquarters that would allow him to fulfil the awful function for which he had been trained.

★

Eddie Challow was on a high as he drove the tanker out on to Quarry Wood Road. True, not everything over the past few days had gone quite according to plan, but nevertheless, he had so far achieved everything he had set out to do. The final score – something he had been dreaming about for so many years – was now just minutes away from being settled and in his mind's eye, he could already see the massive fire-ball blossoming over Tulse End as the village was erased from the face of the earth. His grin broadened even more as he savoured the prospect of his mobile bomb shortly being delivered by the very woman who had had him put away in the first place – her wrists secured to the locked steering wheel with the very last pair of handcuffs he had in his pocket before he released the handbrake halfway down the lower hill and jumped clear with his precious radio transmitter, ready to trigger the explosive on board at the critical second.

Then his brief moment of self-indulgence was shattered as the police helicopter thudded by overhead, so close that he felt the heavy lorry actually shake. Twisting his neck again to peer up through the windscreen, he saw the machine flash off towards the quarry, its spotlights blinding him as they washed over the vehicle.

Swinging the tanker in a wide tyre-screeching turn at the site entrance and heading off in the same direction, he threw Tania's shadowy figure a swift searching glance, surprised by her continued silence. With the knowledge that her beloved Mike had already been burned to a crisp in the house and that she faced a similar fiery death herself in just a few minutes time, he had expected some sort of reaction from her; a further violent assault, hysteria, even just a tirade of abuse. Instead she simply sat there, her eyes staring straight ahead and her hands instinctively gripping the edge of the seat on either side of her thighs in an effort to maintain her balance. It was as if her mind had gone into limbo – had once more retreated into its inner self – and though in that condition she presented less of a problem, her unresponsiveness both irritated and disturbed him.

Then abruptly his gaze jerked back to the windscreen and he braked instinctively. The helicopter had dropped to a hover position right across the road, some three to four hundred yards ahead, and appeared to be waiting for him. Remembering the uniformed figure he had glimpsed leaning out of the machine earlier on, it was his turn to feel his skin crawl. Sitting at the wheel as he was, his head and shoulders exposed to full view through the broad windscreen, he made the perfect target and he didn't need to be a firearms expert to know that a trained police marksman, using a rifle equipped with powerful night-sights, would be able to pick him off with one squeeze of the trigger. Yeah, but the *Old Bill* had forgotten one thing. He still held the ace card.

Reaching across the cab with his left hand, he grabbed Tania tightly round the neck and pulled her towards him. 'Get over here,' he snarled. Let's remind them who we've got on board.'

Forcing her to climb on to his lap, he held the shotgun close to her side with his right hand while he readied himself to steer the tanker

284

with his left. 'Just like old times, isn't it?' he breathed close to her ear, then abruptly urged the monster lorry forward, feeling the thrill of it slowly gathering speed as they headed straight for the still hovering helicopter, headlamps on full beam and spotlights blazing aggressively in support.

*

Assistant Chief Constable Dennis Stanford Parkes had finally lost it. Only too aware of the hideous carnage that would result from a tanker explosion in the middle of Tulse End and the career-consuming public outrage that would be directed against him for allowing it to happen, he was equally conscious of the condemnation he would face for authorising the cold-blooded shooting of Eddie Challow and the killing of an innocent hostage. Torn by doubts and under pressure from both the demands of the Control Room Inspector and the repeated calls from X-ray One-Four, his mind finally capitulated and, for the first time in his police service, he froze completely, self-destructing his career at the same moment.

In the helicopter, twenty miles away, Parkes' indecision had a critical impact on the final course of events, for it resulted in the police sniper missing his one split second opportunity to fire before the head and shoulders of another figure, undoubtedly that of the hostage, thrust up into his sights, blocking off his target altogether. Then, as the front of the tanker dissolved in a blaze of light and Dave Cornish desperately hauled the machine skywards, the huge artic thundering towards them on a collision course almost brushed their skids as it passed underneath. 'Damn HQ, he's through,' yelled Paul Grey, his frustration boiling over. 'Nothing can stop the bastard now!'

But Grey's doom-laden assessment turned out to be premature, for as the helicopter recovered from its emergency climb and staggered off in pursuit, it suddenly became apparent that something was very wrong with the tanker, which had now begun to swerve from side to side along the narrow road.

*

Eddie Challow had made many mistakes in his life, but his biggest was to underestimate the slim pale-faced woman sitting on his lap as the tanker virtually brushed the police helicopter aside and rumbled towards its objective unchecked.

Although outwardly displaying the signs of mental limbo, as if her mind had become uncoupled from reality by the trauma she had been subjected to, nothing could have been further from the truth. Behind the bleak expression, the cold calculating mind of the other half of her personality, which in her degenerative regressive state had finally taken over completely, was dangerously active and the big blue eyes now stared at the windscreen in the same vacant way that they had stared at Ron Ferguson's writhing body as the match was applied to his petrol soaked mattress over twenty years before.

She had found the small can of windscreen de-icer trapped between the cushion and the back of her seat shortly after being dumped in the cab and had managed to slip it beneath her sweater without Challow being any the wiser. Her opportunity to use it came as the helicopter launched itself skywards – practically from under the front wheels of the tanker. Pumped full of adrenalin, Challow couldn't resist a show of bravado, thrusting the shotgun through the open window of the drivers door and discharging a barrel at the fast disappearing shadow.

She turned on him with the can before he realised his mistake, directing the lethal spray over her shoulder, straight into his face. Temporarily blinded and screaming in agony, his hands went straight for his eyes, the shotgun connecting with the window frame and spinning off into the darkness. Before he had a chance to recover, she seized the steering wheel with both hands and, as his foot came off the accelerator, slammed her own foot hard down on the pedal, sending the tanker careering off along the narrow road like a runaway express train, the giant trailer fish-tailing dangerously as she fought to keep control.

Still screaming his pain and rage, but unable to tear her grip from the wheel, he began to batter her head and back mercilessly with his fists, his eyes on fire as he desperately tried to see through the acid mist eating into the retinas. But she seemed impervious to the blows and clung to the wheel with limpet-like determination, kicking his foot away every time he tried to step on the brake pedal.

Then the intersection leading down to the village was there, but instead of slowing to negotiate the turn, Tania accelerated past, smashing through the wire gates of the quarry and on to the rutted potholed track that cut through the pine trees a few hundred yards beyond. 'You're mad!' Challow shrieked, clawing open his door, then jerking back into the cab as the branches of the trees caught it and slammed it shut again. 'This goes nowhere.'

'Mad?' She shouted back. 'We're both mad, Eddie. We always have been. And we belong in the same place.'

Then suddenly they had cleared the belt of pine trees and were bumping crazily across a bare plateau scattered with a mixture of ruined brick and corrugated iron buildings and derelict machinery. The road now swung away in a sweeping left-hand curve before dipping steeply between scarred rock walls on the first stage of a staggered descent to the quarry floor, but Tania made no attempt to follow it. Instead she sent the tanker ploughing through a large wooden warning sign and recently restored safety railings, heading straight for the rim of the pit.

Even as Challow threw open the door for a second time and gripped the edges of the frame in a desperate effort to haul himself out from under her, the lorry launched itself into space and the last thing he heard was Tania's mocking voice as she seized the little radio transmitter from the dashboard. 'Bye, Eddie,' she shouted. 'See you in hell!'

★

Mike Dexter was sleeping soundly when the nurse poked her head through the door of the small private ward. In the armchair beside the bed, Mary Lane held a finger to her lips in warning. The nurse smiled in acknowledgement and dropped the bundle of cards into her lap. 'A few well-wishers, I think,' she said softly, then discreetly withdrew again.

Just forty-eight hours had elapsed since the nightmare of Quarry Wood Hill and Mary still found it difficult to believe that Mike and herself had actually escaped from the horror house with their lives. The Almighty must certainly have been watching over them this time and no mistake. Even now she could still vividly remember the force of the explosion that had hurled them off the balcony as they were racing for the window. By rights they should have broken their necks, but their fall had been arrested by a clump of four foot high thorn bushes growing close to the wall of the house. When the police helicopter had finally spotted them crawling away from the burning building and rushed them to Heaton General Hospital, they had been found to be suffering from nothing more serious than shock, coupled with superficial burns and extensive lacerations – though in her case, the leap from the window had not exactly helped what had turned out to be a cracked rib from her earlier fall.

Their physical wounds would soon heal, of course, but the mental scars would take a lot longer – especially where Mike was concerned. Some proper professional counselling, plus a lot of support and encouragement from Mary, would be essential if he was ever to come to terms, not only with the tragic loss of Tania, but the circumstances under which she had died.

Sadly, a muckraking police enquiry into the business could only make things worse, but there was certain to be one after all the blunders that had taken place. The national newspapers lying around the hospital day room were full of it all and now that Chief Constable John Pullinger had actually died, following the massive stroke he had suffered, the media were thirsting for the blood of a suitable scapegoat. With the Home Office fiercely rejecting any suggestion of a government inspired conspiracy over the secret release of Eddie Challow and their panic-stricken spin doctors desperately trying to divert press attention by calling for a thorough investigation into the conduct of the multiple murder enquiry instead, not surprisingly, the knives were already out for Assistant Chief Constable Dennis Stanford Parkes and the hapless Detective Superintendent Brian Moffat, and it was difficult to see how either of them could survive the flack. Whatever happened, however, Mary was determined that Mike would be shielded from any police enquiry for as long as possible and if that meant ensuring he remained in hospital even after she had been discharged, then so be it.

Sifting through the small pile of cards in her lap, she read each of the get well messages in turn before placing them on Dexter's small bedside table, heartened by the fact that so many people had taken the trouble to write. Many of the well-wishers were personally known to her – Detective Chief Inspector Dick Lawson, for example, and John Durrell from the Headquarters Press Office – but there were several names she didn't recognise and her attention was specifically drawn to one card that wasn't even signed. In fact, apart from the flowery picture on the front and the standard "Get well soon" message inside, there was nothing written on it at all and, turning it over curiously to see if there was anything on the back, she froze as her gaze focused on the chilling inscription at the bottom:

Designed by patients at Bramley Heath Psychiatric Hospital.
Your purchase will help us to help them.